TAMARA Tilley

Criminal Obsession

Evergreen
PRESS

Mobile, Alabama

ISBN 978-1-58169-285-3
For Worldwide Distribution
Printed in the U.S.A.

Evergreen Press
P.O. Box 191540 • Mobile, AL 36619
800-367-8203

Note: This is a work of fiction. Names, characters, places, and incidents are productions of the author's imagination. Any resemblance to actual persons, living or dead, and how they relate to events and locales, are entirely coincidental.

Dedication

To Walter, my amazing husband. Your continual support
means everything to me. You are so willing to make sacrifices to see my
dreams accomplished. I can think of no one I would rather share this journey
with. You are my happily ever after.

Acknowledgments

Wow! I am yet again given the opportunity to thank in print the people who are so important to me and have been such an encouragement.

I have been blessed this year with two wonderful additions to our family. The Lord has given my youngest son, John a wonderful wife. Alex is a blessing to our family. Thank you both for your encouragement and excitement over my accomplishments. You bring joy to my life. I pray your relationship will continue to grow with Christ as your center.

The Lord also brought a little one into our lives this year. My son and his wife, Christopher and Jennifer, were able to bring Jade home on April 1st of this year. A precious little girl the Lord has allowed us to love and nurture. We do not know for how long we will be able to enjoy this incredible blessing, but we do know God has ordained her future and we will be thankful for whatever time God allows us. Thank you, Chris and Jenn, for being so supportive. It thrills my heart to see how God moved to bring you two together, and I know He has a perfect plan for your lives.

To my mother, Nancy Archer, who encourages me always. Thank you for tirelessly reading and rereading my work. Thank you for your eyes . . . and your heart.

To my in-laws, Stan and Betty. Thank you for your constant prayer support. I know you go before the Lord daily with prayers for your family. It is wonderful to know you are so faithful on my behalf. You have been a wonderful example of dedication to each other and to the Lord.

To April, my sister. I know we don't always see eye to eye, but I know you love me and support me in your own special way. Thank you.

To the rest of my family—John, Diana, Nancy, Jennifer, Lesley, Ron, and Patti. Thank you for being readers and encouragers. Your support means the world to me.

To all my friends who support me and get excited with each new book I write. Your feedback and enthusiasm continues to buoy me and give me the confidence to press forward on this journey. Thank you, Michelle, for being so willing to go over my manuscripts and help me as we learn together the rules and the ways of publishing.

I would also like to thank Nancy Stoeckel, F.N.P. for making sure my medical information is accurate and for being a reader as well. I really enjoy our snippets of time when we get to talk.

To readers of *Full Disclosure* and *Abandoned Identity*, what can I say but thank you, thank you, thank you. Your faithful support and encouraging emails mean more to me than you will ever know.

And to my Lord and Savior, Jesus Christ, thank you for giving me a passion for storytelling. I pray through my stories and characters others will see Your awesome power and the love and redemption You desire to bestow on all who call on Your name.

CHAPTER ONE

Tyler Henderson decided that he'd had enough of Los Angeles. He'd been a cop all his life and a detective for the LAPD for the last five years. He'd loved it, but he'd finally grown weary of big city crime. Having seen the worst the city had to offer, he knew it was time for him to get out.

It had been a difficult year for Tyler. His father had lost his battle with cancer, his partner was killed in a senseless car accident, and his fiancée decided she didn't want to be the wife of a cop. It was the perfect time for a change of scenery.

Though his captain had tried to convince Tyler to stay, he couldn't fault him for wanting the simpler life. Accepting a job with the Emerald Lake Police Department, Tyler would be one of only two detectives and have a normal nine-to-five schedule. No more overtime. No more crazies. No more politics.

Tyler sat on his back porch taking in the view. *This is the life*, he thought to himself. What could be better than enjoying a lakefront cabin, a four-wheel drive truck in the driveway, and a three-day reprieve from work? He lowered his feet from the railing and stood up to flip the burgers grilling on the barbeque. His phone rang just as one wrong move sent one of the burgers through the metal grate. Grabbing his phone from his pocket, he tried unsuccessfully to rescue the burger from a charcoal grave.

"Yeah, Henderson . . ." Tyler said as he skewered the burger that was falling apart every time he grabbed for it.

"Wow, I thought you'd be in a better mood than that!"

"Hey, sis. What's up?" His tone lightened up at the sound of his sister's voice.

"Just checking up on you. I'm making sure you don't have cabin fever yet."

A huge grin covered Tyler's face. "Not a chance. You should see it up here. It's incredible. I'm never coming back."

"Sure, that's what you say now. Just wait until you get the munchies at night or want to impress a date by taking her to a great restaurant. Then you'll wish you weren't in the middle of Timbuktu."

"No, that's where you're wrong," Tyler said as he gave up on the mangled burger and chuckled at his sister's obstinate attitude. "I've given up on women. In fact, I saw a sign for a kennel down the road. I'm going to get me a dog. Good company is just a pedigree away."

1

"Great. My brother is going to turn into a monk or some kind of sexual deviant." Hailey laughed at her own joke. "So, you're sure you're all right?"

"No, I'm a manic-depressive, hiding from the world," he teased.

"I'm serious, Ty. I'm worried about you."

"I'm fine, Hailey," Tyler reassured her. "Couldn't be better. So when are you going to visit me?"

"Never," she huffed. "I don't do back woods. I'll wait and see you at Thanksgiving."

"It's your loss, Hailey. You know you shouldn't knock something until you've tried it."

They talked a few more minutes before Tyler hung up and removed his now blackened burgers from the grill. He sat before his barbecued "masterpiece" with all the fixin's and bowed his head in prayer.

"HEY, MIKE, ARE YOU READY TO RELEASE the remains of John Kemper?" Nathan, Mike's lab assistant, asked.

Michal "Mike" Madigan was the county medical examiner and a force to be reckoned with. She was tops in her field and recognized for her expertise. She was equally as passionate about her job as she was private about her personal life. Only the few who really knew her understood the demons she battled.

Mike looked over her shoulder as she snapped off a pair of latex gloves and tossed them in the trash. "Yeah, I signed him off last night."

"Well, I just wanted to make sure. You know the son is still sticking to his story."

Mike laughed. "I don't care what he says. His father was not murdered by his stepmother. John Kemper died of liver disease. End of story."

It was a family feud that had John Jr. accusing his stepmother of murder. But he knew as well as anyone that his father had finally succumbed to his long years of drinking.

Mike went back to the lab and got ready to work on her next case—a victim of an apartment fire. What first looked like an accident now appeared to be a cover-up for another crime. The vic had no I.D. on him and wasn't a resident. All the apartment tenants had escaped the fire and were accounted for. The body wasn't found until the next day when the fire department overhauled the site.

Nathan walked back into the lab and started laying out the instruments Mike would need. "I already took x-rays. They should be ready in just a minute."

"Thanks, Nathan. You're too good to me."

"Well, one good act deserves another. What about dinner at my place? I could throw some steaks on the grill, get some wine coolers, and maybe fire up the jets on the Jacuzzi. How about it?"

Mike just laughed. "No . . . no . . . and absolutely not."

"Come on, Mike, why are you so uptight?" Nathan asked with a smooth voice and a sensual bounce of his brow. "You've heard the talk; you know I'm very accommodating. Why do you keep turning me down?"

"Because I've *heard* the talk, I know you're *very* accommodating, and you also have the reputation of wanting a little *dessert* at the end of each date. Look, Nathan, I don't do that, and you don't take rejection well. You're a great assistant and a good friend. Let's just leave things the way they are."

Nathan reached for the x-ray film and punched it onto the viewing wall. "Man, Mike, you are one hard nut to crack. Are you sure that's just a nickname? Maybe I've been barking up the wrong tree."

"I'll bring in my birth certificate if that will make you feel any better. But then again, maybe you'd prefer to have an excuse." She looked at him with that *can we get back to business* look before turning her attention to the light board. Nathan turned on the back light. The x-ray revealed exactly what they were looking for.

"Bingo!" Mike said as she pointed to a spot on the screen. "We've got lead."

TYLER WAS UNLOADING A BOX of personal items at a desk across from his new partner. Jim Thompson was a veteran with the Emerald Lake police force and the only other detective. He was a great guy and someone Tyler was looking forward to working with. Tyler had only been at the station a week when Jim informed him he was having a second desk moved into his office so they could work together. Tyler was surprised. Jim was the senior officer at the station and had every right to have his own office. But Jim didn't seem to take his title too seriously and welcomed the company.

"Hey, Tyler, how are ya doin'?"

Jim came in with a cup of coffee in one hand and the classifieds in the other. Hanging his jacket over the back of his chair, he took a seat behind his weathered desk and threw his large Dexter loafers on the desktop.

"Good. Now that I have my own space, I thought I'd bring in some of my personal stuff." Tyler looked over at Jim, who seemed to be studying the paper. "What's so interesting?"

It took a minute before Jim realized Tyler had asked him a question.

"I'm looking through the classifieds for a puppy."

Tyler laughed. "A puppy! What on earth do you want with a puppy?"

"Not for me, dummy, for my grandson. He's turning six on Friday. I've been wearing my daughter down for a whole year, and she's finally caved in. I've got exactly three days to find the perfect pup."

"Hey, there's a kennel down the road from where I live. I've been meaning to check it out since I moved here. How about we take a look at it together?"

"What kind of dogs?" Jim asked, sounding uninterested as he continued skimming the ads.

"Labs."

Jim's eye caught Tyler's. "You're on." He lowered his feet to the floor and took one last swig of his coffee before grabbing for his jacket and following Tyler out to the parking lot.

LATER THAT AFTERNOON IN THE BREAK ROOM, the appearance of Bridges, the chief medical examiner, caught both Mike and Nathan by surprise.

"I just wanted to let you guys know the work you did on the Cumming's case last week was exceptional."

To Mike it had been routine stuff. She had been able to remove the bullet from the burn victim and send it to ballistics. The victim's fingerprints were undistinguishable, but the dental imprints she had taken and DNA extracted from the femur had been enough to I.D. the victim. It had been basic forensics for Mike, but she had heard through the grapevine that the victim had been someone on the FBI's most wanted list. The captain was garnering many kudos for solving the case. The fact that he was making sure to pass the "that-a-boys" down the line was commendable.

Mike sat in the break room for a few moments longer. Nathan had already moved on to his next subject for the day—not a person to examine, but someone he was trying to secure a date with for the weekend. Mike couldn't understand why Nathan insisted on being such a lady's man. He was very attractive and a pleasant guy when he wasn't delivering pickup lines. It was a shame. He would never find someone to settle down with if he didn't do something about his developing reputation as a player.

Mike glanced at her watch and decided to call it a day. She had put in enough overtime in the last few weeks to justify getting off a little early. This was one of the few times she was caught up on her workload and decided to take advantage of it. She locked up her office, let Nathan know she was leaving, and walked out to her car, pleased that she would actually be getting home before dark. Sliding into her truck, she slipped in a CD, cranked up the volume, and headed for home.

JIM AND TYLER PULLED INTO THE HEAVILY RUTTED driveway of the kennel. Though they had left the station hours ago, they'd been radioed about a suspicious package left in front of the Quick Mart. It turned out to be nothing more than a bag of trash, but the store owner had let his imagination get the better of him. He insisted he'd heard the package ticking, only to realize that his own wrist watch was the culprit. Well, one thing led to another, and before Jim and Tyler knew it, the day was shot. It was almost

5:00, and they were just now getting the chance to see what the kennel had to offer. Jim was glad that Tyler had volunteered to drive, knowing that his sedan never would have been able to handle the potholes in the old asphalt.

They could hear the dogs barking even before the kennels came into view. Tyler pulled up next to another truck and crossed the driveway to the fenced kennel. There were at least ten different Labs of various colors and sizes. Tyler was immediately drawn to a chocolate colored, full-sized Lab that was running the length of the enclosure. Jim craned his neck to see if he could spy any puppies when he heard a robust voice behind him.

"Can I help you, gentlemen?"

Both men turned around to see an older man in jeans and a flannel shirt.

"Why, Jim, you old son of a gun," the kennel owner said with an outstretched hand. "What brings you out here?"

Jim grasped his hand and gave it a hearty shake. "I wanted to get a puppy for my grandson. When Tyler told me about the kennel down the street from his place, I didn't even put it together that it was you."

They talked like old friends while Tyler played with the chocolate Lab through the fence.

"Frank, this is my partner, Tyler. Tyler, this is Frank Madigan."

Tyler stood, wiped his wet, dog-kissed hand on his pants, and shook Frank's hand.

"So, Frank, got any pups?" Jim asked.

"Three females."

"Can I see them?"

"Sure thing. They're in the inside pen."

Jim followed Frank around the back of the fenced kennel. Tyler squatted down next to the chain link running cage and extended his hand to the Lab that had already connected with him. The dog wiggled and whimpered, excited by Tyler's attention. Stroking his silky coat for some time, Tyler could feel himself getting attached. He wanted to get in the pen, but there was an alarm on the gate and the other two men were nowhere to be found. Tyler walked around the back of the house and knocked on the door, but no one answered. He poked his head inside the large ranch-style kitchen and yelled to see if he could get anyone's attention. Still nothing. Finally, he stepped inside and took a quick look around. Walking a few steps across the kitchen, he could see what looked like a family room. He took a swift glance from side to side before stepping back into the kitchen.

"What do you think you're doing?"

Tyler turned around to see a petite blonde standing in the doorway with a gun in her hand. She was out of breath but didn't seem the least bit nervous. Tyler decided he wouldn't take any chances. He put his hands up and started to explain who he was.

5

"I'm Detective Tyler Henderson. I work for the Emerald Lake Police Department. I'm going to reach inside my jacket to get my—"

"Bull! Don't move!"

"Excuse me?" Tyler said confused.

"You're messing with the wrong chick, mister. I'm quite familiar with the ELPD, and you're not one of them."

"But I can show you my badge." Tyler tried for a second time to reach inside his jacket.

"Uh, uh, uh. Keep your hands where I can see them."

"This is ridiculous! I have I.D."

"Mike, is that you?"

Tyler was relieved to hear Jim approaching.

"Who's there?" she yelled but didn't take her eyes off Tyler.

"That's my partner, for cryin' out loud!" Tyler shouted.

Jim came into view over her shoulder but instead of calling her off, he started laughing hysterically. Tyler was ready to explode. "Grab the gun, Jim, before she blows my head off!"

"You know this perp?" she said, still holding the gun on Tyler.

"Yeah, he's my new partner," Jim said still laughing.

The blonde cringed. "You're the new guy?"

"Yeah, I'm the new guy!" Tyler's voice rose as he lowered his hands to his waist. He looked at the woman who had held him at gunpoint and watched her squirm as she lowered the gun.

"Hey, I'm sorry, it's just that—"

"Yeah, well, maybe next time you should try listening instead of doing your impersonation of Dirty Harry." Tyler's reply was clipped and left no room for apologies.

"Maybe next time you'll think twice before entering someone's home without permission. Because if I remember the code book correctly, unless you have a warrant or just cause, you just broke the law."

Tyler was hot. "Look ..." he said, wagging his finger at her.

"Okay, okay, enough you two. Allow me." Jim stepped between the two of them. "Detective Henderson, this is Mike Madigan, the county M.E.; Mike, Detective Tyler Henderson."

Mike extended her hand to welcome Tyler, hoping he would let the matter drop.

Tyler looked at Mike's hand and then at his partner. "I'll be waiting for you in the truck when you're ready." Passing them both, Tyler exited through the back door, whizzing by the confused kennel owner, who was carrying a black Lab puppy.

"Hmm, not a very friendly guy, is he?" Mike said as she put the small handgun back into the holster that was concealed behind her back, under her oversized tank top.

Jim watched as Tyler walked away. He was going to go after him and reprimand him for his behavior, but when he reviewed the scene he had just witnessed, he started laughing all over again.

"What are you doing here?" Mike said as she reached into the refrigerator for a bottle of water.

"What just happened?" In walked Mike's father, who handed the pup to Jim.

"Mistaken identity," Jim said as he playfully nuzzled the docile pup that he would be taking home to his grandson.

"Dad, you remember Detective Thompson."

"Of course, I do, but what about him?" Frank tossed a look over his shoulder to where Tyler had stormed away.

"That's my new partner."

"Well, tell your partner he'd better take a refresher course on unlawful entry. I could have shot first and asked questions later," Mike said as she swigged her water.

It took a minute for Jim to explain why he was there, who Tyler was, and why he thought Tyler was in the house. After all was said and done, Mike felt guilty for being so gruff with the new guy. She grabbed another bottle of water from the fridge and headed to where Tyler was sitting in his truck.

Tyler watched as she crossed the yard. She was cute, he had to admit that. She was maybe all of 100 pounds and had obviously been out running. She wore blue nylon running shorts and a white tank top that had to be ten times too big for her. Her almost platinum ponytail bobbed up and down as she walked. She was very attractive—that is, until she opened her mouth.

Walking to the side of Tyler's oversized truck, Mike closed one eye to block out the glare of the sun.

"I came to apologize," she said as she stuck the bottle of water through the rolled-down window as a peace offering.

Tyler tried to ignore her, but she didn't budge. "Look, I said I'm sorry. If you can't handle that, then you've got bigger problems than procedures and policies." She turned to walk away.

"And you've got a smart mouth."

Tyler was still mad, and her second indictment of his actions didn't help matters.

"Excuse me?" she said as she turned back to Tyler. "You're the one who should be apologizing to me. You were the one who was where he didn't belong. You scared me half to death, and then you stormed off like some kind of spoiled brat. You can't be a very good cop if you can't admit to screwing up."

Mike turned to leave for the second time when Tyler jumped out of his truck and grabbed her arm. He spun her around, sending the water bottle flying. "Talk about spoiled. Who do you think you are, telling me how to do my job? It's obvious why you work with dead people. Your people skills stink."

Mike twisted her arm free from Tyler's grasp. She was ready to unload on him when Jim yelled at them both. "Knock it off, you two!" Jim walked up to them with the Lab pup in his arms and stretched his neck, moving his head from side to side, trying to dodge the pup that was trying to lick his face. "Look, this was a simple case of mistaken identity. Can't you two give it a rest?"

Mike looked at Tyler, and Tyler looked away. "Hey, I did my good deed. I apologized, but that's obviously not good enough for your Detective Henderson. It was nice seeing you again, Jim. I'm glad you finally made it out here. Don't be a stranger." Mike walked away.

Jim looked at Tyler with concern. He wasn't sure he wanted a partner with such a short fuse.

They were almost back at the station when Jim finally broke the silence.

"So what are you going to do with your days off, Tyler?"

"I'm not sure. I still have some unpacking to do. Probably just hang around the house." Tyler's plans *had* been to go to the kennel and pick out a dog, but that wasn't going to happen now.

"Then let me give you a piece of advice. Take it easy. Relax. I've worked with my share of hotheads, and as you can see, they're not around here anymore. I like you, Tyler. I like you a lot, but I won't put up with any of that flying-off-the-handle garbage."

Tyler was frustrated with himself as he drove home. He'd lost his temper with the M.E. and he knew it, but to have Jim reprimand him made him feel like a rookie. He thought about his argument with Madigan. She had gotten completely under his skin. The accusations she leveled at him incensed him, and he didn't like the fact that he had been shown up in front of Jim. Although he had never thought of himself as a chauvinist, to be so easily cut down to size by a woman really ticked him off, even if she had been right.

CHAPTER TWO

Tyler had been at the new job a month and was loving it. Normal hours. Great people. Just what he had hoped for when moving to Emerald Lake. The camaraderie at the station was comfortable, although he was having a difficult time with one of the patrolmen. He just wrote him off as a person who took a little longer to get to know. And then there was Mike Madigan, the medical examiner.

Their paths had crossed a few times, and the tension between them was obvious. Tyler knew her actions were understandable at the house. She had thought he was an intruder and was just trying to protect her property. But because she had been so ready to remind him of that, he wasn't willing to concede that she was right. Her overconfident attitude was not an attractive quality.

Jim and Tyler had just finished up at the M.E.'s office regarding the body of a transient found on the far side of town. Mike gave them the specifics on what she had discovered and told them she was ruling his death natural causes. Tyler questioned her analysis and thought she might be jumping to conclusions.

"The man just ran out of time, Tyler. His body had deteriorated under the conditions in which he had lived for the last several years. It was his lifestyle that killed him, but that isn't exactly a formal cause of death. My ruling is natural causes."

Jim and Tyler pulled away from the county facility and headed back to Emerald Lake. Jim had had enough of the friction between Mike and Tyler, so he decided to bring it to an end.

"I'm going to give you a little assignment to take care of on your days off, Tyler. It shouldn't take much of your time, but I want it done before you come back to work."

"What's that?" Tyler asked as he turned into the parking lot and pulled up alongside Jim's sedan.

"I want you to apologize to Mike Madigan."

Jim walked to the back door of the station and left Tyler standing in the parking lot, speechless. When he was finally able to react, he stormed into the station, straight to the office he shared with Jim. "You want me to do what?"

"You heard me. You've got two days. Before you come back to work, I want to know that you and Mike have cleared the air."

"But—"

"No, buts! Look, Tyler, I know this is a small town, but as you can see, we still have our share of drownings, car accidents, and unexplained deaths. Mike is not a person you're going to be able to avoid, and quite frankly, I'm tired of the tension that I feel whenever the two of you are in the same room. I'm going to put an end to it right now."

Tyler tried to rebut what Jim had said, but Jim quickly stopped him with a raised hand. "This is not up for debate, Tyler. I'll see you in a few days."

Tyler stood in the office for a moment, dumfounded by Jim's statement. He was going to have to go back to the kennel and apologize to the smart-mouthed M.E. Boy, what a way to ruin a couple of days off.

MIKE HAD TAKEN HER SHOWER BUT STILL felt agitated. She knew it was because of the new detective. They had exchanged words again today, and each time they did his superior attitude grated on her nerves. He had the uncanny knack of making her feel as though she had to defend her work. She was good at her job and she knew it; but with cases that involved him, she was taking no chances. She left no room for error. She wouldn't give him the satisfaction of correcting her or questioning her findings.

It was a shame he was so defensive and headstrong. If it weren't for the way they wore on each other's nerves, Mike would have thought Tyler deserved a second look. In fact, a few times she'd found herself losing her train of thought because of the way his piercing hazel eyes studied her as she spoke. He was definitely her type: strong, fit, and appreciative of the outdoors. His incredible good looks couldn't be denied. Too bad his personality was so flawed.

Mike shook off her morose mood as she walked the path from her place to the kennels where she knew she would find her father and Arnie, his helper. She watched for a few moments as he and his assistant exercised the dogs. She smiled as she saw her dad work with dedication and affection. Breeding dogs had become his life after her mother had left. Mike and her dad had suffered through quite a bit in the last fifteen years. But they had each other, and that always seemed to be enough.

"Hey, Dad. I'm cooking dinner tonight. So be at my place at say 6:30?"

"Sure," he said as he tried to wrestle a sock away from Sally, his prize Labrador.

"You're welcome to come too, Arnie," she said with a smile.

Arnie dipped his head the way he always did when Mike talked to him. Arnie was in his forties but slow by nature. Frank had befriended him and given him a job working with the dogs. He was still shy around Mike, even though he'd known her for years.

"Thanks, Mike, but I'll be going now."

His response was always the same. He was always polite around Mike but never took her up on any of her offers.

Mike's place was just down the path from her father's house. She had converted the old barn-style shed into a small studio apartment—the only time she'd used her talents as a decorator to design anything. Her passion for interior design had taken a back seat when she decided to pursue a career in forensics. Thrilled that she hadn't moved far away, her father felt blessed that she lived close to him. After all, she was all he had. Her and the dogs.

Mike gathered all the ingredients for her dad's favorite meal. Manicotti wasn't the easiest dish, but for him it was worth the effort. She dropped the pasta in a large pot of boiling water and prepared some bread for grilling. Whipping together a cheesecake from an ordinary boxed mix, she planned to smother it with a strawberry glaze to give it a little extra pizzazz. While her red sauce was simmering, she stepped out onto her balcony overlooking the lake. This is why she never wanted to move.

Emerald Lake was a small suburb on the outskirts of the county. On the rare occasions that Mike toyed with the idea of moving closer to work, she always asked herself why. She bordered the county that she was responsible for and could be at work in thirty minutes when necessary. But, on her off time, she was able to enjoy a small paradise that few people had stumbled across.

Returning to the kitchen, Mike checked to see if the shells were al dente. *Perfect*, she thought and drained them in a colander. She filled them with a creamy mixture of ricotta, mozzarella, and freshly grated Parmesan cheese, and then topped the pasta with marinara sauce and more cheese. While her pasta shells baked, Mike tossed a small green salad with cucumbers and cherry tomatoes.

Thirty minutes later Mike put the bread under the broiler, just as her dad walked in.

"Smells good, sweetheart."

"Thanks, Dad."

"It's a shame that you waste talent like this on me."

Her dad had that look in his eye that Mike was so familiar with.

"Don't start, Dad."

"What? I just think you need to get out more. You need to—"

The ringing phone interrupted his "you need to find someone and settle down" speech, much to Mike's relief.

"Madigan." Mike waited for someone to talk on the other end, but no one responded. "Hello?" Mike was ready to hang up when she finally heard his voice.

"This is Detective Henderson."

Mike rolled her eyes and sighed. "What, questioning my work isn't enough for you; now you're going to crank call my house?"

"I'm not crank calling you. I was going to start talking to you about something when my call-waiting line clicked. How about you give the attitude a rest."

Tyler had been sulking around his place, made himself dinner, and realized he wanted to get this monkey off his back. The sooner the better. As soon as he dialed Mike's number, his other line began to ring. He told his sister he would call her right back, but before he could get to the other line, Mike had already answered.

"Fine, so talk. I have a dinner guest, and we were just getting ready to eat, so I'd appreciate it if you would get to the point."

Henderson brought out the worst in her. She was running out of patience, and he was ruining her delicious dinner. Her father laughed at her, and she quickly silenced him with an oven mitt to the side of the head.

"Fine. I called to apologize."

"So you're sorry?" she said with just the smallest grin. "It takes a big man to admit when he's wrong. Apology accepted."

"Hey, I never said anything about being wrong. I'm just sorry that we butted heads." Tyler's voice bristled.

"That's got to be the most meaningless apology I've ever heard." Mike planted her hand on her hip. Her father could tell she was ready to unload on someone.

"I'm just following orders."

"I get it now. You're not really sorry. Thompson told you to apologize, didn't he?"

"Look, I'm just doing what I was told."

Mike was ready to sound off again when she got a whiff of smoke from the broiler. "Shoot, now I've burned my dinner. Thanks a lot, Henderson. You've turned out to be one heck of a guy."

Mike slammed down the phone and yanked out the broiler tray. The blackened toast was burned beyond recognition. She grabbed a dish towel, took the tray out of the broiler, and dropped it onto the stove top with a few choice words.

"It's okay, honey. I like it well done." Her father was trying to be loving.

She slumped her shoulders in frustration. "It looks like one of my case files."

TYLER SAUNTERED AROUND HIS KITCHEN agitated by his conversation with the M.E. He scolded himself for letting her once again get the better of him.

He decided to work off his pent-up aggression by going for a jog. He changed into his black running shorts and an old black T-shirt that read, "Handcuffs are my specialty." The shirt had been a joke from his sister. She had bought it at some trashy novelty store, but thought the irony was too good to pass up. She knew Tyler's conservative nature would never allow him to wear it, so she bet him dinner and a movie that he wouldn't wear it in public. Tyler actually thought the shirt was pretty funny, won the bet, and it quickly became his favorite running shirt. It was big enough to conceal his firearm, and it was a great deterrent from unwanted conversations.

Tyler headed for the path that would take him completely around the lake. It definitely beat running around the streets of L.A. Signs of fall were beginning to show on the trees that dotted the shoreline. Jet skiers and small sailboats were scattered about the lake, their occupants trying to grasp the last warm days before the chilly air of fall arrived. Tyler finally felt some of the tension leave his shoulders as he took in the beauty of what he now called home.

The houses along the lake ranged from rustic cabins to immense vacation homes. Some houses stretched almost to the water's edge and showed off their own well-equipped docks and party cabanas. Others looked as if they would fall down if the wind hit them just right. Of course, every house faced the lake and had a huge deck or patio—that was the whole point of living lakeside.

Tyler had taken his time and hadn't made it completely around the lake when he heard voices up ahead on the trail. That was the only problem with this path: the narrow way was so wooded you usually couldn't see people until you were right on top of them. Tyler turned the corner and saw four dogs playing up ahead. The scene reminded him that he really needed to get himself a running companion. Of course, now he would have to look some-where besides the kennel down the road.

Tyler recognized Mike and her father, but it was too late to disappear. One of the dogs darted ahead and ran to Tyler's side. It was the chocolate Lab that he had played with at the kennel. Tyler spied a stick along the running path, picked it up, and sent it sailing up ahead. The dog took off like a shot and quickly brought the stick back to Tyler's outstretched hand. Tyler continued to play with the dog, but only until Mike and her father got closer. He didn't want another confrontation with her, so he changed directions and headed back the way he came. The only problem was that the dog now thought he had a friend and started following him down the path.

"Skyler . . . Skyler, come." Mike saw the dog following a jogger. She hurried down the path to follow the dog, disappointed with his disobedience. "Skyler, heel!" The dog ignored her as the jogger continued to run in the other direction.

"Excuse me!"

Tyler had heard Mike yelling at her dog, but this time she was talking to him.

"Excuse me!"

Tyler stopped where he was but didn't turn around.

"I'm sorry to interrupt your run, but could you stop for a moment? My dog seems to be taken with you and is not following my commands."

Mike was approaching the jogger, who had his hands at his waist and was breathing rapidly. When he turned around, Tyler saw an expression on her face that could be described as surprise, but he was sure it was disgust.

"Oh, it's you," Mike said as she pulled a strand of hair out from the corner of her mouth. "You know what? You're really beginning to bother me. First you invade my house, and then you treat me like a rookie at work—my place of work, mind you. You call my house with an empty apology and now you're here. What is your problem?"

"Look, I was just jogging when your dog started following me. Obviously he was looking for better company."

Frank had followed Mike as she tried to retrieve the dog. He recognized Tyler. "Hey, aren't you the guy . . . the cop from—"

"Yeah, unfortunately, that was me."

"Unfortunate is right," Mike said with a huff.

It seemed as if Mike had to have the last word no matter what.

"So, what brings you around these parts?" Frank was trying to be friendly, more than Tyler could say for his daughter. Tyler tried to be polite in return.

"I bought the Franklin cabin across the lake. I like to jog when I'm frustrated, and I've had my fill of that lately."

Mike's eyes narrowed. She knew he was speaking about her.

Tyler turned to leave, but Frank kept talking. With an extended hand, he introduced himself. "Hi, I'm Frank Madigan."

Tyler received a sturdy handshake from Frank. "Tyler Henderson, nice to meet you." Mike wasn't saying a word. She just walked to the water's edge with the other three dogs and ignored Tyler all together.

"You've got some great looking dogs there, Frank."

"The best in the state," he said as he stuck out his chest with pride. "Skyler looks as though he's taken to you like a fish to water."

"Well, I did introduce myself to him the other day when I was at your place. You see, I was interested in getting a dog before I was interrupted."

Mike was pretending not to be interested in their conversation, but Tyler could see her backward glances. He decided to see how intently she was actually listening.

"This dog looks great, but I kind of thought I wanted a female. They're so much easier to handle. I mean, with the right discipline and the right encouragement, they'll do just about anything for you. Kind of like women, right Frank?" Tyler winked to let Frank know he was only kidding. Frank knew Tyler was just trying to irritate his daughter. He should've been offended but instead found it rather amusing.

"Come on, Dad, let's go. It's getting late, and I'm sure Detective Henderson has better things to do."

"Wait a minute. Is this dog for sale?" Tyler asked as he crouched down to pet the Labrador. Skyler almost bowled him over with his size and exuberance.

"Well, yeah, but are you sure Skyler is the one you want?" Frank asked as he watched the dog jump all over Tyler. "As you can see, he has a problem with discipline."

"They'll be perfect together." Mike finally decided to join in on the conversation and walked to where the two men were talking. The three other dogs wrestled and played while Tyler inquired further.

"What do you mean by a discipline problem? I just laid hardwood floors in my house. If he's not house trained, I'm gonna have to pass."

"Oh, nothing like that. He's very well trained when it comes to that and barking, and obedience within the home. He's just easily distracted and sometimes won't pay attention to you if he's off on his own hunt. Kind of like now."

"Does he always come back?"

"Oh, yeah. He'll come back. He just might have a small varmint in his mouth when he does."

Tyler bent down again and began inspecting the dog. He was full grown, had an amber sheen to his coat and bright, energetic eyes. Tyler stood and looked directly at the dog. "Skyler, sit." Skyler obeyed. Tyler looked at Mike and then back to Frank. "How much?"

Simultaneously, Frank and Mike began talking. The only problem was they said two different things. Tyler raised his eyebrows at Mike. "I guess I'll be doing business with your father. He seems a little more reasonable."

"Well, you two do what you want; I'm going home. Oreo, 'Nilla, Sally, come." Mike threw one more glance Tyler's way. "Nice shirt. Did you lose a bet, or is that really the extent of your talents?" Mike turned before Tyler had a chance to answer her. She gave a playful holler to the dogs and headed in the other direction. Skyler started to follow and then looked back at Tyler. He seemed unsure what to do.

"Why don't you follow us back home?" Frank suggested. "We can go over the details there."

"But I don't have my wallet or my car. Why don't I jog home and then I'll drive over?"

"Or you could walk with me now, and I could drive you back to your place."

The offer was tempting. It was already dusk, and Tyler would have to hustle to get back before dark. "Are you sure you don't mind?"

"Not at all." Frank turned to walk towards home. He liked this guy. Maybe if Mike was quiet long enough, she would see something in him too. Frank decided that striking up a friendship with Tyler might not be a bad idea.

"Come on, Skyler. Let's go get you packed up."

Tyler walked with Frank back to his place while Frank filled him in on everything Tyler needed to know about Emerald Lake. Tyler found out where he could find the best fishing hole and the location of some back-road short-cuts, what the hours of the worship services were at Frank's church, and where to go when he wanted really good Mexican food.

"That's great, but Italian's my favorite. Where would I go to get a really good fettucini or a big bowl of tortellini?"

"Well, that's hard to say. Mike makes the best Italian food in town, so I don't even bother eating out when I want Italian. I just wait until she gets good and frustrated with work, and I know a home cooked meal is in the works. Like today. Out of the blue, she's cooking me—"

Frank stopped, realizing what he was saying. Tyler chuckled and admitted that he knew he had been the object of Mike's frustration.

"I didn't mean to upset her, but I'm glad it worked out for somebody." Tyler pondered something that had been on his mind since the first time he and Mike had squared off. "Let me ask you this. Is Mike her real name, or is it just a nickname?"

"It's a nickname. Her real name is Michal."

Tyler was puzzled. "But that's just as bad. I mean, I'm not blind. She looks nothing like a Michael. Why did you choose such a masculine name? I mean why not call her Michelle?"

"Michelle was her sister's name. You see, when my wife was expecting, we found out she was having twins. The doctor told us we were having a boy and a girl. Michal kind of surprised us all. Anyway, we had grown so attached to the names, we decided to go ahead and call her Michal. We decided it wasn't all that strange. People these days call their kids Moonbeam, Dakota, Love—with names like that, Michal seemed pretty normal to us."

"So you have two daughters I'm going to have to avoid?" Tyler was only joking when Frank's demeanor changed completely.

"Michelle was killed nearly fifteen years ago."

"Hey, Frank. I'm sorry. I had no idea."

"Of course you didn't. Don't worry about it." Frank and Tyler continued to walk in silence. They took a private path that led to Frank's property. Tyler noticed that Mike had gone into a small cottage-style home that was closer to the water. Frank continued to walk up the path to the large ranch-style home and the kennels in which Tyler had first seen Skyler.

"So, Mike lives here with you?"

"Yeah, that's her place over there."

"It must have been hard for her to lose her sister. I hear twins have a unique connection."

"Changed her life. It changed all our lives."

Tyler glanced back at the cottage with French doors and a balcony covered with flowers. Mike ducked from view, but not before Tyler had seen her watching him.

Frank put together a care package for Tyler to take home. He did that with all the dogs he sold. He confirmed that Skyler was $300 and told Tyler he could bring the money by anytime that week.

"Are you sure that's the right price? Because I'm willing to pay the $400." Tyler was referring to the quote Mike had given him.

"$300 is just fine," Frank confirmed with a smile.

Skyler was raring to go. He paced the back of Frank's truck bed all the way to Tyler's house. Frank slowly pulled into the driveway and took in the house at the end of the drive.

"Hey, this place looks better than I remember it. Old George had let it go for several years."

"Some broker bought it last year and started renovating it. He got the outside completely restored, and then I came along. I decided to finish the inside myself and bought it from him about nine months ago. I have a few more things I would like to do to the place, but I'm satisfied with it for now."

Frank pulled to a stop, and immediately Skyler jumped out. He raced down the drive and then back again. He took off around the front of the house and sure enough, came out the other side.

"Are you sure he's not going to bug out on me?" Tyler questioned.

Frank laughed. "Well, if he does, you'll know where to find him."

"Want to come in and have a look around? Then I can get you that check," Tyler offered.

"There's no hurry for the money, but yeah, I'd love to see what you've done with the place."

Frank walked with Tyler into the huge rock entry. It looked as though slate on the front porch continued into the house. When they entered the living room, Frank could see straight through to the large picture windows that overlooked the lake. The view was spectacular. Skyler followed them in, running from room to room, taking in his new home.

Tyler was on the stairs. "I'll be right down, Frank. Make yourself at home." Skyler bolted up the stairs, beating Tyler to the top. He poked his nose in every room and finally disappeared in the same room as Tyler.

Frank continued to roam around, looking at the detailing that Tyler had added to the old cabin. He was impressed. Tyler reemerged from upstairs,

Skyler right on his heels. He handed Frank a check for $350. Frank tried to refuse. Tyler interrupted him.

"I decided to split the difference. Consider it my thanks for the ride home, the pointers, and the friendly conversation."

"My pleasure, young man. You know, I don't believe in coincidences. I believe God allowed our paths to cross for a reason." Frank put a hand on Tyler's shoulder as they walked back out to the driveway. "Don't make yourself a stranger, now, you hear me? You come around any time you want and bring that mangy mutt of yours," Frank teased before bending down and wrestling with Skyler's jowls. "He's a good dog. You two will do just fine together."

Frank waved good-bye before heading down the driveway. Skyler chased him halfway down the dirt road and then obediently came back to Tyler when he called him.

MIKE WAS SITTING ON HER BALCONY watching the moonbeams dance on the water. She didn't hear her dad as he strolled onto the balcony.

"Can I join you?"

"Sure."

He took the seat next to her, leaned his head on the back of the chair, and stared into a sky decorated with an incredible amount of stars.

"I never get tired of this view."

Not answering, Mike just sighed.

"That Tyler fella seems like a pretty decent guy. You should see what he's done with George's old place."

"Not interested, Dad." Her eyes were closed and irritation was evident in her voice.

"Come on, Michal. Look at you. You're young and beautiful and intelligent, but you're closing yourself off." Frank got to his feet and started striding across the balcony. "You don't date, you don't go out, you don't have friends, and you stopped going to church."

"I'm not closing myself off, Dad. I have a very strenuous job that people don't understand. When I have time off, I want to be able to decompress, relax, and not have to make small talk with people who think what I do is gross."

Frank plopped down in the chair. "But look at this Tyler guy. He's a cop, so he understands how important your job is. He likes jogging; you like jogging. His favorite food is Italian; you make great Italian food. He loves dogs; you love dogs. And you should see what he's done with his house—hardwood floors, open beam ceilings, slate tile—"

Mike got up before her father could finish. "He sounds like a wonderful catch, Dad. You two should be very happy together." She leaned over and placed a kiss on his forehead. "Good night, Dad."

"But, Michal—"

Good night, Dad," Mike said as she walked through the open French doors.

Frank felt defeated. His daughter's stubbornness seemed to be hedging on self-destruction. It brought him close to tears. Michal had always been the outgoing one. She was a cheerleader, class president, and dance chairman— she did everything, that is, until Michelle was killed.

Frank understood Michal's anger and grief. Michelle's investigation had been compromised, and her murder went unsolved. Michal changed her life-long ambition of becoming an interior designer and switched her major to forensic pathology. She studied with a passion and scored at the top of her class. She had made up her mind that she never wanted another family to live with the unanswered questions that she did.

At first, Frank admired his daughter. She didn't allow her grief to debili-tate her; she allowed it to empower her. That's what he thought back then. Now he wasn't so sure.

Frank headed home, knowing prayer was still the only way he could help Michal—unless he could peak Tyler's interest.

TYLER PLAYED WITH SKYLER until they were both exhausted. He sat on his deck looking over the lake with Skyler at his feet. He had enjoyed his conversation with Frank who reminded him of his dad. He was obviously a man of faith, but Tyler wondered if it had preceded his daughter's death or came as a result of it. If walking with the Lord was his lifestyle, it certainly hadn't rubbed off on his daughter, not that having a child rebel from their childhood upbringing was strange. His sister was the perfect example.

Tyler's thoughts reminded him that he had never called Hailey back. He looked at his watch and saw that it was 11:30. That was pretty late, but Hailey would rather be awakened than wonder all night if something had happened to her brother.

Tyler pushed the preset number of her cell phone and waited.

"Hel-lo." She didn't sound as though she were asleep.

"Hailey, it's me."

"Well, what do you know; you didn't fall of the face of the earth."

"Hailey, where are you? I can hardly hear you." Tyler strained to hear her above the noise in the background.

"If a club were quiet, it wouldn't be much fun now, would it?"

Tyler could tell she'd been drinking. "Who's with you, Hailey?"

"Amy and some other friends. You don't know them."

"Let me talk to Amy, Hailey."

"Look, Ty, I'm glad you called and that you're okay, but that doesn't give you the right to give me the third degree or interrogate my friends. What do you want, anyway?"

"You called me, remember?"

"Oh, yeah. Kelly called looking for you. Says she's having second thoughts and was missing you. She wanted to know if I thought it would be okay if she gave you a call."

"What did you tell her?"

"I told her to drop dead, but I figured I should leave that decision up to you. No one at the station is giving out your new number, and you're not listed in Emerald Lake. Should I give her your number?"

"I don't think so, Hailey. I don't feel like dealing with her right now. I'm surprised she hasn't called the Emerald Lake Station. She could have reached me there."

"I think she's afraid of causing waves."

Tyler thought it over for a few more minutes, barely being able to hear his sister through all the noise coming over the phone. "I think I'll pass for now, Hailey. If she gets desperate enough, she knows where I am."

"She always seemed a little desperate to me anyway. I think you're better off without her." Hailey laughed, but Tyler wasn't amused.

"Hailey, are you sure you're all right? I can't handle being this far away wondering if you're going to make it home tonight."

"Don't worry, Ty. Amy's not drinking." Hailey's voice became a little more compassionate to her brother's concern. "I'll give you a call later."

Tyler hung up and immediately said a prayer. His sister had not taken their father's death well and was using it as an excuse to self-destruct. Tyler and Skyler headed upstairs, ready to call it a night.

Tyler showered and came out of his bathroom to find Skyler lying at the foot of his bed, nuzzled in his comforter. He raised his amber head with eyes that asked the question.

"Yeah, you can stay there," Tyler said as he walked over and scratched Skyler's head. "But if you move anywhere near my pillows, you're going to find yourself out in the cold."

Skyler cocked his head as if he understood and waited for Tyler to climb into bed. Once he did, Skyler stretched out alongside Tyler's legs and sighed before going to sleep.

CHAPTER THREE

Tyler arrived at the office a few minutes after Jim because he had stopped off at the pet store to get some items for Skyler. They had spent the rest of his days off getting to know each other.

"So, how's it going in puppyland?" Tyler asked Jim.

"Are you kidding me? That little scamp has been in, over, under, behind, and on top of every piece of furniture we have."

Tyler was confused. "I thought you bought her for your grandson?"

"I did. We just get to puppy sit whenever they're out of town. She's adorable but a handful. Just like having another kid in the house." Jim got situated behind his desk and started going over some reports. "How 'bout you? How were your days off?" Jim said.

"Interesting."

"Did you complete the assignment I gave you?" Jim questioned as he looked over the glasses that hung off the bridge of his nose.

"Yep. Even spent some time with Frank. In fact, I got myself that Lab I was looking at."

Jim was relieved to know that Tyler had righted his standing with Mike. She was a decent girl. She and Tyler had just gotten off on the wrong foot.

"Anything interesting happen while we were off?" Tyler inquired as he logged onto his computer.

"Just the usual. A couple DUI's, a party that got out of hand down at the lake, and a couple punks pitching rocks broke some windows out at the old boarded-up gas station on Easton. Normal stuff."

Jim and Tyler's day continued at a slow pace. Tyler figured by this time back in L.A. he would have had at least one meeting, fifteen calls, or some kind of case follow-up. He and Emerald Lake were getting along just fine.

Jim cut out early, wanting to give Irene a hand with puppy detail. He invited his partner over for dinner, but Tyler declined. He knew it was a considerate gesture on Jim's part, but he didn't want to intrude on family time. Instead, he decided to use the time to get acquainted with some of the officers and the procedures at his new station.

Everyone was really pleasant. Genuine. Tyler fit in just fine with these guys. There were more patrolmen than he had thought for such a small community. But with the lake and all the recreation that went on there, they needed the extra manpower. Most of these guys were locals. There were two women patrol officers, one married and one single. Jenny made it more than obvious that she was unattached. Tyler caught her staring in his direction several times. He found it flattering.

After all, Tyler was a good-looking guy: six feet, four inches tall and in excellent shape. Women were immediately attracted to him. He had a very businesslike attitude—that is, until he smiled. He had the greatest smile that made him look like the boy next door. His hazel eyes sparkled but had an intensity that was piercing. He wavered back and forth about shaving, sometimes leaving behind more than a five o'clock shadow. Jenny was admiring how good he could make a simple dress shirt look.

Most of the men were curious about Tyler and why he would leave the big city for a small town like theirs. They peppered him with questions regarding some of the investigations he had pursued. Tyler couldn't tell if they were truly interested or just comparing notes. Either way, Tyler didn't mind. He enjoyed the conversation. A couple of the guys expressed their interest in transferring to a larger department. They wanted to do more than write tickets and break up fights. Officer Billings continue to keep his distance from Tyler. He didn't join in the conversations with the others or even acknowledge that Tyler was there. His disposition and mannerisms seemed to keep people at a distance.

The weekend started off without any hiccups. Tyler, being the neat freak that he was, decided to clear some space in the file room and organize the department. Jim was all for it and offered to help. Anyone who was willing to do paperwork was okay with him. Jim and Tyler found themselves going through files that dated back almost twenty years. The files were so old they needed to be packed up for deep storage.

After the files were categorized, boxed, and labeled, they were placed in a stack designated for their storage facility at the city yard. Next, Tyler applied his expertise to rearranging the remaining files.

"Doesn't this make better sense, Jim?"

"So, is that why we hired you, because of your housekeeping skills?" Billings made the comment as he walked through the backroom. He mumbled the words under his breath, but Tyler heard them anyway. He glanced at Jim. Jim's nod told him he should just ignore it. Tyler waited until Billings left before he questioned Jim.

"What's his problem? He's avoided me like the plague since I got here."

Jim stacked one more box before answering. "He applied for the detective's position. He's still a little put out that he got passed over."

"I guess I'd be ticked off too if some stranger took the position I was gunning for. So, why wasn't he promoted?"

"He's had a few situations where he was taken before the disciplinary review board."

"Anything serious?" Tyler wanted to be aware of behaviors he should watch for.

"Let's just say he's had a problem with his temper flaring a few times."

"Wow, then I guess you were serious about not tolerating loose guns."

"What—your little communication problem? That was nothing compared to what Billings did. The department stood to lose a lot by his last incident."

"That serious?"

"That serious."

"That's a pretty big flaw if you're going to be in law enforcement. If you can't stay objective, you're going to screw up."

"Okay, now you know what Billings is all about. Don't expect him to warm up to you. In fact, it probably won't be long before he's on his way out of here."

"He's transferring?'

"No."

Jim didn't elaborate, but Tyler could only assume what he meant. Billings was walking a thin line.

Paul ducked his head into the back room. "Jim, Tyler, you've got a call. We've got a gunshot wound at Lake Memorial."

"So much for an easy Saturday," Jim said as he put down the stack of files he was organizing. "Let's go and see what this is all about."

Tyler drove them both to the hospital. A nurse motioned to them as they entered the E.R. She led them through a set of double doors and pointed out the examination room that accommodated the injured party.

"Man, this is nothing like the hospitals in L.A. Those places had patients lining the hallways. They didn't have exam rooms either. They had exam areas. The only separation between you and the next guy was a flimsy piece of curtain."

Jim knocked on the door and then let himself in. When the patient looked up from where he was laying on the table, he knew he'd been nailed.

"Good afternoon. I'm Detective Thompson and this is Detective Henderson. I hear you've had a little accident." Jim was taking the lead on this one. Tyler would be taking notes.

"Man, why did they call you guys? I told them what happened. It was an accident."

"Don't blame the hospital. They were only following procedure. Doctor, do we need to wait until you're done?" Jim asked the attending physician.

"No, I've deadened the area. The bullet isn't very deep, so it shouldn't be that difficult to extract." The doctor cut open the remainder of the patient's shirt sleeve and started working.

Jim moved to the other side of the table. Tyler got a look at the wound and then took a chair in the corner.

"What's your name, son?"

"Dorian ... Dorian Thomas."

"Where do you live?"

Jim continued with his questions, getting all the background information from the patient. Then he asked the real questions.

"So, why don't you tell me what happened."

"Like I told the doc here, I was thinking about buying a gun from this guy I met at a party. I was looking it over real good. Didn't want to buy me a piece of trash. He thought I was disrespecting his merchandise and tried to grab it away from me. The gun went off, and it ended up catching me in the arm."

"So, he shot you?"

"No, man, it was an accident."

"What's his name?"

"I don't know."

"What do you mean, you don't know? The guy had to have a name."

"I only know him as E.Z."

"Where is this E.Z. fella now?"

"He split, man. He got all crazy on me, said something about getting his license suspended, and he split."

"Where did this happen?"

"At my place."

"So were you holding the gun or was this E.Z. character holding it?"

"We both were."

"So you still had possession of the gun when it went off?"

"Well, yeah, I guess."

"Was the other guy injured at all?"

"No. He was fine."

The doctor recovered the bullet from Dorian's arm. Tyler heard the piece of lead clink as it was dropped into a stainless steel tray. The doctor used a few stitches to close the wound and then bandaged the kid as Jim continued his questioning.

He repeated the same questions from other angles to see if Dorian's story would change at all. When the doctor was finished, he helped the kid to a sitting position. That's when Tyler noticed the blood on the back of Dorian's shirt.

Tyler was out of Dorian's line of vision. He got Jim's attention and rubbed his thumb and index finger together. Then he pulled on his own shirt, signifying there was something on the kid's shirt. Jim got the message. Tyler excused himself from the room while Jim finished up.

"Okay, Dorian, we're going to let you go for now. But we'll be in touch. You're not planning on going anywhere, are you?"

"Well, actually, I was planning a trip."

"That's not a good idea." Jim got a stern look of his face. "Now, I could arrest you to get you to stay put, but I don't think you want that on your record."

"You can't arrest me, man. I haven't done anything wrong."

"I've also told you to stay put for a few days, and if you're not going to take my suggestion, I'll have to take serious measures."

"Okay, man. I'll put off my trip until next weekend. But I don't like it."

"I didn't ask you to like it; I just asked you to do it."

Tyler walked in just then and tossed the kid a shirt. "Here, I don't want you having people staring at you as you leave. I'm sure you already feel bad enough." Tyler was dripping with sincerity. Jim just rolled his eyes.

"Thanks, man. You're pretty cool. How'd you get stuck with him?" Dorian sneered in Jim's direction.

Tyler chuckled. "I lost a bet."

The kid tossed his shirt in the large trash can next to the doctor's stool. The lid spun around as the shirt disappeared inside. Dorian pulled on the shirt Tyler handed him and then signed the release forms the doctor gave him. He strolled past Jim, giving him an antagonizing look. He was going to be trouble and Jim knew it.

Tyler carefully retrieved the bloody shirt from the trash can. "So, what do you think?"

"He's lying through his teeth. There's no way he could have gotten that wound if he were still holding the gun," Jim argued.

"That's what I thought. And this blood on the *back* of his shirt—it can't be his hand print."

"Doc, I need some of—"

"I'm way ahead of you. This gauze has only come in contact with the wound itself. It never touched the perimeter of the wound or the shirt—nothing. This is 100 percent his blood. And here's the bullet."

"Thanks, Doc."

Jim and Tyler left with the evidence in hand. "So I guess you know that doctor?"

"Yeah. His name is Dr. Nicholas. I'm sorry, I should have introduced you."

"No problem."

Jim was already on the phone securing a patrol officer to keep an eye on Dorian's place. Tyler walked around to the driver's side of his vehicle. "So, where to now?"

"We're going to pay Mike Madigan a visit."

INWARDLY TYLER CRINGED AS HE DROVE to the coroner's office. He knew if Jim felt he'd been lied to, Tyler would be in hot water. He had done what Jim had asked of him. He had apologized. He just hadn't relayed to Jim the fallout that had ensued after that.

Jim entered his pass code at the back door of the county building. He had called ahead so Mike was expecting them. Tyler followed him down the hall until they reached the office door labeled, Dr. Michal Madigan, Forensic Pathologist.

Jim knocked on the door and then stuck his head in the office.

"She's not in there, fellas. She's got a floater in exam room one," Nathan volunteered as he walked by.

"Thanks, Nathan."

Jim and Tyler walked past the coolers to the exam room. Jim opened the door and got Mike's attention.

"Hey, come on in. I'm just finishing up."

Tyler and Jim silently approached the table as Mike finished dictating her finds into the overhead microphone. When she was done, she pulled off her gloves and looked up at Jim. "I have just a few more things to do and then I'll be done. I'll meet you out in the hallway."

Jim and Tyler exited the room and waited in the corridor. Tyler knew he needed to come clean with Jim. He had to let him know he and Mike were still at odds with each other. If Jim thought he'd been deceived, he might lump Tyler in with the likes of Billings.

"Jim, when I talked with Mike on Tuesday—"

"Hey guys. What can I do for you?" Mike quickly looked at Tyler and then back to Jim.

Tyler wasn't sure what he was expecting, but Mike's appearance caught him completely by surprise. She pulled off her lab coat to reveal a silky, pink blouse and a form-fitting black skirt. The heels she was wearing accentuated her long, shapely legs. Her hair was pulled back in a silky bun, and the little amount of makeup she wore brightened not only her eyes but also her smile. She wore a delicate gold chain with the initials M and M on it. Obviously a reference to her moniker. Tyler could feel his face heating up. He wasn't sure if it was because of Mike's appearance or the fact that she could expose his behavior at any moment.

"We need to compare some blood samples, and we need them yesterday."

"So what are we looking at?"

"Gunshot victim. He says it was an accident, and he was the only one hurt."

"And you don't believe him?"

"Let's just say I'm betting those two samples don't match."

Jim noticed Tyler wasn't making eye contact with Mike. He knew this had to be awkward for him.

"Hey, Tyler tells me you guys had a good talk on Tuesday and that he even bought one of your dogs."

"Yeah, we talked. My dad seems to have taken a liking to him. But I'm not surprised. He's used to taking in strays." Mike settled a piercing look on Tyler.

Jim laughed at her comparison. "Well, I'm just glad you guys got things squared." Jim's phone vibrated at his side. "Hey, hang on just a minute."

Jim turned to answer his phone. "Wait, I can't hear you. Let me try to get better reception." He walked further down the hall.

Tyler turned to Mike. He had his hands stuck in his pockets and for a moment, Mike could see the slightest bit of charm glimmer from his eyes. "Thanks for not saying anything. I owe you one." His smile was breathtaking. Too bad it was wasted on such a hothead.

 "No, you owe me two."

Before Mike could say any more, Jim was off the phone and walking towards them.

"So when do you think you'll have the blood comparison done?" Jim asked as he flipped his phone shut.

"Is tomorrow morning soon enough for you?"

"Are you sure, Mike? I mean I know I'm anxious, but I don't want to rush you unreasonably."

"No big deal. I have some other things that I need to finish up, and I planned on working late tonight anyway. I'll fit it in somehow. Look, I've got two more floaters to do, and then I have to be in court. So I've got to go."

"Are you working on that party barge accident?" Jim asked.

"Yeah. It's a no-brainer. There was no alcohol involved, but two of them already tested positive for marijuana. It's hard to steer a boat when you're stoned."

Mike turned a mischievous glance towards Tyler and then smiled at Jim. "I'll let you know in the morning." She turned and disappeared into one of the exam rooms.

Tyler was quiet as they drove back to the station. Jim interrupted his thoughts.

"What are you so perplexed about, Tyler? You've had that strained look on your face ever since we left the coroner's office. Don't tell me the big city cop has a weak stomach." Jim reached across the front seat with a good-natured jab to Tyler's arm.

"No, it's not that. Believe me, I've seen my share of autopsies and exam rooms. No, I'm just trying to figure out why Mike would be interested in such a gruesome profession. I mean, I'd have to be dead not to notice how attractive she is, and she's obviously intelligent. To become a forensic pathologist takes years of schooling. She got her M.D. She could be working at a hospital or have her own practice. Why would she choose to be a coroner? It just seems so odd."

"She's got her reasons."

"Does it have something to do with her sister's death?"

Jim looked surprised at Tyler's question. "How did you know about that?"

"Frank told me."

"I'm surprised. They usually don't talk about Michelle, especially to strangers."

"Well, that was kind of my fault. I asked Frank a few questions. One thing led to another, and he told me Mike's twin had been killed." Tyler paused for a moment. "It sounds as though you've known them for a long time."

Gazing out the window, Jim said softly, "I was the one to investigate the murder."

"Murder!" Tyler was shocked. He assumed she had been in a car wreck or maybe an accident at the lake. He never considered the possibility of murder. "What happened?"

"We don't really know. Her body was dumped along the frontage road by the lake. We knew that wasn't the location of her death because of the limited amount of blood." Jim stopped. That picture in his head of Michelle was one that would bother him forever.

Tyler looked at him and realized Jim was visualizing the scene. "How'd she die?"

"There was evidence of a struggle and sexual assault. Her throat and her torso had been slashed and her hands severed—a sure way to slow down an identification."

"Did you find the guy who did it?"

"No," he said as if he were reliving the nightmare. It took him a minute to continue. "You've got to understand, Tyler, our coroner then was an older gentleman, back when the coroner was an elected official. He'd been on the post for as long as I could remember. We didn't have any of the high-tech people like the pathologists or forensic specialists we have today. Emerald Lake was a sleepy little town. Our crimes involved bike snatchings and shoplifting, or maybe a fight once in a while at the high school. We were the typical small town USA. That was before the lake renovation project."

Jim stared out the window, a look of regret on his face.

"Well, anyway, the coroner had never dealt with a murder before. He was horrified. Michelle was a local girl, someone he knew. It was more than he could handle. Her body had been found naked and brutally assaulted. He was so worried about protecting her privacy and that of her family, he just kind of checked out."

Jim paused again. It was obvious, even after all this time, the thought of Michelle's death was difficult for him to handle.

"By the time I was called in, the coroner had already taken her to the morgue and cleaned her up. He knew she would need to be identified and didn't want her parents seeing her like that. The evidence that he hadn't contaminated at the scene had been washed down the drain."

"You're kidding?" Tyler was shocked. He'd never heard of such a bungling of evidence.

"Stratford, the coroner, resigned immediately. He never recovered from what he had done. When the lake expansion project was done and our population and crime rate exploded, we teamed up with the county coroner's office."

"And Michelle's case was never solved?" Tyler added.

"I tried, Tyler, really I did. But without the necessary evidence, there was no way of following a lead or narrowing in on a suspect. Anything I could have done at that point would have only hurt the family further. I decided to label it unsolved and put it to rest.

"Mike, on the other hand, did not. She changed from being the most popular girl in school, a homecoming queen with an outgoing personality, into a distant and moody person. She decided to major in forensic pathology in college, graduated with honors, and came to work for the county. She's the youngest and the most educated they have." Jim took a breath and sighed. "Her mom left about a year after Michelle's death. She was distraught and depressed. At times she would blame Mike, saying she should have looked out for her sister better. Mike was away at school when she got the call from her dad that her mom had taken off. She couldn't live with the memories or with Michal, the walking reminder of the daughter she'd lost."

"Wow!" Tyler was overwhelmed. He couldn't imagine losing his sister, but there were times he was terrified of that very thing. He kept placing Hailey in the scenario of Michelle's death, praying that it would never come to that.

"Now you know a little about Mike Madigan."

"So, why hasn't she ever married?"

"Says she's married to her job."

"That's just an excuse," Tyler shot back.

"I guess," Jim said, rubbing his chin. "I know she's dated, but I guess some guys have a hard time with her line of work. They figure she's some kind of a freak to want to mess with dead people. At least that's what Frank has said on occasion."

"But cops understand her job is valid and very necessary. I know the guys at my last precinct would have jumped at a chance to date her. Of course, some of those guys I wouldn't even trust with a dead body."

Jim chuckled softly. "I can't say I understand all of Mike's choices. But she's one tough cookie and an expert in her field."

And a beautiful woman, Tyler thought to himself as they entered the back door of the station.

CHAPTER FOUR

After a jog with Skyler, Tyler had taken a quick shower. He opened every cupboard in the kitchen and realized he really needed to do some shopping. He looked up the name of a local pizza place that delivered. Then he thought of an even better idea.

MIKE WAS FINISHING UP HER final report on the boating victims. Three kids had died because of reckless behavior. One of the kids was responsible for the accident, but the other two drowned due to their impaired condition.

Mike went to get a soda and a snack from the break room when she heard someone being buzzed in the back door. Nathan came around the corner just as she pulled some cookies from the vending machine.

"Hey, Mike, got another vic for you. He looks like a real stiff."

She closed her eyes and whined, "No more sneaking men in at all hours of the night, Nathan." Mike snickered to herself. She and Nathan bantered all the time. "Besides, you know you're the only man for me." Mike continued her joking in a low, seductive tone. "What will people think?"

When Mike turned around, Tyler was the one who was standing there, not Nathan. Her mouth dropped open and her palms got sweaty. She tried to swallow but her mouth was bone dry. Tyler had an amused look on his face that let her know he'd heard every word she had said.

"Far be it from me to come between you and your man. I just came to offer you dinner." Tyler was standing with a pizza box in one hand and a liter of soda in the other.

"Aah . . . I didn't really mean that. Nathan and I are always joking like that. Right, Nathan?" Mike chuckled a nervous laugh. She was mortified.

"That's for sure," Nathan said as he grabbed his instant meal from the microwave. "She won't let me get to first base with her. Man, she won't even let me in the ballpark. In fact, I don't think she's participated in the world's favorite pastime since I've known her."

"Nathan!" Mike was horrified that he would say such personal things to Tyler, of all people.

Nathan only smiled as he left with his food. "I'll meet you back in exam room number two after dinner, okay?"

"Yeah. Thanks, Nathan. You've been such a great help." Her exaggerated tone let Nathan know they would have words later.

"Hey, I'm just calling them as I see them."

Mike couldn't bring herself to look at Tyler. She was too embarrassed. He walked over to the break table, put the pizza box down, and turned to her. "I knew you'd be working late, so I took a chance. I hope you like pizza?"

"I love pizza. But you didn't have to do this. I have stuff here for dinner."

"Oh, I see that. You must be on that new Oreo diet that I've heard so much about." He was referring to the bag of cookies she had in her hand. "Look, you're doing Jim a favor by pushing through those tests. I thought I would try the good cop/bad cop technique. He's the bad cop for making you work. I'm the good cop for bringing you dinner." Tyler pulled back the lid of the box and grabbed some paper plates from the counter. "I got pepperoni. I figured I couldn't go wrong with that." He pulled two pieces of pizza from the takeout box, plopped them on a paper plate, and slid them over in front of her. She pulled out a chair and sat down.

"That was really nice of you," she said as she looked at the plate in front of her.

"Good. Then that's one," Tyler quickly said before he bowed his head in prayer.

First, she was surprised that he prayed. Then, she was curious why he hadn't asked her to join him. When he was done praying, she decided to clarify something. "What do you mean 'that's one'?"

"That's one. You said I owed you two, and that's one." Tyler bit into a piece of the deep-dish pizza.

"No way. When I need a favor called in, I'm going to come looking for you, and you'll have to do what I say. I mean this is nice and everything, but you still owe me."

"Oh, I agree. I still owe you." Tyler knew that just one more deed would settle their score.

Mike decided to let it drop. The pizza was too good, and she was too hungry to spend her time talking.

They ate in relative silence, each of them enjoying their meal. After taking a swig of her soda, Mike decided to find out a little more about Tyler.

"So, why Emerald Lake?"

"What?"

"Why did you transfer there?" Mike clarified between bites.

"I was fed up with city life. I wanted a place where I could slow down."

"You got lazy," she said in an argumentative tone.

"I got tired." His tone was more along the lines of "don't push me."

She decided to change the subject. "How's Skyler doing?"

"He's doing great. I don't understand why you thought he was such a disciplinary problem. He hasn't disobeyed me once since I got him."

Mike smirked. "Just wait until he decides to have some fun outside. Then you'll see what I'm talking about."

Again, a silence hung in the room. They were almost done eating, and then they wouldn't have anything to use as a distraction.

"Your dad seems like a really nice guy. Reminds me a lot of my own dad," Tyler said.

"He is. Sometimes he can be a bit smothering, but he's a pretty good guy." Mike quickly changed the subject from family. "So, what is your take on this shooting suspect?"

"He's lying for sure. My hunch is the other guy is worse off. If I went with my instinct, I would say he's dead."

"How come?"

"The guy goes to the hospital to get help even though he knows gunshot wounds have to be reported. He says he was the only one hurt, but he has blood stains on the *back* of his shirt. I don't know. He seemed too sure of himself, as if he'd thought everything through. That's usually not the case when there's been an accident."

Mike played with a piece of crust on her plate while Tyler drained his paper cup of soda, crushed it in his hand, and tossed it in the trash can in the corner. He didn't like the silence any more than Mike did, so he tried to keep the conversation going.

"So, what's the weirdest case you've ever investigated?" he asked as he folded up the empty pizza box and cleaned off the counter.

"Well, I don't know about weirdest, but I would have to say my most awkward moment came when two wives showed up to identify the same husband."

"Really! How'd you handle that one?"

"Actually, I pride myself in having a hand in solving that case."

"How so?" Tyler sat back down at the table and stretched his large frame out in front of him, clasping his hands behind his neck.

For a brief moment, Mike was distracted by how attractive Tyler looked. When he caught her eye, she shook off the feeling and went on to explain.

"Well, the first wife comes in all distraught. While I have her in the viewing room, Nathan calls me and tells me the deceased's wife is waiting for me in my office. I excused myself for a moment to meet with the other 'wife.' I'm confused and trying to console her, and she is near hysteria, going on and on about her husband. This lasts for a few minutes when her cell phone rings. She composes herself and tells the person on the line that she's with the coroner and then bursts into sobs again. She sets her cell phone down on my desk as she tries to compose herself. I glanced at her phone and saw the name of the other 'wife' on the screen. I thought that was suspicious or a very big coincidence."

Tyler leaned forward to follow the story. Mike took a swig of soda before continuing.

"I excused myself for a minute and asked Nathan to step into my office so wife number two wasn't left alone. I headed back to wife number one and continued my conversation with her, finding out where she wanted the body sent."

"Wait a minute. What was the cause of death?" Tyler broke in as he tried to follow the story.

"Self-inflicted gunshot wound. Suicide. The cops found the note and everything. The husband admitted to having a secret life and could no longer live a lie. Anyway," Mike regrouped, "I'm talking to wife number one who seems to have gathered her composure remarkably well, when all of a sudden I have an urgent phone call to make. I'm without a phone, so I asked to borrow hers. Of course, she lets me, and while she's not looking, I scroll the history button and place a call to the last outgoing number. Guess where it rings?" Mike says smugly.

"Wife number two?"

"You got it. Nathan was even there to witness it. I asked to speak with Nathan, and unknowingly she repeated his name out loud, said I had a wrong number, and hung up."

"So the two wives already knew about each other?" Tyler chimed in.

"Bingo. The two distraught wives obviously knew each other. Of course, that evidence would have been shaky in court, but it gave the detectives something to go on. They found out later that the two wives had known about each other for some time. They had been plotting their husband's death for months."

Tyler shook his head up and down. "Good job, Madigan. Maybe you went into the wrong branch of the department."

Mike's casual demeanor changed instantly. "No, I'm where I need to be. I think families deserve answers when they lose their loved ones. They shouldn't ever have to live wondering about the truth." Mike got up from the table, washed her hands, and then headed for the door. "Thanks for the pizza, Tyler. It was good. Now if you'll excuse me, I have some work to do."

Mike exited so quickly that Tyler wasn't able to say much in return. He had thought things were going so well. Then, in an instant, it seemed as if he had lost what little ground he had gained.

TYLER WAS JUST WALKING INTO THE STATION when Jim got the call. "We were right. That was Mike, and she said she has two different blood samples and a few more surprises for us. Jim was pulling his jacket from the back of his chair. "Let's go."

They entered through the back door and walked towards Mike's office. She was on the phone and signaled for them to take a seat. Tyler took in the surroundings that made up Mike's office. It was sleek and modern, nothing like what he'd expected. There were no personal touches or family photos. The only things that identified the space as her office were her numerous degrees and plaques that hung on the wall.

"Sorry, guys. When the captain calls, you don't put him on hold."

"So, what do you have for us, Mike?" Jim asked.

"Let's go to the lab, and I'll show you. I don't have much time, though. I'm due in court." When Mike stood up, Tyler noticed she was once again without her standard lab coat. She had on a pair of navy dress slacks that fit in all the right places and a light blue sweater set. Not one hair was out of place. She looked stunning.

As she walked ahead of them down the hall, she was saying something to Jim that Tyler didn't hear. He was too busy trying to get his heart to stop racing.

"—anyway, when I was examining the blood before swabbing it, I noticed a partial thumbprint. It wasn't likely to be decent enough since it was grabbed in a fluid, but I took a stab at it."

"And?"

"And I got one. I gave the print to Derek to work on, but that's not all." Mike looked like a kid in a candy store. "I noticed there was a residue on the front of the shirt and on the sleeve. When I tested it, it was gunshot residue."

"And you're saying it was on the shoulder as well as the front of his shirt?"

"Yeah, about waist high."

Jim was perplexed. "If the other guy was holding the gun . . . and Dorian was shot in the arm—"

"That means there were two guns," Tyler said. "Why didn't you tell me any of this last night?"

Tyler looked to Mike for an answer, but Jim looked at Tyler, a satisfied grin on his face.

"I don't say things until I'm sure."

"And now you're sure?"

"Absolutely. I agree with you. There had to have been two guns involved."

"Thanks, Mike," Jim said turning to Tyler. "I think we better pay Dorian a visit."

As the two detectives headed for their vehicle, Jim's curiosity got the better of him. "So, how is it that you two were together last night?"

"I felt sorry for her putting in so much time, so I brought her dinner."

"How gallant," Jim said sarcastically, though inwardly he was smiling. He was glad that Tyler had taken an interest in Mike. Maybe Mike would follow suit.

THE CASE WAS COMING TOGETHER QUICKLY. In just a few days, Mike had gotten a match on the partial print. It belonged to a Vince Ortega, a known criminal who just happened to have gone out of town sometime the week before. Dorian had been brought in for questioning. When he stuck to his original story and refused to take a lie detector test, Jim booked him on suspicion of foul play. Mike was meeting Jim and Tyler at Dorian's place to go over it with a fine-tooth comb. Dorian would have had plenty of time to remove any evidence, but some evidence is harder to obliterate than most people realize. Hopefully, Mike would get lucky.

Mike pulled up in her huge Dodge truck. She jumped out wearing a pair of old faded jeans and a T-shirt that read, "Scientists do it with precision."

Tyler smirked. "Nice shirt."

"Look who's talking." Mike opened the shell of her truck. "It was Nathan's idea of a birthday present." She reached in for something that was just out of reach. "Hey, grab that case over there, will ya?" Tyler reached in and took hold of what looked like an old tackle box. Mike took it from Tyler and also pulled out some coveralls and a handful of Tootsie Rolls.

"What are those for? Oh no, let me guess, you use Tootsie Rolls to extract evidence from carpet fibers." Tyler's tone was sarcastic.

"It's called lunch, smart aleck. I've hardly had two minutes to call my own these last few days, so these are going to have to do."

Dorian's apartment was pretty run-of-the-mill for this side of town. A couple of bean bag chairs tossed around the living room, a mattress on the floor of the bedroom, and beer cans everywhere. "Quite the chick magnet," Mike said as she put down her equipment and gazed around the room.

"Here, hold these." She handed Tyler her handful of candy while he watched her step into her dark coveralls. Tyler couldn't help but watch her shimmy her petite figure into the shapeless coveralls with the word *Coroner* emblazoned on the back. She took the candy from Tyler's hand, but before she slipped them into her pocket, she unwrapped one and popped it into her mouth. Then, she got to work.

She started in the living room. She was looking for less obvious places where fingerprints could have been left but not necessarily cleaned up. Jim and Tyler slipped on some latex gloves and helped gather up beer cans, hand towels, trash from under the sink, and containers from the refrigerator.

Mike worked meticulously in the living room. When she felt she had exhausted every inch of it, she moved to the bathroom. It was only a second before she marched back across the living room, obviously irritated. She grabbed a mask from her kit and snapped. "What is it with men and their aim? Can it really be that difficult?" Tyler looked at Jim and laughed.

They had been in the apartment for almost an hour when Mike procured her first lead. "I've got blood," she yelled from the other room.

Tyler and Jim went to the bedroom door. Mike was spraying a large area on the wall with fluorescin. When she hit it with the light, it turned the guiltiest shade of blue. "Bingo."

Mike was able to gather other pieces of evidence in her search, but the blood was going to be the lead that Jim and Tyler needed.

It was almost 6:00 by the time they wrapped up their investigation. Jim received an urgent call from Irene as they headed for the cars. The puppy was missing, and Joshua was hysterical.

"Irene, it's going to take me at least an hour. I'm on the far side of town. Tyler drove, so I'm without a car. I'm gonna have to go back to the station."

"Why don't you take Tyler's truck? I'll give him a lift home," suggested Mike as she loaded her equipment back into her truck.

"Would that be okay with you, Tyler? Irene sounds pretty upset," Jim said.

"Sure . . . yeah. That would be fine."

"Okay, hon, I'm on my way." Jim flipped his phone shut. "Thanks, Mike. I owe you." Jim grabbed Tyler's keys from him and jumped into Tyler's truck, quickly pulling away from the curb.

"Hey, what about me? You owe me too, you know," Tyler yelled after Jim as he pulled away. When Tyler turned back to talk to Mike, he saw her tripping on her coveralls that hung around her knees. He laughed as she danced around trying to regain her balance—that is, until she fell down forcefully, and he heard her knee crack against the curb. She grabbed for it immediately and tried to muffle some choice words.

"Mike, are you all right?" Tyler pulled the tangled coveralls off of her feet and asked her again, "Are you all right? You hit pretty hard."

Mike had difficulty answering due to the excruciating pain in her knee and because Tyler was so incredibly close. "I'll be fine."

Tyler scooped her up without warning and sat her on the tailgate of her truck.

Mike tried to hide her discomfort. "I'm fine, Tyler, really. I just lost my balance." She was anything but fine, but she was not willing to admit that to him. She tried to step off of the tailgate, but the minute she put pressure on her knee, it buckled. She fell against Tyler's chest as he reached out to catch her. For a moment their eyes caught.

"Let me take a look at that," Tyler said as he helped her back up on the truck.

"Don't be so dramatic. An alcohol swab and a bandage will do just fine." She leaned over to look at the bloody hole in her jeans and ended up knocking heads with Tyler.

"Hey, watch it," Tyler said irritated. "Can't you sit still for just a minute?" He yanked at the rip in Mike's jeans and made the tear even bigger.

He was trying to see the cut on her knee better. It was deep and bleeding profusely.

Mike slugged at Tyler's shoulder. "Dang it, Tyler. These are my favorite jeans."

"Not anymore they're not. Looks as though you're going to need some stitches. Tyler opened Mike's black box and rooted around for something he could use to stop the bleeding. He pressed a wad of tissues against her knee.

"Ouch!" Mike jumped. "What are you trying to do, paralyze me?" Mike knew she was in trouble. Her knee was on fire, and she became lightheaded.

"You're bleeding pretty bad. I was just trying to stop the flow."

Mike pushed his hand aside and looked at her own wound.

"Let me secure the apartment, and then I'll drive you to—." Tyler didn't finish what he was saying. Mike's eyes were beginning to water, and Tyler could see the color starting to fade from her complexion. "Are you going to be okay?"

"Yeah . . . I'm just feeling a little . . . nauseated." Just then, Mike leaned over as far as she could to the side of the truck and lost it. Tyler felt horrible for her. She looked to be in a lot of pain and now was sick on top of it. Tyler hurried to lock up Dorian's apartment and put the crime scene tape across the door. When he got back to the truck, Mike was in a fetal position, and her face was as white as a sheet.

"Hey, how are you doing?" Tyler's voice was filled with concern as he knelt down next to the truck and brushed back Mike's hair from her face.

"I wouldn't get too close if I were you. I have throw-up breath."

"I think I can handle it," Tyler said softly. "Look, I need to get you to the cab of the truck, so let's go slowly, okay."

Very carefully, Tyler helped Mike to a sitting position. Once he knew she handled that okay, he slowly lifted her into his arms and carried her to the passenger side of the truck. He wondered if Mike could feel his heart beating rapidly against his chest. He felt like a cad. Here she was in pain, bleeding, and sick to her stomach, and all Tyler could think about is how good she felt in his arms.

He carefully slid her into the truck and then dashed around to the back, flipped up the tailgate, and jumped into the driver's side. He turned on the radio, hoping for a distraction when loud, horrendous, rock music came blaring from the speakers. "You listen to this stuff?"

"It's a good distraction when I'm heading to a scene," Mike said with her eyes closed and her head against the back of the seat. Tyler reached over and turned it off.

He glanced at Mike a few times while driving. He was surprised how badly she was reacting to her injury. Obviously, the sight of her own blood was not something she dealt with easily.

The trip to the hospital was slow and quiet. Tyler knew Mike was struggling to keep her stomach in check. When they arrived, Tyler gently lifted her out of the truck and headed through the emergency room doors.

Tyler copied down Frank's phone number while she filled out the medical forms. He tried numerous times to reach her dad but was unsuccessful. It was an hour before Mike was seen by the doctor, and by then she'd reached her pain tolerance level. The doctor used fifteen stitches to close the gash under her knee and gave her two Percocets for the pain. He sent her home with a bottle of medication and a pair of crutches.

Tyler drove Mike home while wondering how he was going to get home himself. Jim still had his truck, and Mike would be in no condition to drive.

He glanced over at Mike and saw that she was beginning to relax. The pain medication was apparently doing its job. He drove down the long driveway to the path that led to her house. When Tyler picked up Mike, they clunked heads again, causing Mike to giggle. Obviously, she was feeling no pain.

The path to Mike's place was dark and uneven. Tyler stumbled a few times, causing Mike to hold on tighter to his neck and laugh hysterically at the same time.

"If you don't stop strangling me, I'm gonna drop you right here." Tyler couldn't help but laugh. Mike's giggling was infectious. "I've got you, Mike, so loosen that death grip of yours."

They continued to laugh and stumble all the way to her cottage.

"What's your code?" Tyler asked when he saw the keypad on her door.

"Just use the key."

Tyler juggled with the key while Mike rested her head against his chest. He was finally able to open the door and walk into her perfectly decorated living room. Mike didn't loosen her hold on Tyler when he placed her on the couch. He lost his balance and nearly landed on top of her. He braced himself on the arm and the back of the couch. Mike started giggling again as Tyler placed a pillow under her knee.

"You're so nice. You should have been a nurse instead of a cop." Mike's conversation was getting less lucid. She grabbed Tyler's hand before he could move.

"You're not going to leave me, are you?" Mike's eyes were glassy but still mesmerizing. He wished it wasn't her reaction to the medicine that made her reach out to him.

He sat down on the oak coffee table as Mike held his hand. "I won't leave until your dad gets home, okay?"

"O-kay." Mike let out a heavy sigh. She looked at him with one eye open and began to drift. "You know . . . you're even cute with one eye shut." Tyler knew he was blushing, but at least Mike wouldn't notice since she could barely focus. "I like you, Tyler, you know that? I tried not to, but . . . I do." It was the last thing Mike said before she closed her eyes. Tyler pulled a blanket over her and watched as she slept. He had an overwhelming desire to kiss her, but knew he would be way out of line. He got up and went outside. He needed some fresh air. His emotions were on overdrive and he needed to cool off.

He pulled out his phone and hit redial. "Hey, Frank. This is Tyler. Look, Mike had a little accident today. Nothing major, just a few stitches. I'm not sure what time you're getting home, so I'm going to sack out at her place until morning. Don't worry about coming over if you get in late. She really needs her sleep. I'll see you in the morning." Tyler hung up the phone. He hated to leave a message like that, but he knew Frank needed to know. His next call was to Jim.

"Hey, Jim. Did you find the puppy? Hey, that's great. Yeah, well, we never made it back to the lab. Mike had a little accident. No, no, she's all right, but we got hung up at the emergency room, and then I drove her home. I'm waiting for Frank to come home now. Yeah, seems like it. Hey, I'll talk to you tomorrow. Go ahead and take my truck to work. I'll catch up with you as soon as I can. Thanks, Jim."

Tyler walked back inside and locked the doors behind him. His eyes wandered around the cozy little cottage. It was filled with personal touches and mementos—nothing like her office. Creamy yellows and muted blues added to the picket fence-style furniture. This is where Mike lived. This is where her heart was.

Tyler turned off all the lights except for a small table-side lamp. He made sure the front door was locked and checked on Mike one more time before he got comfortable in one of the oversized chairs. He stared at her until he fell asleep himself.

TYLER HEARD MIKE STIRRING. He glanced at his lighted watch and saw that it was only 3:00 in the morning. He waited a few minutes and then heard a groan.

"Mike, are you awake?"

"Yeah," said a groggy voice from across the living room.

Tyler got up and moved to the coffee table so he could see her. "How are you feeling?"

"I'm feeling. That's just it. Can you get me some medicine?"

"Sure."

Tyler got up and looked around. He couldn't remember if Mike had laid the packet of medicine down somewhere, or if he had it. "Hey, Mike, where is that packet the doctor gave you?"

"That's right. I've got it." Mike pulled back the blanket that surrounded her and stuck her hand in the hip pocket of her jeans. Tyler came from the kitchen with a glass of water.

"You're going to have to sit up, unless you want water all down the front of you." Mike handed him the small white pouch before pushing herself up on her elbows. Tyler could see the pain the movement caused her. He dug two pills out of the little pouch and handed them to Mike. She tossed them to the back of her throat and then quickly reached for the glass of water Tyler was holding. She swallowed hard and tossed her head back. Her body shuddered before she collapsed back down on the pillow with a sigh.

"I can't believe I feel so wiped out. What time is it?"

"It's only 3:00. You've got a few more hours before morning."

"My stomach is killing me."

"It's probably the medicine fighting with the Tootsie Rolls. Why don't you try to go back to sleep." Tyler got up and moved back to the chair he had been using.

"You can go home, Tyler. I'll be fine."

"I told your dad I'd wait with you until he got home."

"When did you talk to him?"

"Well, I didn't talk to him. I left a message, but I told him I'd be with you until he got home."

"Well, that was big of you. There's only one problem . . . He won't be home until Monday."

"Monday!"

"Yeah. He and some of his fishing buddies went deep sea fishing for the weekend. He won't be back until sometime on Monday. So why don't you go on home. I'll be fine." Mike's voice was getting softer, and Tyler could tell she was drifting back to sleep. He waited a few more minutes to make sure she was out. Then he carefully pulled the blanket back over her and allowed his hand to graze her cheek. He sat back down in the chair and stared at her once again as she slept. *Lord, help me. I think I'm in over my head.*

MIKE WOKE UP TO THE SMELL OF BREAKFAST. She looked down and saw that she had slept in her clothes, but why? And who was cooking? Then it started coming back to her. She'd hurt herself, had stitches, and Tyler brought her home. She peered over the back of the couch to see him making himself at home in her kitchen. She fell back to the pillows and covered her eyes with her hand.

What had she said last night? What had she done? At least she was still wearing the same clothes she had the night before. That was some consolation. She knew what pain medicine did to her, and if Tyler had any ulterior motives in being so helpful, he could have easily gotten what he wanted from her. She slowly moved her feet from the couch. Her knee felt stiff as a board.

Of course, the inch of gauze that was wrapped around it was rendering it unbendable. She noticed the crutches lying along the coffee table. She tried to get to a standing position, only to lose her balance and plop back down on the couch.

"Whoa, whoa, whoa, what do you think you're doing?" Tyler came from the kitchen with a dishtowel over his shoulder. "You need to stay put. Doctor's orders."

"Well, unless you're volunteering for bedpan duty, I need to get up." Her words were direct and to the point.

Tyler chuckled. "Oh, in that case, let me give you a hand." He picked up the crutches that had fallen to the floor. "Here, hold onto my arm. I'll pull you up." Tyler extended his muscular forearm and with one swift move brought Mike up to within inches of him. She quickly grabbed the crutches and slowly hobbled around the couch. Tyler could see her wincing and knew she was still feeling the pain.

When she started heading up the stairs, Tyler stopped her. "I thought you were going to the bathroom? There's one down here."

"But I'd like to change my clothes and comb my hair. I feel like I just fell out of a dump truck."

"Then let me help you."

Tyler moved to her side, but she motioned him away. "I can manage just fine."

"Okay, but don't be long. Breakfast is almost ready."

"I don't eat breakfast."

"You do today. You can't afford to live on food from a vending machine; you're liable to melt away. You're skinny enough as it is." Tyler couldn't believe what he had just said. He didn't mean to say it out loud—it just happened. He waited to get an irate rebuttal from Mike but heard nothing. Luckily, she hadn't heard him. He was going to have to be more careful. He had to make sure he didn't make his thoughts known. At least not yet. ·

Mike hobbled up the stairs and to the bathroom. She clung to the sink feeling as if she were going to faint. The exertion of climbing the steps had proven to be too much for her.

When she saw her reflection in the full-size mirror, she stood still for a moment. *I am not too skinny . . . I'm trim.* She had heard Tyler's comment but hadn't known how to respond. She turned on the faucet and held a washcloth under the spigot while reflecting on the interactions she'd had with Tyler over the last few weeks.

Mike knew he was trying to make an impression on her, but she had acted nonchalant. He'd only known her a little over a month, but the way they kept bumping into each other seemed a little too noticeable. She thought back to their conversation on the jogging path and smiled. *Was he really watching her that closely?*

Mike wasn't sure how she felt about that. She had always kept her feelings closely guarded, never really meeting anyone on the job that interested her. The guys she worked with were either married or crazed. Nathan was the perfect example of the macho "I can get any woman that I want" mentality that she was up against day after day. But somehow, Tyler was different. He hadn't tried to charm her at every turn; in fact, as Mike remembered their first encounter, she laughed out loud.

No, Tyler was different. He didn't make lewd jokes or talk about his sexual exploits. Even last night, with the perfect opportunity to beguile her, he was every part the gentleman, at least she thought he was. She couldn't remember much but was thankful to have woken up fully dressed and downstairs.

Mike's mind continued to wander as she freshened up. She pulled off her shoes and carefully inched out of her torn jeans and T-shirt. She slipped a pink floral sundress on because it was easy and would cover her bandage when she went in to work. She pulled her hair back in a large clip at the base of her neck and applied a little makeup to cover her pale cheekbones. She hobbled back down the stairs and then used the crutches to cross to the kitchen.

Tyler looked up from where he was positioned over the stove and did a double take. "Wow, you look good. I mean . . . you look like you're feeling a little better." Tyler turned to butter the toast, mentally kicking himself for sounding like such an idiot.

"Thanks, I do feel a little better." She was lying. She felt horrible and had no idea how she would make it to work. She sat at the bar with her leg outstretched and watched Tyler as he finished up with the meal. "My gosh, Tyler. Do you think you have enough food there? Omelets, ham, toast, fruit—no wonder you jog all the time."

Tyler turned to her as he slid a cheese omelet onto the plate in front of her. "How do you know I jog all the time?" he asked, puzzled.

"Well, I don't mean all the time, but I do see you on occasion. I mean, not just you, but anyone who goes by. I have a view of the entire lake from my balcony. I can see everything."

"Everything, huh?"

She *had* been watching him. Maybe what she said last night about liking him wasn't just the painkillers talking. Tyler decided to let it go for now. He served up the rest of their breakfast and sat down beside her. "Do you mind if I pray?"

"Go ahead." Mike seemed a bit cold.

"Dear Lord, thank you for this food, and may it nourish our bodies. Help Mike's knee to heal quickly, Lord. And thank you for the invaluable work that she does for us. Amen."

Tyler sensed Mike's change in attitude after he prayed. He decided to find out why.

"So, I guess you don't share your father's faith?"

"Who said my father has faith?"

"When we talked the other day. I got the impression that he—"

" My father and I are different in more ways than one. Don't get me wrong. I have a tremendous amount of respect for my dad. I just choose to believe in myself more than some higher power."

"Is that because of what happened to your sister?"

Mike was surprised by Tyler's question. "How do you know about Michelle?"

"Your father told me about her the other day. When I said something to Jim, he gave me some of the details. That must have been really hard on you."

"Look, I don't want to talk about it, okay?" Mike was angry that Tyler had been poking around in her private life.

They ate in silence. Tyler gobbled up what he prepared while Mike just pushed her portion around on her plate. When she could take the silence no longer, she got down from the bar stool and hobbled across the room with her crutches. "I've got to get to work."

"You can't go to work like that."

"My legs are moving slower, not my mind."

Tyler almost growled at her stubbornness. "What about the medicine you're on? You can't take those and drive."

"I'm feeling fine. Tylenol will be good enough for the rest of the day. Look, I have things that need to get done—namely, your case against Dorian Thomas. Now, I can give you a ride to your place or the station, what will it be?"

"Let me at least clean up these dishes." Tyler turned to the kitchen.

"I don't have time for that. I'm going to be late as it is. Just leave them, and I'll take care of it when I get home. Come on, Tyler. I appreciate your help, but I've got a job to do and so do you."

"Fine." Tyler threw the spatula in the sink and left the kitchen. Mike grabbed her purse, slipped on some shoes that were lying by the stairway, and headed out the door. Tyler offered to help her up the path to the truck, but she refused.

"I'll drive," Tyler offered.

"I'm perfectly able to drive," she retorted.

"No, you're not. I have the keys." Tyler dangled the keys in front of her. He headed straight for the driver's door while Mike tried to figure how she was going to get up into the truck.

"Do you need a hand?"

"No! I can do it myself."

She tossed her crutches inside the cab, almost hitting him. Then she backed into the seat far enough so that she could swing her legs around in front of her. She closed the door, straightened her dress, and wiped the sweat from her forehead. Tyler didn't dare laugh, but there was nothing he could do to hide a smile.

"You think this is funny, don't you."

"Yeah, I do. If you weren't so bullheaded, that wouldn't have been so difficult." Tyler put the truck in gear and headed for his house. "I need to check on Skyler and change my clothes. I promise I won't be more than fifteen minutes. Then you can drop me off at the station. Jim should be there by then."

Mike acted as if she weren't listening. She just stared out the window.

Tyler pulled into his driveway. Skyler came dashing out to meet him at the car.

"You left him loose outside all night?" Mike blurted.

"No, I installed a doggie door for him." Tyler got out and wrestled with his dog for a few minutes.

"You know from a security point of view, those aren't very safe," she hollered out the window as she tried to get comfortable.

"Boy, aren't you in an argumentative mood?"

"I am not!"

"Right." Tyler walked away, Skyler racing him to the door.

Mike leaned her pounding head back against the seat. She could feel her knee throbbing. She hadn't taken any medicine since three that morning, and she was beginning to regret it. She could feel herself being drawn to Tyler, but his questions about Michelle and her faith were definitely a problem.

Mike grew up believing in God. Her parents took her and Michelle to church all the time. She loved the Bible stories and the pictures of Jesus holding the little lambs or gathering children to his side. That was the Jesus she believed in. That was the Jesus she prayed to. But when he stopped answering prayers, Mike gave up on him. Not only did Michelle die, she suffered. God did nothing to protect her from being victimized. That was not the God she wanted to rely on. She could take care of herself better than that.

When Tyler returned to the truck, he was out of breath. "Sorry, it took a little longer than I thought." Tears glistened on Mike's cheeks when Tyler turned to her. She tried to brush them away and continued to stare out the window. Tyler allowed her the privacy she clearly wanted.

CHAPTER FIVE

Tyler saw his truck as soon as he drove into the parking lot. He pulled up next to it and put Mike's truck in park. "Are you sure you're going to be able to drive?"

"Yeah," Mike said as she slid over into the driver's seat. "I'll call you when I have something on the blood samples."

"Would it be okay if I swung by tonight? Just to see how you're doing."

"I really have a lot of work, Tyler. I won't be home until late."

Tyler looked disheartened. "Okay, then I guess I'll see you around."

Mike rode out on the main highway and U-turned her truck back towards the city. Tyler went to his desk and plopped in his chair. Jim was staring at him with a smirk on his face.

"What?" Tyler blurted.

"I don't know. You tell me."

"There's nothing to tell. She got hurt and I made sure she was okay."

"And conveniently stayed at her place."

"Look, Jim. You had my truck, she was whacked out on pain pills, and Frank is gone for the weekend. What was I supposed to do?"

"Is she okay?"

"Yeah . . . she's hurting more than she'll admit, but she insisted on going to work."

"That's good for us. I want to get to the bottom of the Dorian Thomas case."

Tyler decided to focus on work instead of Mike. "So, what do we have so far?"

"First of all, we've got a liar. Then we have two blood samples, two different points of discharge, and Vince Ortega is still missing."

"So, if the blood from Dorian's apartment matches the other sample not Dorian's, we can book him with suspicion of murder."

"Yeah, but I don't feel good about it. The district attorney will have a field day with it. Without a body, we don't have enough to nail this one down."

Tyler and Jim went about the rest of the day doing follow-up work on some smaller cases. Jim went over reports and Tyler went back to straightening the file room. When they had lunch at one of Jim's favorite burger joints, Tyler couldn't help but wonder if Mike had stopped to eat. He must have missed something Jim said because before he knew it, Jim had bounced a burger wrapper off his forehead.

"You know if you're that distracted, we could swing by county and see how she's doing."

Tyler's head popped up.

"Who said I'm thinking about her? If she wants to be stubborn and independent, let her."

"I was talking about the analysis," Jim said with a grin. "You just broke rule number one. Never give up more information than is necessary. You, my friend, just indicted yourself."

"Fine," Tyler said with a smile. "So I was thinking about Mike."

"So what are you going to do about it?" Jim asked as he finished off the last of his fries.

"I don't know, Jim. She's a pretty complex person. Right about the time I think I've made a little headway, she throws up another wall. She won't talk about her sister, and I found out she has no interest in God." Tyler shook his head. "No, I think I'm better off leaving things where they are. It seems the only thing we do well together is fight."

"You know what they say about that, don't you?" Tyler raised a brow waiting for Jim to finish. "If you fight like cats and dogs, you're either related or in love."

"Then I better check my family history because believe me, as far as she's concerned, there's no love lost between us."

WHEN MIKE SHOWED UP FOR WORK ON CRUTCHES, Nathan wouldn't let it rest. She wasn't ready to match wits with him so she tried to ignore him. "Make yourself useful, Nathan, and go unload my truck. We have a lot of stuff to go through."

"Oh, come on. Aren't you going to tell me what happened?"

"No! I'm in no mood, Nathan. I'm in a lot of pain, I've had little rest, and my head is ready to fall off my shoulders." Mike went straight to her office and took some Tylenol.

When Nathan had everything out of Mike's truck, he poked his head into her office.

"Nice dress, Mike. I'm flattered. But you don't have to get all dolled up for me. I'll take you any way I can get you."

"You wish." Mike laughed at Nathan's feigned levity. "Sorry to disappoint you, Nathan. It was out of necessity. There was no way I was getting slacks on over my knee."

"So how bad is it?" Nathan asked, turning a little more serious.

"Fifteen stitches."

"And you're not going to tell me how you did it?"

"Nope. Now come on, we have work to do."

Nathan went to the lab. Mike listened to her voice mail before she joined him. As she was leaving her office, she swung her leg around and nailed her knee on the corner of her desk. She gasped and pinched the bridge of her nose. She could feel her eyes begin to water but refused to cry. She knew if she started, she would totally lose it. *Come on, keep it together. You've got to make it through the day.*

Mike and Nathan spent most of the afternoon inspecting the items that she had pulled from Dorian's apartment. Everything was handled in a slow, methodical manner. They pulled some latent prints off the beer cans from the trash and were looking for anything else that might help. Nathan now spread out the contents that had been removed from the bathroom.

"Well, looky what I found." Nathan held up his tweezers for Mike to see. "Latex. Seems as though Dorian did a little partying before Jim and Tyler hooked him up."

Nathan left the lab to check on some of their other cases. Mike was glad he did. Her knee was killing her, and she needed to sit down. Lifting her dress, she saw that blood had seeped through the gauze. She pulled at the bandage and winced.

"You know you're not supposed to play with that."

Tyler and Jim walked into the exam room. Mike didn't look up right away. Swallowing back her tears, she let her dress slip down over her leg and stood.

"What are you guys doing here already? Nathan and I haven't finished yet." Mike had a smile on her face, which was a dead giveaway that she was hiding something.

"Tyler was getting antsy," Jim said as he looked at the pile of trash on the table.

"Well, these things take time, Tyler. I told you I would call when I had something definitive." Mike wasn't making eye contact, and her mannerisms were all business.

Tyler noticed Mike was leaning heavily against the table. "How's the knee?"

"Fine."

"Don't believe her, guys. She's been hobbling around here all day," Nathan said as he walked back into the lab.

Mike looked at him with disgust. "Nathan, I think I can speak for myself."

"Look, I'm already in trouble with boss lady." He turned to Jim and Tyler. "So I might as well go for broke."

"Nathan, if you say another word, you'll be deep cleaning the coolers with a toothbrush."

"Go ahead, Nathan," Jim said. "Me and Chief Bridges go way back."

"Jim! I can't believe you're working against me."

Tyler couldn't tell if she looked shocked or hurt.

"Fine, fine. Go ahead, Nathan," she said in a sharp tone. "Trash talk all you want, but you can't make me stand here and listen to it."

Mike limped out of the room to her office. She couldn't believe that Jim would go to her superiors.

The three men watched as she hobbled from the room. Then Nathan voiced his concerns. "Look, she's been in tears twice today." He leaned against the counter as he spoke. "She's usually hard as nails, but she's been working herself like there's no tomorrow. I don't think she's had a day off in over two weeks, and her Tootsie Roll supply is gone. I told her to go home, but she just glared at me. She should be resting that knee and she knows it, but she's been hobbling from one table to the next, each time gritting her teeth and wiping her eyes. She is the most stubborn woman I've ever met, but this time I think she's met her match. One false move and her knee is going to give out. Then she's really going to have some recuperating to do."

"Can you handle things here? I mean, can the department spare her for a day or so?" Jim asked, not wanting Mike to get in trouble.

"Of course, I can. We've taken care of almost all of the evidence for your case. All we have left is what's here. We've got everything else logged in. Once we do tests, it's a waiting game for results."

Tyler had heard enough. He headed down the hall to Mike's office and gave the door a light tap. "Leave me alone, Nathan. You've really ticked me off this time."

"It's not Nathan. Can I come in?" Tyler answered softly.

"I'm busy." Her words were anything but soft.

"Mike, this is ridiculous. I'm not going to talk through a door." Tyler swung the door open to find Mike's desk chair turned facing the wall.

"Please just go away." Mike had her back to the door, and Tyler could hear the tears in her words.

"But Mike— "

"Look, I've already embarrassed myself enough over the last few days. Please just let me have this pity party alone." Mike sat with her leg extended and her head in her hands.

Tyler walked over to Mike's chair and carefully spun it around so he could see her. He crouched down next to her.

"Look . . . Nathan told me you've been in pain all day, you haven't had a full day off for weeks, and this has been the extent of your food supply," Tyler said as he shook the empty Tootsie Roll tub.

"Boy, and people say women gossip," Mike muttered, not looking up.

"Let me take you home." Tyler waited for an answer.

Mike wiped the tears from her face and sniffled. Her first reaction was to refuse, but who was she kidding—she couldn't take it anymore. She needed to go home and she knew it. It took a moment for her to speak.

"Okay, but you're taking me home, dropping me off, and then you're going home. No babysitting. I want to soak in a nice hot bath and then if I feel like having a good cry, I don't want anyone around to witness it."

"Can I negotiate on two points?" Tyler asked but didn't wait for a reply. "I get to fix you something to eat, and I don't leave until you're out of the tub. I want to make sure your bath is relatively crash free."

Mike took a deep breath and sighed. "And then you'll leave me alone?"

"Just you and your pity party," Tyler said with a grin. He noticed the bloody bandage peeking out from under the hem of Mike's dress. "Let me see that." Tyler cradled Mike's calf in his hand and discreetly pushed back the hem of her dress. "Mike, that was a pretty thick bandage for that much blood to have seeped through. Did you do something to it?"

"I caught it on the corner of my desk." Mike was looking at the bandage as Tyler gently rolled her leg from side to side. "I think I might have pulled a stitch. I figured I could just butterfly bandage it when I got home."

"Okay, I have an addendum to my deal. I get a look at this before I leave to make sure it isn't more serious."

Mike didn't have any fight left in her. All she wanted to do was go home. "Whatever," she finally answered. "Just let me shut down my computer and make sure Nathan has things handled."

"Just get what you need, I'll go talk with Nathan. I'll meet you by the back door in five minutes. Will you be able to make it that far?"

"I've made it around all day. Another sixty feet isn't going to kill me."

Tyler got up from where he had been crouched by Mike's chair. She ignored the smile on his face; she wasn't going to give him credit for the minor victory he apparently thought he'd won.

Tyler joined Jim and Nathan back in the lab. They were deep in conversation as Nathan went over some of the evidence he hoped would pay off.

"So, is she leaving?" Nathan asked, looking up from the microscope.

"Yeah, I'm going to take her home now. Are you sure you can handle everything here?"

"I'm sure." Nathan got up from where he was sitting and removed the gloves that had covered his hands. "So, what's your secret, Detective Henderson?"

Tyler was confused. "What do you mean? I don't have any secrets." He looked back and forth between Jim and Nathan.

"I don't know," Nathan continued. "Jim told me you two have been spending time together. Said you were at her house last night, making sure she was comfortable. I've known Mike for more than three years, and you've gotten more out of her in a couple weeks than a dozen guys in this department have gotten in a couple of years."

"Hey, I think you might have misunderstood what Jim said. Mike was zoned out on pain medicine, and I was afraid that if I left, she might hurt herself. I slept in a chair all night, not anywhere else." Defensiveness came through every word Tyler spoke.

"Hey, I'm just talking about time, Tyler. Your chivalry isn't at stake here. Relax. I didn't say anything about you hitting it out of the ballpark." A buzzer went off and Nathan crossed the room to grab something from a piece of equipment. "I'm just saying that Mike is a very private person. She's never allowed anyone that I know of to invade her personal space. I mean, I've been to her place because we work together. I might tease her about gettin' it on, but she knows I'm joking. We work well together, and I'm not going to screw that up. But you, my friend, have somehow found yourself an inside track. I applaud you. Mike needs a life away from this place. She allows it to consume her and at times becomes obsessed. She needs to have something to look forward to at the end of the day other than nailing criminals to the wall or grieving with stricken families."

Nathan moved back across the room. "She takes things so personal sometimes that I think she's going to melt down, and then voila, the hard-as-nails Mike shows up and locks all her emotions away." Nathan gave a good-natured shove to Tyler's shoulder. "I say keep up the good work. Maybe she'll realize there's more to life than these four walls."

Tyler looked at Jim as if he had spoken out of turn. Jim put up his hand in self-defense. "He asked me a direct question earlier, and I gave him a direct answer."

Jim and Tyler walked out of the lab together. "Nathan is Mike's friend, Tyler. He's only concerned. I told him he had nothing to be afraid of with you. You're not an opportunist."

Mike was already waiting by the back door when Jim and Tyler appeared. With her crutches under her arms, she hopped down the gurney ramp and over to her truck.

Jim spoke up before leaving. "Nathan said Mike is good for two days off. He's got things covered and will explain it to her superiors. I'll handle things on the case and let you know if Nathan comes up with anything. We worked through our last days off, so you have some time coming to you."

Jim walked away while Mike pulled herself up into the passenger seat of her truck. Her head was back on the seat and her eyes closed. She balanced her left foot on top of her right, trying to keep it as straight as possible. The drive to her place was done in complete silence. She had almost dozed off by the time they reached the long rutted driveway.

MIKE EASED OUT OF THE TRUCK and put her crutches under her arms. She was determined to do it by herself. Tyler walked close behind, knowing the path was steep and Mike was exhausted. She almost made it to the door when her right crutch wedged itself in between two pieces of the slate path. She was falling forward when Tyler grabbed her around the waist and pulled her back against him.

"That was close," he whispered, since she was now standing only inches from him. He allowed his hands to linger a moment. He could feel her body up against his and inhaled the tropical scent of her shampoo. "How about I take over from here?"

Tyler didn't wait for an answer. He just lifted her into his arms and carried her the last few steps to the front door.

Mike wanted to protest, but she couldn't find her voice. She enjoyed the feeling of Tyler's arms around her and the way he held her firmly but gently. She reached down and slid her key in the lock. Tyler stepped sideways through the entryway, careful not to hit her extended leg on the doorjamb. Mike found herself fantasizing about spending time with Tyler. He was handsome and strong. His eyes were tender yet sensual. She wondered what it would be like to be swept off her feet by someone like him.

"Where to?"

"What?" Mike was brought back from her daydreaming.

"Should I put you on the couch or do you want to go upstairs?"

"My bedroom is upstairs," Mike said, sounding confused and a little skittish.

"I know. Is that where you'd like me to take you?" Tyler answered. He could still see the discomfort on Mike's face. Then he realized what she might be thinking. "I'm not propositioning you, Mike. I just want you to be where you will feel most comfortable."

She felt completely off balance. "Of course, you weren't . . . I knew that." She looked at Tyler standing there with his disarming smile and felt her body heat up with embarrassment.

"Right, that's why you've turned three shades of red in less than three seconds. I'll reserve the right to make a pass at you later. Right now, I just want you to get comfortable." Mike's eyes narrowed, and she was ready to unload on him. Tyler said, "Come on, I was only kidding. Now can we keep the fighting to a minimum and get you comfortable? I know you can't weigh more than a hundred pounds, but that's a hundred pounds more than I am used to carrying around. Where do you want to go, lady?"

His try at a New York accent made her laugh. "Upstairs."

He carried her up the simple staircase that opened up to an expansive loft that ran the length of the house. "Wow, this is incredible." Tyler sat Mike near the pillows of her bed and started walking around, taking in the architecture. "Who designed this? I've got to get his name."

"I did."

Tyler turned an approving look at her. "This is really great. Are these

51

pocket doors?" he said fingering the molding. Tyler had walked to the large panes of glass that stood between the foot of her bed and the balcony over-looking the lake.

"Yeah. As a kid I loved sleeping outdoors. I wanted to be able to have that same feel here. So I had the pocket doors installed and the bed put on large, easy-to-maneuver casters. In the summer, I can actually roll my bed out onto the deck and sleep outside."

"You're kidding!" Tyler was dumfounded. "This is great." He looked at a wall of what looked to be shutters that had met him when he reached the top of the stairs. "And what's with all these shutters?"

"That's my closet." Tyler looked at her in disbelief and opened one of the doors slightly. "I wanted the room to be as open as possible," she explained. "It was just one open room when I got done with the renovating. I knew I needed an enclosure for the bathroom for privacy, but I didn't want to lose any more square footage for a closet. So, I had utility shelves installed the length of the room and bought plantation shutters for doors. Now it just looks like a long bank of windows with closed shutters."

Mike was enjoying describing the design of her bedroom. She was very proud of it, but not many people had seen it. Tyler walked to the far side of the room that was a sitting area, complete with an oversized chair, ottoman, and a piece of furniture he hadn't seen before. "What's this funny looking couch thing?" Tyler raised his voice so Mike could hear him from the other side of the room.

"It's called a tête-à-tête. It's an antique and supposedly was used as a reading couch for lovers." Tyler's look was inquisitive, so she explained further. "When a gentleman would come to call on his lady in the evening, they could enjoy being close to each other without compromising their repu-tations."

Tyler raised a bushy brow. "Interesting." He stepped into the bathroom and continued to be amazed. The tub had frosted glass blocks on one side of it, but in front of it was a wall of pebbles and sea glass that had water trickl-ing down it. *She has her own water sculpture. Amazing.*

The shower was a walk-in shower. Again, a wall of glass blocks was used to enclose it, and multiple shower heads were focused in on the bench against the back wall. The pedestal vanity was flanked with a large oval mirror and two sconces for light. He assumed the toilet was behind the shut-tered door. It was the most inventive, romantic bathroom Tyler had ever seen. He walked out of it with a look of amazement on his face.

"So, what do you think?" Mike asked.

"Are you kidding me? I've never seen anything like it, and believe me, I've been dragged around enough model homes to know what's out there." Mike's eyes were brimming with satisfaction. She was very proud of her designs, even if she was the only one who benefited from them.

"You could have gone into interior design with concepts like these."

Mike didn't say anything because she didn't want to think about it further. "You know, Tyler, you can go ahead and go. I'll lay here for a little while and then take a nice hot bath. I appreciate your wanting to help me, but I'm going to be fine."

"Of course, you are," he said as he came and sat on the edge of her bed. Pointing to her knee, he said, "I'm going to check this out, run your bath, and then make you a nice dinner. When I'm satisfied that you've eaten something besides Tootsie Rolls and are comfortable enough to sleep, then I'll leave." Tyler had a no-nonsense look on his face. "Do you have a first-aid kit some-where?"

Mike knew it was useless to argue with him, and she didn't have the strength. The sooner she gave in, the sooner he would leave. "In the cupboard in the bathroom."

When Tyler stepped away from the bed, Mike situated herself in a better sitting position against her pillows. In an attempt to make sure she didn't show more leg than was necessary, she made sure her dress was lifted just above her knee. She started picking at the tape that was holding the gauze together.

"Don't pick at it. Cutting it off will be easier." Tyler sat on the bed again, but this time closer to Mike. He pulled a pair of bandage scissors from the first-aid box and carefully slid the tip under the folds of gauze. Mike sucked air in through her teeth.

"Did that hurt?" Tyler asked with concern.

"No, the scissors were cold."

Tyler could see goose bumps rising up on Mike's skin. He gently unwrapped the gauze from the back of her knee, leaving the stitches still covered. He pulled on it slightly, causing Mike to jump.

"Sorry." He looked more intently at the bandage. "The blood has dried on the gauze; this isn't going to be easy." Tyler tried again. Again Mike jumped and her eyes watered. "Okay, this isn't going to work." Tyler got up and in one quick swoop, scooped Mike up in his arms.

"What are you doing?" Her voice raised an octave.

"I'm putting you in the tub." Tyler carried her through the door of the bathroom.

"You're what?" Mike asked as she clung to him for balance.

"I just want to run some water over the bandage. We need to loosen the dried blood." Tyler set her down on the edge of the tub but couldn't find a good vantage point from which to work. So he took off his tie and jacket, revealing the badge on his belt and a holster at the small of his back. He removed his shoes and socks and started rolling up his slacks.

"Now what are you doing?" Mike wanted to laugh because he looked so ridiculous. She put a hand over her mouth to hide her smirk.

Tyler rolled up his sleeves and carefully stepped into the tub. "I have to be able to see what I'm doing." He moved closer to the faucet. Leaning over, he turned it on and then carefully held Mike's leg. He took a handful of water and poured it over the dried bandage.

Mike jerked her leg and almost lost her balance. "Tyler, that water is freezing!"

"It is not. Just hold still." He poured another handful of water onto her leg and made her jolt again. "You're going to fall over if you keep that up. It's not *that* cold. I'm standing in it."

"Yes, but you are wearing more than a flimsy dress." Mike put her hand on Tyler's shoulder for balance and leaned over to adjust the water temperature. Her dress shifted and she pleaded, "Don't let my dress get wet."

Tyler mumbled something under his breath as he continued to pour water over the wet gauze.

"What did you say? Did you just call me a baby?"

Tyler didn't deny it. "Look, it's just a little water. It's not that cold, and it's not going to ruin your dress."

"I'll show you who's a baby." With that, Mike took a handful of water and splashed it in Tyler's face. He was so surprised he jumped back and nearly lost his footing. Mike couldn't help but laugh. Tyler had water dripping from the end of his nose and little beads of water in the scruffy hairs on his chin. He turned a mischievous eye on Mike. She knew she was in for it.

"I'm sorry. I shouldn't have done that," she said through her nervous giggles.

"You're right, you shouldn't have. He held her leg firmer. "You're in a very precarious position, Miss Madigan. I could easily lift your leg just high enough for you to go over backwards." Tyler was beginning to raise her leg just a little.

"Tyler, don't . . . Tyler, please . . ." Mike reached out for Tyler's neck and held it tightly. She couldn't help but laugh, but her words were definitely pleading. "Tyler, someone could get hurt!" Mike was screaming and laughing at the same time.

"It's not going to be me." He was laughing too and obviously enjoying the power that he held at the moment. He was leaning extremely close to her as she tightened her hold on him. They were almost nose to nose when their laughter abruptly stopped. Tyler stared deeply into her clear blue eyes. She could feel the warmth in his eyes like she could feel the warmth of his touch against her leg. He said in a whispered tone, "Now are you going to behave yourself?"

She couldn't answer. She was afraid of what she might say. Behaving was the farthest thing from her mind. She nodded slowly and could feel him lower her leg so that she was able to regain her balance.

Tyler had to get refocused on what he was doing. He had so wanted to kiss Mike just a moment ago but wasn't sure how she'd react.

The water had unfastened the bandage slightly. Tyler gently pulled at the loosened corner of gauze and slowly pulled it away from the stitches. Mike tightened her muscles as tears came to her eyes. The corner of the gash on her leg was bleeding, and Tyler was trying to examine it.

"You did pull some stitches, but like an idiot, I left the first-aid kit in the other room." Tyler stood up straight and looked around for a towel he could use to dry his feet, but all he saw was white. "Do you have a towel I could use?"

"Any of the ones hanging up would be fine."

"But they're all white. How can you live with white towels?"

"Because they're easy to wash. I just bleach them and they look like new."

"Huh, never thought of that." Tyler took a towel from what looked like an old-fashioned warming rack near the tub. He tossed it on the floor and carefully stepped onto it. He quickly walked to the bed to retrieve the kit. Then he slowly climbed back in the tub and went to work on Mike's stitches. He dried the area around the cut and got a couple of butterfly bandages ready. He pressed the two sides of the wound close to where the stitches had come out. He didn't dare look at Mike, knowing the pressure he was applying had to hurt. She didn't say a word while he pressed the strips in place, but Tyler could see the whites of her knuckles as she clung to the side of the tub. The butterfly strips were in place and looked to be holding. Tyler carefully dabbed a liberal amount of antibiotic ointment around the stitches to help prevent the gauze from sticking the next time. Knowing he was almost done, he looked up at Mike while he picked up a roll of gauze from the kit.

"Are you doing okay?"

She nodded.

"You're awfully quiet."

"It's hard to talk and hold your breath at the same time."

Tyler lightly wrapped gauze around the wound and continued wrapping past her knee so she wouldn't bend her leg and pop another stitch. Finally, he applied adhesive tape.

"There. Good as new."

Tyler stood up to admire his handiwork and then instinctively searched Mike's eyes. She seemed so tired.

"Tell you what. Since you're already here, why don't you take a long, relaxing bath? I'll go start on dinner, then you can call it an early night and get some much needed sleep." Tyler stepped out of the tub and onto the towel he'd already used.

"Why are you going to all this trouble?" Mike studied his face, her expression serious. "I mean, I haven't been exactly nice to you." She was beginning to feel guilty for the way she'd been treating Tyler.

"Are you getting used to having me around?" he said as he rolled down his pants legs and picked up his tie and jacket.

"Yeah."

"Then I guess my plan is working." He placed his items on the bed.

"What plan?" she said loudly, thinking he was leaving. He then walked back into the bathroom.

"Do you want me to start your water for you or get you something to change into?" He was gathering up the wrappers and trash and putting the first-aid kit back in order.

"No, I want you to answer my question." Mike felt ridiculous trying to carry on a conversation with him while she sat on the side of the tub.

"Make sure you don't let your bandage get wet. I'll be downstairs cooking dinner. Yell if you need help on the steps." Tyler shut the door as he left.

"Wait!" Mike yelled. "You didn't answer my question." It was no use; she could hear him bounding down the steps. *What did he mean by a plan?*

Tyler entered the kitchen to be greeted by the mess he had left from breakfast. He looked in the refrigerator to see what he could fix for dinner. Teriyaki chicken and rice would be easy enough. He pulled some chicken from the freezer and stuck it in the microwave. After setting it to defrost, he started in on the dishes.

Tyler's mind was working overtime where Mike was concerned. He shouldn't even be entertaining the thought of getting involved with her, knowing she felt no need for God in her life. He continued what he was doing, but all the while his thoughts were on the woman upstairs.

MIKE SOAKED IN HER BATH BUT found it almost impossible to relax with her leg hanging over the edge and her head spinning with thoughts of Tyler. Her first impression of him as an arrogant, smart-mouthed, city cop was quickly diminishing. He'd been caring and considerate to her, bringing her dinner and helping her physically. He'd stayed with her through the night out of concern, not so he could put moves on her. He had been a complete gentleman in situations where other men would've tried to take advantage of her. Even though she found Tyler incredibly attractive, she still wasn't sure she was ready for another relationship. Her last one had been such a mistake. Jason had really messed with her emotions and her head, but Tyler seemed so different. Maybe it was time to reconsider and give a relationship another chance.

She carefully stepped out of the tub, lifting her bathrobe from the hook on the back of the door and wrapping it around her. Her crutches were downstairs, so she would have to be careful. The slightest amount of pressure on her leg sent sharp pains through her knee. Slowly, she made her way to her closet and pulled out the easiest garments to reach. Khaki shorts and a white polo shirt would have to do. She reached her bed, tossed her clothes on the comforter, and tried to get dressed while hovering on one foot. Even the simple task of pulling on her shorts was expending what little energy she had. She hobbled back to the bathroom and held on to the sink. She pulled the clip from the nape of her neck and allowed her hair to fall over her shoulders. She brushed it out and decided to keep it down. One more trip back to bed and she collapsed. *No more Tootsie Roll lunches and dinners,* she thought to herself. Her sparse diet and leg injury had taken their toll. With her head resting on her cushiony down pillows, she quickly fell asleep.

THE KITCHEN WAS CLEAN AND THE RICE was steaming. Tyler chopped up the chicken breasts and put them in the pan. He braised the chicken in his own concoction of Teriyaki sauce, Worcestershire, and brown sugar. He glanced towards the ceiling from where he had been able to hear Mike walking around, but now it was quiet. He waited until dinner was done before checking on her. He stood at the foot of the steps to determine if he could hear any noise from up above. Nothing. He whispered Mike's name as he ascended the stairs. Still nothing. Wanting to respect her privacy, Tyler stood in the stairwell for some time before finally climbing the last stair. When he saw her fast asleep on the bed, he smiled.

He cautiously walked over to her bedside and for a moment watched her sleep. She was beautiful. Her petite body seemed to be swallowed up by her huge featherbed. Her shiny blond hair framed her delicate features. She looked so vulnerable, not like the self-assured, no-nonsense M.E. he'd come to know. Knowing how badly she needed her rest, he didn't want to disturb her, so he quietly crept back down the stairs.

He dished up two bowls of chicken and rice, placing Mike's in the oven to keep it warm. He wandered around her home, trying to get a feel for who Mike really was. Coastal landscapes were the theme of the art that hung on the walls. The memory box coffee table had been cleverly filled with sand and seashells. Though Mike lived on a lake, it was obvious her desire was to be near the ocean.

MIKE HAD BEEN ASLEEP FOR AT least an hour when Tyler decided to prepare a tray for her and take it upstairs. He found a TV tray and popped the legs off of it. He pulled her chicken bowl out of the oven and poured her some soda. He went outside and grabbed some wildflowers he'd seen growing alongside the fence and arranged them in a small vase he found on the kitchen windowsill. Grabbing some napkins and Mike's medicine, Tyler headed upstairs.

Mike was still asleep when he got there, but his steps on the hardwood floors made her stir. She woke up slowly at first, but when she saw Tyler standing by the bed, she quickly shook the cobwebs from her mind.

"I'm sorry. I must have fallen asleep." Mike scooted towards the edge of the bed, feeling a bit embarrassed.

"You don't need to get up. Relax, I brought you dinner." Mike adjusted the pillow behind her back while Tyler set the tray down across her lap, careful not to put pressure on her knee.

"Tyler, you didn't need to go to all this trouble." She looked at the meal on her tray, but it was the flowers that made her smile.

"It was no trouble. Besides, it was great working in a fully stocked kitchen for a change. I still haven't made time to do any real grocery shopping."

"This looks delicious."

Mike started eating but felt self-conscious with Tyler just hovering at the edge of her bed. "Tyler, why don't you sit down?"

Tyler looked around for a place to sit. He could sit on the balcony or in the sitting area across the room, but both seemed so far away. Mike watched as he awkwardly scanned the room.

"You can sit on the bed, Tyler. I promise I won't bite."

With her permission, Tyler went to the other side of the bed and sunk into the comfort the down offered.

"This tastes really good. Where did you learn to cook so well?"

"Necessity. I'm a fast-food junkie by nature, but when I ended up gaining forty pounds and could no longer keep up in a street chase, I decided I needed to reevaluate my eating habits.

Mike was eating as she spoke. "No way. I can't image you being overweight. You're so muscular... I mean ... fit." Mike regretted her comment.

"Thanks for noticing," Tyler said was a smile. "Anyway, I started eating better, jogging, and weight training; now it's just a way of life." Tyler relaxed while Mike enjoyed her meal.

Feeling full, she paused for a moment with only half of her chicken and rice gone.

"You're not finished, are you?" Tyler asked as he rolled to one side and propped himself up on his elbow.

"You gave me too much. There's no way I could finish it all. But it was very good. You can cook for me anytime."

"I'll remember that."

Tyler enjoyed being this close to Mike. She was much softer around the edges than she would have people to know. "I put your medicine on the tray. It's right there next to your bowl."

Mike saw the two small pills. "I don't want to take them anymore. They got me through the first night, but I don't like the way they make me feel."

"Then let me get you some Tylenol." Tyler started to get up.

"No, that's okay. I don't need them right now." Mike realized she didn't want Tyler to leave. "Would you like to finish my chicken and rice? I really am stuffed, and I would hate for it to go to waste."

"No wonder you're so skinny." Tyler took the bowl and started picking at her leftovers.

"Why do you keep saying that? I am *not* too skinny!" Mike waited a moment but with a more uncertain voice asked, "Do you think I'm too skinny?"

Tyler didn't look up from his bowl of rice. "No. You felt pretty good to me." Tyler tossed a look Mike's way, wanting to know if he were in trouble for his comment. Mike's pink cheeks and soft smile let him know she didn't seem to mind.

"Okay, Henderson, one more time. Why are you being so nice to me, and what is this plan of yours?"

Tyler put the bowl back on Mike's tray and pushed himself up farther on the pillow, closer to Mike. He looked into her deep blue eyes and said, "My plan is to wear you down. I like you, Mike. I thought maybe if you got to know me, you might see I'm not that bad to have around."

Mike swallowed hard before speaking, her voice barely above a whisper. "Well then, I guess your plan is working."

An awkward silence filled the room. Mike laid her head back against her pillow, willing the pain in her knee to go away, but with no success. As much as she hated pain medication, she knew she had to concede. She lifted the pills to her lips and swallowed them in one gulp. She knew she would be out of it soon and felt a little disappointed. She was enjoying Tyler's company, maybe enjoying it too much.

Tyler didn't like seeing Mike in pain. He gathered up her dishes and took them downstairs, straightening the kitchen one more time. He moved back upstairs and took in the view from the balcony, allowing himself a little relaxation as a soft breeze came up from the lake.

HE HAD BEEN OUTSIDE FOR QUITE SOME TIME when he heard Mike stirring. He moved to her bedside and sat where he had before. Mike opened her eyes and smiled. She reached across and stroked the stubble on Tyler's face, offering him a sultry grin.

Tyler knew she was still under the effects of the medication. Allowing things to go any further would be taking advantage of an inviting situation. But he moved closer anyway. He leaned towards Mike and reached across to feel the delicate form of her neck. Her eyes closed as he brushed his thumb across her cheek.

Mike was in a dreamlike state, her senses somewhere between fuzzy and aware. She felt the softness of Tyler's caressing and leaned into it, not wanting him to stop. The next thing she felt was the press of his lips to hers. It was a slow, lingering kiss that she had no desire to resist. When Tyler pulled away, they looked into each other's eyes.

Mike felt as though she had cotton balls in her mouth but was conscious enough to know she liked the way Tyler made her feel. She could barely speak, her words a husky whisper. "That was nice, Tyler."

He continued to stroke her warming cheek. "Then let me go for good." He leaned into her again, this time allowing a little more passion in his kiss. Mike was responsive, even though she had an idea where this moment of intimacy was leading. Tyler massaged the back of her neck and slowly allowed his hand to fall over her shoulder and caress her arm. Mike felt herself getting lost in feelings that she didn't think even existed anymore. She allowed Tyler to continue because she wanted it herself. But with one last gentle kiss, Tyler pulled away and swung his feet over the side of the bed.

Mike was confused. *Why did he stop?*

Tyler stepped out into the fresh air and inhaled. *That was close*, he thought to himself. He had felt himself slipping away from what he knew to be right. But somehow feeling Mike accept his kiss made his mind whirl too far ahead. He was glad he'd been able to stop. Not just for his sake, but for hers. Tyler wanted Mike to know that a real relationship was based on more than just the physical, and a relationship is what he wanted.

Mike carefully got up from her bed and hobbled her way to the open glass doors.

"Why did you stop?" she asked.

"What?" Tyler was surprised by the question.

"Why did you stop? I gave you no reason to stop, but you did. Is it me?" Her last question was barely audible.

"Yes . . . it's you."

Mike's head sunk to her chest. She appreciated his honesty, but it hurt just the same.

"You're special, Mike, and I'm totally captivated by you. I just don't want to ruin that by allowing our relationship to get ahead of itself." Tyler moved in close and lightly laid his hands on her waist. He lowered his face closer to her ear and whispered what he had to say. "I don't want you to think that you're not desirable enough or beautiful enough, because that's not the case. I just don't want to mess things up by moving too quickly."

Mike remained silent, not knowing what to say. Tyler decided to be honest with her about his past.

"I don't want you to think I'm a saint or anything, because I'm not. I've had my share of relationships, the previous one lasting over two years. I just don't want to do that again. I've changed, and I can see now how that was a mistake."

Mike didn't know what to say. Her last relationship had fallen apart over the very same issue. She had become a conquest to Jason. He had waited for her, and when the time came, Mike felt obligated. Once they slept together, things had changed. Jason expected sex whenever they were together. They no longer had caring, intimate moments or times when they just held each other. That was no longer enough. Their last night was something Mike had worked at forgetting. It was still perched in the corner of her mind, but she refused to think about it.

"You're awfully quiet, Mike. Have I offended you?"

She looked up into Tyler's hazel eyes and rested her hands on his arms. "Tyler Henderson, you're obstinate, bullheaded, opinionated, and stubborn. When I first met you, I thought you were a real jerk. But now, I realize you're a fun-loving, caring, and compassionate jerk." Mike laughed at her own joke and then turned serious. "I've enjoyed having you around, Henderson, as much as I've tried to resist it. I guess I'm glad that you're stubborn and that you didn't give up on me." Mike pressed at the back of Tyler's neck, drawing his face down closer to hers. Their kiss was tender and their embrace comforting.

Tyler said a quick prayer. He knew he was treading dangerous water. After his breakup with Kelly, he vowed he would only date women who shared his faith. Now he was getting close to someone that had a grudge against God. Hopefully, between him and God they would be able to get Mike back on the right path.

CHAPTER SIX

"So, what should we do with the rest of the evening?" Tyler said as he continued to hold Mike close.

"You could tell me your life story and put to rest the other preconceived ideas I have about you."

"That depends if they're good ideas or bad ideas."

Mike got a silly grin on her face. "I think you'd better set me straight."

"If I share, will you?" Tyler asked quietly, knowing some of what her sharing might include.

Mike stiffened slightly. "I can try, Tyler, but a lot of it is difficult to talk about."

"I understand." Tyler gave her an encouraging smile and brushed back her bangs from her eyes. "How about if I fix us some popcorn and hot chocolate, and we go sit out on the patio?"

"How did you know I like hot chocolate? Most people would offer coffee."

"Well, considering I found every flavor of hot chocolate imaginable in your cupboards and no sign of coffee, I took a wild guess. Would you allow me the honors, or do you want to use your crutches?" Tyler asked as he glanced at the stairs. He thought it was a good idea to move their visiting away from the bedroom.

"Oh, I don't know. You made it abundantly clear that you weren't used to carrying around so much extra weight. I would hate for you to throw out your back or something else on account of me."

Tyler picked Mike up and held her in his arms as he laughed at his own words being used against him. "Hey, I wanted to kiss you so badly I had to say something. I think if I would have made a move on you then, you would've slapped me and that would have been the end of it. I was just protecting myself."

"Oh, so you lied to me?"

They continued their good-humored bantering as he carried her down the stairs.

Tyler set Mike on one of the oversized chaise chairs out on the deck. He went inside to prepare their snacks while Mike took in the shimmers of light that danced on the water. She really wasn't hungry, but she didn't want Tyler to leave either. Tyler returned with a tray of drinks, a large bowl of popcorn, and a blanket tossed over his arm. He could still see the discomfort on her face. The pain medication was helping but not completely.

"Is there enough room there for me?"

Mike moved over carefully so they could both fit on the chaise. Tyler got comfortable lying beside her and pulled the blanket over their legs. He handed Mike her cup of hot chocolate, dropped his arm around her shoulders, and gave her a little squeeze.

"So, tell me about your family," Mike said before Tyler had a chance to say anything.

"Well, it's just me and my sister now. Hailey is thirty and lives in Redondo Beach. That's where we grew up. My mom died of breast cancer when I was eighteen. It was difficult on all of us, but I think Hailey took it the hardest. She was only thirteen and didn't have a mother to help her through all the girl issues of life. Hailey's still a wanderer today. I worry about her because her behavior can be self-destructive at times."

"And what about your dad?"

"He lost his battle with cancer in February."

"Tyler, I'm sorry." They were both quiet for a moment, and then Mike spurred him on. "What was your relationship with your dad like before he got sick?"

"He was my world. He helped me train for the police academy. Ran right beside me every day. We did everything together. Watched sports. Played golf. Debated politics. Everything."

"What about church?" Mike asked hesitantly.

"No, my dad wasn't a Christian then. When he was in the hospital, a preacher would visit him every week. He talked to him about life and eternity. My dad would share with me what the preacher had said. I was pretty resistant at first. I hadn't really given spiritual matters much thought. Then I started to realize that my dad was not going to recover. He had been my rock, my counselor, and my advisor all my life. Now I didn't know where to turn." Tyler stopped for a moment as he recounted the memory.

"When my dad had gotten so weak he could no longer focus to read, he asked me to read the Bible that the preacher had left for him. He was in a lot of pain, and it seemed to bring him comfort. After a while, I began to read for my benefit as well as his. I realized then that my dad would not always be with me but God would. Both my dad and I accepted the Lord a week before he passed away."

"What about your sister?"

"I tried to explain what I was feeling, how the Bible was helping to comfort me, but she wasn't buying it. She said she was not going to change her life for a God that left her stranded. I pray for her and watch out for her, but I'm afraid she's headed down a very dangerous path."

Mike thought about what Tyler had shared. It was obvious he too had experienced tremendous personal loss. He could understand how she was feeling, except that she felt more like his sister did—abandoned by God, not comforted. She sipped on her chocolate, knowing Tyler was waiting for her to share, but she didn't want to. She didn't want to think about Michelle. For once, Mike wanted to think only of herself.

She was enjoying how it felt to be next to Tyler, to feel his arm wrapped around her and the warmth of his body radiate to hers. She didn't want to think about what she could have done, how she could have stopped Michelle, how if she had spoken up sooner, maybe Michelle would still be alive. Guilt overwhelmed her when she spoke about Michelle—guilt she had never shared with anybody.

"I know it has to be hard losing a sister," Tyler said as he pulled Mike closer to him, "especially since you two were so close. But you have to get past it, Mike. You have every right to mourn and grieve, but you can't allow that to stop you from living."

Mike felt a twinge of resentment. Tyler was trying to apply textbook psychology to her feelings regarding Michelle. "You don't understand, Tyler, it ripped our family apart. When I went to college, I decided to live on campus because my mother could hardly stand to look at me. She took prescription drugs to help with her depression, but she started abusing them. She would sit for days at a time in her room and cry. Dad had to keep working to make a living, but he was devastated too. Finally, my mom couldn't take it any longer. She packed up and left. We haven't heard from her since. I don't know if she's dead or alive."

"But your dad held onto his faith."

"I understand what you're saying, Tyler, and I'm glad you found a sense of peace after your dad died. I guess it's the same peace my dad talks about, but I just don't feel it. I just don't see the need to rely on someone or something that didn't come through in our situation."

"But look at the outcome of our two situations. What have you done since Michelle's death? It's been nearly fifteen years. Have you been able to move on with your life?"

"Yes," Mike said defensively. "I got my education and I'm working so others don't have to deal with the unanswered questions I did."

"But have you moved on? My father has been gone less than a year, and even though I miss him terribly, I've moved on with my life. I enjoy every day, even though I have to deal with a crummy job at times. You on the other hand, are so wrapped up in your job that you don't eat, you don't sleep, and you don't allow yourself any fun. You're punishing yourself, Mike. You've taken on a job to try and right the wrong that happened to Michelle, but you can't. You've got to let it go."

Mike's shoulders were rigid and her lips were tightly pressed together. She was angry that Tyler had dug deep enough into her personal life to find out these things about her.

"I don't want to talk about this any more." Her words were sharp and brimming with emotion.

"But you need to deal with it, Mike."

"Look, it's late. Maybe you should go."

"But Mike—"

"Tyler, I'm more tired than I thought, and the pain is getting to be more than I can handle. I really need to go to bed."

Tyler knew it wasn't just the pain from her injury. Mike was continuing to dwell on the loss of her sister. That was where her real pain originated.

She finally turned to look at him. Her eyes were glassy with unshed tears. "Could you give me a hand getting upstairs?" Her look was pleading with Tyler to let the subject drop.

"Yeah, I'll give you a hand." Tyler got up from where he'd been lying next to her. He felt chilled, but it wasn't from the air. He left the blanket over Mike as he lifted her into his arms. She gently rested her head on his chest as they made their way up the stairs. He laid her on the bed and then sat by her. She swiped at a few runaway tears as she looked into his eyes. She knew he was only trying to help.

"Don't be angry with me, Tyler. I just haven't spent much time talking about Michelle; and when I do, the wounds seem as fresh as the day she died. I know I need to find a better way of dealing with it. Someday I'll figure out how."

He leaned over and put a kiss first to her forehead, then to a cheek that tasted like tears, and finally to her lips. "I'll give you as much time as you need. You just have to promise not to shut me out."

"I'll try. But you have to promise to let me deal with it my way."

Tyler placed another quick kiss to her lips. He went downstairs and came back with a glass of water and more medicine. "Here, you should be able to take these around 10:00. I'm going to clean up a little and close everything up downstairs. I'll lock the door on my way out. By the way, who takes care of the dogs when Frank is gone?"

"Arnie comes and does it. I'm too unreliable."

"Who's Arnie?"

"He's a man my dad befriended. He's a little slow and a bit shy, but he's great with the dogs."

Tyler acknowledged her with a nod before walking towards her sliding doors.

"I'll call you tomorrow to see how you're doing. You're not going to try and go to work, are you?"

Mike sighed. "I know when I'm beat. I think I'll stay home tomorrow. One more day and I should be able to handle this better."

"Smart choice. I'll come by in the morning so I can fix you some breakfast."

"That's not necessary, Tyler," she said as he made sure her sliding glass doors were secured in place. "If you keep feeding me like this, you'll really have something to complain about."

"We'll find a way to work it off." The playfulness was back in Tyler's voice. With that, he was down the stairs, and Mike could hear him shutting windows and closing doors. He puttered around the kitchen and then yelled up the stairs before he left, "I turned on the dishwasher timer, so don't get startled if you hear it later tonight. Good night, Mike. Sweet dreams."

She smiled to herself. Tonight she actually thought it was possible.

Tyler shut the front door, jiggling the knob to make sure it locked before heading up the walk. He didn't get very far before he heard a stirring alongside the house. In an instant, a flashlight beam shone in the eyes, momentarily blinding him. He reached for his gun when a timid voice questioned him.

"What are you doing here?"

"Excuse me?" Tyler asked stunned.

"This is private property. What are you doing here?"

"Are you Arnie?"

"Yeah. Who are you?" Arnie lowered the light, distracted by the fact that the stranger knew his name.

Tyler released his grip on his gun and answered, "I'm a friend of Mike's. I was just leaving."

Arnie glared at him. "Mike isn't like that. She doesn't have men over to her house." The man's voice revealed his nervousness.

"Well, I'm obviously Mike's friend. How else would I know who you are?"

The question seemed to puzzle the man.

"Look, Mike had a little accident at work. I'm just making sure she takes care of herself."

Arnie's eyes darted in the direction of the house. "Mike's hurt?"

"No. She's doing okay now." Tyler extended his hand to the man, trying to get him to calm down. "My name's Tyler. I work with Mike, and I know her dad, Frank. In fact, I bought one of his dogs the other day."

"You bought Skyler?"

"Yeah."

"He's a good dog you know. Not the problem Mike thinks he is."

Arnie seemed to relax as he spoke.

"I agree. He's been a great companion to me." Tyler paused. "Look, I need to get home. It's good to know someone is looking out for Mike when Frank's gone." Tyler shook Arnie's hand again.

"You can be sure of that," Arnie said as he walked back to the kennel.

Tyler watched him and felt a twinge of concern. The man seemed easily riled, and Tyler wondered if he could be trusted. He decided he was being suspicious for no reason. He glanced back at the cottage before leaving, hoping Mike would be able to get some rest.

TYLER DROVE HOME ON AUTO PILOT. *Lord, you're gonna have to help me here. I'm new at this kind of thing. I know Mike's fighting you, but I also know the Bible says you'll never abandon one of your children. Don't let me push too hard, but help me to make her see. Help me to remain physically strong. Thank you for saving me. In your Son's precious name, Amen.*

When he arrived at his cottage, Tyler was greeted by an adoring Skyler.

MIKE WENT TO SLEEP WITH TYLER ON her mind, but her subconscious was remembering the last time she saw Michelle alive.

"Michelle, what are you doing?" A Volkswagen van pulled to the curb and honked. Michelle gave the guys a wave.

"Just going to have a little fun."

"Michelle, you don't even know those guys."

"Yes, I do. I met them last week."

"What are their names?"

"Tom and Jerry," Michelle said with a chuckle.

"I'm serious, Michelle."

"I'm being honest." Michelle giggled. *"I thought it was funny the first time they introduced themselves to me too."*

"Look, Michelle," Mike's face was covered by a wounded expression, *"I know what you've been doing and it's wrong."*

"Lighten up, Mike. Must you always be the consummate goody-two-shoes? I'm just having a little fun. It's our senior year for crying out loud. We should be enjoying it."

"Enjoying it, yes; getting stoned, no. I just don't get you, Michelle. What's come over you? It's as if you're somebody I don't even know anymore. You're never home. You're ditching school. And the only time you spend with me anymore is when I'm doing your schoolwork. What's gotten into you?" The tone of Mike's voice reflected the desperation she was feeling.

"Get off it, Mike. You've always helped me in school."

"Yes, when I thought you cared about learning, not so you could go off and get loaded with some loser guys."

"Look, Mike," Michelle became defensive, *"just because my friends aren't in the honors society or student council doesn't mean they're losers, and if it does, then I guess your sister is a loser too."*

"Michelle, that's not what I meant."

"Look, I know you have your life all planned out for you. You're the one that got accepted into State. You're the one who has Jason falling at your

feet. And you're the one Mom and Dad have always looked at with pride. Not me. I'm not like you, Mike. Everything doesn't come that easy for me. We knew from the start you were the one with the brains. I tried, but I just can't cut it. So, if I want a little fun once in a while, just leave it alone, okay? I know what I'm doing." Michelle turned to join her friends in the van.

"Michelle . . ."

Michelle turned to see Mike standing with tears in her eyes. "I love you. I just don't want to see you hurt." Michelle came back and gave her sister a hug. "I love you too, Mike. You're getting way too upset. Look, I'll be home late tonight, but what if tomorrow we have a day just for us. No friends, no Jason, just you and me. We'll go shopping and out to dinner, and then maybe we can talk, okay?"

"Sure, Michelle, that would be great."

Mike watched as Michelle jogged to the van and jumped in with the two guys before slamming the door shut.

Mike sat straight up in bed. Tears were in her eyes, her body covered in perspiration. It was the same nightmare she'd had for the past fifteen years—her last conversation with Michelle. If she had stopped her that day and convinced Michelle not to go, she would still be alive.

This was Mike's reality. She blamed herself for her sister's death. She had seen all the signs of a problem: a change in behavior, different friends, and drug abuse. But instead of telling her parents, she covered for Michelle. She thought she was protecting her but now realized she was a factor in her death.

Mike got up from bed, carefully walked to the glass doors that overlooked the lake, and cried. She cried as she had so many times before—out of guilt, anger, and loss. Ultimately, she blamed God for not protecting Michelle. He knew she was struggling, but instead of helping her out of the hole she was digging for herself, he allowed her to fall in it to her death.

Mike grabbed the comforter folded at the foot of her bed and opened the sliding door. She stepped carefully to the chaise on the balcony and curled up on it with just the comforter and her raw emotions surrounding her. If they had only found her killer, then Mike would be able to blame someone other than herself and God.

CHAPTER SEVEN

Tyler was up early. He figured he could go for his morning jog and then stop by Mike's house to fix her some breakfast before he left for work. She might not be a breakfast person, but Tyler would use any excuse to drop by and see her.

When he arrived at the cottage, all was quiet. He had taken her house keys with him the night before, so he carefully let himself in and shut the door behind him.

He crept upstairs to see Mike, assuming she was still asleep. When he looked over the wall of the landing and saw her bed empty, he was surprised. Then he saw her on the balcony. She was lying with her comforter wrapped around her and appeared to be asleep.

Tyler slowly walked over to the chaise. Her nose seemed red, but that could be from the slight chill in the air. His impulse was to bend down and kiss her, but he was sure that would startle her. He gently tried to wake her.

"Mike . . . Mike, wake up."

She stirred for a moment, then opened her eyes. They were red and glassy. It was obvious she had not gotten the night of rest she needed.

"Mike, what's wrong? Did you sleep out here?"

She tried to wrap the comforter tighter around her. She was cold, but the chill came from within her. Tyler nestled himself up against her and pulled her to his chest. She welcomed the warmth and the comfort.

"What happened last night?"

"It was awful, Tyler. I had a horrible nightmare—the same nightmare I've had since Michelle died."

"So you want to tell me about it?" Tyler asked as he held her close. "I'm a good listener."

"I've never told anyone about the last conversation I had with Michelle. I didn't want my parents to know what she'd been doing. They had already lost their daughter. I didn't want to damage their memories."

"What happened?"

For the first time ever, Mike felt as if she wanted to talk to somebody about that day. Maybe if she talked about it, it wouldn't keep haunting her.

Mike took a deep breath and told Tyler about the last conversation she had with her sister. With moments of silence and many shed tears, she recounted the way she felt when she saw her sister drive away. She had been chilled that day, same as she was now. It was as if she knew something were going to happen. She always felt she should have been able to do more to stop Michelle, but she'd been worried her sister would shut her out of her life. Instead, Michelle paid with her life.

Tyler knew what Mike was thinking. "It's not your fault. There was really nothing you could have done."

"I could have stopped her."

"You tried. It was her choice to go with those guys." During the silence between them, Tyler thought about the investigation. *Yes, the physical evidence had been contaminated, but what about the fact that Mike had seen the men and the car? Had any of that been followed up on? Jim had said he was on the case. Surely, Mike would have at least told him about her last conversation.* "Did you ever tell Jim about the two men and the van?"

"Yeah. I didn't tell him why Michelle was with them, though. It didn't matter anyway. I couldn't have identified them, and all I remember about the van was the make and the color. I didn't think, Tyler. I didn't think that was going to be the last time I saw Michelle." Mike started crying again.

Tyler held her tighter, trying his best to comfort her.

"I'm sorry, Tyler. This isn't fair to you. This is something I need to deal with. It's not your problem."

"Of course, it's my problem. I care about you, Mike. I want you to feel as though you could share anything with me. I just want to be able to help you move forward. I'm not telling you to forget about Michelle, I just want you to remember the good things. That is what she would want you to remember." They held each other for a few moments more. Mike couldn't believe the ease she felt when talking with Tyler. It was as if she had known him her entire life.

Time passed as they sat in stillness.

"So, are you ready for some breakfast?"

Mike grinned at his casual way of changing the subject. "Maybe a small one, but why do I get the feeling you're trying to fatten me up like a Thanksgiving turkey?"

"Naw, I would never call you a turkey—a chicken, maybe—but never a turkey." Tyler laughed as he stood. He carefully pulled Mike to her feet and wrapped his arms around her shoulders. She allowed her cheek to rest on his chest and could hear the pounding of his heart.

"Thank you, Tyler."

"For what?"

"For this," she said as she breathed deeply, taking in the scent of his cologne. "It feels good to be held." She turned her head up and smiled at him. He sealed their embrace with a memorable kiss, one that made his heart race.

"Okay, I believe you said something about breakfast, and I need to take a shower," she said as she put some space between them.

"When you're done, I'll change your bandages, so don't worry about keeping them dry."

Tyler headed for the kitchen while Mike hobbled to the bathroom. By the time she was done and made her way downstairs, she knew she would not be able to handle a day at work. She pushed herself up onto the barstool and allowed her head to sink between her hands. Tyler looked up from the bagel he was spreading with cream cheese and sighed.

"If you don't mind me saying so, you look terrible."

"Gee, thanks, Tyler. It's not as if I don't already know that."

He pushed the bagel in front of her and laughed. "Well, you wouldn't want me to lie to you, would you?"

"Oh no. I'd much rather you be brutally honest."

She took a bite of what was usually her favorite evening snack and felt as if she were chewing on cardboard. She swallowed, then took a swig of orange juice and dropped her head back into her hand. "There's no way I can go to work today. My knee is throbbing, and I can barely hold my head up it hurts so bad."

"I thought we decided last night you weren't going to go to work today?"

"I know, but I thought maybe I could pull it off. I hate to think of how much work will pile up by tomorrow."

"No one's expecting you to be at work today. Jim said you were to take a few days off. Stop trying to be superwoman."

Mike got a disgusted look on her face. "And since when is the lieutenant of Emerald Lake in charge of the county M.E.'s schedule?"

"Since Jim called Bridges and told him how banged up you are. Look, Mike, you're the one putting so much pressure on yourself. Swallow your pride for once and let yourself be human."

Mike wanted to lash out at Tyler. He had no right to judge her. She was not trying to be superwoman. She just took her job seriously and didn't want the lab to get backed up or Nathan to get overwhelmed on account of her.

Tyler could read her expression but didn't wait for her rebuttal. "You can be mad at me all you want, but it won't change anything. You need to take a few days off and that's that." Tyler finished his last gulp of orange juice and cut Mike off before she could unload on him. "I've got to go; some of us have to work." He grinned, knowing she was getting more agitated. "Let me rebandage your leg, and then I'll go."

"I can do it, Tyler. Really, I'm not as helpless as you think I am."

He laughed. "Helpless is the last thing I would call you." He rinsed out his glass and put it in the sink. "I'll call before I leave work tonight to see if something sounds good for dinner." He placed a tender kiss on Mike's forehead and looked into her eyes. "Try to rest, okay."

What could she say? Tyler could get her all worked up and then with a gentle word or a sideways smile, he could make her forget that she was even mad at him.

She returned the smile and watched as he walked to the door and stopped. "Are you going to be all right?"

"Yeah. I'm going to be fine."

"I'll call you." He slipped out the door, leaving her with her thoughts. These thoughts both confused and excited her. She never would've thought after their first encounter that he could become such a good friend, and so fast. He was really doing a number on her heart, and there was nothing she could do to stop it . . . not that she wanted to.

WHEN TYLER SHOWED UP AT THE STATION, Jim was already pouring himself a cup of decaf. Tyler headed for the coffeepot and waited his turn.

"So, how is our patient this morning?" Jim said as he added heaps of sugar to his steaming cup.

"Very impatient." Tyler chuckled as he poured himself a cup of the strong, black liquid.

"Did she stay home?"

"Yeah. She stayed, but she didn't like it."

"So what about you?" Jim said with a raised brow.

"What about me?" Tyler tried to act unaware, but he knew what Jim was implying.

"For two people that were ready to deck each other a month ago, you seem to be getting along pretty well now."

Tyler tried to hide his grin behind the cup of coffee raised to his lips. "I guess you could say that we've worked out our differences." He headed to his desk and turned on his computer. Jim followed behind him and waited for details, but Tyler wasn't giving any. It didn't matter to Jim. The smile on Tyler's face pretty much said it all.

MIKE SPENT HER DAY IN AND OUT OF SLEEP. She took the pain medicine, not caring that it would affect her mental sharpness. She wasn't expected back at work, so she had no reason not to take it.

Her thoughts bounced from one subject to another. Her ego was feeling a little deflated that she wasn't needed at work. She had convinced herself that the work she did was so important that the county could not do without her. That obviously wasn't the case. *I guess it's true. Everyone is dispensable.*

Once she pushed her pity party aside, she allowed her mind to drift back to times spent with Michelle. They had been best friends since the time they were born and had done everything together. They shared dance and gymnastics classes, were junior lifeguards together, and had been inseparable. But when they reached high school, subtle changes began to take place. By their senior year, she and Michelle were traveling in completely different social circles. Mike continued to excel both socially and academically, while Michelle began to drift to a different group of kids. She struggled in her studies and relied on Mike to get her through some of her classes. She no longer wanted to participate in group activities like the student council or cheerleading. Instead, she hung out with friends who had the reputation of being outsiders and troublemakers. Michelle felt comfortable with this group of misfits because that was who she had felt she'd become.

Their parents were pressuring them to choose a college, assuming they would go to the same one. Mike had already been accepted at State and was pushing Michelle to finish the application process. Michelle had already decided not to go to college but didn't know how to tell her parents or her sister.

Mike's mind fast-forwarded to the argument, the van, Michelle walking away, the way she looked at the morgue, the devastation on her parents face, and for Mike, the sense that she had lost a limb, an essential part of her being.

Mike sat in a funk for most of the afternoon. It wasn't until after some much needed rest that she allowed her thoughts to move to Tyler. The smile she could feel on her face and the warmth that melted her heart let her know he had broken through the arms-length barrier she kept between herself and others.

Though he was opinionated and stubborn, Tyler was also charming and caring. He was more chivalrous than chauvinistic and was what she would describe as gallant—something missing in this day and age. The emotions she was feeling were a surprise. She had never thought a man could touch her the way he had been able to in such a short amount of time. She was embarrassed at her reaction the previous night. She had assumed he wanted to sleep with her. She thought that was a given in today's society, but Tyler had politely turned her down. The embarrassment she felt was softened by his gentle explanation. It was his depth, his charm, and his incredible smile that made Mike's heart twirl when she thought of him. The fact that he was drop-dead gorgeous hadn't escaped her attention either.

She glanced at the clock and wondered what time Tyler would call to check in on her. She longed to hear his voice. She giggled silently and chided herself for acting like an adolescent. But she didn't care. She had never felt this way before and was anxious to see where it would take her.

TYLER HAD GLANCED AT THE CLOCK for the hundredth time.

"That's it. Why don't you go ahead and get out of here for the day," Jim barked from behind his desk. "It's not as though I'm going to get any work out of you if you stay."

Tyler looked at him sheepishly. "I'm sorry, Jim. I'll be fine. I just keep wondering how she's doing. I don't want to call her and wake her up if she's sleeping, and I'm sure she probably hasn't eaten anything all day."

"Like I said, go ahead and go. It's already 4:00. There's nothing else for you to do around here anyway."

"But I don't want to leave you short-handed."

Billings leaned into the office shared by Jim and Tyler, and signaled to Jim that there was a call for him. Jim finished his conversation with Tyler before picking up the phone.

"Tyler, we've managed all these years without you. I don't think another hour at the end of your shift is going to matter."

"Well, if you feel that way about it, maybe you won't mind me taking tomorrow off too. I think it would be nice to take Mike out on the lake before all the good weather is gone."

"Go ahead. Take the time now because I have a feeling when this Dorian Thomas case heats up, we'll be putting in some long hours."

Tyler didn't ask twice. He turned off his computer, grabbed his phone, and headed for the parking lot. He couldn't wait to see Mike. He hoped she felt the same way about him.

Tyler dialed Mike's number the minute he got in the car. She answered on the third ring, sounding a little groggy.

"How are you doing? You sound sleepy."

"I was just resting."

"Are we still on for dinner?"

Mike tried to make sure her reply didn't sound overly anxious. "Sure . . . if you want."

"Does anything sound good to eat?"

"Not really."

"What have you had to eat today?"

"A bagel."

"That's what I thought. Look, I'll pick something up and see you in about twenty minutes."

Mike tried to make herself look presentable. Earlier she had put on her favorite pair of cut-off jean shorts and a tank top. Now she looked as though she had just rolled out of bed. She dragged herself upstairs, ran a brush through her hair, and put some blush on her cheeks. She really wasn't into makeup, but today she needed the help. She pulled an oversized sweatshirt on that hung well below her shorts, making her look a little more presentable.

She slowly got herself downstairs and could feel a slight improvement in her mobility. The day off her feet had really helped. *Maybe there really is something to this rest and relaxation thing,* she thought.

By the time she was settled downstairs, she heard a slight knock at the door. Before she could get up to answer it, Tyler was already letting himself in the house. When he saw the perturbed look on her face, he explained.

"I took your house keys this morning. I figured you weren't going to be using them, and I knew I could return them tonight."

"You sound pretty sure of yourself, Henderson. What if I had said you couldn't come over tonight?"

Mike was standing at the foot of the couch when Tyler approached her. He moved to within inches of her steely blue eyes. "I took my chances." He leaned down and placed a kiss on her lips. "Do you want me to leave?"

Mike knew what Tyler was doing. He wanted her to admit she wanted him there as much as he wanted to be there. Her first reaction was to give him a nonchalant reply, as though it didn't matter. But she didn't. She wanted him to know how she was feeling. "No. I'm glad you're here."

"Me too," he said with a smile while he headed towards the small dining room table. "I picked up Chinese. I wasn't sure what you like, so I got a little of everything. I like all of it, so I'll have whatever you don't want."

He started unloading the small white boxes from the large sack he was holding. By the time Mike had gotten some plates and some sodas from the refrigerator, Tyler had opened up at least nine different cartons.

"My word, Tyler. Do you think you got enough?"

"I guess I was hungrier than I thought. It all sounded so good. Besides, they'll keep. You can have them for leftovers tomorrow." Mike slowly lowered herself into one of the dining room chairs.

"I'm going to pray, okay?"

"Sure," was her curt reply.

His prayer was short and to the point.

After dishing up his plate and taking a few bites, Tyler commented, "You look as if you're getting around pretty good."

Mike played with her food and finally used her chopsticks to grab at a pot sticker. "I'm actually feeling a little better. At least not as stiff."

"Are you still taking the pain medication?"

"I took some around 3:00, and I'll take some before I go to bed tonight; but I think I'll be able to make it at work tomorrow without it."

"I'm glad. So you admit a day off helped?"

"I admit it—a day off helped. It wasn't the R and R I was fighting; it was my ego that I was struggling with."

"What . . . afraid Nathan's going to try and move in on your territory?" Tyler was only joking. He could see that Nathan and Mike had a good working relationship.

"It's not Nathan that I'm worried about."

"Then who?"

"Anyone who thinks I'm in a job better suited for a male. I'm afraid if I show any signs of weakness, certain people will start doubting my capabilities."

"Has that happened before?" Tyler asked as he continued scooping rice up with his chopsticks.

"I've had a couple incidences of chauvinism."

"But that can't be the norm. Not in this day and age."

Mike continued between bites, "Even so, I don't want to do anything that would open me up to scrutiny."

Tyler could begin to see Mike's shoulders tensing. "Okay, time to change the subject. I didn't come over to talk about work."

"So why did you come over?" Mike's question was intended to put Tyler on the spot, so he decided to turn the tables on her.

He leaned over from where he was sitting, placed a firm hand to the back of Mike's neck and pulled her closer. He pressed his lips to hers and gave her a kiss that spoke volumes. It was long and lingering, but still ended with Mike wanting more. Tyler was staring at her as she opened her eyes. By her satisfied expression he could read the pleasure she felt. "That for starters."

"Starters, huh." She swallowed deep. "If that's where we're starting, then I think we better say good night right now."

"I promise to behave. I'm not going to take advantage of you since you're not one hundred percent."

"Oh, but you'd take advantage of me if I were?" Mike bantered.

"No one could take advantage of you. You're too bullheaded. You'd have to be unconscious for someone to get the upper hand on you."

"Or drunk."

All teasing was gone from Mike's voice. It was her way of admitting something to Tyler. She stood up slowly from the table, barely having eaten any of her dinner, and hobbled to the living room.

Tyler knew what she was doing, but it wasn't going to work. So she had a past. So what. So did he. He was a different person now than he was when he was with Kelly, and if Mike was trying to admit mistakes from her past, then it was obvious she had changed too. He wasn't going to give into her self-deprecating mood.

Tyler noticed she still moved slowly yet with more force than she had earlier that day. There would be no convincing her to take another day off. He would have to come up with a plan that gave her no way out.

He left Mike to her funk and cleared the table of the white cartons and dishes. He put the leftovers in the refrigerator and rinsed the plates and silverware.

Mike sat on the couch with her arms crossed on her chest and her leg resting on a pillow on the coffee table. Tyler walked up behind her and gently placed his hands on her shoulders. He started massaging the strained muscles of her neck. When he felt the rigidness begin to melt away, he spoke up.

"Mike, if you want me to leave you alone, I will. You don't have to try and scare me away with whatever is in your past. So, if there's something you want to tell me, fine, but you have to know that I'm interested in you for who you are now. Not who you once were or who you hope to be someday. I don't want you to feel any pressure by my being here. Do you understand what I'm saying?" Tyler voice was firm. He was serious and wanted Mike to know it.

Mike felt as if she had just gotten a lecture from her dad. As much as she wanted to be angry, Tyler was right. She had a habit of pushing people away. She had convinced herself that she was fine by herself. She didn't need anyone to complete her as a person. Even though she'd spent the day thinking about him, her first instincts were to sabotage the feelings they shared.

"You're awfully quiet," Tyler said as he circled the couch and sat down next to her. "I didn't mean to hurt your feelings. I just feel we're too old to be playing games. I think you know how I feel about you, Mike, and I would like to be able to pursue those feelings, but not if you're going to live in the past." Mike turned to him to make a point but Tyler interrupted her. "I know you've had your share of sorrows that I could never even begin to comprehend. But living in the past is not the answer. I will be here for you to help you deal with it, but if that's where you're going to live, I can't do it. I won't watch you waste your life on things that can't be changed."

Mike didn't know what to say. She wanted to be angry with Tyler. He had no idea what she had gone through, yet here he was telling her to get over it. Yet in her heart of hearts, she knew he was right. As painful as it was, he was right. She needed to live again. And her heart told her this was the man that could awaken in her the joy that had been missing from her life. She tried to quiet the turmoil of the feelings inside her. Tears began to wet her cheeks, and she closed her eyes to gather her composure. She felt Tyler move away from her, and she quickly reached out to grab his hand before he could leave the couch. When their eyes met, she could see the redness that circled his.

"I don't want you to go, Tyler."

Tyler's embrace blanketed her with a feeling of peace—a peace she had not had for so many years.

He spent a few more hours at Mike's but called it an early evening. As much as he wanted to be with her, she needed her rest. And he needed to give her some space to think. He told her he would be by to pick her up in the morning. Of course, she had no idea how early he would arrive.

CHAPTER EIGHT

Tyler awoke raring to go. He had a lot to get ready for the afternoon he had planned with Mike. He went to the grocery store and loaded up on crackers, cheese, fruit salad, and snacks. He went to the deli section to have some fresh sandwiches prepared and grabbed a bottle of sparkling white grape cider and a bouquet of pink roses. He headed to the dock and made arrangements to rent a pontoon boat for the day, stowing his purchases on the boat before he left. He had everything they needed for a romantic cruise up and down the lake. Now, for the challenging part—getting Mike to agree to miss another day of work.

WHEN MIKE STEPPED OUT OF THE SHOWER, she heard a light knock at the front door. She quickly wrapped herself in a towel and hobbled to the landing of the stairs. By the time she did, Tyler was already standing at the base of the stairs, staring up at her.

"Tyler . . . what would you have done if I were standing here naked?" she asked, holding the towel closer to her chest.

"My face probably would have turned red," he said with a shrug. "And then I would have had to apologize for not turning away quickly enough."

"Tyler!"

"Hey, you asked. I'm only human." Tyler smiled and held up the bag he was holding in his hand. "I brought breakfast. Why don't you come eat before you get dressed."

"What?"

"You know what I mean."

"Yeah, I know what you said. But what you meant is another story."

Tyler headed for the kitchen and put two breakfast croissant sandwiches on plates while Mike pulled on her robe and slowly worked her way down the steps.

"You know, Tyler, you can't just keep barging in here. I do enjoy having some privacy."

"I know. I was going to give your key back today anyway. Now let's eat before this gets cold."

Tyler bowed and prayed, not even asking this time if Mike minded. She really didn't as long as Tyler didn't try to preach to her.

They chatted over breakfast until Mike got up to get dress. Tyler wasn't sure how he was going to accomplish the rest of his plan. He was just going to have to play it by ear.

It took Mike another twenty minutes to get ready for work, but for Tyler it was well worth the wait. She looked incredible. She wore a simple polo dress that hung just below her knees, but boy did it hug her body in all the right places. Tyler whistled his approval.

Mike was embarrassed by his show of appreciation. Her reddening cheeks were proof of that. Tyler decided to tease her even further.

"You sure are moving easier today. The way you glided down those stairs was absolute poetry in motion."

"Okay, Tyler, that's enough. All this flattering is going to get you on my bad side."

"Oh, I don't know. I don't think you have a bad side—or at least I haven't found it yet."

Mike's cheeks were inflamed, and Tyler couldn't contain his laughter. Mike grabbed for her crutches by the door and gave him a punch to the gut. He let out a grunt.

"Hey, I could arrest you for assaulting a police officer," he said as he followed Mike out the door and turned the key in the lock.

"And I could charge you with sexual harassment," she said as she limped up the slate steps leading to the driveway. She hid the smile on her face by keeping her back to Tyler. Her heart was hammering away, and she could feel herself falling for him. With every touch of his hand and every word of concern, she was falling deeper under the charming spell of Tyler Henderson.

"Here, let me give you a hand." Tyler bent down and swung Mike up into his arms.

"That's more than a hand," she said as she wrapped her arm around his neck. "But I'll take it."

He climbed the steps slowly, making sure he didn't lose his footing, or at least that's what he tried to convince himself of. After helping her into his truck, he situated Mike's crutches in the back of his extended cab. He was ready to back out of the driveway when he stopped. "Dang it, I left my phone in the house. Hold on a minute. I'll be right back."

Mike handed him her keys. Tyler jumped out of the truck and trotted down the steps. Once inside, he bolted up to Mike's room and looked around. *Nothing.* He moved to the bathroom, looking around. *Bingo.* Hanging from the hook on the back of the door were the discarded shorts and tank top she had been wearing the day before. A black bikini was also hanging from the hook. He thought about grabbing it but figured there would be no easy way for Mike to slip into it.

He looked around the floor of her room for sandals of any kind but found none. He quickly searched through the bank of shutter doors and finally found her stash of shoes. He pulled out a pair of flip flops, but not before something else caught his attention. There, hanging in a clear garment bag, was a wedding dress.

Tyler had to take a breath. Had Mike been married? Or engaged? And if so, what happened?

It wasn't as though it would have made a difference in how he felt. He had been engaged too, but it just surprised him that she hadn't said anything. He wouldn't push her. He would wait and see what she had to say about it. If there was anything to even say. He had already told her that her past didn't matter as far as he was concerned.

Tyler came to his senses and gathered up the things he had collected. He headed to the kitchen, found a plastic trash bag to hold the items, and then grabbed his cell phone from where he had purposely left it on the counter.

Mike was confused when Tyler reappeared carrying a trash bag. She questioned him the minute he was seated in the truck.

"What's in the bag?"

"I thought I would dump your trash for you. It was pretty full with all the take out containers."

Mike thought Tyler was behaving strangely but let it go. "Did you get your phone?" Mike asked.

"Yeah, right here." Now to see how good his bluffing game was. "I have just a few errands to do on the way to work. So you might want to sit back and relax."

"Will it take long? I should call Nathan and let him know I'm running late."

"No, and I already squared it with Nathan."

"You called Nathan? Oh great! He must be having a field day with that." Mike lay her head back and groaned. "I won't get a moment's peace at work. He'll give me the third degree when I get there."

"So give him something to talk about. Let's see . . . we were in the tub together and in bed together— " Tyler wasn't able to finishing his teasing because of the hearty slug Mike planted on his arm.

"How dare you, Tyler Henderson! I can't believe you said that." Her expression was shock mixed with embarrassment.

"I was only kidding." Tyler was laughing so hard he could barely talk. "I just figured you could get the upper hand on Nathan. Shock him. That would shut him up."

Mike was completely ignoring him. His diversion had worked. She was so flustered by his comments she was no longer paying attention to his driving. She was sulking with her eyes closed and her head back, exactly where Tyler wanted her. She stayed this way for quite awhile. She looked genuinely hurt. Tyler was almost feeling guilty, but hopefully his surprise would even the score. He was close to the marina when Mike finally started asking him some questions.

"What on earth do you have to pick up down here?"

"Jim asked me to pick up something for him, so I said I would."

"Tyler, do you know how late we're going to be? We are going to end up right in the middle of morning traffic." Mike huffed and crossed her arms sternly across her chest.

Tyler couldn't hold his grin, so he turned towards the window. He pulled into a parking place and quickly got out of the truck. He walked around to Mike's side of the truck and opened her door. She looked at him with disgust.

"You know, Tyler, maybe I spoke too soon. I'm seeing a different side of you, and I'm not sure I like it." Her tone was serious, and Tyler could see he had let things go too far. "You obviously don't take your job as seriously as I do or care about your reputation, which really surprises me. I thought I was a better judge of character. Maybe I better rethink—"

Tyler didn't let her finish. He pulled a single pink rose from behind his back. "Is it too late to sway the jury?"

Mike looked back and forth between Tyler and the rose. She slowly took the stem from Tyler's hand, held it close to her face, and enjoyed its wonderful scent.

"What is this for?"

"It's an invitation to spend the rest of the day with me."

"The rest of the day? Tyler, what about work?" She was in a quandary. Never before would she have allowed work to take a backseat to something she wanted to do. But she was considering that very scenario in order to spend the day with Tyler.

"I told you. I already cleared it with Nathan."

"You're serious. You spoke to Nathan about my taking off? You realize, even if he said yes, I'm his superior. He doesn't have the authority to approve time off for me."

"No, but Bridges does."

Mike cringed. "You went to Bridges?"

"I didn't, but Nathan did. He explained to him the overtime you were putting in for the department and reminded him of the fact that you injured yourself pretty badly on the job. Nathan assured Bridges that he could handle whatever came in and explained that you would never ask for yourself. Nathan also convinced him it was for your own good."

"I wish you hadn't done that." Mike wasn't actually mad. She was just upset thinking that her impeccable record might now have a question mark. Jerry Bridges was the chief M.E. and was well-respected. Would this incident cause him to think she was unstable or unreliable? How did it look to have her co-worker do her bidding? What if he thought she wasn't a team player because she was taking personal time? She was getting nervous thinking about what this might mean to her career.

"Do you want to know what he said?"

"Bridges?" She perked up.

"He said you were more than entitled to some time off. Your record is exceptional, and he should have said something sooner. He sends his apologies concerning your injury and said to take as much time as you need."

"You're kidding?" A huge smile crossed Mike's face. "He really made those comments about me?" Realizing her work had not gone unnoticed, she felt a sense of pride.

"Okay, now that you know you still have a job, and I'm not as undependable as you think, what do you say to a day on the lake?"

"Yes," she said with a smile.

Tyler left his jacket and tie in the truck. He removed his holster and concealed his gun and shield in the bag he was carrying, the supposed bag of trash. He grabbed the other things he would need and started towards the dock, Mike at his side.

She was moving slowly. Her crutches were proving to be difficult to maneuver on the weathered planks of wood. Tyler's hands were full, so he just walked with her, allowing her to go at her own pace.

When they got to the boat, Tyler put everything he was carrying on the deck and carefully helped Mike. Once on the deck, he pulled her close, wrapping her tightly in his arms and staring into her eyes. She looked up into his, wondering what else he had up his sleeve.

"You lied to me, Tyler." The smile on Mike's face was one Tyler had never seen before. Pleasure was evident in her eyes.

"No, I surprised you by withholding key information." He was sure his smile matched hers.

"What about an errand for Jim?"

"Well, maybe it's more like a favor. He told me to get you to take a couple days off, and that's what I'm doing."

They were still holding each other, neither one of them wanting to move. "Are you ready to take off?"

"Where are we going?"

"Nowhere in particular." Tyler tipped his head down towards Mike's upturned face. There was something happening between them, and they both knew it. Mike decided it was time to try a relationship. Michelle had been gone fifteen years, and during that fifteen years Mike had done nothing for herself. Everything she did was to please or help others. It was time she did something for herself. She just hoped Tyler was going to be able to handle the baggage she was carrying. As much as he tried to assure her that her past didn't matter, she felt he might reconsider once he heard it all.

Tyler knew this time things would be different. Mike was nothing like Kelly. He had loved Kelly at one time, but had never gotten that same assurance from her. Her resistance to set a wedding date had shown Tyler she liked the relationship they shared but wasn't sure it was love that she felt.

Tyler thought about the wedding dress hanging in Mike's closet. He wanted to ask her about it but didn't. He wanted to enjoy the day. He was sure she would tell him when she was ready.

Tyler helped Mike to the large bench at the stern of the boat and readied the small craft for their afternoon cruise. Mike pulled her feet up on the bright yellow cushion and tried arranging her dress so she could get some sun.

"Would you like to slip these on?"

Tyler held out the pair of shorts she had been wearing earlier.

Mike recognized her crummiest pair of shorts and felt embarrassed. They were frayed and had paint stains on them. They were a pair she didn't usually wear in public because she thought they were on the short side. "Where did you get those?" Mike asked as she snatched them from his hand.

"You left them lying out along with this." Tyler held out her white tank top.

"So, what else did you lift from my house?" she asked with an amusing tone in her voice. "Should I be counting the silverware when I get home?"

"No," he said as he perched on the edge of the bench cushion. "You shouldn't be thinking about home, or work, or the case, or anything. Today is about us."

"Us? Is there an 'us,' Tyler?" Mike suddenly felt nervous. There was so much that Tyler still didn't know about her. She couldn't ignore it. He would find out soon enough. One moment she was excited about the prospects of having Tyler in her life, and the next she felt she needed to protect him. She felt he deserved better.

"I'm working on it." His smile was relaxed. "Here, let me help you keep your balance while you slide on those shorts. Then you can enjoy the sun while I get us to where we're going."

Mike stood, her cheeks becoming flushed. Tyler knew she was blushing because they hadn't been out long enough for her skin's redness to be from the sun. He was trying to figure out the most modest way for her to slip on her shorts. It was nothing to slip them on under a dress, but her one stiff leg was going to make the task a little more difficult.

She laid her shorts on the deck and allowed her peg-like leg to step into them. She bent down and held them while she stepped into them with her good leg at the same time that Tyler was holding her by the waist for balance. She slid them up under her dress while Tyler gallantly looked away. Then she tackled the tank top. This proved to be a little harder, but after a few maneuvers, she was able to pull her dress over her head.

"Done," Mike said with a breath.

Tyler looked at her with an admiring eye. "Wow, Daisy Duke has nothing on you."

"That's it. I'm changing back." Her face, neck, and chest glowed red.

"No, you're not," Tyler said with a playful voice as he grabbed the dress from her hand. "I was just admiring the view."

"Yeah, well. These are too short. I only wear them around the house." She felt so embarrassed by her appearance that Mike wouldn't even look at Tyler.

"Look, if I had wanted to, I could've grabbed your bathing suit, which would have been a lot more revealing than those shorts. Come on, I want you to relax, enjoy the sun and the lake. It's only the two of us, and I promise not to ogle." Tyler's look turned devilish. "Well... maybe not too much."

Mike swung at Tyler's arm and he grabbed it. He allowed the space between them to disappear. His arm was firmly around her waist, and he tipped her chin up so she had to look at him. She squinted against the sun. "Let's just enjoy the day, okay?" His words were soft and promising. The safety she felt with him was like nothing she had ever known before.

They shared a long, lingering kiss, and then Tyler helped her back to the bench. She stretched out, perched herself on her elbows, and allowed her head to tip back. The sun felt fabulous, and she could feel a light mist coming up from the back of the boat.

Mike enjoyed a quiet, relaxed ride to the far side of the lake. When the engine moaned to a stop, she watched as Tyler dropped a cinder block that was used for an anchor over the side of the boat.

"Can you do me a favor?" he asked.

"Sure." She looked at him, squinting in the sun.

Tyler was unbuttoning the dress shirt he wore while he talked. "I can't change into shorts as easily as you did. Give me a couple minutes while I change into mine." The shirt was gone. Tyler wore what the teens called a 'wife beater' undershirt. His arms were very muscular, his shoulders looking even broader in the slim cut of the undershirt. He undid the clasp of his slacks. "Well..."

Mike realized she was staring when Tyler had asked for privacy. She quickly turned her head towards the back of the boat. She heard the rustle of material and then a silence. A shadow came over her, and she turned to see Tyler, hovering above her.

All he was wearing was a pair of navy board shorts. His chest and his abs were as taut as his arms. He definitely worked hard at staying in shape. Mike felt herself heat up again—this time from the inside out.

Tyler sat opposite Mike, putting his feet up alongside her outstretched legs. He leaned back against the side of the boat and looked out over the water. Mike couldn't take her eyes off him. Her attraction for him had reached a whole new level.

"That's not fair, you know." Tyler was talking to her but his head was still turned looking out over the water.

"What's not fair?"

"If I can't ogle you, you can't ogle me." He turned back and caught her eye with a devilish grin. "I have very good peripheral vision."

"If you didn't want me looking, you would have kept your shirt on." Mike was defending her actions by casting the blame on him.

"And get a farmer's tan? No way. You'll just have to control yourself." Tyler closed his eyes and tilted his head to the sun.

They lounged on the stern for some time, neither of them feeling the need to fill the silence. Mike was beginning to drift. The sun was warm, but the gentle breeze wrapped the warmth around her like a soft summer blanket.

Tyler stirred but Mike continued to bask in the sun, somewhere between awake and asleep. Sleep finally won.

Tyler worked quietly to set up their lunch—sandwiches, cheese, crackers, fresh fruit, sparkling cider, candles, and, of course, a bouquet of pink roses. He set up a small table in the middle of the boat and put the vase full of roses in the middle of the black checkerboard tablecloth. He quietly set the little candles down inside two large slender glasses. He tilted the glasses, lit the candles, and inwardly applauded himself for his ingenuity. The candles stayed lit because of the protection from the tall glasses. He set the food out on the table, the scent seeming to arouse Mike.

She stretched, took in the sky above her and the lake beside her, and remembered that the way she was feeling was not just a daydream. She turned from the water to the boat to be met by the picture perfect picnic lunch.

"Lunch is served." Tyler picked up the table and carefully moved it closer to her.

"How did you do all this? You were at my house by 7:30 this morning. When did you have time?"

"I'm an early riser, and the market up on Fifth Street is open twenty-four hours."

"You're incredible." The pleasure in Mike's voice was exactly the reaction Tyler had wanted. He walked around the table to sit next to Mike as she slowly lowered her foot to the ground. She was able to keep her knee straight enough by moving to the edge of the cushion. Tyler slid in beside her, took her fingers in his, and placed a light kiss to the top of her hand.

"Mind if I pray?"

She nodded her head and found herself bowing as she had done so many times as a child.

"Lord, thank you for allowing Mike and me some time to get to know each other. Thank you for an incredible day and gorgeous weather. Bless this food to our bodies. Amen."

Tyler saw that Mike had bowed her head and closed her eyes. He hoped it was a step in the right direction.

"This all looks so good, Tyler."

"I had to guess on a few things, but I think you'll enjoy it."

Mike turned an admiring look to him as he poured her cider. "I think everything looks wonderful."

Tyler and Mike thoroughly enjoyed their picnic lunch. Tyler talked a little about his time as a beat cop, his promotion to detective, and about the tragic accident that had taken his partner's life.

"When I got the call about Bob, I was stunned. To think he'd been a twenty year veteran of the force, and he was nailed by a drunk driver around the corner from his own house. It just didn't make any sense."

Tyler continued on about his life before he moved to Emerald Lake. He had seen a lot of violence and crime in his fourteen years in the big city.

"How did you handle it? I mean, I see people when there is nothing left to do for them, but you had to have encountered people that were reachable. How did you handle seeing them throw their lives away and not be able to stop them?"

Tyler thought back to Heather. His look was solemn, and Mike instantly noticed the change in his demeanor.

"I'm sorry. I didn't mean to hit a sore spot."

Tyler was quiet for a moment before he told Heather's story. "There was this girl—Heather. I first met her when I picked her up for shoplifting. She was a spunky kid. She tried to make me believe she wasn't afraid, but I could see that she was. I decided to give her a chance. I told her if she could give me three reasons why I shouldn't take her to Juvenile Hall, I would take her home."

"What did she say?"

"At first, she just wanted to be belligerent and told me she didn't care what I did. Then, she started opening up. The reason she had stolen the food was to feed her little brother at home."

"She stole food?" Mike had shock in her voice. She had assumed the girl was caught stealing clothes or a CD, not food.

"Yep. Turns out, her mother was a pothead and would zone out for days at a time. Heather had started shoplifting to make sure she and her brother had something to eat. Then, her second reason for not wanting to go to Juvenile Hall was her mother would beat her if she had to come and get her. That's when I learned this had not been Heather's first incident with the cops."

86

Mike was horrified but not surprised. So many kids today were considered throwaways because of the lifestyles of their parents. "So what did you do?"

"I made her a deal. If her mother came home wasted and she needed money for food, she was to call me. I didn't want her stealing. If I found out she was, I would take her in for sure. Our agreement lasted for awhile. She would call me, and I would meet her with groceries."

Again, Tyler became quiet. He started fiddling with the leftovers on his plate, distracting himself from what Mike sensed was a story without a happy ending. He looked like a hundred-pound weight had been laid across his shoulders.

"Tyler, what happened to Heather?"

"She was killed."

Mike gave Tyler a little time before she asked, "How?"

"Heather was growing up. One night I saw her working the streets. I was enraged. I pulled her into the squad car and tore into her. She sat in my car resilient and unmoving. I gave her all the money I had in my pocket and told her to get herself cleaned up.

"Tyler, you didn't!" Mike gasped. "You could have gotten into major trouble if anyone found out. You could have been questioned for solicitation yourself."

"I know, but I was so upset. Heather and I had known each other for a few years at that point. She had told me how she wanted to go to modeling school or get her beautician's license. I felt as if I were more than a cop to her. I thought I had done something to change a person's life. Seeing her on the street, all made up, and wearing seductive clothes, made me realize I was wrong. The world Heather lived in was more difficult to penetrate than I had thought. The last time I saw her alive, I had stopped by her place to check in on her. When she answered the door, she almost slammed it in my face. I pushed my way in to see that her place was a shambles, her mother and brother were nowhere around, and she had a black eye and a busted lip. Come to find out her mother had herself a new boyfriend, and the scum decided that he was entitled to Heather as well. He had gotten rough with her when she refused his advances."

Tyler leaned on the rail at the bow of the boat. He felt ill from the memory. Mike knew he was on the edge; she could see it on his face. She stood behind Tyler and wrapped her arms around him. She laid her head against his back and brought her hands up to his chest. She could feel his heart racing and wanted to comfort him. He had tried to reach someone and had failed, just as she had done with Michelle.

"She was found in a back alley shot up with heroin," he continued. "Her case was labeled an overdose, but I knew that was wrong. Even with everything Heather had done, she had never taken drugs. She still had hopes and dreams. She wasn't a druggy, and she wouldn't have killed herself."

"Did you investigate it?"

"Yeah. I knew it was her mother's boyfriend. I was sure of it, but I couldn't prove it. They had skipped town, and I never got a name. He was just some dirt bag that latched on to her mother. I had no leads and nowhere to go. The streets were no help because no one saw anything—the typical scenario." Tyler sighed heavily. "I had to let it go. There was nothing I could do."

"How did you let it go?" Mike asked, wondering how he was able to separate himself from something so tragic. She hadn't been able to distance herself from the memory of Michelle's murder after all these years.

"I went on a three-day binge and when I was done, I had a private funeral for Heather. It was all I could do for her."

They stood in silence, and for a moment, Mike thought Tyler might even be crying. He sniffed a few times, turned to Mike, and apologized.

"Wow, what a downer of a date I turned out to be." He was trying to be humorous, but his red eyes exposed the true man that was inside.

"Oh, I don't know. This part is pretty nice." Mike tried to change the subject completely. Mike tipped her head up to look into his saddened eyes. She slipped her hands behind Tyler's neck as he wrapped his arms around her waist.

"Then let me go for good." Tyler smiled, seeming to enjoy this little phrase of his. His kiss was timid at first, but with Mike's consent, it turned more searching, in need of assurance.

Mike realized this is what was missing from her life. She had shut herself off, convincing herself she was self-sufficient. But she had only been fooling herself. She needed this. She needed the love of a man—someone to hold her and comfort her, someone to make her feel safe and protected, and someone to make her feel alive again. She was convinced a part of her had died years ago with Michelle. She knew now that her heart had not died completely; it had only been waiting to be reawakened by the right person.

CHAPTER NINE

He made sure he wasn't seen by anyone as he worked his way down to the shore. He watched Mike and Tyler with binoculars, wanting to know what was going on between them. When he saw their intimate embrace, he knew he had been betrayed. The twig snapped that he had been holding in his hand, his anger rising.

Mike had been the object of his affection for as long as he could remember. She freaked out after Michelle's death and pushed everyone away so she could sort out her feelings. He had given her the space she wanted. But he felt someday she would come to her senses and realize how much she still needed him. He had been willing to wait for her until she could move on. From what he was seeing, she was ready to move on, just not with him.

TYLER STROKED THE LENGTH OF MIKE'S FOREARMS as her fingers intertwined behind his neck. He looked into her eyes and smiled. Her eyes were sparkling in return.

"What would you like to do next?" Tyler asked, relieved that his somber mood had not affected Mike adversely.

"I would love to go swimming, but I know lake water would not be good on my stitches. Besides, I don't have my bathing suit with me."

"How disappointing," Tyler said with a heavy sigh.

"It's no big deal, Tyler. I'm fine just being out on the lake." Mike tried to assure him that she was still having a good time.

"I was talking about me," he said with a beguiling grin. "To think, those stitches are the only thing standing between you, me, and a bikini."

Mike laughed and tried to pull away from Tyler's embrace, but he just held her tighter. "Who said anything about a bikini?"

"Hey, I'm a detective. It's my job to be observant.

His smile was captivating and the warmth of his arms around her was comforting. She liked the way it felt to be close to a man. Intimacy had long been missing from her life.

"Go ahead and go swimming if you'd like, Tyler. I'm more than content to just relax here and enjoy the sun."

"Are you sure?"

"Yeah. Go ahead. I'll be fine."

Tyler gave Mike a quick peck on the cheek. He then moved to the back of the boat and stepped out on the small ledge. Diving into the water, he came up about twenty feet away from the boat. She watched the way his muscular arms cut through the water with ease. He alternated between swimming and floating, looking right at home in the water. Mike stretched out once again in the sun.

She could hear Tyler splashing around as she closed her eyes. He had been in the water for quite some time when she felt the rocking of the boat as Tyler grabbed onto the ladder and heaved himself up on the back ledge, panting from the exertion.

Mike felt a shadow loom over her and then tiny droplets of water splashed on her face. She opened one eye to see Tyler hovering over her.

"Tyler, you're dripping all over me."

"That's the point. If you can't go to the water, I thought I'd bring the water to you." With that, Tyler shook his head like a hound dog, sending a steady stream of droplets over Mike. They were cold and prickly as they landed on her bare skin. She tried to protest, but her laughing just got in the way. Tyler stepped over the rail of the boat and knelt on the cushion on which Mike was laying.

"Oh no, you don't. You're not lying here all wet and soggy."

"Oh come on. A little water never hurt anybody." Tyler stretched out next to Mike and wrapped his arms around her. She struggled to break free as she felt the water soaking into her clothes. The more Mike protested, the tighter Tyler held her; neither one of them could contain their laughter. Weakening in her struggle, Mike finally gave up. Tyler felt her relax in his arms. He rested on his side and looked into Mike's dancing eyes. Instantly, he felt his playful spirit being replaced with passion.

His kiss was deep, her response inviting. The nearness of her body next to his was intoxicating. He felt his way over the curves of her physique, caressing the slope of her waist and hips, letting his fingers brush against the fringe of her shorts.

He could feel himself losing control. He was allowing himself the justification that they weren't doing anything immoral. They were adults and didn't need to follow the same boundaries a parent might set for a teenager, but he knew he was wrong. He knew he was wrong because his mind did not want him to stop. His passions were pulling him further than he knew it was right to go.

Mike was lost in the intensity of her feelings. She held onto Tyler tightly and allowed her leg to become entwined with his. She could feel the intensity of Tyler's movements and wanted nothing more than allowing him the pleasure of indulging himself.

The thought had no sooner passed through Mike's mind when Tyler pulled away from her and stood abruptly. He laced his fingers behind his head and started to pace as he spoke.

"I'm sorry, Mike. I can't do this. This is wrong."

A frigid feeling instantly enfolded Mike. She felt as if she had been doused with a wave from the sea. She sat up and nervously pushed her hair behind her ears and rubbed her hands against her thighs, drying the water that lingered there. She was embarrassed by her behavior. She was ready to give herself to Tyler, thinking that was what he wanted. She realized now that she had been enticing him, not wanting him to stop. She felt stripped of all self-respect. The silence between them as they both struggled with their actions was deafening. Finally, Mike broke the silence.

"I'd like to go home now." She couldn't even bring herself to look at Tyler.

He knelt in front of Mike and tried to look into her downcast eyes. She turned her face from his.

"I'm sorry, Mike. I just lost myself for a moment."

"Maybe this isn't going to work. We're just too different." The coldness in Mike's tone told Tyler that he had blown it big time.

"Don't say that." Tyler's voice was soft but urgent. "This was my fault. I'm sorry I put you in that situation. I should've never let things go that far. I should've stopped sooner."

"But that's just it, Tyler. I didn't want you to stop at all." Mike looked directly at Tyler with deep, cold eyes. "I was enjoying it. I wanted it. This just isn't going to work. You have your moral standards, and it's obvious I don't have any at all. Now can we please go home? Humiliation is something I'd rather deal with alone."

Tyler attempted to help Mike, but his efforts were fruitless. She wanted to be angry, and there was nothing that Tyler could say to convince her otherwise.

The trip home was a quiet one. Tyler couldn't believe the date had taken such a horrible turn. When he pulled into the driveway, he saw that Frank was finally home. He was out tending to the dogs. The smile on his face showed his obvious approval that Tyler had been spending time with Mike. When Mike hobbled from the truck, his look changed to surprise.

"I guess you really did it up good."

"It's nothing, Dad."

"Nothing? Then why the bandages and the crutches?" Frank looked to Tyler for an explanation. Mike hobbled down the steps after refusing Tyler's help. Tyler watched her as she nearly fell twice in her haste to reach her door.

"So, are you going to tell me what really happened?" Frank shifted his attention to Tyler.

Tyler, with hands on his hips and a head hung in dejection, quickly gave Frank a rundown of the incident that had split Mike's knee. Frank laughed, but only for a moment, realizing there was still more to the story that Tyler wasn't volunteering.

"And how is it that she was with you today?" Frank had a feeling he was going to like the answer.

"Well, I would say that we are seeing each other, but we had a little miscommunication today. Now I'm not exactly sure where I stand."

"Don't give up on her, Tyler. She's not as tough as she likes people to think."

A shrill scream pierced the air. Both Tyler and Frank bolted towards Mike's cottage. Mike was standing motionless next to a table that held family pictures and mementoes. There, on the table, was a picture of Michelle with a note attached to it:

It happened once. It can happen again.

Frank held Mike as Tyler quickly sprang into action. He drew his gun and headed upstairs. He searched carefully but found nothing. He checked all the doors and windows, but none of them looked to be tampered with. Tyler slid his gun back into his holster and went over to where Frank was holding a hysterical Mike in his arms. Frank looked at Tyler, knowing he hadn't found anything.

"Frank, what time did you get home?"

Frank looked at his watch. "I'd say about an hour ago, but Arnie always gets here around 9:00 a.m."

If they didn't come in this way, they had to use the lake access, Tyler thought. "I'm going to see if I can find anything."

Tyler slowly walked the path that led to the lake. He scanned for anything that looked out of the ordinary but found nothing. He walked along the lake for a while, but still saw nothing that looked unusual. He pulled out his cell phone and called Jim.

"Jim, it's Tyler. I need a favor."

"I thought you took the day off to woo Mike."

"Look, Jim, we've had a little incident at Mike's place. Someone broke in and left a note attached to a picture of Michelle. Someone is either trying to scare Mike or means business."

"You're kidding!" Jim was shocked. "Is she all right?"

"I don't know, Jim. She's pretty shaken up. Look, could you swing by my place later tonight and bring me the case file on Michelle's murder?"

"Sure, but what do you think you're going to find? There's not much information there."

"I don't know, but I would feel better if I were able to go over it."

"Okay, Tyler. I'll bring it over. I'll see you around 5:30."

Tyler snapped his phone shut and scanned the distance of the lake. He tried not to get too worked up, but the intention of the note was nothing to take lightly. He slowly walked back to the house to find Arnie hovering by Mike's door.

"What are you doing?" Tyler asked with a raised voice.

"I was looking for Frank," Arnie said as he stepped away from the threshold. "What's wrong with Mike?" he asked as he peered into Mike's place.

"Nothing—just a little accident," Tyler said, not wanting to tell Arnie more than he needed to know.

Arnie's reaction was slow. "Is Mike okay?"

"Yeah. She's fine."

"Well . . . okay then. I'm just going to help with the dogs then."

Arnie moved up the path towards the kennels.

Tyler entered to find Mike sitting on the couch and Frank pacing the floor.

"Did you find anything?" Frank asked in a desperate tone.

"Nothing." Tyler moved to Mike's side. "How are you doing?"

"I'm scared to death. Someone was in my home who knows about Michelle and is either sick or dangerous."

Tyler slumped down in the side chair and put his head in his hands. "Who would want to hurt you, Mike?"

"I don't know. I mean I haven't had any altercations or any . . ."

"What . . . what is it?" Tyler scooted to the edge of the chair.

"You don't think this has anything to do with the Dorian Thomas case, do you? It seems like a shot in the dark, but it is the case I've been working the closest on lately." Mike threw her head back against the pillow. "No, that's ridiculous. Now I am just getting paranoid. He has no idea what my involvement is with the case."

"Unless he had someone watching the apartment when you did your investigation." Tyler knew he was grasping at straws, but right now, every observation had to be explored. Otherwise, they would be at a dead end.

Frank was beside himself with worry. The loss of Michelle and the destruction of his family came flooding back to him like a fresh nightmare. He wasn't going to let it happen again. "You need to move your stuff into my house, Mike. Someone has broken into your place once. I'm not going to take the chance of them doing it again with you inside."

Mike didn't put up a fight. She just sat transfixed, looking at the picture of Michelle and realizing her worst nightmare was becoming a reality.

Tyler helped Frank move Mike's necessary items into her old room in the main house. It still looked like a teenager's: posters on the walls and a pink comforter on a canopy bed. He tried to imagine Mike as a teenager, before her life had taken such a tragic turn.

"Frank, where was Arnie when all this happened?"

"What?" Frank seemed confused.

"He was snooping around outside Mike's place when I came up from the lake. You don't think he could have anything to do with this do you?"

"Absolutely not. Arnie might be different, but he cares about Mike. He would never do anything to hurt her."

"You're sure?"

"Positive. Arnie would never do anything to upset Mike or me for that matter."

"Sorry, I had to ask."

"You had to ask what?" Mike hobbled in behind Tyler.

"Nothing. Just thinking out loud." Tyler didn't elaborate, and Mike didn't question him further. Realizing how tired she was, she told Tyler and her dad that she needed some sleep.

"Are you sure you're going to be okay?" Tyler asked. "You could stay at my place. No one would know to look for you there."

Mike answered softly, "I'll be okay. No one's going to try something with Sally, Oreo, and 'Nilla running around." Mike looked at Tyler, who had knelt down in front of her. "I'm sorry for this afternoon. I overreacted," she whispered.

Tyler extended himself from his kneeling position so he could take Mike into his arms. "You don't have to be sorry, Mike. I'm sorry that I handled the situation so poorly. I promise to do better next time." He held her close and could feel Mike's tight embrace. It spoke of fear, not of affection.

"Mike, would you mind if I were to pray for you?"

Her answer was a nod buried deep in his chest. Tyler closed his eyes and spoke to God as he would a friend. "Lord, we know you know all things. We are terrified by this attack on Mike's emotions. Please, Lord, intervene on her behalf. Give her the rest and the peace she needs tonight. Give her the strength and the healing that she needs in her body, and above all, make your very presence real to her in her time of fear. Thank you for being all things to those of us who call on your name. May we be living examples of what it is you have done in our hearts. Amen."

Tyler placed a kiss on the top of Mike's head before leaving. He hoped he had left her with words that would bring her comfort through the night.

TYLER HAD GONE OVER THE FILE on Michelle's death three times. Nothing much was in it and there was even less to go on for leads. It didn't seem feasible that such a violent criminal would be dormant for more than fifteen years and then resurface to stalk another family member.

Tyler walked up and down his living room as he reviewed the details again. Michelle's murder was a violent act, not necessarily one that was thought out very well. Why would the murderer warn Mike if he were planning the same thing for her? No, there was a link, but not in an obvious way.

Tyler collapsed back in his chair and stroked Skyler as he tried to process everything. His mind was too restless to sleep, but his thoughts were too jumbled to make sense. All he could picture was Mike on crutches trying to get away from some madman. He would feel much better when she was at full strength physically. He would also pray that she would one day be at full strength both psychologically and spiritually.

TYLER WAS AT FRANK'S HOUSE BRIGHT AND early the next morning. Frank was already outside feeding the dogs and making his rounds.

"Any trouble last night, Frank?"

"None. The dogs know something's up, though. They sense it, but they were quiet all night."

"How's Mike this morning?"

"I haven't seen her yet. She was in the shower when I got up, and I've been out here ever since."

Tyler turned to leave, but Frank stopped him. "I'm glad you're around, Tyler. Mike is going to need someone to help her process this. I know she won't talk to me. She didn't the first time."

"I'm glad I'm here too Frank."

Both men exchanged a look that spoke of their concern for Mike. Tyler stepped into the house and stopped just inside the kitchen door. He looked around, remembering the first time he saw Mike. She had a gun pointed in his face and a chip on her shoulder as big as the great outdoors.

"What are you staring at?" Mike asked, pulling him from his thoughts.

"I was just remembering out first meeting. I was the unwanted intruder and you were superwoman." Tyler chuckled as he crossed the kitchen and embraced Mike. "How did you do last night?"

"Good. Believe it or not. I actually slept most of the night."

She looked fresher than Tyler had expected. She was dressed and hobbled around without her crutches, but her words seemed strangely distant.

"Are you going to work?" Tyler asked as he poured himself a cup of coffee. He held up the orange juice carton from the refrigerator, knowing that Mike didn't drink coffee. She nodded her approval, so he poured her a glass and brought it to her.

"Of course, I'm going to work. I've already taken two days off. I'm certainly not going to take another. Besides, work will keep my mind off it."

"So, you want me to drive you?"

"No, I'll be all right."

"Are you sure?"

"Yes." Her answer was short.

Tyler could tell she wasn't her usual self, but he didn't want to press her. He decided to change the subject altogether.

"How about if you come over for dinner tonight? You haven't seen my place yet, and I bet Skyler would love the visit. I feel as though I've neglected him ever since I brought him home. You'd be doing us both a favor."

"How about if we play it by ear? I'll see how backed up Nathan is. If things are going well at work and I can get out of there at a decent hour, I would love to see your place. But if work is crazy, I'll have to take a rain check."

"Fair enough."

MIKE CAREFULLY GOT IN HER TRUCK AND started the engine.

"Thanks for being here, Tyler."

Tyler leaned over the rolled down window to kiss Mike. She met him halfway. A simple kiss was all they shared, but it spoke volumes to each of them.

"I'll talk to you later," Mike said as she rotated her head from side to side.

"Are you sure you're going to be okay?" Tyler asked as he leaned on the window frame.

"Yeah."

Tyler watched as Mike pulled away. A sense of wonder filled his heart. He was in love. He knew it. The wonder lasted only for a moment and was quickly replaced with panic. He was in love with a woman who was being stalked. He prayed he would be able to find the scum or that the episode would turn out to be some horrible prank before it was too late.

TYLER BEGAN THE DAY INTERROGATING Jim to see what he knew about Michelle's case. There really wasn't much more to tell. The file held everything that had been reported on the case.

Tyler tried to probe Jim's mind about any hunches he might have had at the time or maybe anything that was odd but never explained, but he kept coming up empty.

MIKE SPENT HER DAY CATCHING UP with Nathan and the caseload that was waiting for her. He asked her a hundred questions about Tyler and teased her about feeling slighted. Mike didn't tell him about the note. She felt it was better left unsaid. If Nathan knew, he would turn into a mother hen and suffocate her. She mentally wrote it off as a horrible joke and tried not to let it interfere with the rest of her day.

Her first priority was to follow up on the blood analysis that was taken from Dorian Thomas' apartment. Nathan had handled it thus far, and now they were ready for some answers. Mike read the final report and smiled.

"Bingo!"

"It's not Dorian's blood?" Nathan said, figuring that was what Mike's smile indicated.

"Nope," Mike said as she left the lab. "I'm calling Tyler."

Tyler reached for the phone mechanically. He was still reading the newspaper accounts of Michelle's death. "Henderson."

"Tyler, it's Mike."

He quickly put down the paper he was holding and turned his full attention to the phone. "How are you doing? Are you okay?"

"I'm doing fine. Look, Tyler, I got the final DNA from Dorian's apartment. It's not Dorian's blood. Someone lost a lot of blood in that apartment, but it wasn't him."

"Yes!" Tyler clenched his fist. "Mike, I found out that Ortega had been in the Corcoran jail. If you don't find anything in the system, put in a call to Corcoran. See if he had been in any fights, anything where they might have a blood sample record for him. I'll check back with you a little later." Tyler hesitated for a moment. "Are you sure you're all right?"

"I'm fine. I've ditched the crutches, though. They were getting in the way. I can get around better if I'm hobbling."

"Did you tell Nathan about the note?"

"No. There's no reason for that. Look, this could just be some horrible prank, a dare that was in bad taste. Kids don't think when they do things like this."

"Don't let your guard down. Dare or not, someone still broke into your house. So, are we still on for dinner?"

Just then, Officer Billings walked into Tyler's office. He noticed Michelle's case file on Tyler's desk and the newspaper articles surrounding her death.

"Let's make it around 6:00. Nathan needs to catch me up on a few things, and we haven't had time to sit down and discuss them yet."

"6:00 it is. You know where the place is, right?"

"Yeah."

"I'll see you then, and Mike, keep your eyes open."

Tyler hung up the phone and looked at Billings.

"What's all this?" he asked, pointing to the mess on Tyler's desk.

"You know Mike Madigan; she works in the coroner's office?"

"Yeah, I know Mike," he grunted.

"And you know about her sister's murder about fifteen years back?"

Billings' voice was on edge as he answered. "Look, Tyler. Unlike you, I grew up in Emerald Lake. This is my town. So yes, I know about the murder. We all went to school together."

Billings' tone was defensive, something Tyler was growing accustomed to. "Well, someone broke into Mike's house yesterday and left a disturbing note by a picture of Michelle. It could just be a prank, but it seemed too ominous for a simple joke."

"Is Mike okay? She wasn't there when it happened, was she?"

"No, she wasn't home." Tyler straightened the papers on his desk. "Look, you patrol the lakefront, right?"

"Yeah, so what?"

"Could you maybe spend a little more time on Mike's end of the lake? Maybe double back in that vicinity when you have the time? I'm sure that the person who broke in used the lake access to her house. Maybe you could keep your eyes open for anything or anyone acting suspicious."

"So, now you're telling me how to do my job?" he said belligerently. "Look, *Detective* Henderson. I know my business and I know my area. If anything suspicious happens, I'll see it—not because you told me to look for it, but because I'm good at what I do."

Tyler again was surprised by the amount of animosity Billings had for him. "Sorry, Billings. You're right. I had no business talking to you that way. I just thought you might want to know what happened, being these are your people and all." Tyler's tone was patronizing.

He walked away, leaving Billings to digest his last statement. Billings left the station with a brisk stride and a slam of the door. A true hothead, just like Jim had said. Well, Tyler didn't care as long as he did his job.

CHAPTER TEN

Skyler alerted Tyler to Mike's arrival. It was a little after 6:00 p.m. when he went running to the front door yelping and barking.

"Okay, okay, I hear ya, Skyler."

Tyler opened the door just as Mike was slowly making her way up the front steps. It was obvious that Mike had gone home to change. She wasn't wearing the dark green pantsuit that she had on that morning. Instead, she was wearing a great pair of jeans and a hot pink T-shirt. Mike walked through the open door, her steps not as stiff as the last few days.

"Your knee must be doing better. Your hobbling is not as noticeable." Tyler leaned over and gave her a soft kiss on the cheek as he closed the door behind her. "You look great."

Mike ignored the compliment but acknowledged that her knee was doing better. "It's feeling pretty good. I don't think I'm in danger of pulling any stitches anymore." Skyler was attempting to refrain himself, but finally he barked to be noticed. Mike turned to him and laughed.

"Same old Skyler. If he's not the center of attention he gets jealous."

She stepped forward and leaned down to stroke Skyler's head. The over-sized puppy relaxed against Mike's side, nearly knocking her over. She regained her balance with the help of Tyler, who was standing behind her. She enjoyed leaning into the comfort that Tyler was giving.

He wrapped his arms around her from behind and pulled her close. Resting his head on her shoulder, he whispered in her ear, "I missed you today."

"I missed you too." Mike leaned back into Tyler's muscular chest, closed her eyes, and sighed. Tyler squeezed her even closer. They started swaying to the music playing on the stereo in the distance. After a minute, Skyler let out another bark and started jumping around the dancing couple.

"Come on, Skyler. You're blowing the mood here."

"I told you he had a discipline problem." Mike turned to face Tyler, giggling at the misbehaving spirit that she had come to know in Skyler.

"That's okay, we can pick up where we left off after dinner. Dinner!"

Tyler quickly headed to the kitchen, leaving Mike to take in the expanse of the living room. Her eyes wandered across the massive beams on the ceiling, the full-length windows, and the spectacular view of the lake. Skyler had stayed by her side, hoping for some more affection. He followed her over to the sliding doors that led to the deck. Mike could see that an intimate setting for two had been arranged outside. Candles were already glowing as the sun sat on the far side of the lake.

"Coming through."

Mike turned to see Tyler carrying a large casserole dish. She inhaled. It was lasagna, if her guess was correct. She opened the door for Tyler and followed him to the outdoor dining area that he had arranged. Bread was already in a basket on the table next to a green salad. Tyler set down the hot casserole, looked around to see if he had forgotten anything, and then turned to Mike.

"Dinner is served."

He pulled out her chair for her before taking the one opposite. Skyler sat at the end of the table and looked back and forth between his former and current owner.

"I think Skyler's confused," Mike said with a slight giggle.

"I think Skyler better make himself scarce if he knows what's good for him. I don't want any more interruptions." Tyler gave Skyler a firm look and pointed towards the house. "Skyler, go inside."

Mike was ready to laugh until she saw how obediently Skyler obeyed Tyler's command. "I don't believe it. He actually listened to you."

"Of course, he did. He knows who's boss. He just needed some firm discipline and a lot of reinforcement." Tyler cut into the lasagna and put a serving on Mike's plate.

"Are you saying I didn't discipline him enough?" Mike tried to act wounded.

"No, I just think Skyler's got an exceptional sense of people. He saw right through your hard exterior and knew you were really a softie."

Mike took the plate from Tyler with a gasp. "A softie! No way! I tried to discipline him, but he always had a mind of his own." Mike set down her plate and placed her napkin on her lap. Tyler dished a hefty portion for himself and then reached across the table for Mike's hand. She gently laid her hand in his. Tyler gave it a squeeze that set her heart racing.

"Let's pray."

Mike bowed her head and closed her eyes. She expected this from Tyler, and a sense of comfortableness seemed to accompany his simple words.

"Lord, thank you for this night and the healing you are bringing to Mike's body. Help us to keep our conversations, actions, and thoughts upright and pleasing to you. Thank you for this food. Amen."

Mike's mind traveled back to their last strained conversation. She felt as though she had thrown herself at Tyler when he had tried to be a gentleman.

"About the other day, Tyler—"

"Forget it, Mike. That's behind us."

"But I feel I should apologize for getting so upset. I was angry at myself, and I took it out on you."

"And I'm sorry that I put you in such a compromising position. I got caught up in the moment and kind of lost control of my senses." Tyler took a swig of the fruity cider he had poured. "There . . . I apologized, you apologized, and we're both sorry. Let's forget it and enjoy the rest of the evening." Mike clinked Tyler's raised glass and smiled.

The rest of the meal was spent conversing about many topics. Mike and Tyler would take turns talking about their favorite sports, their schooling, and their secret aspirations.

Mike felt as if she had known Tyler all her life. She felt as comfortable with him as she did her own dad—in some ways even more. She smiled at the romantic thoughts that were filling her head. Tyler could make a simple pair of jeans and a thermal shirt look oh so good. She listened to Tyler talk as she played with the strawberry that was floating in her glass.

A lull filled the air and brought Tyler to his feet. He started to clear the dishes from the table, insisting that Mike not do a thing. She was easily persuaded and moved to the rail of the deck. She stared out at the lake. It looked like a giant sheet of glass, calm and unblemished.

"I thought we could wait a little while before dessert," Tyler said as he stepped back outside. Instead of going to stand next to Mike, he plopped himself down on a self-suspended hammock. He put his hands behind his head and winked at Mike. "Care to join me?"

"Oh, I don't know about that. I've seen too many comedy skits involving hammocks. I think they should come with a warning label and liability insurance."

Tyler's laugh was deep and full. He carried on so much that Mike found herself laughing too.

"Oh, come on. It's not that difficult. Give me your hand." Tyler extended his hand to Mike. She stepped forward to take it but stopped short of sitting on the sling of canvas. "I'll put my foot out to balance us as you sit down. Then, just lie back. That's all there is to it."

"Tyler, if I screw up my knee further because of this contraption, falling out of the hammock will be the least of your worries."

Tyler laughed at Mike's threat. It was a simple swinging chair, yet he would have thought he was asking her to step out of a moving airplane.

Mike carefully lowered herself to the edge of the hammock. She let out a quick scream when she felt it shift from under her. Tyler couldn't help but laugh. Mike was usually so confident, and here she was scared of an inanimate object.

Once she regained her composure, she lifted one leg and nearly sent them both over the edge. She screamed again and tried to stand up, but Tyler had a hold of her arm and wouldn't let her go.

"You can't give up that easy. Now come on, try again."

Mike let out an exasperated breath and resolved to give it another shot. "Okay, one more time, but if we go swinging like that again, I'm out of here."

"Look, try raising you leg and lying down in one motion. It will even out your balance. Then swing up your other leg and you'll be fine."

Mike mumbled something under her breath before giving it one more try. She did as Tyler said, trying to make one fluid motion of her attempt. Shock of all shocks, she did it. She was lying beside Tyler as he let the hammock take on a light swing.

Mike didn't say anything right away. She wanted to make sure they were out of harm's way before she commented, but Tyler beat her to it.

"Now, isn't this relaxing? Just you, me, the moon, and the soft rocking of a hammock."

"Well, I can't say I'm all that relaxed yet, but it does have a rather soothing effect."

Tyler lowered his arm around Mike's shoulders. She closed her eyes and took in the warmth of his closeness. She began to feel her muscles relax and her mind unwind. She was glad that Tyler didn't feel the need to fill the silence. The hammock rocked them both into a peaceable rest. They both needed to relax after the tension of yesterday's discovery.

Just as Mike felt herself drifting off to sleep, Skyler let out a holler that sent Tyler immediately into defense mode. He was out of the hammock instantly and ran into the house. Flood lights washed over the porch as Tyler reappeared, gun drawn.

"What is it, boy? What did you hear?"

Skyler was whimpering and running back and forth across the front of the railing. He had definitely heard something outside. His low growl caused a chill to streak up Mike's spine. Skyler might be a disciplinary problem, but he was an excellent watch dog.

"Mike, why don't you go on inside."

"But Tyler—"

"Now, Mike! Please! Just do as I say." Tyler words were firm and left no room for argument. Mike carefully tipped herself out of the hammock and walked slowly to the glass doors. Tyler turned to her and looked at her through the glass. "Lock the door. I'll be right back."

"Tyler, please. It was probably just an animal or something."

"It's the *something* that has me bothered. Just lock the door. I'll be back in a minute."

Tyler and Skyler disappeared down the staircase that led to the lake. Mike was allowing paranoia to fill her mind. *What if someone is out there? What if it is the same person who left the note and Tyler is in danger?* Mike crossed the living room as quickly as she could. She made sure the front door was locked and then did the same thing to the kitchen door. She went back to the door that led to the deck and pressed her face against the glass. It was impossible to make anything out through the glare of the floodlights. Suddenly, she saw something streak across the deck. She screamed and jumped back from the door, only to see that it was Skyler with Tyler close behind. She quickly unlatched the door and opened it for the two of them. Tyler's face was red, and he was breathing heavily. Mike's expression asked the question that was on her mind.

"Nothing. I didn't see anything, but there was definitely someone or something there. I've never seen Skyler this worked up, have you?"

Mike swallowed hard and shook her head slowly. "Only once." Mike didn't elaborate.

Tyler headed for the front door.

"I already made sure it was locked," Mike said from behind him. He stopped his forward motion but not his pacing. He looked like a caged animal sauntering back and forth across the living room. Skyler was still whimpering, knowing that something wasn't right. Tyler realized he needed to calm down. There was nothing he could do at the moment, and his nervous energy was just going to make matters worse. He walked over to where Mike was and pulled her to his chest.

"Are you okay?"

She rested her head against him and let out a deep breath. "I am now."

They held each other for some time. Skyler finally calmed down and curled up by the fireplace. Tyler cautiously brought in everything from the deck and stacked the dishes in the kitchen. Mike ran some water and started rinsing the plates. She had everything in the dishwasher when Tyler returned to the kitchen.

Mike laid down the dish rag and observed Tyler's silence. "What are you thinking?"

"I don't know. It just seems strange. I haven't had a problem since I've been here and now all of a sudden this. I guess after the note at your place, I'm just kind of jumpy."

"It was probably nothing, Tyler. Some kids were probably taking a shortcut between property lines and it spooked Skyler."

"Maybe, but I would have thought that Skyler had better instincts than that. He usually doesn't bark at just anything." Tyler thought for a moment. "You said you had seen this behavior in Skyler one other time. When was it?"

Mike didn't want to make Tyler any more upset than he already was, but to lie to him would be wrong. "I was walking with the dogs once along the lake. Out of nowhere, Skyler takes off like a bat out of . . . well, he took off faster than I could keep up with him. When I finally found where he had gone, he was hovering over a body, whimpering and crying like he was tonight." The look in Tyler's eyes was pure horror as Mike continued. "The girl wasn't dead, but she had been beaten up pretty badly. She was semiconscious and barely coherent. If Skyler hadn't found her, she probably would have died. The temperature dipped that night below thirty degrees, and she probably wouldn't have survived in the cold."

Tyler started pacing again. "So, what you're telling me is Skyler doesn't overreact without reason?"

"I'm just telling you what happened that one time. Other times Skyler has run off chasing ground squirrels."

"Yes, but did he holler and whimper the whole time?"

"Well, no . . ." There really wasn't much that Mike could say. She didn't need to be convinced that something had startled Skyler. She was just hoping there was no connection between that and the break-in at her place.

"I'm going to drive you home." Tyler stomped across the tile floor.

"I'm perfectly fine to drive myself home, Tyler. Look, I'll call my dad and tell him I'm on my way, and then I'll call you when I get there. I'll even talk to you on my cell phone the whole time if that will make you feel better."

Tyler was weighing his choices. His hands were planted firmly on his waist, and his jaw was clenched. Mike moved to put her arms around him, hoping to help him relax. "I'll be all right, I promise." Tyler held onto Mike as if he were afraid to let her go. Something wasn't right. He could feel it, but he just couldn't put his finger on it.

"You'll call me as soon as you get home?"

"I promise."

"But you're going to be at Frank's, right? You're not going back to your place, are you?"

"I'll go to Dad's for the night. I'll go home in the morning to shower and change for work."

"Then tomorrow you need to call and get your alarm fixed."

"It's not broken."

"Then why don't you use it?" Tyler was referring to the fact that Mike only used her key to enter her house instead of the security keypad.

"I got lazy."

"Start using it again, will you?"

"I promise."

Tyler held her even closer and looked into her incredible blue eyes. He knew her smile was for his reassurance more than anything, but he enjoyed it just the same. "You're beautiful, you know that?"

Tyler's comment took Mike by surprise. She blushed and tried to wave it off. "I'm sure you say that to all the damsels you think you need to save."

"I'm saying it because it's true." Tyler's tone was firm. "I don't think you realize how beautiful you are. You try to keep people at arm's length with your cynicism and direct attitude. That's your way of fending off men. But if there is someone out there watching you, all he sees is a beautiful blonde with a limp. You're the perfect target right now."

Mike looked at Tyler in disbelief. He had conjured up an entire scenario that had no basis in fact. "Tyler, you're overreacting."

"No, I'm not. Something's not right, Mike. I don't mean to scare you or sound ominous, but I have a feeling about this. I just want you to take extra precautions. You have a permit to carry, so make sure you have your weapon with you at all times."

"Tyler, you're scaring me." Mike pulled away from his embrace and sunk to the edge of the couch.

"Good, I hope I am. That way you'll be on your guard. A little paranoia is not a bad thing in a situation like this." He sat down beside her and gently caressed her back. "For the time being, until we either find out who broke in or if there was someone creeping around the house, would you make sure you're armed when you leave the house? And make sure you always have your weapon in reach when you're in the house."

"I know the drill, Tyler." Mike's tone was even and short.

"You can be mad at me all you want, Mike. I'd rather you be mad at me than unprepared in case anything were to happen." Tyler got up from where he was sitting and extended his hand to her. "Now, let me walk you out to your truck."

Tyler watched as she pulled from the driveway. He called Frank and let him know she was on her way.

TYLER DIDN'T SLEEP AT ALL THAT NIGHT. He was waiting for the light of day to investigate around the house. He took a quick shower, but before he could get dressed, his cell phone rang.

"Henderson," he said as he ruffled a towel through his wet hair.

"Tyler, it's Jim." His voice was all business. "We've got a situation." Jim paused for a moment before expounding. "A girl's body was found by the lake this morning. How soon can you meet me?"

"I just have to get dressed. Where are you?"

"About half a mile from your place. The Willow Bark Picnic Area."

"I'll be right there. You want me to bring Mike? I don't think she's left yet this morning."

"No, just get here as quick as you can. I'll explain more when you arrive."

JIM, BILLINGS, CARRUTHERS, AND SOMEONE sitting on a park

bench were at the scene when Tyler arrived. He walked the trail from his house since it was quicker. He stepped through the brush to see the tarp-covered body.

"What do we have?" Tyler said as soon as Jim walked up to him. "And why didn't you want Mike here? Someone's going to have to come and do the investigation. Why send someone from the city?"

"See for yourself." Jim's look was grim. Murder was nothing you ever became accustomed to, but Tyler didn't expect to see Jim so affected by it. Maybe Tyler was more calloused, since he saw this type of thing all the time when he worked in the city.

He walked over to the tarp, squatted down, and pulled back the yellow plastic. His eyes traveled over the body: slashed throat, slashed torso, hands cut off, naked—except for a note jabbed into her chest. It read:

I told you it could happen again!

Tyler lost it. He lunged to the underlying brush and heaved what was left of his dinner from the night before. His head was spinning, and his pulse points were riveting out of control. He felt as if he were having a panic attack. He stood bent over with his hands on his knees for some time. Finally, Jim came up beside him.

"Are you gonna be all right?"

"Yeah, I just wasn't prepared for that."

Jim handed Tyler a bottled water. He took a couple of swigs and sloshed the cold liquid around in his mouth before splitting it out.

"Now you know why I didn't want Mike here, at least not yet."

Tyler rolled his neck around in a slow circle trying to release the tension that felt like a vice around his head. "I can't believe this is happening. After all this time. I mean what do we have here? Some lunatic that's come back after fifteen years? Or some copycat killer getting his jollies, but why? And why Mike? How is it that she is now part of some psycho's sick joke?"

"I don't know, Tyler. I'm just as confused as you are." The two men stood for what seemed an eternity, rolling over the possibilities of what was yet to come. One scenario was worse than the next.

"How do we tell Mike? We've got to let her know before she finds out on her own. She's in real danger. It's obvious this isn't just a prank." Just then, Tyler's cell phone rang to life. The caller ID brought up Mike's home number.

"Hey, Mike, what are you doing at home? I thought you were going to stay at Frank's?" Tyler tried to control the overwhelming urge to yell at her, warn her, tell her to get out of the house, but he knew he needed to stay calm.

"I did. I came home to shower and change. I told you that last night." Mike was perplexed that Tyler had forgotten that detail of their conversation.

"Well, don't leave for work yet, okay. I need to talk to you about something."

"Can't it wait until this evening? I want to get a jump on today's work."

"No, I need to talk to you before you go to work. I'll be by in about twenty minutes. I've got to go, but stay put until I get there." Tyler snapped his phone shut before Mike could reply. She would probably be mad at him for hanging up, but he was willing to take that chance.

"What are you going to tell her?" Jim had listened in on the call. He was glad he wasn't in Tyler's shoes, but was concerned for him just the same.

"I'm not sure, Jim. Hopefully God will be able to give me the words."

Jim respected Tyler's relationship with God. He didn't see a need for it personally, but he respected his partner's convictions.

"I think I'd better call Nathan in on this one. Mike's the best, but this is going to be hard enough on her."

"So, is that the person that found her?" Tyler nodded his head over to where an elderly man was sitting at a picnic table. A small breed of dog sat stoically at his feet.

"Yeah. He was out walking his dog."

"Everything's the same, right?"

"Yeah."

"So we have a copycat. Someone out there getting a thrill duplicating someone else's crime."

"There's only one thing, Tyler." Jim sighed. "We never reported the shallow grave. That was evidence that was withheld from the public. That was the only thing that we held back in hopes of catching the guy or guys one day."

"So what are you saying? You think this could be the same guy? You've got to be kidding? Why? He got away with murder fifteen years ago. What would he gain by coming back and doing the same thing again? He's got to know he couldn't get away with it this time. Forensics has improved by leaps and bounds since then."

"I hope you're right, Tyler. Something tells me this is not what it seems."

TYLER DECIDED TO WALK TO MIKE'S PLACE. The added time would help him gather his thoughts. He prayed as he walked, keeping his eyes open and his head down. He scanned the pathway and the neighboring shrubs for anything that could possibly be related to the incident. As he reached the lakefront gate that led up to Mike's cottage, he pleaded with God for intervention.

Please God. Help her through this. Don't let this be the breaking point for her. Help me to know what to say and what to do.

Tyler wasn't able to finish before Mike swung the front door open. "What are you doing walking?" Mike asked with a perturbed look on her face. When Tyler looked up at her with a face of uncertainty, she knew something was up.

"You found something, didn't you?"

"Let's sit down, Mike." Tyler brushed past her and walked over to the sofa. Mike joined him and looked at him with steely resolve.

"Tell me, Tyler. What did you find at your place?"

"Mike, I don't know how to say this." Tyler was searching for the words that he had petitioned the Lord to give him, but somehow they weren't within his grasp.

"Just say it, Tyler." Mike put the stoic, "I can handle anything" facade on and sat waiting for Tyler to fill her in.

"A body was dumped by the lake last night."

"What? By your house? Is that what Skyler was so upset about?" Mike was racing ahead of Tyler with her own questions. She stopped when she saw the solemn looked on Tyler's face.

"There's more, isn't there?"

"Mike, you're just going to have to listen for a minute, okay?"

Mike positioned herself to listen to whatever it was Tyler had to tell her. He took a deep breath, held Mike's hands in his, and began speaking what he knew would be the most heart wrenching facts he had ever revealed.

"The body that was dumped . . . we think it's a copycat . . . of Michelle's murder."

Mike didn't move, she barely even took a breath. Tears trailed down her cheeks silently as she tried to comprehend what Tyler was telling her. Mike choked the words out, "Who was she?"

"We're not sure yet. Jim's going to call Nathan."

Mike stood up quickly and wiped the tears from her face. "I want to do the investigation."

"No way." Tyler got up and placed his hands to her shoulders, trying to comfort her. She quickly stepped back from his touch.

"I'm serious, Tyler. I want to do it. I don't want anyone else screwing it up."

"There's no way Nathan would screw this up. He'll know how important it is to you."

"I don't care. I want to be in charge. Let me get my shoes on, and you can take me to the scene." Mike walked across the room, her limp no longer noticeable. She grabbed up the shoes that she had by the door and stood waiting for Tyler to join her. "Well . . ."

"I don't think this is a good idea, Mike. I—"

"I don't care what you think. I'm doing it, with or without your help."

Her tone was belligerent and her words sharp. She opened the front door and leaned on the knob, waiting for Tyler to move, but he didn't. "Fine. I'll go by myself." She turned from him and slammed the door. She was gone before he knew it.

Mike headed for her truck and turned on her scanner. She flipped open her phone and dialed Nathan. "Nathan, where's the scene? . . . Just cut the nonsense and tell me." She revved up her engine as she saw Tyler walking towards her. "Fine, I'll meet you there. Don't do anything until I get there, do you understand? Not a thing."

Mike didn't even look at Tyler. She just put her truck in reverse, turned around, and screeched out of the driveway. Tyler stood there shocked that she left without him.

Tyler knew he could get back to the scene before she did. Mike had to drive the long way around and then had to unload her equipment from the back of her truck so he ran back to the scene. He waited for her at the dirt parking lot nearest the picnic sight. She pulled up in a cloud of dust. She saw Tyler standing there waiting for her but didn't acknowledge him. She got out of her truck, slammed the door, and headed to the back. Tyler circled around the other side of the truck just as she was lowering the tailgate.

She grabbed for one of her black boxes, and Tyler clutched her hand before she could move the box forward. "Just promise me you'll step back if it gets to be too much."

Mike could hear the concern in Tyler's voice and felt a twinge of guilt for the way she had left him standing in the driveway. "I'm fine, Tyler. This is my job."

Tyler ignored her attitude and helped with her equipment as she slid into her coveralls. Nathan pulled beside them and started doing the same. He looked back and forth between Tyler and Mike, trying to see whom he should be taking his cue from.

"Get it in gear, Nathan. I don't want us missing a thing."

Nathan stood directly in front of Mike, stopping her from what she was doing. "You sure you want to do this, Mike? I could do all the groundwork and report back to you every minuscule finding that I uncover."

Mike knew that Nathan was trying to protect her, just like Tyler, but they would both have to realize there was no way she was going to let anyone else handle this case. For fifteen years she'd wrestled with the idea that she was responsible for Michelle's death. If she could find Michelle's killer, then maybe she could live with the thought of knowing she had helped the only way she knew how. She would not leave this case to someone else to mishandle. This was her chance at closure, and she wasn't going to let anything keep her from solving this case.

"I'm fine, Nathan, really I am. I'm not saying it's going to be easy, but I can do this. I have to do this."

Mike, Tyler, and Nathan went over to the perimeter of the scene. The old man was gone, so was Billings, but Carruthers and Jim were still there. Jim was shocked to see Mike on the scene. He looked to Tyler for an explanation, but it was Mike who spoke up.

"Don't worry, Jim, this isn't Tyler's idea; it's mine. I want to do this."

"Why, Mike? What are you trying to prove?" Jim was not holding back. He thought this was the last place that Mike should be, and he was going to let her know it.

"Hopefully, my expertise." Mike tried to ignore his comment, but Jim wasn't going to let it go that easily. If he could make her break, then he would know for sure that she was not psychologically prepared to handle this, regardless of what she thought.

"This isn't going to bring Michelle back, Mike. She's gone. There's nothing you can do about it. No amount of analysis or scientific findings is going to bring her back. If this is your way of proving to everyone how accomplished you are and how incompetent the police force was fifteen years ago, you might as well leave now. I have a dead woman that needs to be handled with respect, not as a stand-in for your own personal—"

"Okay, Jim, I think that's about enough." Tyler was horrified with the brutality of Jim's comments. He was trying to crush Mike before she even got started. "Maybe you're the one that should step aside, Jim. Maybe you can't handle facing the fact that the police botched the first investigation."

Jim was ready to fire back when Mike held up her hands to stop them both. "That's enough, both of you. I don't need anyone patronizing me or defending me. I'm taking this case whether you like it or not, Jim. Go to my superiors, see if I care. This is my case, and if you can't handle that, you might as well get out of my way and leave."

Jim was satisfied. Mike was going to be able to handle the investigation, but would she be able to live with herself if the case went unsolved yet again? That was the real question.

Mike and Nathan pulled sterile booties over their shoes before approaching the body. When Mike got her first look at the body, her stomach lurched and her throat tightened like a vice. The girl was blond like her and Michelle. *Was that a clue? Was it only blondes the attacker would go after? Or was it a copycat that was trying to follow every detail?*

Mike slowly pulled the tarp from the body, letting her eyes travel to the torso area. It had been slit, just like before, between the naval and the pelvic area. Blood loss from the wounds had puddled around the slashed wrists, neck, and hips; but the blood loss was low in comparison to the wounds.

"She was slashed postmortem. The blood loss would have been heavier if they were the cause of her death." Mike talked to no one in particular. Her monotone voice revealed the detachment she was imposing on herself in

110

order to complete the exam. Her eyes followed the curve of the victim's hips, down her legs, and stopped at her ankles.

Nathan took pictures from every conceivable angle. He took overhead shots and lay down right next to the victim to focus at eye level. Mike had done a thorough visual of the victim to make sure no evidence was lost in transport. When she was satisfied with her findings, she sat back with a sigh.

"Okay, I'm ready to bag her, but I want to be extremely careful. If there is any fiber evidence on her that I've missed, I want to make sure it makes it into the bag."

Jim and Tyler slipped on protective booties before approaching the body. Nathan and Mike carefully tipped the body up to one side while Jim and Tyler painstakingly laid the body bag under the victim.

"Try not to disturb any impressions in the ground. If there's trace evidence on the ground, I don't want it brushed aside."

They laid the body gingerly in the blue plastic bag. Mike placed a sheet over the victim before zipping it shut. Carefully, Tyler and Jim picked up the bag and headed for the coroner's van.

"Take off those booties, turn them inside out, and give them back to me. You were both close to the body, and if you picked something up in the grass, I want it."

Tyler and Jim slowly removed the booties before carrying the body the rest of the way to the van where Carruthers was waiting to give them a hand.

Tyler looked at Carruthers and realized why he had left the scene so quickly. His face was green, perspiration beaded on his forehead, and he held a napkin to his lips.

"Sorry I couldn't have been more help, guys, but that was a little too much for me."

"No problem, Andy, even after many years of this you still never get used to it." Jim assured Andy. He was a rookie cop, and the scene had proven to be too gruesome for his stomach.

Nathan walked up to Jim and Tyler, but Mike was still at the site. "I'm going to go ahead and take the body and get set up for the examination. Mike's going over the ground with a fine-tooth comb." Nathan pulled off his coveralls and tossed them in the back of the van.

Tyler questioned Nathan before he left. "How's she doing, Nathan? You've seen her at scenes before—how's she holding up?"

"Like the professional that she is." Nathan jumped in the van and pulled away.

When Tyler returned to the scene, Mike was on her hands and knees. His first thought was of her injured knee. Obviously, she no longer cared about her own discomfort.

"Don't come any closer, Tyler. You took off your booties, so stay away."

Tyler watched her from a distance. She put her face to the ground to see if anything caught her attention—an impression, a snapped twig, or anything that could be related to the incident. Tyler watched her as she zoomed in on something. She moved on her hands and knees closer to the shallow grave. Using tweezers, she picked up the smallest shred of material. She looked at it before putting it in an evidence bag. Scanning the area once more, she decided she had done all that she could. She got back to her feet and slowly walked over to Tyler.

"I'm done here."

"Do you think you got anything?"

"I doubt it. This is a picnic area. All kinds of people tromp through here daily."

Tyler put his arm around Mike. "Are you ready to head back?"

"Yeah."

The confidence was gone, the monotone voice replaced by a frail whisper. She had held it together so far, but a meltdown would be only a matter of time.

TYLER HAD TO WALK HOME AND GET HIS TRUCK before he could head to the lab. The drive seemed longer than usual. He used the time to pray for Mike and for Frank. This was going to be difficult on him too, especially when he found out that the person who broke into Mike's place was capable of murder.

Tyler pulled up to the dock behind the coroner's van and Mike's truck. Jim had called Tyler to let him know he was heading back to the station to check out any missing persons reports that matched the description of the victim. Tyler buzzed the back door. A lab tech he didn't recognize stood in the doorway and asked for his ID. Tyler showed him his badge and was escorted in. Nathan was hurrying down the hall with his white lab coat lapping at his knees.

"Lab room number two, Tyler. We're just getting started."

"How's Mike?"

"She's holding it together. She'll be fine as long as she's in search mode. When she's working, she's as steady as a rock. It's when she takes the lab coat off and heads for home that worries me."

"Me too." Tyler followed Nathan into the lab. Mike looked up but only briefly. She was examining something under a microscope.

Nathan's voice dropped to a whisper. "I'm sure you've been in on these things before, Tyler, but if it gets the better of you, the can's over there." Nathan pointed to a large stainless steel trash can. "Don't even think of heading to the sink or the other cans. Mike doesn't dispose of anything until she's confident that she's done with it. If you contaminate her area, she'll have your hide."

112

Nathan left the room for a moment and returned with the stainless steel gurney that held the Jane Doe. He positioned the gurney next to the autopsy table and carefully rolled the victim onto the cold, medicinal surface. Tyler rubbed his eyes. The nudity of the victim didn't bother Tyler; the fact that an innocent woman had died a brutal death was what was making his eyes sting.

Mike got up from where she had been hovering over a microscope. Tyler noticed the stain mark on her slacks just below the knee. Her knee had been bleeding again. He made a mental note to check on it once Mike was done. Mike pulled on an apron and long rubber gloves. She started rattling off vitals as Nathan wrote them down: sex, race, height, estimated weight, hair color, and eye color. Mike reported all the key ingredients for a missing persons report. She was all business, barely acknowledging Tyler's presence.

Mike switched on the recorder and started talking so the overhead microphone could pick up her statements as she proceeded with the exam.

"Cause of death is a broken neck. Hands severed postmortem. Lacerations to the neck and pelvic regions postmortem. Lacerations measuring in depths of one to three centimeters. Bruising to pelvic area and chest seems to show the lacerations were made while the victim was lying down."

Mike used tweezers to extract a few loose hairs that she found on the body. One had been wrapped around the victims earring, probably her own. But another hair, possibly the assailant's, was found attached to the woman's bracelet.

Mike moved to the head of the table and opened the victim's mouth. She swabbed the interior of her jaw, and with a separate swab, ran it across her teeth front and back. Each swab was snapped back into its sterile container and handed to Nathan for labeling. She moved to the genital area of the victim and took internal and external samples.

"Initial examination shows no signs of forced entry into either the vaginal cavity or anus. No bruising, tearing, or abrasions."

Next, she extracted a urine sample with a large syringe, which she handed to Nathan to transfer to a specimen bottle. Mike detailed each bruise with explicit detail, including where it was found, its size, and its coloring. She continued her slow and methodical probing of the body, noting anything she felt would be pertinent evidence when questioning a suspect.

"This concludes the initial exam of Jane Doe, case number 1045. Dr. Michal Madigan. Assistant, Nathan Armstrong." Mike clicked off the microphone with an exhausted sigh.

"How did you know she was lying down when she was cut?" Tyler asked.

"Come over on this side, I'll show you." Tyler walked around the table to stand next to Mike and the victim. "See the bruising just below each laceration?"

113

"Yeah?"

Mike took Tyler's hand and held it below the victim's throat. Tyler realized the bruise matched the outline of his hand. He looked at Mike for an explanation.

"The killer leaned on the body as he slashed it. Both here and here." Mike pointed out the same bruising pattern under the laceration to the torso. "He leaned on the body with his right hand and pulled the knife across the body towards him."

"So you believe the suspect is left-handed?"

"Exactly. He would have cut with his stronger hand. And from the laceration measurements, I can tell he used a large knife—perhaps a butcher knife."

"If the incisions have varying depths, why do you feel it was a large-bladed knife? Couldn't he get those same markings from a regular steak knife?"

"I don't think so." Mike when on to explain. "The wounds are completely clean and they start shallow, grow deeper, and then minimize again. If he had used a small knife, chances are he would have stabbed the victim and then dragged the knife across the torso, making the deepest point of entry on the far side of the victim. But, if a butcher knife was used, he would have sliced the victim, causing the wound to graduate in depth. Also, there are no blunt tears or bruising at the surface of the wound. It was a clean cut, showing that the handle of the knife never got near the surface of the skin. I think it was a large knife. The killer was positioned above the body and cut her like so." Mike once again showed how she felt the lacerations were made.

Tyler was quiet. He was taking in all that Mike had showed him. It was amazing how she could almost visualize the crime by what appeared to be little or no evidence at all.

"Do you have an idea how she was attacked?"

"I think he grabbed her from behind," Mike said as she peeled off her rubber gloves and tossed them in the sink. "See this large bruise across her midsection and the discoloration around her mouth?" Tyler nodded his head that he was following her so far. Mike turned her back to Tyler and said, "Grab me around the waist and cover my mouth with your hand."

"What?"

"Just do it." Mike was insistent.

Tyler put his left arm around Mike's waist and then used his right hand to cover her mouth. Nathan watched the demonstration. He too was curious about the point Mike was trying to make. She pulled Tyler's hand back from her mouth so she could speak.

"Now, I'm going to try and get away, but don't let me go." Mike jerked forward and Tyler instinctively tightened his gripped, which made his arm press hard against her rib cage. Mike stopped resisting. "Now, cover my mouth. I'm going to try and scream. You have to make sure I'm not heard." Mike glanced back at Tyler. "Ready?"

He nodded his head and placed his hand over Mike's mouth. Her head thrashed from side to side. Tyler again had to tighten his grip on her mouth to make sure her screams did not escape. Tyler felt water trickle down his hand and stopped instantly. He spun Mike around and saw that she was crying.

"Did I hurt you? Mike, I'm sorry . . ."

Mike was shaking her head in disagreement. She pulled away from Tyler and ran out into the hall. She leaned against the corridor wall and inhaled the fresh air. Tyler found her staring at the ceiling taking deep breaths, tears running down her cheeks. He didn't say anything. He waited for her to gain her composure.

"I'm sorry, Tyler. All of a sudden I realized that could have been how Michelle spent her last moments."

Tyler pulled Mike to his chest and held her. He rocked her back and forth as she cried silently into his shoulder. She had kept it together until now. She had done her job, and now it was time for her to mourn the loss of her sister all over again.

CHAPTER ELEVEN

Mike sat on the stoop as she watched Tyler install the new deadbolt on her door. She wasn't his only audience. Oreo and 'Nilla had stationed themselves on either side of Mike like sentries on duty. Tyler thought it was incredible how keen the animal instinct was. They were no longer just pets and companions; they were now part of the new security system. Tyler had already chastised Mike about the condition of her knee. She assured him it was okay and hardly even hurt anymore. He looked at it for himself after she had changed into something more comfortable. It was healing, even with its setbacks.

"What are you thinking?" Tyler asked as he observed Mike's faraway look. They hadn't talked any more about the case. Tyler had gone back to work, and Mike continued to work on the trace evidence she had removed from the body. She stopped by the station after work so Tyler could follow her home. He came loaded with deadbolts and window locks and now was making his rounds installing all the new devices.

"This was a copycat; it's not the same man," Mike said matter-of-factly.

"How can you be sure?" Tyler asked softly as he continued working.

Mike took a moment to answer. As she stroked 'Nilla, Oreo put his head in her lap. "Michelle's murder was an act of passion—this wasn't. This girl was killed first and then wounded. And she wasn't sexually assaulted."

"Her name's Elizabeth Jordan," Tyler added quietly. "She ran away from home two days ago after an argument with her mother."

"Déjà vu." Mike turned her head away.

"Mike . . . Michelle wasn't running from you. She just made some bad choices and ended up at the wrong place with the wrong people."

"But she was running. She was running from the pressure my parents were putting on her. We were twins, Tyler. They expected us to be identical. When I got good grades and Michelle didn't, they would tell her she wasn't trying hard enough. When I ran for class president or the debate team or cheerleading, they just expected Michelle to want to do the same. They would argue that she wasn't applying herself or that she was trying to slide by in life. They never let Michelle be Michelle. I should have seen it earlier and done something about it."

"But what could you have done, Mike? You couldn't give up doing the things you wanted to do because Michelle didn't excel."

Mike snapped her head away from Tyler. She was angry—angry that Tyler wouldn't allow herself to shoulder the blame.

"You're still trying to blame yourself for something that wasn't your fault. It was Michelle's choices that ultimately led to her death, not your success." Tyler's words were harsh, but he knew he had to convince Mike to let go of the blame. "Look, Mike, it's obvious you loved your sister very much. No one doubts that. It's just that we can't make other people follow our ideals."

"What do you want for dinner?" Mike got up from where she was sitting and brushed off her hands. Obviously, their conversation was over.

"I'm not picky," Tyler said as he pulled the door closed, then opened it again with the key. "There, that's done. But I still want you to use the keypad entry as well. Now to the windows."

Mike walked past Tyler into the house, her loyal sergeants following her. Tyler went upstairs and worked on the doors and windows. It took him about an hour before he descended the stairs to the smell of grilled cheese. He walked over to the kitchen to see cheese sandwiches and tomato soup prepared and ready to be served.

"You said you weren't picky. This is what sounded good to me." Mike's demeanor had softened a little. She was still quiet, but her words weren't as biting.

"Looks great to me. Do you want to eat out on the patio?"

"Sure."

Mike and Tyler made their way out to the patio. Mike had poured them each a big bowl of soup and gave Tyler two sandwiches to her one.

They sat their things down at the table, and Mike went back into the house to grab some sodas. When she returned and sat down, the dogs relaxed at her feet. Tyler again asked if he could say a prayer. Mike shrugged her shoulders, clearly not seeing a need for it. They ate in relative silence, each of them reviewing the events of the day.

"Do you think you acquired any evidence that might be from the perpetrator?"

"I don't know. There's that one hair and that piece of material, but odds are they might not mean anything to our case. The material could have come from anywhere."

"And the hair?"

"Possible. It seemed to have a different texture than the vic . . . Elizabeth's."

"Anything else?" Tyler was trying to keep Mike hopeful that somehow they would get a break.

"The swab I took of her teeth produced blood. It's not hers. If she was able to bite her attacker, we could have some DNA. It could be difficult to type, though, which makes it a long shot."

"But it's something." Tyler turned his attention to his meal. It was good, better than the normal cheese sandwich. He was about to compliment Mike on the meal when she blurted out what had been on her mind since Tyler prayed.

"How does God allow something like this to happen? I just don't get it, Tyler. I mean you say that Michelle's death was the cause of her own bad choices, but what about Elizabeth's death? She's a random victim, someone who fit a profile. How do you explain that?" Mike's words were laced with cynicism. Tyler thought for a moment. He hadn't been a Christian long, and he wasn't sure he was going to be able to give Mike a satisfactory answer.

"That's the sin of the world, not the lack of God in the world."

"But he could have stopped it. He could have intervened."

"You're right, but his intervention interferes with free will. He's given all of us free will. We have the will to choose right and wrong, truth or lie, his way or the world's way. Unfortunately, as unfair as that might sound to you, that's the way it is."

"And you agree with that? You don't see anything wrong with a God that would allow innocent people to be tortured and murdered because some crazed person has the power to do it?"

"Yes, I've accepted it as the evil that is part of this world." Mike shook her head and stood to clear her dishes. Tyler continued, "You're confusing the idea that since God allows it, He condones it. It's not that way." He followed Mike into the kitchen with his own dishes. "Let me ask you this— did you know Michelle was ditching school, partying with the wrong type of people, getting in over her head?"

"I told you I did." She was angry that Tyler had made the argument personal.

"So you condoned it?"

"Of course not. I tried to talk her out of it at every turn, but in the end she did what she wanted to do."

"So, you allowed it, but you didn't condone it?"

"That's different."

"How? Didn't you love Michelle with everything that you are? Didn't you cry over the decisions she made? But ultimately you had to allow her to make her own decisions?"

"Yes! But I'm not God. Why should I worship someone who is as power-less as I am?"

"Well, let me ask you this—what would you say if I were to tell you that I am falling in love with you?"

Mike looked at Tyler with irritation. He was taking a cheap shot at her emotions. "That's not fair, Tyler. You're changing the subject."

"I'm not," Tyler continued as he loaded the dishes into the dishwasher while Mike scoured an already clean countertop. "How would you feel if you had the power to make me love you? If you could say a wish or a spell that guaranteed my love, would you use it?"

"No! That's stupid. If I did that I would never know for sure if you really loved me, or if it's because I wished it on you."

"Exactly. So, if God did not give people free will—the will to choose him freely—if he made everyone love him and because of that eliminated all the wrongs in the world, would he have true believers or puppets doing as he instructed?"

"You're confusing me, Tyler. You're not making any sense."

"Think about it. If God made a perfect world for his people and everyone loved God because of this perfection, they would not be serving God for what he saved them from, only for what he was giving them. He would be this giant Santa Claus."

Tyler could see that Mike wasn't following him, so he tried a different angle.

"Look at it this way. If you were a millionaire and told your secretary that she would inherit everything you had when you died, what do you think her motivation for serving you would be? Would it be a genuine love and respect for you or would her love be motivated by what her payoff would be?"

Mike tossed the rag on the counter and moved to the living room and sunk into the cushions of the couch. Tyler followed her and sat on the coffee table in front of her.

"You see, Mike, God wants his people to love him and serve him because they recognize that he's God; and to insure that, there's free will in the world. We all make a thousand decisions a day. What motivates our decisions? Self? Others? Or love of God and what he would have for us?"

Tyler was sure he still wasn't getting through to Mike. Her hands were crossed tight against her chest, and her eyes were on her lap.

"Yes, there are horrible things going on in the world because of the sin in the world, but don't confuse who's in charge of that sin. Satan is more powerful than people give him credit for. You see, he knows his ultimate future will be in hell. His goal is to take as many people with him as possible. If he can plant doubt in the hearts of people, he wins. He's using the sin that ensnared him to ensnare others. It's our choice. Follow the one who saves us or the one who destroys us."

Mike sat still for some time. She was trying to comprehend all that Tyler had said. It blurred together with memories of Sunday school lessons and bedtime stories that her father used to tell her and Michelle. She remembered praying to God and staring at the picture of him holding the little lamb tightly in his arms. She remembered the childlike innocence she had experienced as a little girl before her world took such a tragic turn. Could she really believe again? Could she really cry out to a God that stood by and allowed the sins of the world to take one of his own? She wanted to; she really did. She wanted to believe again, but to believe would mean to forgive; and she didn't think she would ever be able to forgive those responsible for Michelle's death—and that included God.

TYLER DECIDED TO CALL IT AN EARLY NIGHT. Mike was falling asleep in his arms, the weight of the day more exhausting than she was willing to admit. He offered to stay the night on the couch, but Mike refused. She felt confident she would be fine with Oreo and 'Nilla on watch along with the security measures Tyler had installed.

He drilled her on what to do if the dogs alerted her to something. She was to arm herself, call him, then 911. She was not to prowl around on her own. If someone was in the house, she was to let him come to her and shoot if necessary.

Mike listened to Tyler, knowing he didn't feel comfortable about leaving her. She walked him to the door.

"So, what are you telling me . . . that you're in love with me?"

Tyler turned around with a chuckle. "Where did that come from?"

"Our conversation earlier. You alluded to the fact that you were falling in love with me. Is that true or was that a hypothetical analogy? Because you hardly know me, Tyler. And I must say I haven't showed you my best side in the short time we've been together."

"And I'm not running. That should tell you something."

Mike smiled at his assurance. "But what about our differences? Doesn't that worry you?"

"Not enough to give up on us." Tyler leaned down and placed a gentle kiss on Mike's lips. "Now, are you sure you're going to be okay?"

"Eventually."

Mike closed the door, turned the key in the deadbolt, and set the alarm. She looked at her two companions. They twisted their heads from side to side as if they were asking her the same question. "Come on, guys. Let's call it a night."

IN A SHROUD OF DARKNESS, THE FIGURE WATCHED as Tyler pulled away from the driveway. He swore to himself, hating the way Tyler had weaseled his way into Mike's life.

Tyler radioed the black and white that he had asked to patrol Mike's neighborhood. "Yeah, this is Henderson. Everything's secure at the moment. I'll check in with you tomorrow. If anything even remotely suspicious comes up, call me."

Skyler greeted Tyler in his usual fashion. Again, Tyler felt a twinge of guilt that he wasn't spending nearly the time with Skyler that he should. He hadn't gone running for days, and his workouts were nonexistent. He knew he would get back in a routine once things were back to normal. Hopefully, that would be soon.

THE NEXT MORNING, TYLER SET OUT TO SEARCH around the perimeter of his house. He had intended on doing so the day before, but with the discovery of Elizabeth Jordan, his plans had been sidelined.

Skyler followed along. He seemed as determined to find something as Tyler was. Tyler came across some footprints. Strangely, they looked like his, but he hadn't remembered walking around this outcropping of bushes. Obviously, he must have; he just couldn't remember doing it. Tyler searched until he was satisfied there was nothing to find.

He spent a few moments wrestling with Skyler and promised to himself that he would spend more time with his pet later. He glanced at the clock; it was already 7:30. He wanted to call Mike but didn't want to disturb her if she were still getting some much needed sleep. He raced Skyler up the stairs and took a quick shower. He was just stepping out and grabbing a towel when his phone rang. He twisted the towel around his midsection and answered the phone.

"Henderson."

"Good morning, Tyler."

"Is it?" Tyler asked Mike with hesitation.

"Nothing happened out of the ordinary, if that's what you're asking me."

"How did you sleep?"

"Pretty good. I'm just not used to sharing my bed." From the silence over the line, Mike could tell Tyler was taken back by her comment. "The dogs, Tyler. They insisted on pinning me in between the two of them. I couldn't move edgewise."

"Were they disturbed at all?"

"Nope. They didn't move all night."

"That's good," Tyler said with a sigh of relief. "So, how about if I meet you for lunch? You name the time."

"Let's just wait and make it dinner. I'm not very good with lunch dates. I have a tendency to lose track of time and work through them."

"Okay, I'll try not to take that personally, but you have to promise me you'll grab something other than Tootsie Rolls."

"How'd you know Tootsie Rolls are my normal meal replacement?"

"You had them at Dorian's place, and Nathan told me about your addiction."

"Boy, he's really turned into quite the snitch, hasn't he?"

"Hey, he cares about you."

"I know, I know. Besides, I'm out of Tootsie Rolls and haven't had a chance to replenish my supply." Mike grabbed for her keys and purse. "I should be no later than 6:00. If I am, call me and I'll let you know how much longer I'll be. My place or yours?"

"Let's say your place. That way when I leave, I'll know you're all locked in for the night."

"Okay, then why don't you bring Skyler. He can play around with Oreo and 'Nilla. Maybe we could even take a walk by the lake."

"Sounds great to me. Are you sure you feel up to it?"

"Yes, Doctor Henderson. I think I can handle a little walking."

"Okay, okay, no reason for name calling. Look, I'll bring everything to your house and have dinner ready by 6:00. Just don't be late—and Mike, don't forget to set the alarm."

TYLER WAS ALREADY AT WORK WHEN JIM showed up. Jim shuffled to his chair, fired up his computer, and moaned. "Grandchildren can be so exhausting. I swear that Joshua has two speeds—fast and faster."

Tyler gave him a slight chuckle to show he was listening but never let his eyes leave the folder he was holding in front of him.

"How's Mike doing?" Jim asked, the tone of his voice changing from playful to serious.

"As well as can be expected. She's had her moments, but nothing that's interfering with her job. If anyone is going to solve this case, it will be her."

Just then there was a tap on the open door. Carruthers leaned in and addressed both Jim and Tyler, "Billings has something that I think you two will be interested in. A car belonging to one Vince Ortega is being pulled from the lake."

Both Jim and Tyler jumped to their feet. "Where?" Jim asked as he pulled his jacket from the back of his chair.

"The old launch. It's been closed for repairs, but some kids decided to use it anyway. When they did, they backed right into Ortega's car.

"Thanks, Carruthers. Tell Billings we're on our way."

Jim drove quickly to the other side of the lake. Finally, something other than the blood traces would link Ortega to the vicinity. They pulled up behind Billings' patrol car. Some kids with a boat were there, obviously the ones that found the car. A tow truck was sitting by the launch with a chain attached to the back end of a partially submerged car. Billings was standing on the launch. The wet rings around the hem of his pants showed that he had already gone into the water. When he saw Jim and Tyler, he started rattling off what he knew. Of course, he only directed his information at Jim. He didn't give Tyler the time of day.

"Those kids went to use the launch, even though the sign said it was closed." Billings gestured to the barricade off to the side of the launch. "When they lowered their boat, it ran into the car. When they saw it was a car, they called it in. The tow truck pulled it out far enough for me to get a license reading. When I ran it and found out it belonged to your missing person, I left things where they were."

Jim nodded his appreciation. "Did you get pictures of it?"

"Yeah, plenty." Billings lifted the camera that was in his hand.

"Okay, tell the driver to pull it all the way out."

Billings signaled for the tow truck driver to start up his winch. It was slow going. All the windows of the car were down, making the car completely waterlogged. When the car was far enough up the ramp for the back doors of the old sedan to be exposed, Tyler and Billings approached the car and opened the rear doors. With a swish, a torrent of water flowed from the car. Tyler took a quick look. No bodies were in the front or back seat, but the key was still in the ignition. The tow truck driver pulled the car completely up the ramp. It moved with more ease once the water had dissipated.

The three men stood staring at the old Ford Fairlane. It was in beat-up condition, but anyone who had a love for the old classics could see the potential in the vehicle.

"What a waste." Jim shook his head.

Tyler called the lab. Nathan answered the phone, sounding more professional than he did in person.

"Nathan, is Mike there?"

"Yeah, but she doesn't want to be disturbed."

Tyler panicked. "Why, what's wrong?"

"Nothing's wrong. She's just working on some meticulous specimens. She doesn't want to be interrupted."

Tyler released a sigh of relief. "What about you—are you busy?"

"Why, what do you have?"

"We might have found our missing victim from the Dorian Thomas case. At the very least, we have his car. You can retrieve fingerprints even if the area got wet, right?"

"Yes, if the area wasn't wiped clean or smudged."

"Okay then. Grab your little black bag and meet us out at the lake, the east side launch."

"What's with Emerald Lake all of a sudden? It seems to have turned into a hotbed of crime this month." Nathan had spoken what Tyler was already thinking.

"Yeah, lucky me. I leave the big city for the simple life, and crime decides to follow me."

Tyler gave Nathan instructions on how to find the launch. The drive would take him at least twenty minutes. It would be completely worth it if they could have something solid to pin on Dorian.

Tyler walked back to where Billings and Jim were discussing something. They quieted as Tyler approached.

"Nathan will be here in about twenty minutes."

"No Mike, huh?" These were the first words Billings had spoken directly to Tyler.

"No, she's working on something and doesn't want to be disturbed."

"Well, I'm going to split. After all, you two are the *detectives*. I'm just a street cop."

Tyler continued to feel the animosity that Billings was directing at him.

"You'd better get that hand checked." Jim's comment made Tyler look at Billings' hands. He had a slight gash on his left hand between his index finger and thumb.

"How'd you get that?" Tyler said quizzically.

"It's nothing." Billings looked at his bloody hand and then back to Jim and Tyler. "When I cleared some lake weed off the frame of the license plate, it caught and gave me a pretty decent cut. Looks worse than it is. I just need to get it cleaned up. I already had a tetanus shot, so I'm not too worried about it. So, if you guys don't need my expertise . . . oh, that's right, I've already been told that I'm not good enough. Then I guess I'll be leaving." Billings revved up his squad car and left in a cloud of dust.

"When is that guy going to cut me some slack? I didn't choose me over him. The advisory board did. If he has a beef with them, he needs to take care of it, not take it out on me." Tyler was hot. He had enough to worry about right now without Billings talking smack all the time.

"Don't let him get to you. He's done this to himself, and he's just looking for someone else to blame. Ignore it. Sooner or later he's going to get himself in enough trouble of his own. You have what he couldn't get and that bothers him. I say that he doesn't make it until the end of the year. You'll see."

"Hey, man." One of the kids that discovered the car was heading towards Jim and Tyler. "Can we leave? We've already lost a couple hours on the lake. We don't have all day." The kid's arrogant attitude grated on Jim's nerves.

"You can go, but the next time a sign tells you to stay out, I suggest you do it." Jim's voice was stern and laced with the disciplinary attitude of a father.

"Yeah, man, I know. But hey, looks like we did you a favor." The kid walked away with a very cavalier attitude. Tyler's bet was he would use the launch again if he felt like it.

Tyler and Jim waited for Nathan to show up. They okayed the tow truck driver to go out on another call. He would come back when Nathan was done. Twenty minutes had already passed, and Tyler was getting antsy. An odor was now discharging from the car, and though it could be the lake water, Tyler's guess was that it was Mr. Ortega himself. As much as he wanted to pop the trunk and confirm his suspicions, he waited. He didn't want to take any chance of tainting possible evidence.

Tyler noticed something floating in the small wake at the edge of the launch. When he bent to pick it up, he realized it was a bloodied bandage. He carefully picked it up and set it on the hood of the car. He would have Nathan bag it to see if it had any bearing on the case.

Nathan finally arrived and tried to do what he could to remove prints from the steering wheel, gear shift, the key itself, and the hood of the trunk. Nathan put the key in an evidence bag. "I might be able to get something off of this if I take it back to the lab." He wasn't that hopeful, but even a partial on any of the items could be enough to pin Thomas to Ortega.

With Jim's permission, Tyler used a crowbar on the trunk. It didn't budge at first, but with a little extra pressure, the trunk finally popped open. Out spewed a stench that spoke of death. There, in the trunk, was most likely the remains of Vince Ortega. The corpse was bloated from the water, and the skin was already beginning to pull away from the body; but Nathan was sure he could make a positive identification.

A couple more hours were spent on the scene. Photos were taken of the body before removing it. More photos were taken of the trunk and anything that could be used as evidence. The body was finally loaded into Nathan's van and the car hitched up to be taken to the evidence impound.

Jim and Tyler decided to pay Mr. Thomas a visit in county lockup. A confession would still be a useful piece of evidence to hand to the district attorney. Tyler was sure he could get Dorian to break under interrogation.

While Jim was making his way to county, Tyler tried to give Mike a call but still couldn't reach her. He would have to wait and talk to her tonight. If he were lucky, he would have at least one case wrapped up by then.

DORIAN WAS ACTING UNAFFECTED by the detectives' summons to the interrogation room. He had fooled them thus far and was confident he was going to get away with murder.

"Good afternoon, boys. Nothing better to do than harass the locals?" Dorian stretched in his chair. Tyler wanted to pop him but decided watching him squirm would be better.

"Well, before we get started, would you like to have your lawyer here?"

"I don't need a lawyer. I told you what went down. You ain't got nothing on me."

Tyler waited a moment before saying anything. Then, very casually, he began.

"We met with your friend today."

"What friend?"

"Vince Ortega."

Dorian stiffened slightly. They were trying to trip him up. He knew Vince was dead. "Really. And what did he have to say?"

Tyler leaned across the table and looked directly into Dorian's eyes. "Well, let's just put it this way . . . the blast to his chest had pretty much guaranteed his silence."

Dorian sneered. "You've got nothing on me or you wouldn't be here talking to me. You'd be arresting me."

"Oh, we're going to do that too. I just have one question for you."

Dorian acted as if he weren't paying attention.

Tyler continued, "If you were willing to kill him over drugs, why didn't you remove the seven kilos from his car before you dumped the body?"

Dorian's look turned ashen. He swallowed hard and with an irritated tone lashed out, "How stupid do you think I am? I'm not going to fall for that. You've got nothing on me. Now let me out of here. I'm not gonna saying another word without a lawyer."

"A lawyer, Dorian? Why would an innocent person like you need a lawyer? Maybe you're afraid that the more you talk, the more you're going to indict yourself? Doesn't matter, we found your prints everywhere."

"Of course, you did." Dorian's fingers nervously pattered on the tabletop. He was ready to spill it; Tyler could taste it. "I never said I wasn't in his car. I just never drove it. So, if you think you're going to pin this on me, you're wrong."

"So the fingerprints we found aren't going to be yours?"

"No, man, I told you. I never drove that car."

"Who said we found the prints on a car?"

Dorian slammed his fist down on the table. "You just did, man."

"No, I said we found prints, and I asked you why you left the drugs in the car when you dumped the body. I never said I found prints on the car."

Dorian glared at Tyler, who was fighting back a grin. "You're under arrest for the murder of Vince Ortega," Tyler said with satisfaction.

"I want a lawyer," Dorian said.

CHAPTER TWELVE

Tyler ran across the street to the warehouse store to get something for Mike. He quickly found what he wanted and grabbed a bundle of flowers on his way out. He hustled back across the street and through the parking lot. The county coroner's building sat catty-corner from the county lockup, and he wanted to check in and see how Mike was doing. He buzzed the back door and waited for someone to let him in. He hadn't been assigned his own code yet and needed to wait for someone to identify him before he could go inside. Showing his badge to a lab tech, he wandered down the hall to Mike's office. He tapped on the door, but there was no answer. He tried the doorknob and found that it was unlocked, so he decided to leave his quirky gift as a surprise. He placed the flowers in a discarded Slurpee cup and left a note that read:

See you at 6:00.

He went back to the precinct where he caught up with Jim, who was talking to an old buddy. When he saw Tyler, Jim said his good-byes and walked with him to the door.

"Where did you disappear to? Like I didn't know."

Tyler just smiled as they climbed into the truck.

"How's Mike?"

"I don't know. She wasn't in her office."

"Then what took so long?" Jim asked as he pulled into traffic.

"Oh, I just picked up a little something for her. I didn't want to disturb her, so I just left it in her office." Tyler would love to have seen her reaction, but hearing about it from her would be good enough.

MIKE HAD SPENT ALL DAY GOING OVER each piece of evidence that was collected from Elizabeth Jordan. They definitely had trace evidence from another person, both at the scene and on Elizabeth's body. Now it was up to her to find that person and make him pay for Elizabeth's death as well as find out what his connection was to Michelle.

It was after 5:00 before Mike dragged herself out of the lab. She went into her office to collapse for a few minutes before driving home, only to be greeted by a tub of Tootsie Rolls and a bouquet of flowers. The note made the hours of exhaustion melt away. She had thought about calling Tyler and canceling, but now she looked forward to seeing him more than ever.

TYLER'S TRUCK WAS IN THE DRIVEWAY WHEN she got home.

127

Even as tired as she was, she liked the idea of coming home at the end of the day to someone she could spend time with.

The door was locked, so she dug around in the bottom of her purse for her key. Finally finding it, she was able to let herself in. A menagerie of dogs greeted her at the door. Tyler had brought Skyler, and 'Nilla and Oreo were pressing towards her for attention. She talked and hugged on them for a few minutes before seeing Tyler at work in the kitchen.

"You didn't set the alarm," Tyler said the moment he saw her.

"I thought I did."

"Dang it, Mike. That's not good enough." He was trying not to get upset but was concerned that she had been so careless.

"I'm sorry. I guess I was preoccupied with getting to work and going over a few things," she said as she kicked off her shoes and walked to the kitchen. "Smells good." Tyler stopped what he was doing and pulled her into a bear hug. He decided not to lecture her. He gave her a welcoming kiss instead and whispered in her ear, "Are you hungry?"

"Starved. But, of course, I already had dessert." Mike stretched up and gave him another kiss. "Thanks for the Tootsie Rolls and flowers."

"You're welcome," he said with a satisfactory grin.

"Why didn't you come and find me?" she asked as she peeked at what was being served for dinner.

"I didn't want to disturb you. Besides, I only had a few minutes."

Tyler pulled cornbread from the oven and started ladling out bowls of chili. "Did you find anything?"

"Oh sure. Now all we need to do is find out who it belongs to."

Tyler could hear the cynicism in her voice.

She quickly changed the subject. "This looks wonderful, Tyler." She pulled at the corner of a piece of steaming bread.

He simply smiled as he carried the basket of cornbread and one of the steaming bowls of chili to the table. Mike grabbed the other bowl and joined him. He reached out for her hand. Tyler bowed his head for prayer. Out of courtesy, Mike followed.

"Lord, you know what we're up against and how difficult this is for Mike. Show her you care. Show her your power, Lord. And help us to solve this crime and maybe bring closure to Michelle's death. Keep Mike safe, and thank you for this time that Mike and I can spend together. Amen."

The warm chili was soothing to Mike, along with the company. She found herself thinking ahead about her relationship with Tyler. She knew she was falling in love with him. He brought joy, strength, and security to her life. But he also brought another relationship. She knew what the Bible said about being unequally yoked. She knew that Tyler had a strong and committed relationship with God. She wouldn't come between that.

"What are you thinking?" Tyler asked as he finished his chili.

"Just going over some details in my mind," Mike said in a distracted tone.

"Well, how about I clean up the dishes, and you go change into something more comfortable. That is, if you still feel up to that walk?"

"Sounds good." Mike headed upstairs, still thinking about Tyler. The dogs followed after her, vying for her attention. She changed into some comfortable sweatpants and a sweatshirt and soon found herself wrestling with the dogs on the floor of her bedroom. She was laughing and carrying on when Tyler found her. When he entered the room, Skyler obediently went to his side.

"Boy, he sure knows who's boss," Mike said as she picked herself up from the floor.

"Yeah," Tyler said as he goodheartedly pushed at Skyler and played with him. "He's a good dog. He knows when he has a good thing." Tyler trained his eye on Mike. "He learned that from me." He raised his eyebrows to make his point.

The five of them headed for the lakefront. The dogs ran ahead of Tyler and Mike but would circle back when they were called. Tyler held Mike's hand in his as they walked, enjoying the silence, the company, and the scenery.

"I've been thinking about what you said about God and free will."

"And ..." Tyler prompted cautiously.

"I understand what you said, and I know that I believe in God. I don't think that has ever changed. I just can't get past the fact that he allowed this to happen. I want to be angry at him, and I think he is ultimately to blame."

"That's because you haven't been able to look at Michelle's killer and place the blame where it belongs. You're transferring your anger, Mike. If you can't blame the killer, you blame yourself and God. But don't you see, that's wrong. That's like blaming Ford when a car kills a pedestrian or blaming Smith and Wesson when an innocent child is killed by a misused handgun. You're blaming the Creator instead of the one who ultimately misused his power. There is a person responsible for Michelle's death and the death of Elizabeth Jordan. Are you going to be able to transfer blame to them, even if you never find them, or are you going to keep blaming yourself and God? That's the issue, Mike. It's not your belief in God that's being challenged here. It's your belief in the fact that even though we don't understand it, God has allowed this to happen. And you might not ever fully understand why."

Mike was clutching Tyler's hand as if he were the only thing that kept her from running once again from the issue at hand. "I'm trying, Tyler. I just need some time."

Tyler pulled her close. He tipped up her chin and stared into eyes that were brimming with tears. "I'll wait as long as it takes." Tyler's kiss was warm and soothing. He wrapped his arms around her and held her to his chest. "I'm in love with you, Mike. I know that sounds crazy since I've only known you a little while, but I know it's true. I won't rush you, though. Your relationship with the Lord is the most important thing to me right now."

MIKE HAD LEARNED NOTHING FROM ELIZABETH JORDAN. Didn't she realize that it was her fault Elizabeth was dead? Maybe Mike would need more proof that she'd never be able to put Michelle's death behind her.

The man in the shadows stalked away from where he was watching Mike and Tyler. He would remind Mike once again why she was by herself.

MIKE COULDN'T DECIDE IF IT WAS HER ALARM buzzing or the phone ringing that woke her. She quickly tapped the alarm and then reached for the phone.

"Hello."

"It's all your fault you know," a low, guttural voice spoke over the phone. "This never would have happened if you hadn't decided it was up to you to save the world. Well, here's your chance. Don't blow it. The wrong person paid for Michelle's murder. You don't want that same mistake to happen again."

The voice was angry and defiant. Mike sat straight up in bed. She was terrified. She knew she was talking to Elizabeth Jordan's killer. Mike gathered her composure. She had to talk to him. She had to find out why this psychotic killer was targeting her. "Why are you doing this?"

"I told you. You want to make people pay for their crimes? Then how about you? How about the crime of lying? You're a liar, Mike, and I think you need to pay for your crime too."

The phone went dead, even though it was still cradled against her ear. Mike was trying to remember all that was said, but her mind was cloudy. She was being blamed for Elizabeth Jordan's death and accused of letting the wrong person pay for Michelle's death. But how could that be? Michelle's killer was never found. How could the wrong person have paid for her death, and how did Elizabeth Jordan's killer know that?

Her phone rang again, causing terror to flood over her. She slowly reached for the phone, afraid of what she would hear. "Hello."

"Mike, there's been another killing."

Mike allowed herself to breathe at the sound of Tyler's voice. Tyler waited to hear Mike's reaction, but there was nothing but silence. "Mike, did you hear me? Another body was found by the lake." Tyler held his phone close to his ear. Mike's whispered reply was hard to hear. "Mike, I can barely hear you."

"He called me, Tyler."

"Who called you?"

"The killer. He called me. He said it was my fault."

"I'll be right there." Tyler bolted for the front door. "Stay on the line with me, Mike. Don't hang up." He was in his truck and skidding out of the driveway before Mike could say anymore.

"He said it's my fault, Tyler. He said the wrong person paid for Michelle's death. He called me a liar and said it was my fault."

Tyler could barely make out what Mike was saying. She was repeating herself and talking from what sounded like a state of shock. "Mike, I'm almost there. Where are you?"

"I'm upstairs."

"Where's your gun?"

Mike glanced to the nightstand and saw her gun by the phone. "It's right here."

"Good. Don't move. I'll let myself in and I'll announce myself. If you hear any other noise downstairs, get your gun and stay put. I'll make sure you know it's me in the house. If you hear anyone else . . . get ready to use your gun."

"But the alarm is set. No one could've gotten in."

"We don't know that. Stay put until I get there."

It took only a few more minutes before Tyler was skidding into the driveway. Arnie spun around from his position by the kennels and was startled by Tyler's appearance.

Mike jumped when the dogs scrambled from her room. Their instincts told them someone was outside. She took her gun from the nightstand and slowly descended the stairs.

Tyler ran to Mike's door, turned his key, and entered the code Mike had given him. "Mike, it's me." Tyler stood in the doorway.

Mike threw her arms around Tyler's neck and held him with all the strength she had. Tyler reassured her with soft words, trying to calm her down. He closed the door behind him and held Mike as if he would never let her go.

"I don't get it, Tyler. Why is someone doing this to me?"

"I don't know, Mike, but before we talk about it, you need to write down everything he said before you forget." Tyler pulled out the small notepad that he always kept in his pocket and handed it to Mike along with a pen. Mike moved to the couch and sat down. Her hands were shaking as she feverishly began to write. Oreo and 'Nilla were whimpering and pacing throughout the room. They could sense that something wasn't right.

When Mike felt as if she had remembered everything, she handed the notepad back to Tyler and watched him as he read. When he was done, he looked at her with compassion and confusion. He sat down next to her, pulled her close to his side, and let her release the tears that had been hovering just below the surface. He could see the chills that were on her arms and felt her tremble in his embrace. He held her for several minutes before Mike pulled away and stood. She looked like a little girl in her oversized flannel pants and spaghetti-strap camisole.

Right before Tyler's eyes, he saw a transformation take place. With every pacing stride that Mike took, the emotional Mike began to disappear, only to be replaced by the analytical Mike.

"He's trying to confuse me, Tyler. He knows no one paid for Michelle's death. There was no trial; no one was arrested or even detained for anything but questioning. He's trying to make this personal to throw me off."

Mike bolted up the stairs and started pulling things out of her closet.

"What are you doing?" Tyler asked as he watched her from the bottom of the stairs.

Mike yanked clothing from hangers and shelves. "I'm getting dressed. We have a murder scene to investigate."

Anger would be the tool that Mike relied on to get her through another autopsy.

THE SCENE WAS THE SAME AS THE Elizabeth Jordan case: shallow grave, slash marks to the torso and neck, and hands severed from the body. The victim was a girl in her late teens, possible early twenties. She had fair skin, blond hair, and blue eyes.

Mike worked the scene in silence and precision. She had to distance herself from the idea that these girls died because someone was playing a sick game with her. She and Nathan gathered trace evidence from the scene and carefully loaded the body into the van.

Tyler watched Mike as she stopped to talk to Officer Billings. He had been involved with both the crime scenes, and her approach to him was with care and concern. She talked to him for a few minutes and then headed to the coroner's van.

"I'm going to ride with Nathan. Maybe you can pick me up tonight and give me a ride home." Mike's voice was rigid and unattached.

"Are you sure?"

"Yeah. I don't know who this idiot is, but the only way I'm going to be able to stop him is to wait for him to make a mistake. And when he does, I'm going to have the evidence to nail him."

"Are you sure you're all right?" Tyler stopped her so he could judge for himself.

"I'm scared to death, Tyler," she said as her eyes met his. "But scared is good. Scared will keep me on my toes."

TYLER FOUND HIMSELF BACK AT THE OFFICE with Michelle's case file in his hand. He looked through the minimal information. A full list of students at Emerald Lake High School was included, along with the list of people that were questioned. Tyler's eyes stopped on Billings' name as he scanned the list. He felt his jaw set. He could feel Billings' animosity towards him beginning to rub off on him, but he brushed his feelings aside so he could concentrate on the case. He started running names through the computer to look for anything out of the ordinary.

"What are you doing?" Jim asked as he peered over Tyler's shoulder.

"I don't know. Just trying to find anything that might have been over-looked. I keep thinking if I look at Michelle's case file long enough, something will jump out at me. The connection's here. I know it is."

"Well, if you find it before 5:00 p.m., let me know," he said in an exaggerated tone. "I have to make a statement to the press."

TYLER BUZZED THE BACK DOOR and was let in by Nathan. "You're becoming quite the fixture here, Tyler."

"Nice to see you too, Nathan."

Nathan laughed. "Don't get me wrong. I'm glad that she isn't going home at night by herself, especially now." They walked down the hall together and stopped at Mike's office. "Go ahead and have a seat. I'll tell her you're here."

Nathan continued down the hall while Tyler leaned back in Mike's leather swivel chair. He rocked for a few moments, feeling tired and worn out. He pivoted to look at the large shelves behind him and noticed the Tootsie Roll bucket on the bottom shelf. He decided that Mike probably never stopped for lunch. He would make sure she had a dinner a little more substantial than a handful of candy.

Tyler was resting his eyes when Mike finally stepped into her office. She plopped down in the other chair across from her desk and laid her head back to rest.

"Are you okay?" Tyler asked after a few moments of quiet.

"No . . . I'm not," Mike admitted as she sat staring at the ceiling. Tyler was surprised by Mike's candidness. "I want to go home, take a nice long bath, and curl up with you and not talk about work."

"I think I can arrange that," Tyler said as he got to his feet. He walked around the desk and extended his hands to Mike. She took them and allowed Tyler to pull her up to her feet. She stood for a moment, her head resting against him, not wanting to move.

"I could fall asleep right now, right here," Mike said as she listened to Tyler's heartbeat.

"Then let's get you home before you fall asleep standing up."

MIKE SUNK INTO HER BUBBLE BATH while Tyler worked in the kitchen. Frank was downstairs keeping Tyler company and checking on the progress of the case. He was shaken that Mike was the target of a psychotic person and that she again had to think about Michelle's death. He was glad that Tyler was a part of her life at the moment. Although he had never thought she would take the step into another relationship, he could see Tyler was the perfect fit for her. She might have sworn off cops once, but Tyler was different. He brought security to Mike instead of pressure.

"I'm glad she has you right now, Tyler. You're good for her. I just wish you didn't have to worry about some psycho at the same time." Frank munched on chips while Tyler worked on dinner. His expression changed, and it took him a minute to verbalize what he was thinking. "Do you think the same person who's committing these murders is the one responsible for Michelle's death?"

"I don't think so, Frank. Neither does Mike. Though the similarities are great, there are still some factors that differ."

"Like what?" Frank inquired.

Tyler wasn't sure what to say. The major difference in these crimes was the fact that Michelle had been sexually assaulted. He wasn't sure how to tell Frank this without causing him further anguish.

"Hi, Dad," Mike said as she walked up behind him. Her hair was twisted up on top of her head, and she wore tattered sweatpants with a shirt that said, "Crime pays . . . my salary. " She placed a tender kiss to his cheek and smiled. "Are you joining us for dinner?"

"If that's an invitation, I am." Frank watched as his daughter moved closer to Tyler, completely at ease in his company. She deserved this. He wished she would leave her job with the coroner's office and make domestic pursuits her full-time job.

Tyler laughed when he read her shirt. "Do you have a drawer full of shirts with wisecracks?"

"You're just jealous," she said with a playful nudge.

The smile on Mike's face warmed Frank's soul. Even in the turmoil that he knew she was dealing with, she seemed to have an air of contentment.

The three of them enjoyed a casual dinner, everyone trying to ignore the obvious subject. Frank told childhood stories of Mike that embarrassed her and made Tyler laugh. When they were done with their meal, Frank excused himself for the evening.

"You want me to send over Oreo and 'Nilla?" he asked as he reached for his jacket.

Both Tyler and Mike answered at once, but with different words. Tyler looked at Mike and again replied to Frank. "Yes, I want the dogs in with Mike until we find this guy."

"But you changed all the locks, Tyler, and I'm using the security code. There's no way someone can get in here without me hearing them."

"Be that as it may, the dogs can forewarn you about anything they might hear outside." Tyler turned back to Frank. "Just leave the door cracked. I'll close it after the dogs are in."

Frank turned to his daughter and gave her a kiss on the forehead. "I'm going to be gone for a few days."

"You are?" Mike said with surprise.

"Yeah. Remember I told you I would be going to Bakersfield to look into the breeding ranch there."

"I'm sorry, Dad. I guess with everything else going on, I just forgot."

"That's okay. I can understand that with all you're dealing with right now. Just say the word, Mike, and I'll stay home." Concern was written all over Frank's face.

"No, Dad, I'll be fine." Mike placed a kiss on her dad's cheek and gave him a reassuring smile. "I've got the dogs, the security measures, and Sergeant Friday here to keep me safe. I'll be fine."

Tyler waited for the dogs to make their appearance and then closed and locked the door behind them. He joined Mike in the kitchen and could tell by her mood that she was agitated by his decision to have the dogs in the house.

"Come on, Mike. It can't hurt to have them here. Besides, look how excited they are to see you." Mike and Tyler both turned to the two dogs sitting in the living room. Just then 'Nilla yawned, causing both Tyler and Mike to laugh.

"Oh, they're excited all right. They can hardly contain themselves."

Mike threw the dishtowel at Tyler and loved on the dogs for a few moments before moving over to the couch. Tyler sat close to her and wrapped his arm around her. "Now, is this so bad? A quiet evening after a nice dinner, just the two of us." Mike's eyes traveled back and forth between Tyler and the dogs. "Okay, the four of us, but I don't mind an audience."

Tyler leaned in close to Mike and placed a long, lingering kiss on her lips. Mike enjoyed the way Tyler made her feel. She felt desirable and passionate. She returned his kiss, wrapping her arms around him and bringing her body closer to his. They allowed themselves to get lost in the feelings they had for each other, but not for long. Tyler struggled with the temptation of going further, but reined himself back from allowing the situation to go too far. Mike realized the exact moment that Tyler caught himself. He gently pulled back from her and allowed his passionate kisses to subside.

Mike sat beside Tyler, not sure how she was feeling. It wasn't rejection, because she knew in her heart how much Tyler cared for her. She realized it was disappointment in herself. She didn't want to spoil her relationship with Tyler by allowing things to go too far. She had allowed her feelings of intimacy to slip away from her once before, and nothing good had come of it.

She was the only one to blame for that night. She had given Jason every part of her, and when it came time to take it back, he wasn't willing to concede. She didn't blame him; she blamed herself. Though she knew what he had done was wrong and unforgivable, she realized it was a consequence of her behavior. She wished she could offer Tyler a pure heart, something that hadn't been violated; unfortunately, she couldn't go back and change the past.

Mike felt she needed to be honest with Tyler and let him know how far her involvement had gone with someone else. She didn't want to keep secrets from him and somehow she felt she was being dishonest by not letting him know that at one time she had been engaged.

"You're awfully quiet, Mike. Talk to me, because if I offended you, I need to know so we can talk about it."

"You didn't offend me, Tyler. It's just that I need to tell you something that I should have told you sooner." Tyler waited for Mike to continue. It took her a moment because she wasn't sure what to say. Finally, she just blurted it out. "Tyler, I was engaged once."

In a casual tone, completely different from what Mike expected, Tyler answered back. "Then I guess that explains the wedding dress hanging in your closet." Mike turned to Tyler, surprise on her face. "I saw it when I was hunting around for your shoes the other day when we went to the lake."

"Why didn't you say anything? Why didn't you ask me about it?"

"Because I knew you would tell me when you were ready. Mike, I told you that I was involved with someone for over two years. We're not kids. It's pretty normal to have more than one relationship in a lifetime."

"But you know him," Mike said quietly.

Tyler's calm demeanor turned to confusion. "You mean I know the person you were engaged to? Who?" Quickly, before Mike could answer, a slide show of men appeared in his mind. He had only met a handful of people since being in Emerald Lake and had no idea who it could possibly be.

"Jason Billings," Mike said.

At the mention of his name, Tyler's mind started replaying the few conversations and interactions he had with Billings. Now things were a little clearer to him. The argumentative and aggressive behavior that Jason had been showing him wasn't just work related. Maybe Jason was jealous of his and Mike's relationship. But how would he know? Tyler hadn't paraded around the office announcing it. Tyler thought back to his previous station. Gossip had been rampant there. Obviously, the rumor mill was alive and well in Emerald Lake too. Tyler thought for a moment and then asked, "Who broke it off?"

"I did."

"Well, that explains a lot. I thought he was just belligerent towards me because he had applied for the detective's position and was overlooked. Maybe it has to do with the fact that I'm seeing you?"

"Maybe." Mike thought for a moment. "It was a long time ago though. We were going to get married after high school, but things didn't work out. He went away to the academy, and I got involved in school. Our relationship just wasn't the same."

Mike decided not to tell Tyler how she and Jason's relationship had ended. It was a bad memory for Mike, and she decided not to relive it right then. She would tell Tyler eventually, if it became necessary. But at the moment, she figured he had enough to think about. Tyler sat in silence. She gave him a moment to digest what she told him but was curious to know what he was thinking.

"Are you okay with this? I mean working with Jason and all?"

"Yeah, sure. I mean it will make me look at him in a different light, but I'm not going to let it bother me. I was just wondering why Jim hadn't said something to me."

"Maybe he forgot. After all, it was a long time ago."

"I don't know. Jim doesn't seem like the forgetful type."

"Maybe he thought I had already told you?"

"Well, it really doesn't change anything—I mean between us."

Mike sat quietly, her head resting against Tyler's outstretched arm and soaking in the comfort of just being with him. He was right. They were adults. They both had past relationships. She couldn't let that ruin or interfere with what they had with each other now.

"I've been going over Michelle's file." Tyler's comment broke the silence.

"But I told you, it's not the same guy." Mike was annoyed that Tyler was second-guessing her judgment.

"Don't take it personally, Mike. I'm just looking for anything that might have been overlooked. Whoever's doing this knew about the shallow grave. Jim said that was evidence withheld from the public."

"But, Tyler, after all these years, I'm sure some of that information has leaked out. People talk. Especially when they think they know something no one else does. Michelle's case has almost reached myth-like status at the high school. They use the information from her case as the 'Don't let this happen to you' poster campaign."

Tyler could hear the hurt in Mike's voice. He couldn't imagine what she'd dealt with over the years. "So why did you stay in Emerald Lake? With your expertise, I'm sure you could have gotten a job with other departments. Why stay here?"

Mike thought for a moment before she answered. "I guess I didn't want to leave Dad or Michelle." She sighed and closed her eyes. "I worked on her case when I was first assigned to the coroner's office. I thought I would be able to discover something no one else had. After a while, I realized that sometimes it doesn't matter how much you know. Sometimes things happen that just can't be explained. I put Michelle's case aside and concentrated on my relationship with my dad. He's lost a lot over the years—first Michelle, then my mom. We were all we had left. I guess that's what kept me here."

Tyler thought over Mike's conversation. "But you never struck things up with Billings again?"

Mike couldn't help but smile. She knew Tyler had been curious earlier. He was just trying not to sound too obvious. "I knew that bothered you more than you were letting on," she said in a kidding tone.

"It doesn't *bother* me. I just can't imagine the two of you together. You're both hotheads. That must have made for a volatile relationship."

"People change, Tyler. I wasn't the same person in high school that I am now."

"What about Billings? Has he changed much?"

The tone of Mike's words grew a little cold. "I wouldn't know. I've tried to steer clear of him over the years."

"So I guess things didn't end on a very positive note for the two of you?"

Mike realized she needed to be truthful with Tyler. She shifted to the edge of the couch and turned to look at him. "I was struggling with Michelle's death one night after graduation and got drunk. I was in self-destruct mode." Mike stumbled over her next words, never having said them out loud. "Jason and I slept together that night. I felt horrible about it the next day. I knew it was wrong, that I was wrong, but Jason didn't see it that way. He had finally gotten what he wanted from the relationship and wasn't willing to take a step back. We spent the next week arguing. He didn't see the big deal about having sex if we were going to get married anyway. I was still trying to deal with Michelle's death so my emotions were all over the place. One night, he decided to prove his point. He got pretty physical with me and tried to convince me that I couldn't live without him."

Tyler's words were soft. "Are you telling me he raped you?"

"No . . . I mean . . . yes. No, it's not as simple as that, Tyler. I mean I didn't want to . . . but I deserved it because I put myself in a vulnerable position."

Tyler sprung from the couch, angered by what Mike was saying. He began walking swiftly up and down the room. Mike gave him time to regain his composure, but not time enough to say what was on his mind.

"Look, Tyler, I know what you're thinking. But I don't agree. It was my fault. I put myself in a position of compromise."

"But he had no right to—"

Mike cut him off before he could finish. "You're right—he had no right, but I have no one to blame but myself."

"So if you blame yourself, why did you break it off with him?" Tyler stood with his shoulders rigid and his hands crammed into his pockets.

"Because Jason's behavior terrified me that night." Mike shuddered and wrapped her arms around herself trying to ward off the chill of the memory. "He tried to apologize and even cried along with me afterwards, but I saw a side of him that night that made me realize that his outburst was about more than just sex. He had turned violent and wasn't able to control it until he got what he wanted. I decided right then and there that I wasn't going to become a victim like Michelle. I would never give anyone that kind of power over me. I broke off our engagement the next day, changed my major in college, and tried not to look back."

"And he left you alone . . . just like that?" Tyler was still clearly agitated.

"Not exactly, but he finally got the point. He wanted a career in law enforcement, and when I threatened to press charges, he backed off."

"What were you talking to him about at the scene the other day?"

Mike thought back, realizing that Tyler had been more observant than she thought. "I asked how he was doing. Finding two bodies isn't the easiest thing on a person. I was just making sure he was okay." Tyler was silent, almost distant. "I don't have feelings for him, Tyler, if that's what you're thinking."

"Yeah, but does he still have feelings for you?" Tyler moved out onto the balcony and stared into a pitch black night.

"Tyler, our relationship ended years ago. I'm sure he's moved on."

Mike moved to where Tyler was standing. She wrapped her arms around his chest and pressed her body close to his. "This is why I hesitated to even say anything to you. I knew you would want to read more into it than was necessary. It happened a long time ago—a lifetime ago."

Tyler turned to Mike. Her eyes were searching him for some kind of affirmation that he understood her. He caressed her cheek with the back of his hand before wrapping her in an embrace that assured her that they were still on track.

HE WATCHED THEM UNDER THE COVER OF DARKNESS. He was angry that Mike was not listening to him, not taking his warnings seriously. His plan was not working. He left in a rage, knowing that he would have to do more to make his point.

JUST THEN, TYLER'S PHONE RANG.

"Henderson . . . Yes, this is Tyler Henderson . . . What? . . . Is she all right? . . . What hospital? . . . I'm on my way." Tyler snapped his phone closed as he moved towards the front door. The dogs jumped at his sudden movement and whimpered at the unnerving vibes in the room.

"Tyler, what is it? What's happened?"

"It's my sister. She's been in a car accident."

"Oh my gosh, Tyler, is she okay?"

"She's pretty banged up, but the doctor said she's going to be okay." Tyler pressed a number on his phone and then put it to his ear.

"Jim, this is Tyler. Look, I have to head to L.A. It's kind of an emergency, but I wanted to let you know that Mike was going to be by herself . . . That's right. I shouldn't be gone longer than a day, but I'll call if I get delayed . . . I'll talk to Frank. He can keep an eye on things . . . Are you sure? . . . I mean . . . is he . . . competent? Okay . . . Give him my number and have him call me if anything suspicious happens around here, okay? I'll check back with you when I get back in town." Tyler clicked his phone closed a second time.

"I can call my dad," said Mike.

"Yeah, well, I think I'll do it. I don't want anything to get lost in the translation." Tyler put both of his hands to Mike's forearms and squared her shoulders so that she was looking directly at him. "You have to promise me that you'll call me if even the slightest thing seems out of place or if something doesn't feel right, okay? I'm not going to be able to concentrate on Hailey if I think you're trying to be wonder woman."

Mike wanted to debate what she knew she could handle, but she knew this wasn't the time. She just smiled and agreed.

Tyler pulled her tight and whispered in her ear. "I love you, Mike. Please be careful."

He had said it again. He was in love with her, even with the differences that dotted their lives. Mike held onto him, trying to convey to him without words how she felt. She would not pledge her love to him without knowing she could satisfy every part that was Tyler Henderson. She would have to research her feelings, dig deep down, and see if she still had a love for God that she once knew as a child. Or find out if that love and trust were gone forever.

"I'll call you as soon as I see Hailey."

"Okay. Drive carefully. Concentrate. Don't let this distract your driving."

They shared one more kiss before Tyler left. Mike shut the door, locked it, set the alarm, and stared into the quiet that surrounded her. She would use her time alone to sort out her feelings.

Tyler charged up the driveway, not even seeing Arnie by the kennels. Arnie stepped back into the shrubs so that he wouldn't be caught in Tyler's headlights. He looked back at Mike's place, realizing she was alone. He would make sure she was safe—safe from people like Tyler Henderson.

CHAPTER THIRTEEN

W hen Tyler arrived at South Bay Hospital, he was escorted to Hailey's room. The doctor told him most of her injuries were minor cuts from the shattered windshield, but seeing Hailey bandaged and lying in a hospital bed was difficult just the same.

She heard him shuffle into the room and opened her eyes. She wore a look of embarrassment. "I'm sorry, Tyler. I shouldn't have let them call you. It's just that I was so afraid."

She looked like a little girl again, fragile and without her savvy attitude. "Hey, that's what big brothers are for." He moved to her side with a smile. "Are you okay?"

"Yeah."

"Anyone else hurt?"

"Justin. They had to pry him from the car. He's in surgery right now."

Tyler took Hailey's hand in his, and in a calm voice asked for an explanation. "I promise not to get mad or even give you a lecture . . . yet. I just want to know what happened."

"We'd been to a party. Justin shouldn't have been driving." Hailey closed her eyes and relived what had happened. "He was speeding and went through a red light. When other cars started honking, he freaked out and lost control of the car. We slammed into the signal pole."

"No one else was with you guys?"

"No, it was just the two of us."

"Had you two been dating?"

Hailey shrugged her shoulders and turned away. Tyler was ready to fire away when he caught himself. He promised no reprimands at the moment. He would let her off for now, but would get to the bottom of this when Hailey could handle a good old-fashioned browbeating.

"Well, the important thing is that you're okay. We can deal with the other issues later."

Hailey was both surprised and relieved that Tyler wasn't going to interrogate her on the spot.

MIKE WAS UPSTAIRS WHEN THE DOGS WENT running for the front door. Their barking subsided quickly. They had heard something, but obviously nothing had given them the sense of danger. Before she got to the bottom landing of the stairs, she saw Arnie standing in her entryway. His presence startled her.

"Arnie, how did you get in?"

"It was unlocked," Arnie said, unable to make eye contact with her.

Instantly, Mike was angered. "It was too locked. I locked it myself and set the alarm."

Arnie started rubbing his hands and rocking back and forth. He knew he shouldn't have walked in. Now she was mad at him. All he wanted to do was protect her. "I saw Tyler leave in a hurry. I thought that maybe something was wrong. Is there anything wrong? I mean . . . he didn't hurt you or anything?"

His statement distracted her momentarily. "No, why would Tyler want to hurt me?" She hadn't realized that Arnie had been watching them. She wasn't sure if she should feel concern or relief.

"Frank told me some creep was giving you a hard time. It makes me angry when I think of someone hurting you, Mike. When I saw Tyler leave, he seemed angry. Are you sure you're okay?"

"I'm fine, Arnie. Tyler would never hurt me," she said with a heartfelt smile.

"Okay, but if anyone does . . . you know . . . anyone, you just let me know."

Mike knew that Arnie had a simple mind and a big heart. Somehow, he had misunderstood her relationship with Tyler.

"You just tell me if you need any help, Mike. I'll help you whenever you need it. It makes me angry to think someone might be hurting you." Arnie was beginning to repeat himself. It was a nervous habit he had when he was upset.

"Well, I'm all right, Arnie. Everything's all right. I was just going to go to bed." Mike waited as Arnie opened the door and started to leave.

"Arnie, you never told me how you got into my house."

"Don't you remember, Mike? When we installed the alarms, you were afraid you would forget the codes, so we used the same code on all the doors to Frank's house, your house, and the kennels. Don't you remember?"

She thought back to when they had upgraded the security all around the property. Why hadn't she remembered that earlier?

"But we changed the locks. Where did you get a key?"

Again, Arnie looked embarrassed. "Frank has keys in the house. I used it. I just wanted to help."

Mike had given her dad a key and knew that he had probably hung it with all the rest in the house. She would make sure that her dad put the key away in the future.

"Good night, Mike. I hope you sleep better knowing that there's someone here to protect you." Arnie closed the door behind himself. Mike heard him reset the alarm from the outside. She knew that Arnie meant no harm. He was just trying to look out for her, but it bothered her that he seemed to have such a low opinion of Tyler.

Mike shook if off, made sure the house was secure, and climbed the stairs with Oreo and 'Nilla at her side. They jumped on the bed and made themselves comfortable. She laughed. She knew she would be pinned to the sheets again until morning. But she would wait until she heard from Tyler before calling it a night.

After taking a quick shower and dressing in her favorite baggy sweat-pants, she pulled a familiar book from the shelf on the wall. She crawled between the sheets just as the phone began to ring. She smiled, knowing it would be Tyler.

"Hello," she said with a smile in her tone.

The line was silent. Chills crept up her spine. She knew who it was. She slammed the phone down, staring at it as it began to ring again. She didn't want to answer it, but what if it was Tyler? If she didn't answer, he would panic.

"Hello?" This time her voice was cold and brittle.

"Hey, sorry about that. I dialed and then dropped my phone." Tyler's voice never sounded better. "Are you doing okay?"

Mike closed her eyes and allowed the tension in her shoulders to melt away. "I am now." Mike's racing heart began to calm down. Paranoia was beginning to get the better of her.

Tyler explained that the extent of Hailey's injuries were minor. They hadn't had much chance to talk, so he would probably be staying another day. "Are you going to be okay?"

"Of course, I am." Her words sounded more confident than she felt. "I have my two faithful companions pinning me to the bed as we speak."

"I wish I could be there." Tyler's voice was low and sultry.

"Mm hmm, then I guess it's a good thing that you're not because my resistance is awfully low right now." Mike knew the sexual tension was growing between them. They were adults and both desired the depths of an intimate relationship.

"Maybe this is something we need to talk about when I get back?"

"Maybe *I'll* give us something to talk about?" Mike said as she stared at the worn cover of her Bible as Tyler said his good-byes.

It had been a while since she had read it, but she knew it was time. It was time for her to have some open communication with God.

THE PHONE RANG EARLY THE NEXT MORNING. Mike rolled over to get it, and as anxious as she was to hear from Tyler, she wanted to have a little fun at his expense. "I know you said you would call in the morning, but did you have to make it so early?"

"Sorry, Mike, this is Jim. I guess you were expecting a call from Tyler." Mike sat straight up in bed, causing the dogs to jump. "We've got another body."

MIKE MADE IT TO THE SCENE IN RECORD TIME. Jim and Billings were there waiting for her. She stepped out of her truck and went to grab her gear. Jim met her at the tailgate.

"Who found her?"

"A jogger. She called it in. Billings was here within minutes."

"Did she see anything or anyone?" Mike asked as she pulled on her jumpsuit.

"No. She was hysterical so Jenny took her back to the station. We'll ask her some more questions when she calms down."

Mike reached for one of her bags while Billings approached them.

"Mike, there's something I need to tell you," Jim said.

Mike stopped what she was doing and looked to him for an explanation.

"The killer left a note for you."

"Again?"

"Yeah. It's addressed to you, personally."

Mike swallowed and took a deep breath. "This really is personal, isn't it?"

"Looks like it, Mike," Jim said as he rubbed the furrow of his brow. "Look, I can call Nathan."

"No! Like you said, this is personal."

Mike grabbed one of her bags. Billings picked up her black kit and led her to the victim. She was covered by a tarp and situated next to a shallow grave. Before Mike leaned down to undercover the victim, Billings stopped her.

"Mike, I'm sorry all this is happening to you. Maybe if you took a leave of absence or some time off this guy might give it a rest."

"I'm fine, Jason. I'm not going to let some psycho get to me."

"Well, if you need someplace to go, you know, just to get away from it all, I still have that houseboat my parents had on Shasta. We could take it out for a few days. Get far away from here and everyone else."

Mike was stunned. Jason was actually talking about them going away . . . together . . . after all these years. "Jason, I'm fine, really." She squatted down, uncovered the victim, and took a breath. She had a job to do, but her head was swimming with thoughts of failure and the idea that these deaths were her fault.

"So I see you finally got rid of your shadow?" Jason said smugly. He had lowered himself next to Mike and was watching her as she worked. Mike was zoned in on the victim and didn't even hear him. "Mike?"

"What?" She said in a monotone voice, clearly not paying attention to him.

"I asked you a question." He fought to keep his composure.

Mike turned and snapped at him. "What?"

"Henderson? Where is he?"

"What does that matter?"

Jason's presence was a distraction. It was as if he didn't even realize that they were hovering over the body of an innocent victim. "Look, Jason, you're blowing my concentration. Would you mind waiting over there?" She pointed to where Jim was standing.

Jason yanked at her arm to get her attention. She looked at his grip and then into his glaring eyes. "Look, Mike, you don't need to treat me like garbage. We used to mean something to each other, or have you forgotten that?"

"Jason, you're hurting me."

"Well, what goes around comes around." His look was menacing as he tightened his grip. "So, how's it feel? To be hurt by the one you love?"

"I don't love you, Jason. In fact, right now I can't even stand to look at you. You haven't changed a bit—you know that? Intimidation is not going to get you anywhere, except into more trouble."

"Why you little—"

"Is there a problem here?" Jim asked with a questioning look to Mike. Jason's raised voice had gotten his attention, and he didn't like the hold he had on Mike's arm.

"No problem, Jim. I was just asking Jason to wait over there so I could finish my investigation. Right, Jason?" She looked at Jason to make sure he got her point.

"Yeah. No problem." He let go of her arm. "I won't waste my time around here any longer. Mike's made it clear that she doesn't need me for anything." He stared at her with eyes that were cold and unemotional.

Billings got to his feet and left the two of them next to the body. Jim could see that Mike's hands were shaking as she gathered the evidence bags. Nathan showed up before she was done and noticed the tenseness in her demeanor.

"What is it, Mike? You look distressed."

"He's getting angry."

"Who?"

"The killer. Look at these marks here on her neck. He held his strangle-hold long after he snapped her neck. And here, this knife wound goes completely through the victim. He almost sawed her in half. Something's disturbing him, Nathan, and I have the feeling it's me."

"You?" Nathan was shocked.

145

"He left me a note. This is not about Michelle. This is about me."

Mike and Nathan bagged the body. Jim helped Nathan carry her to the van while Mike looked at the scene one more time. *What am I missing? Why would someone want to terrorize me?*

"Mike . . . you ready?" Nathan called to her.

She gathered her thoughts and walked up the hilly path.

"I'm going to go ahead." Nathan looked at her with concern. "Are you okay?"

"Yeah. I'll be right behind you."

Mike stepped from her coveralls and leaned on the tailgate of the truck. Jim stood by, worried about what he had witnessed.

"Are you going to tell me what went on between you and Billings?"

"It was nothing."

"Are you sure? It didn't look like nothing to me."

"Miscommunication, that's all."

Jim knew she was covering for him. His behavior had been far from professional. Jim knew they had a history together but had thought it was all in the past. Maybe he was wrong. Billings was headed for even bigger trouble if he didn't do something about his temper.

Jim turned his attention back to the case. "So what did the note say?"

"I don't know. I'll read it when I get to the lab. I didn't want to handle it before I had a chance to examine it."

"Okay. You know where to find me if you come up with anything." Jim started towards his own car.

"Jim?"

"Yeah?" He turned around.

"Don't say anything to Tyler about . . . you know . . . Jason. He has enough on his mind with the case and his sister's accident. He doesn't need anything else to stew about."

Jim thought about it for a moment and then answered. "Okay, I won't say anything to Tyler, but I'm going to speak to Billings."

"That's really not necessary, Jim. Nothing happened."

"Look, he still falls under my authority. What I saw was disrespectful and hedged on harassment. He's going to know that I won't put up with that. If it continues, he's going to be looking for employment elsewhere. This is something the review board will not take lightly."

Jim walked away before she could say anything. Letting out a deep breath, she braced herself for what she feared could be the end of Jason's career. He would not take disciplinary action lightly.

TYLER LISTENED AS THE DOCTOR EXPLAINED to Hailey the extent of Justin's injuries. He was lucky to be alive. Tyler was surprised by

Hailey's lack of emotion and realized that she was listening as if the doctor were talking about a stranger. He waited for the doctor to leave before questioning her.

"You barely knew him." His comment was more of a statement than a question.

"What?" Hailey asked, knowing full well her brother's intuition was right as usual.

"I watched you as the doctor explained to you this kid's injuries. How long had you known him before you jumped in the car with him? An hour, maybe two?"

Hailey recoiled under Tyler's accusation but blurted out the truth. "I'm sorry, okay? It was stupid of me, and now I'm paying for it. Isn't that enough for you?"

Tyler yelled, "I don't know, is it enough for you?"

Hailey burst into tears, making Tyler almost feel sorry for her. He waited for her to regain her composure before he said what was on his mind. "I want you to come live with me."

She wiped the tears from her face. "I can't do that, Tyler."

"Why?"

"Why ... because I have a job and an apartment and ..."

"And what? Friends that take you down and a lifestyle that's destructive? Come on Hailey, you're not going to be able to turn yourself around if you don't distance yourself from the things that are destroying you."

"Who says I want to turn myself around? I just need to be a little more careful next time."

"And you expect me to stand by and wait for a next time? I've already had to bury both Mom and Dad. Are you going to make me put you in a grave too? I can't take this anymore, Hailey. I can't live wondering when I'm going to get another call like the one I got last night. It's not fair, it's selfish." Tyler realized he was pacing around the room. He stopped in front of Hailey's bed, grabbed her hand, and finally allowed himself to let go of the tears that had fueled his anger. "I love you, Hailey. I can't lose you too."

Hailey couldn't control the sobbing that had risen inside her. Her brother meant so much to her, and for the first time she realized how much her behavior was hurting him. With what voice she could muster, she gave into the one request that Tyler had made of her numerous times before.

"So ... can I have my own bathroom, or do I have to share one with you?" she said with a conciliatory smile.

Hailey embraced Tyler and apologized for the self-destructive behavior she had allowed herself to sink into since her father's death. She knew she'd made a mess of her life and wasn't sure she could turn things around. But what she did know was she loved her brother very much and would do whatever she could to get her life back on track. She wanted to be someone who would make him proud.

Tyler thanked God for the small victory as his mind jumped quickly to the future. He couldn't wait to introduce Hailey to Mike, the woman with whom he was sure he would spend the rest of his life.

NATHAN FOUND MIKE STARING OFF INTO SPACE. She was exhausted, looking for answers. She read the note again, knowing it had to hold a clue.

Why won't you let me protect you? Why are you changing things now? I was satisfied looking out for you from a distance, but now you've changed everything. I want things to be the way they used to be.

"Mike, are you okay?"

She held the note in her hand and looked at Nathan. "This is about Tyler."

"What?"

"The note. He says he wants things the way they used to be."

"What does that mean?"

"Think about it, Nathan. This all started happening when Tyler and I started spending time together."

"So you think this guy is jealous?"

"No. I think he's deranged."

"CAN I HELP YOU?" Arnie asked as the uniformed officer stepped from his car.

"Is Frank here?"

"No. He's gone. I'm in charge," Arnie said with authority. "Can I help you?"

"Maybe you can. But this is important police business, and I have to have your full and complete cooperation."

"Of course, officer. My name is Arnie." They shook hands.

The officer continued in a firm voice. "We believe Michal Madigan could be in danger. I've been sent here to set up surveillance on her house."

Arnie wanted to help but wondered why Tyler or Jim wasn't handling this. He scrutinized the officer. Arnie had seen him before but couldn't quite remember where. "Why isn't Jim or Tyler here?"

The officer tensed at his question but quickly regained control. "I can't divulge that information at this time. But let me assure you that Mike Madigan is our primary concern at the moment."

Arnie felt important. He was being asked to do something to help Mike— something even Tyler wasn't doing.

"Do you have access to Ms. Madigan's home?"

"Yes," Arnie said as he pulled a single key from his pocket. "But she has an alarm on the house too."

"Do you know who might have access to that code?"

"Yes," Arnie said with downcast eyes. "I have it. I want to keep her safe. I watch her at night."

His plan was working better than he expected. He thought Arnie would be a hurdle to cross. Now he realized that he was going to prove to be quite helpful.

MIKE WAS DEEP IN THOUGHT. Nathan glanced at her when all of a sudden, Mike let out a gasp.

"What is it?"

Mike covered her mouth trying to control her emotions.

"You've thought of someone?"

"No. It's impossible." Mike couldn't believe she was even thinking it.

"What's impossible?" Nathan stepped in front of her, knowing her eyes would reveal what she was thinking. "Tell me, Mike. Remember you have to talk out all possibilities. That's a cornerstone of investigative deduction."

Mike hesitated before reasoning out loud. "Do you know Arnie?"

"Yeah. He helps your dad with the kennel."

"Well, something strange happened last night."

"Strange . . . strange how?"

"Tyler left in a hurry after receiving the phone call about his sister. When Arnie saw him rushing out, he assumed that something happened between us. He questioned me, asking me if I was okay." Mike paced the room, feeling more confused with each sentence. "He thought Tyler might have hurt me. He came to make sure I was all right and let me know that he would help me if I ever needed it." Mike looked at Nathan, waiting for some kind of response.

"This could be something, Mike."

"But how? Do you realize what I'm saying? There is no way that Arnie is capable of murder."

"How can you be so sure?"

"Come on, Nathan. Look at him. He's a grownup child."

"Yes, a child with the strength of an adult. A child without the reasoning power to help him control his anger."

"Nathan, I've known him for years. I've never seen him lose his temper. I've never witnessed him angry or violent. He works with the dogs day in and day out, and I've never seen him get even mildly frustrated with them."

"Just because you haven't witnessed it doesn't mean he doesn't have that capability. I think you need to tell Tyler about this. If anything, Arnie should be watched. If he's under some kind of surveillance and our murderer strikes again, then we'll know it's not him."

"And if word gets out and Arnie isn't involved, I've destroyed his trust and a valuable friendship. I can't take that chance." Mike left the lab and found solace in her office. The silence was short-lived. Nathan wasn't about to let their only possible lead go unchecked.

"Let me talk to Jim." Nathan's voice startled Mike. He continued when he knew he had her full attention. "I'll tell him our suspicions and that you want to keep this confidential."

"But Tyler's his partner. He's not going to keep this from him."

"And neither should you. Tyler cares about you, Mike. If there's the slightest chance that Arnie could be involved in all this, he needs to know."

Mike weighed her options. She really didn't see that she had much of a choice. This wasn't just about her. If she withheld what could be valuable information, another innocent girl could end up dead.

"Okay . . . talk to Jim. But explain to him the sensitivity of this matter. I'm putting a friendship on the line here. I don't want it jeopardized due to speculation."

"Got it." Nathan left quickly, relieved that Mike was finally taking action.

Mike knew she should have told Nathan that Arnie also had let himself into the house, but she didn't. She knew if Tyler or Jim found out that Arnie had the code to her alarm, they would bring him in for sure. No, she would wait and see what Jim had to say.

JIM WAS GETTING MORE PERTURBED BY THE MINUTE. Jason had not radioed in for hours. He was treading a thin line. Jim was tired of his slip-ups and his lack of respect. Peering through the open blinds, Jim finally saw Jason pull into the parking lot. He met him at the front door.

Jim barked, "My office. Now!" Jason had no choice but to follow. "Shut the door."

The agitation in Jim's voice left little imagination to what was about to take place. Jason stiffened his resolve and took a seat across from Jim's desk, knowing he wouldn't have to put up with this much longer.

Jim lit into him for half an hour. He told him in no uncertain terms that he wished he was out of his station. He was tired of the tension that Jason brought to a room, especially where Tyler was involved. Jim would be reporting the incident between him and Mike to the disciplinary review board and if asked, he would recommend a suspension from duties.

Jason listened to everything without saying a word.

"Don't you have anything to say for yourself, Billings?"

"Would it matter it I did?" he said with a smugness that almost sent Jim across the desk to take care of the disciplinary actions himself.

"I'm reassigning you to desk duty until your review can be arranged. I suggest you make as little waves as possible until then." Jim flung his hand in the direction of the door, letting Jason know he was being dismissed.

Jason had to control every muscle in his body to keep himself from slamming Jim's door and storming out of the office for good. He plopped down into a desk chair and wondered why he was still there. It was apparent his days were numbered. He might as well leave.

He stood and started walking towards the door when the phone rang. No one else was around, and he knew Jim wouldn't answer it in the mood he was in, so he grabbed up the phone himself.

"Yes, this is Nathan Armstrong with the coroner's office. Can I speak to Detective Thompson, please? It's important."

There was a shuffling of phones before a muffled voice came over the line. "Thompson."

"Jim . . . is that you?" Nathan could barely understand him.

"Yeah. I got some kind of head cold. It's doing a number on my throat. What can I do for you, Nathan?"

"I'm calling for Mike. She has a situation that she thinks you should know about." Nathan went on to explain Mike and Arnie's strange exchange. His words were met with verbal nods throughout the conversation but very little discussion. When Nathan was done, he explained how hesitant Mike had been to say anything. "This has to be handled with extreme care, Jim. Arnie is a family friend, and Mike doesn't want to do anything to hurt him or cause him to distrust her."

"I understand completely," came the answer through harsh and repeated coughs. "Look, Nathan, tell you what, I'm going to do some investigating of my own. I understand Mike's apprehension, and I want to make sure this doesn't get blown out of proportion. In fact, I think we'll keep this just between us for now. I'm not going to say anything to Tyler. He might overreact because of Arnie's closeness with Mike. I'm afraid he's losing his objectivity where this case is concerned. I don't blame him, but I want to use caution wherever possible." Nathan heard more hacking and sputtering. "I'll get back to you when I find something out. In the meantime, keep this under your hat. The department has a way of leaking this kind of thing, and I would hate for Arnie to get hurt if we're barking up the wrong tree." He cleared his throat. "I'll be in touch."

Nathan hung up the phone. He stared at the receiver wondering why he still felt apprehensive. He figured it had to do with the personal matter of the case. His job rarely hit so close to home. He made his way back to Mike's office and filled her in on his conversation with Jim. He assured her that Jim understood and let her know that Jim agreed not to say anything to Tyler right away. "I told you he would understand."

Mike smiled politely and realized the situation was now out of her hands. Hopefully, she was completely wrong and Arnie's actions would prove him to be a friend, not a murderer.

"WHO WAS ON THE PHONE?" Jenny returned from the break room just as Jason was hanging up.

"Some nut," he said. "You know, someone thinking they saw strange lights over the lake. I told him we would check it out and thanked him for his concern." Billings smiled as Jenny made her way to her own desk. He couldn't believe he had been able to acquire such key information.

So, Mike suspected Arnie. Good, then she won't be apprehensive to meet with me . . . well, maybe.

Jason knew that Tyler was going to be out of town for another day. This was his opportunity to meet with Mike without interruption.

As he left the station, probably for the last time, he headed for home to take care of some last-minute details before he went to see Mike.

THE REST OF MIKE'S DAY WAS DISRUPTED BY her conscience nagging at her. *How could she have implicated Arnie in the serial murders that were now haunting Emerald Lake? How would she be able to explain to him or her dad if they were to find out about Nathan's conversation with Jim?*

She tried to put it out of her mind before she headed for home. Nathan was coming down the hall as she left her office. "Okay, Nathan. I'm out of here."

"Wait a second, Mike. I might have found something." Nathan had been going over some of the trace evidence from the Elizabeth Jordan case. He was making fiber comparisons with the most recent victim.

Mike followed him back to the lab and to the microscope that held the evidence slides. "Tell me what you see," Nathan said.

Mike hunched over the scope and studied the slides side by side. She shot a look at Nathan. "Now look at this," Nathan said as he changed the slides and again moved out of the way so Mike could study them.

"They match?"

"Yep. A fiber and a hair fragment that were found on two of the victims match."

"So they must belong to the killer," Mike said with renewed enthusiasm. "What do you make of the fibers?"

"It's synthetic wool. My bet is it came from the lining of a jacket or a blanket."

Mike's smile quickly diminished. "Now all we have to do is wait for that jacket or blanket to walk into the lab, and we'll have our killer. Just like that."

Mike knew her sarcasm was uncalled for. Nathan had found an incredible clue and she should be ecstatic, but her exhaustion and her accusations towards Arnie had made her a little edgy. "I'm sorry, Nathan. That was out of line. This is great work. I'm just a little bent out of shape. This Arnie thing really has me bothered."

"That's understandable, Mike." Nathan put his hands to Mike's shoulders and gave them a quick massage. "Look, go home, get some rest, and then maybe tomorrow we'll have something more to work with."

Mike headed to her truck, disappointed with herself. She should have made the connection. She should have been the one to make the match. Her personal involvement in this case was impairing her work. Nathan had found a valuable clue while she was in her office sulking. She knew she had to distance herself from the cases, but how? This was a critical issue, especially since she could be the next victim.

WHEN MIKE REACHED HOME, ARNIE'S CAR WAS in the driveway. *Why should that bother me?* she wondered. She slowly got out of the truck and saw Arnie approaching her from the kennels.

"Hi, Mike," Arnie said in his usual shy manner.

"Hi, Arnie."

"Frank's gone."

"Yes, I know," she said as she moved across the driveway.

"That's why I'm here—to take care of the dogs," he said with a smile.

"I'm glad, Arnie."

Arnie's look brightened. "You are? You're glad I'm here?"

"Well, yes," she said as she continued towards her house. "I know how much it means to Dad that you watch the dogs."

"And I watch you."

Mike stopped and turned to Arnie. She couldn't believe he had just admitted to watching her. "You what?"

"I told Frank that I would watch you. I won't let anyone hurt you, Mike."

Mike hurried into the house. She locked the door and set the alarm, but realized it wouldn't stop Arnie from entering. She felt her heart racing and her mind whirling. Arnie had just admitted to her that he was watching her and again made the point that he felt he had to protect her. *Why would he feel the need to protect me unless he knew I was in danger?*

Mike thought about calling Tyler. She needed to talk to someone, but she knew that wouldn't be fair to him. She was overreacting. Everything would be fine. Arnie was not a killer. It wasn't possible.

She dragged herself upstairs and got everything ready for a hot bath. She had undressed and had wrapped a towel around her as she put her hair up in a clip on top of her head. She released the towel and stepped into the tub, but then stopped. She stepped back onto the cold tile and grabbed up her towel. She walked leisurely to her bedside table and pulled out the revolver that she kept there. Her eye caught the Bible that lay on the tabletop, and she said a little prayer.

She'd had a long conversation with God the night before, and though she still held resentment towards him for Michelle's death, she felt as if their line of communication had been restored. She would now try to draw on the comfort that it could bring.

She walked back into the bathroom, dropped the towel once again, but this time she laid the weapon within hands reach. Now she was able to sink into the steaming water and try to let some of the day's troubles wash off of her.

TYLER HELPED HAILEY WITH HER SUITCASES while she looked at the house.

"I thought you said you bought a cabin. This place is huge."

"Does that mean you approve?"

"I'll withhold my comments until I see my own accommodations." Hailey was only teasing Tyler. She was nervous and trying to deal with the idea of leaving everyone and everything she knew behind and moving in with her brother.

He unlocked the door and pushed it open for Hailey. She was in awe. His little cabin in the woods turned out to be a lakefront retreat. It was warm and inviting, filled with character and style.

"Tyler, this is incredible."

"I'm glad you like it. I would hate to think you had to lower your standards to move in with me."

Skyler ran up to Tyler and Hailey, excited to see his master safely home. Skyler demonstrated his obedience by not jumping on Hailey—that is, until she lowered herself to his level and showed him some affection of her own.

"He's beautiful, Tyler, but I thought you told me you were going to get a girl. You know, a woman that you could demand obedience from." Hailey chuckled as she scratched Skyler's head and played with his ears.

Tyler smiled seeing Hailey laugh and look relaxed. She needed this more than she was willing to admit. "Skyler kind of grew on me; besides, I decided to look for female companionship elsewhere." Hailey continued to stroke Skyler while Tyler reached for her suitcases. "I'll take your stuff upstairs, but you can take your time and look around."

She did just that. Hailey wandered around Tyler's home, running her hands over countertops and caressing moldings. The expansive sliding windows at the back of the house looked out over the shimmering lake. She stepped out onto the deck and inhaled the fresh air that swirled amongst the trees.

"Don't breathe too deeply; your lungs aren't ready for pure oxygen. They'll wonder what happened to all that black stuff they're used to inhaling," he teased.

"It's beautiful, Tyler," she whispered, afraid to break the silence.

"I know. That's what I've been telling you." He moved to the hammock and sat in its web, but he was far from relaxed.

Hailey glanced at Tyler and saw his faraway look. "Go ahead and call her, Tyler. I know you're dying to."

"No. I want to spend this time with you," he said with a sincere smile.

She laughed out loud. "You are so full of bull. You know it's killing you not to talk to her."

Tyler couldn't contain his feelings. "Is it that obvious?"

"That you're in love? Yes. It's written all over your face." Hailey sat down next to him with ease. "So where do you go from here?"

"You mean with Mike?"

"No. I mean with your dog, stupid. Of course, I mean with her," Hailey said with a good-natured shove to his arm. "Does she feel the same way about you?"

"Yes and no. I mean I know how she feels about me, but I don't think she's willing to admit it to herself yet. She's had a difficult life and because of it, she's become very self-sufficient. I don't know that she's ready to give up that independence."

"Who says she can't still be independent and have a man in her life at the same time?"

"I was talking more about her relationship with God."

"Oh, so she's one of those. Somehow I got the impression from you that she was more of the rebel type."

"What do you mean, 'one of those'?"

"You know ... conservative ... like you."

Tyler laughed. "She's far from conservative." Tyler's mind wandered to some of their more intimate moments together. "She's running from God, Hailey. Just like you. And once the both of you realize God's plan for your lives is far better than anything you could accomplish, the better off you'll be."

"Hey, since when were we talking about me?"

"Just an observation," Tyler said as he hugged his sister to his side. "You know, you remind me a lot of Mike."

"Then I guess I'll have to meet this woman so I'll know if that's a

155

compliment or not—but not tonight. You can go see her if you'd like, but I just want to take a nice long bath, unpack my stuff, and crash."

Tyler gave her a twisted look.

"That was a bad choice of words, but you know what I mean."

Hailey slowly moved up to what would be her bedroom. Her limbs were still stiff from her injuries.

Her room was huge with a window seat that overlooked the lake. She moved into the bathroom and smiled at the distinct touches that Tyler had added to the decor.

"So, does it pass?" Tyler was leaning in the doorway as she walked from the bathroom.

"I don't get it. You had no idea that I would say yes to staying with you. How is it that this room is completely decorated in my favorite colors and style?"

"It's been this way since I moved in," Tyler said. "I was praying that you would eventually come here and hoped that you would like it well enough to stay."

Hailey wrapped her arms around her brother and cried. The emotions that she was usually so good at hiding were stronger than she was at the moment.

"Hey, no need for the waterworks," Tyler said as he looked into her glistening eyes. "I just wanted you to feel at home here."

"Well, I do, Tyler," she said, wiping her eyes. "I don't deserve you, you know. For all the junk I've put you through, you should have washed your hands of me a long time ago."

"Hey, we're family. That's not what family does." Tyler pushed Hailey's hair back from her face and rested his hands on her shoulders. "Why don't you go ahead and take that bath. I'll start working on dinner."

Tyler left Hailey in her room and headed for the kitchen. He quickly pulled his phone from his pocket and dialed Mike.

The ringing phone made Mike jump. Her nerves were frayed, and her bath was doing little to soothe her. She grabbed the towel from the floor and quickly wrapped it around her. By the third ring, she was able to answer the phone. "Hello?"

"Hey, what's wrong?" Tyler was instantly concerned.

"Tyler." The relief in her voice could be heard through the phone lines.

"What is it, Mike?"

"Nothing, now." She relaxed on the side of the bed.

"Are you sure? You sounded pretty stressed."

"It's nothing. I'm just missing you." Mike would wait and tell Tyler about her suspicions when she could explain herself in person. "Where are you?"

"Home."

"Home? I thought you were going to spend another day in L.A.?"

"We were going to, but if I was going to convince Hailey to come home with me, I needed to get her out of there as soon as possible. I didn't want to give her a chance to talk to her friends or get too comfortable."

"So, she's with you?" Mike sounded hesitant. "She agreed to leave?"

"Yeah." Tyler could detect an edge in Mike's voice. "You're okay with her being here, right?"

"Sure," she said, not sounding too convincing. "I guess I'm just a little nervous to meet her."

"Why? You two will get along just fine. You're both opinionated, obstinate, and headstrong."

"Hey. Is this the only reason you called, to give me a hard time?"

"No. That's just a perk." He laughed.

"When do I get to see you?" Mike was anxious to feel the strength of Tyler's arms around her and feel the protection he was so willing to provide. "I have a few things I want to talk with you about."

"About the case? Has there been a break?" Tyler stopped what he was doing in the kitchen and gave her his full attention.

"Actually, I wanted to talk about something else with you, but it can wait. I'd rather talk to you in person."

"You know I'd love to come over. I just feel I need to make sure Hailey's comfortable first." Tyler sounded torn.

"No, Tyler. I totally understand. You need to be with her right now. I'll just have to get used to sharing you," she joked. "Can I see you tomorrow?"

"Absolutely."

THE LINE WENT DEAD. *So, does Tyler have himself another girl? Mike doesn't seem that upset by it,* Jason pondered to himself. *That leaves Mike available for me.* The tracing device he had installed in her phone proved to be a valuable tool. He stretched in his car as a smile crept across his face. Maybe a little house call was in order. Especially since he knew Tyler was busy with another woman.

MIKE GOT DRESSED IN HER BAGGY SWEATS and spaghetti-strapped tank and wandered around her house, unable to relax. Even after talking with Tyler, she still felt uneasy. She toyed with the idea of calling him back to ask if he could stop by for just a few minutes. As she was reaching for the phone, there was a knock on the door. Sure that it was Tyler, she smiled to herself. He was missing her as much as she was missing him.

Without even thinking, she unlatched the door and deactivated the alarm. Anxious to see Tyler's face, she swung the door open and was shocked to see Jason standing there.

"Jason! What are you doing here?" she said as she hung onto the frame of the door, pulling it close to her.

"Jim sent me," he said as he stepped around her and into the house. He stood with his hands on his hips, pushing back his heavy jacket from his waist. He allowed his eyes to travel the length of the room. He was remembering the time he spent in the place. Of course, back then, it was a run-down work barn. "You've really fixed the place up, Mike."

"Why would Jim send you here?" she said, ignoring his comment.

"Surveillance," Jason said as he made himself comfortable on the couch.

She thought back to earlier that day and the conversation she had with Jim. He was angry with Jason and ready to sideline him. Why would Jim send Jason to carry out surveillance? Mike knew something wasn't right.

She stepped outside and whistled for the dogs.

"I asked Arnie to take care of the dogs," Jason said as he glanced in her direction. "I figured it would give him something to do."

Mike wasn't sure what was going on, but she was ticked. She marched to where Jason was stretched out and pointed to the door.

"Get out. Get out right now, or I'll call Tyler."

"Fine. Then you can explain to him why I'm here and why you suspect Arnie but didn't want to tell him. I'm sure he'll be thrilled to know that you didn't trust him with those details."

"Jim told you?" Mike dropped into the chair, stunned that Jim would have told Jason—of all people.

"Yep. I'm sure I wasn't his first choice, but since you wanted to keep it such a secret, he had to use someone that wouldn't look suspicious spending time at your house. After all, Mike, we used to hang out here a lot. Or have you forgotten?"

Mike didn't know whom she was more upset with: herself for letting Nathan talk to Jim, Jim for recruiting Jason, or Jason for taking advantage of the situation.

Mike's head was spinning. She certainly didn't want to sit there and listen to Jason lecture her about honesty, but what could she do? It would be unfair to call Tyler and spring all of this on him over the phone. He had to be concerned with Hailey. He shouldn't have to deal with issues regarding Jason and her past.

She walked to the French doors and pushed them open. Stepping out onto the deck, she lay down on a chaise lounge and tried to get herself to calm down. Her mind was playing a movie reel from her past. Flashes of Michelle, Jason, her mother, and the funeral all jumped from her subconscious. Then, as if changing gears, the movie played pictures of the victims that had died because of her. Why was it that the killer had chosen her to shoulder the blame for the killings? Why was he targeting other women to get to her? Why didn't he just come after her himself? The most terrifying part was she knew it was just a game to the killer. Those girls died because they were in the wrong place at the wrong time. When would it be her turn? When would he finally be able to get to her when nobody could stop him?

"You know, you shouldn't be out here by yourself."

She jumped at Jason's voice. He grinned at her, glad that he had startled her.

"You did that on purpose."

"Of course, I did. I wanted to show you how careless you are. Some madman is after you, and you're out on a patio, completely in the open. It's a good thing I'm here to protect you. There's no telling what could happen to you . . . if you don't pay attention."

She gritted her teeth, not wanting to give Jason the satisfaction of seeing her angry. "I thought you were supposed to be keeping your eye on Arnie?"

"Why? The view from here is so much nicer." His eyes traveled over Mike's body and back to her eyes. "Besides, if he tries anything, I'll be right here." He stared at Mike—a deep, penetrating stare. Mike felt as if he were undressing her with his eyes.

She couldn't take it any longer so she got up from where she was sitting and moved inside. She reached for the phone and began to dial—that is, until she realized there was no dial tone. She rattled the phone and then watched as Jason closed the French doors and locked them. He moved across the room and took the phone from her hand and gently laid it back in the cradle. His eyes were filled with anger.

"Why wasn't I good enough for you, Mike? I've waited patiently for you all these years, thinking you would change your mind about us." His words sent shivers up her spine. She slowly backed away from him, but his steps matched hers until she was standing pinned against the wall.

"You see, I thought you would come around, realize that we were meant to be together, and then Tyler showed up and ruined everything."

Mike's mind was in overdrive. She had just told Nathan that the killer was getting angry, and that she felt that Tyler was the cause of it. She quickly turned her eyes down. She didn't want Jason to see her discovery register in her eyes. The pieces of the puzzle were fitting together in her head. *The note said, "He wanted things the way they used to be." The killer felt the wrong person had paid for Michelle's death. Did Jason think he had paid for Michelle's death because of their breakup?* Her mind replayed snapshots of the crime scenes. Jason had been the one responsible for either finding the bodies or being the first one on the scene. *Was that because he was the one who had dumped the bodies? Would he lie in wait until someone stumbled across the victims and then show up as the officer on duty? The murderer was left-handed, just like Jason.*

159

Then she thought about the way Jason had erupted at her the other day when she ignored his offer of a weekend away. *Was he feeling jilted all over again?* Surely, he had to know that she had feelings for Tyler and anything she had felt for him had died years before.

Mike chided herself for trying to judge Jason with the characteristics of a rational person. If he were the killer, he was obviously irrational and capable of gruesome behavior. Her downward look caught the bandage on his right hand. *Could that be where Elizabeth Jordan had been able to bite him?* She felt as though the answers were coming together in a matter of seconds. *I have to get out of here, but how?*

All her thoughts had passed through her mind in an instant. When she met Jason's eyes, she tried to hide her terror and her realization that he was responsible for the murders. She would have to lead him to believe she didn't suspect. It was her only chance of survival.

CHAPTER FOURTEEN

J im pored over the file again and again. What was he missing? The murders had to be connected by a common thread. He studied photo after photo of the crime scenes of the unsolved murders. The only reoccurring constant was Billings at every scene. Jim didn't acknowledge this as evidence. Billings' beat was the lakefront. Of course, he would be the first one on the scene since all the bodies were dumped around the lake.

The phone rang just then and pulled Jim from his concentration.

"Jim, it's Nathan."

"Hey, Nathan. What's up?"

"I just thought of something. I can't believe it didn't come to me sooner."

"What's that?" Jim said giving Nathan only half his attention.

"I know how we can eliminate Arnie as a suspect without Mike jeopardizing their friendship."

"Arnie? Who said anything about Arnie being a suspect?" Jim was puzzled. How Nathan how gotten misinformed was beyond him.

"Jim ... our conversation ... Mike's uneasiness ..."

"What are you talking about, Nathan? You never told me that Mike felt uneasy about him." Jim was getting irritated and so was Nathan.

"Jim, I called you and told you in confidence that Mike was beginning to suspect Arnie. Are you telling me you don't remember any of that?"

Jim slammed his fist on his desktop with frustration. "What the heck are you talking about, Nathan?"

Nathan was beginning to panic. He had told someone he thought was Jim about Mike's suspicions. "I talked to someone earlier today. I thought it was you. I told him—"

"Why did you think it was me?" Jim interrupted.

"Because the person who answered the phone supposedly transferred it to you. I didn't think it sounded like you, but the person on the line said it was just a cold that was distorting his voice."

Jim was ready to start cracking skulls in his own station. He didn't know what was going on, but he would get to the bottom of it as soon as he found out what Nathan had to say. "Okay, Nathan. I'll figure out what happened here, but clue me in on why Mike suspects Arnie."

Nathan told Jim of the uneasy conversation that Mike had with Arnie. He told him she was reluctant to think that Arnie could be so violent, but that she had to admit that his dislike for Tyler and his self-imposed need to protect her were a little unsettling. He told Jim how the timing of the murders started right after she and Tyler started seeing each other. She felt that was a key. One of the notes said that the killer wanted things the way they used to be. Mike felt that meant before Tyler was in the picture.

Nathan went on to explain that the matched hairs and fibers they had found on both the first and the last victim had to belong to the killer. If they could get a strand of Arnie's hair, they could analyze it and hopefully eliminate him as a suspect.

"Where's Mike now?" Jim asked.

"Home, I guess. She left a little while ago."

"Okay, Nathan. I'll see what we can do about getting that sample. Thanks for the heads-up."

"What about—"

"I'll take care of it, Nathan. Someone has a lot of explaining to do. What time did you say that you called? Okay, thanks. I'll get back to you."

Jim immediately went to the schedule board to see who would have been at the station during that time. There were only three people: Jenny, who, of course, could never disguise her obviously feminine voice for Jim's low growl, Officer Tran, whose Asian dialectic could never come close to his, and Jason Billings. The hairs on Jim's neck rose several inches. *Why would Jason try to impersonate him?* Again, Jim thought about the crime scenes and the constant that appeared in all of them—Jason Billings.

Jim went back to his office and closed the door. He sunk into the confines of his chair, his mind spinning and his stomach turning. *Was Jason capable of such crimes?* Jim started reviewing the evidence with Jason as a suspect. He definitely had personal ties to Mike. They had been engaged to be married before Michelle's death. Though he was known for his temper, he had become even more agitated after Tyler arrived. Jim had attributed Jason's anger to being passed over for the detective's position. Was it actually because of Tyler's involvement with Mike? He thought back to the scene just earlier today. Jason was angry with Mike. She had not given him the attention he wanted. He had been so upset that he wasn't even able to mask his rage. He had grabbed her. She brushed it off as nothing, but now Jim wasn't so sure. Jim was out of his chair and pacing when it hit him. *The shallow grave!* It was the only part of the evidence withheld from the public all these years. Jason had access to the files. He would've known about the shallow grave. Jim was now convinced they had a copycat, and the copycat was Jason.

Jim rushed from his office to look for Jason. "Anyone see Billings?" Jim asked.

Jenny sat behind a computer and mumbled something about lights over the lake. "He wrote it off as a nut case but decided to check it out anyway. I figured he thought it was the perfect excuse to get some air after your little chewing out."

Jim didn't bother explaining to Jenny that he had assigned Jason to a desk. If his hunch were right, none of it would matter. Jim knew he needed to call Tyler, but he had to find Jason first. Jim dialed Mike's number ... busy.

Well, at least he knew she was home. He would try again in a few minutes. Now, he had to get to Tyler's and explain to him what he suspected.

"WHAT ARE YOU THINKING, MIKE?" Jason asked, standing dangerously close to her. He sensed she was beginning to put the pieces together.

"I don't know." Mike tried to sound perplexed. "It's just ..."

"Just what?" Jason's voiced raised an octave.

"It's just that I'm feeling a little confused right now." Mike tried to move away from Jason, but he raised his hand above her shoulder and held it against the wall.

"What are you confused about, Mike? You're a smart girl. I thought you would have figured this out by now." Jason was sure he had seen a switch go off in her eyes. He assumed she had finally pieced the puzzle together.

"I'm confused about . . . us." She looked at him, deep inside him. She wanted him to believe that she was having feelings for him once again. She didn't know if she could pull it off, but her only chance to get out of this alive was for him to think his plan had worked.

"Us?" Jason asked dumfounded.

"Yes. Us. You see, Jason, I've been thinking about you all day, ever since we got upset with each other at the crime scene. I saw how much you truly care for me after all these years. As much as I wanted to deny my feelings for you . . . for what we once had . . . I can't. They've been stirring in me all day. As much as I've tried to fight it, I still have feelings for you."

She tried to look convincing, although inwardly she felt like she was in a box that was shrinking. She felt herself suffocating with Jason's nearness, and she was terrified that he wouldn't believe her.

Jason stared at her with no expression on his face. His heart was telling him to believe her, but his mind was telling him it was a trick. Mike saw that he was wavering. She had to do something more to convince him.

She reached for Jason's hand and brought it to her lips. She kissed his hand and held it to her cheek. "Jason. I want us to start over."

"You mean it? Just like that, you're willing to dump Tyler and let us get back to where we were?"

"Not where we were, Jason. I want us to start over, from the start. I think we should take it slow."

He leaned closer to Mike. She knew he was going to kiss her. Her stomach was ready to retch, but she had to make him believe she was for real. He pressed his lips to hers, gently at first. Then his kiss became more searching, more urgent. He pressed himself up against her, wanting to feel what he had been missing all these years. Mike placed her hands on his shoulders and gently pushed him away as she whispered, "Not like this, Jason. I want us to take our time."

"I've waited long enough, Mike. I want you now." He pulled her close to him, kissing her as his hand traveled the length of her side. Tears fell from Mike's eyes. She didn't know what she could do. If she let him continue, he wouldn't stop until he had what he wanted; but if she stopped him, would he turn violent?

"Jason, please . . . please stop . . . for a moment."

He pulled back and saw the tears in her eyes. "Mike, what is it, why are you crying? Isn't this what you wanted?"

"No, Jason. This is not what I wanted." She took the opportunity to move away from him and sat down on the couch. She took a deep breath and tried to control her shaking.

He hovered over her. "Why did you lie to me? Why did you tease me if this isn't what you wanted?"

Mike did everything in her power to look like a fragile female. "I said I wanted to start over, Jason. Don't you remember . . . when we first dated, we went to the lake and took long walks? We picnicked and cuddled by an open fire. We fell in love with each other. That's what I want. I want to fall in love with you all over again."

He sat beside her and turned her chin so he could look into her eyes. "But we were kids then. We're adults now. I want to make love to you, Mike."

"But don't you want me to be in love with you first, Jason? Otherwise, it's just sex. If sex is what you want, you could get that from any woman in town. I thought I was different. I thought you wanted to love me." Mike hung her head and tried to look dejected.

Jason paused for a moment, confused. He wanted to believe Mike was telling him the truth about still wanting him after all these years, but her resistance was aggravating him. He laced his fingers together and rested them on his head. He walked across the floor and stood in front of the French doors.

Mike allowed her eyes to rise up just enough to see Jason standing at a distance. He was rocking and muttering to himself. He was ready to snap. She turned to the front door, knowing she hadn't locked it or secured the alarm. All she would have to do is make it to the door. She knew she wouldn't be able to outrun Jason, but as long as she could get help from Arnie and the dogs, she would have a good chance at getting into her dad's house to get the gun that he kept in his bedside table.

Before she was able to move, Jason crossed the room and pulled Mike up to her feet. "You're all I want, Mike. Just you and me." His embrace was stifling. Mike tried to put some space between her and Jason, but he pressed himself against her even closer. She was struggling to get away. She could no longer pretend to have feelings for him. Finally, she used a maneuver she had learned in self-defense. One quick blow and she was able to drop Jason to his knees.

She bolted for the door. Jason lunged at her, catching her foot. She kicked him in the face and broke free from his hold. She struggled with the door and quickly ran up the path to the driveway. She heard Jason behind her and turned to see him closing the distance between them. She hurried around the side of the kennels but tripped and fell over something in her path. When she tried to regain her footing, she found herself face to face with Arnie. He was dead. She screamed for the dogs as Jason quickly approached her. She tried to get her feet underneath her but stumbled. Jason now stood over her, hovering with a look of satisfaction.

"That wasn't a very smart thing to do, Mike. Oh . . . and I wouldn't expect the dogs to help you either. They've been disposed of."

Mike's mind was whirling. Arnie was dead. Oreo and 'Nilla were too. She couldn't move. She just stared at Jason and realized the monster he had become.

He pulled her to her feet and led her back to the house. She lost her footing a few times, her legs unable to hold her because of the way Jason was dragging her across the uneven ground. When they made it to the house, she tried again to break free. Jason held her from behind as she flung her arms in every direction and reached back to pull at his hair.

Finally, Jason had enough. He jerked her head back against his chest and put his lips to her ear. "I could end it right now, Mike. Just as I did all the others. Just one yank of my arm, and your neck would snap like a toothpick. The others didn't have a choice, Mike, but you do. What's it going to be?"

Her body went limp as she gave up her struggle.

"Good choice, Mike. I always knew you were smart."

Mike knew she had to bide her time—for what, she wasn't sure. No one had even suspected Jason. She had just talked to Tyler and wouldn't be talking to him again until tomorrow. She was sure by Jason's behavior that tomorrow would be too late.

"Now, I wouldn't scream if I were you. That would be a mistake." Jason lowered his hand from her mouth, allowing his fingers to brush softly against her chest. "Upstairs." His whispered command caused terror to rise inside of her.

JIM DROVE TO JASON'S PLACE on the other side of the lake. He pounded on the door but received no answer. He peered through the windows to see a typical bachelor's house: pizza boxes on the counter and beer cans on the coffee table. Jason wasn't home and he wasn't answering his radio. Jim knew this wasn't good.

He climbed into his car and quickly speed dialed Tyler's cell number. "Tyler? Jim. We've got a problem."

JASON PUSHED HER TOWARDS THE STAIRS AND followed her as she ascended the steps. *Where did I leave my gun? Was it still in the bathroom or did I put it back in the bedside drawer?* Mike tried to retrace her steps of earlier that evening, but her mind was racing in all different directions.

When they got to the top of the stairs, Mike tried to get a glimpse of the bathroom. She saw her revolver sitting where she had left it on the side of the tub. Now all she had to do was get to it.

Jason pushed her, making her sit down on the bed. The strap of her camisole slipped from her shoulder, and she quickly pulled it back in place. He stepped closer to her and pushed the strap off once again. He caressed her shoulder and then brought his hand up under her chin. He tipped it slightly, forcing Mike to look up at him. He saw hate and fear, which made him angry. His hand quickly came across her face, snapping her head to one side. Instinctively, she brought her hand up to her now burning cheek.

"Why do you look at me like that, Mike? I hate it when you look at me like that. This is all your fault, you know. It never would have come to this if you had just kept your promise."

"What promise?" Mike answered confused.

"You said you just needed time to sort things out and time to get past what happened to Michelle. Well, I gave you time—a lot of time. I waited for you. I waited for you and you lied to me."

"I never promised you anything, Jason. You no longer cared about me or what I was going through. All you cared about was having sex and getting drunk. That's why I broke it off with you. You wouldn't take no for an answer."

He pulled his hand back to strike her again but caught himself as Mike's eyes squinted in preparation for it. "Why do you have to be like that, Mike? Why do you make everything we had together sound so ugly? I've waited for you, Mike. Doesn't that tell you anything?"

She sprung up from the bed, no longer able to sit there and be made to feel that she was the one responsible for all that Jason had done.

"You've killed four people with your bare hands. You've destroyed the lives of dozens of others, and you want to tell me you did that out of love? You're crazy!"

The first blow sent her to the ground. She curled up in a fetal position to protect herself from Jason, who was lashing and kicking her body. He was muttering about love and hate and that sometimes they are the same thing. Soon he was in tears and sounding like a fearful child. He fell to his knees and started stroking Mike's hair.

"I'm sorry, Mike. I didn't mean to hurt you . . . you just don't understand. You need time. I know you'll see that I'm right." He pulled her up to her knees and embraced her. She winced at the sharp pains in her back and side. She was sure Jason had broken some ribs in his tirade. "We're going to go away from here, Mike. We're going to start over somewhere where it will be only you and me. Then you'll see. Then you'll know that everything I did, I did out of love."

He stood and pulled Mike to her feet. He held her close and kissed her— first her lips, then her cheek, then her shoulder. His hands were moving over her body, and his movements were proving to be more urgent.

Mike felt as if she were going to vomit. *Please, Lord, no!* She would die before she would allow him to force himself on her again. But just when she felt her stomach turning in revulsion, he stopped and stepped away from her.

"We need to get out of here, Mike, before someone figures me out."

"Who would even suspect you?"

"Jim. He has all the pieces but just hasn't put them together yet. If Nathan calls him with any more information, he'll know for sure."

Jason pulled his gun from the small of his back and leveled it at Mike. "Put some clothes in a bag."

The gun startled her. She thought his vicious hands and the sharp blade of a knife were his weapons of choice.

"Where are we going?"

"Away."

"CALM DOWN, TYLER. I'M ON MY WAY to your house right now, and then we can head to Mike's."

"Did you call to warn her?"

"I tried, but her line was busy."

"If you're not here in five minutes, I'm leaving without you." Tyler hung up the phone and took the stairs two at a time, Skyler right on his heels. He speed dialed her phone and got a busy signal. He disconnected with a huff. Hailey heard the commotion and appeared in the hallway.

"Tyler, what's wrong?"

"It's Mike." He ran to his room and pulled on his hiking boots, not taking time to put on socks. He pulled a sweatshirt over his head and reached into his dresser for another clip of ammunition. He met Hailey back in the hall, again Skyler right at his side. He speed dialed Mike's cell phone number and got her voice mail. "Where are you, Mike?"

MIKE HEARD HER PHONE RINGING FROM HER PURSE. She shot a look at Jason and then to the purse. "Don't even think about it!" Jason snarled.

Mike prayed right then and there. Someone was trying to reach her. *Please, Lord, let it be Tyler. He knows I would never ignore my cell phone.*

"WHAT'S HAPPENED?" HAILEY QUESTIONED.

"Jim thinks he knows who the murderer is. He also thinks that same person might be on his way to Mike's or is already there."

Hailey knew about the investigation and how closely it was related to Mike. Tyler had filled her in on all the details and explained to her his apprehension that Mike could be one of the future victims. Now his fear was becoming a reality, and Hailey was afraid for Tyler. She was terrified that he would lose the love of his life and possibly his own life in the process.

Tyler could see her alarm and placed a kiss on her forehead. "I've got to go, Hailey. I'm going to take Skyler with me. The house is locked down, and I'm going to set the alarm. Stay put and stay close to the phone. I'll call you when this is all over."

Tyler bounded down the steps with Skyler close behind. He set the alarm, shut the door, and headed for his own truck when Jim's came roaring into the driveway. Tyler scooped up Skyler effortlessly and put him in the back of Jim's truck. He climbed in and turned to Jim. "So, what do we know?"

"At the minute, not much."

"Something's wrong, Jim. She's not answering her cell phone. She wouldn't have it turned off and would never ignore a call if she could get to it."

"We'll be there in five minutes."

"Make it three." Tyler began to inwardly pray or plead—he wasn't sure which. Jim continued to fill him in on more details. He told him about Mike's earlier suspicion about Arnie . . . how Jason had intercepted a call from Nathan . . . and on his crackdown on Jason earlier that day.

"I'm sorry, man. I'm afraid my dressing down might have been what pushed him over the edge. I'll never forgive myself if something happens to her. I should have seen this earlier."

"You had no way of knowing, Jim."

Jim thought about the altercation he had witnessed between Jason and Mike. He should have been a step ahead of Jason, not playing catch-up in the aftermath.

"Let's not talk like this is a done deal, okay. We just need to get to Mike's." Tyler refused to think the worst.

MIKE SLOWLY PUSHED SOME CLOTHES INTO A duffel bag. Jason

was getting impatient and was pacing. "Hurry up! You're wasting time!"

Mike swung around and yelled. "I'm sorry! It's a little hard to move fast with broken ribs. You should have thought of that before you used me as a punching bag."

She knew she was pushing him, but the side of her that had always said she would never be a victim refused to stand by and passively take what he was dishing out.

Her sharp words only angered Jason further. He took her arm in his hand and twisted it tightly until she whimpered from the pain. Then, with what control he could muster, he gritted through his teeth. "Don't push me, Mike." He flung her against the wall.

"Now change your clothes, and let's get out of here."

This was her opportunity. She walked into the bathroom, slowly, trying not to look too anxious.

"Oh no, you don't." He blocked the door. I'm not going to give you the chance to shimmy through some window."

"But there's no window in the bathroom. Here, I'll show you." Mike quickly walked over to where the gun sat on the tub's edge but didn't reach for it. She stood in front of it to block Jason's view. "See . . . no windows."

Jason looked around the room and then back to Mike. She stared at him blankly, trying not to give herself away. One more minute and she would have the upper hand.

He turned to walk out, but as he did, his eye caught the reflection of the revolver in the bathroom mirror. Mike knew she had been caught but reached for the gun anyway. Before she could turn to face Jason, he had his hands wrapped around hers and was struggling with her for the gun. She had her finger on the trigger, hoping to get the barrel turned toward Jason. She held on for dear life as Jason smashed her hand repeatedly against the porcelain of the tub. She felt her grip slipping but fought for all she was worth. They fell to the floor, the gun just inches from Mike's face. Jason was wrenching the gun and slowly turning the barrel towards Mike. She watched as the gun moved closer and closer to her. At the last minute, she slammed her head to the tile, hoping to dodge the bullet that was meant for her.

The explosion from the gun was deafening . . . and then there was silence.

Blood pulsed from Mike's shoulder. She turned to see the gaping wound the point-blank shot created. Her shock was replaced with fuzziness. She could feel herself losing touch with reality. She prayed the Lord knew she was serious when she recommitted her life, because he was going to see her sooner than she had expected. She looked to see tears running from Jason's eyes before her eyes closed shut.

Jason held Mike to his chest and wailed. This is not what he wanted. He wanted Mike to love him, to want him. He didn't mean to hurt her. He looked around in a panic, knowing his time was running out. Mike was losing blood quickly, causing a puddle to form on the floor. He pulled Mike up into his arms and cradled her against his chest. He grabbed the bag she had been packing and went downstairs. He struggled to pull open the front door and set out for the lakefront.

"Hold on, Mike. I'll take care of you, I promise. That's all I've ever wanted to do."

TYLER'S STOMACH CHURNED WHEN HE SAW Jason's patrol car in the driveway next to Mike's truck. Jim blocked in the vehicles and then quickly radioed for backup. He explained that Officer Billings was considered a suspect and was armed and dangerous.

Without a word to each other, Tyler and Jim exited the truck and pulled their weapons. Skyler jumped off the tailgate and padded up the driveway ahead of them. They hadn't taken but a few steps when Tyler heard Skyler wail.

Tyler followed the noise and found Skyler lying by Arnie's lifeless body, his head resting on his still chest.

"Jim," Tyler whispered.

Tyler was crouched next to the body when Jim saw Arnie for himself. Two fingers to his pulse told Tyler the man was dead. Skyler next led them to the bodies of Oreo and 'Nilla. Tyler swallowed hard. *Please, Lord, protect Mike. Help us to find her. Help her to find you.*

Jim and Tyler signaled each other silently. They walked the path to the house as quickly and as quietly as gravel and slate would allow. The door hung open. The house was silent.

Tyler entered first, eyes straight ahead, his gun firmly in his grip. He eyed the living room, kitchen, and deck. Nothing.

"Tyler," Jim spoke.

Tyler turned around to see Jim bent over a trail of blood leading from the stairs.

They crouched as they climbed the steps. The drops of blood were everywhere. Tyler crouched down on his belly when he reached the landing, not wanting his head to get blown off if Jason was waiting for him. He peered around the corner and saw no one. He could see the trail of blood led to the bathroom, and he proceeded in that direction. Jim quickly searched the rest of the room, including the sitting area in the back of the house.

Tyler saw Mike's revolver lying on the bathroom floor next to another large puddle. Someone was definitely losing a lot of blood. Tyler touched the tip of his finger to the deep red liquid. It was warm. It had to have just happened. They weren't far behind.

Jim and Tyler met up in the bedroom. "The blood's fresh and Mike's gun is in the bathroom."

"Maybe she was able to wound Jason before he got to her." Tyler prayed the blood belonged to Jason.

"Then we have a wounded maniac on our hands."

They headed down the stairs together. Tyler ran to the truck and snatched the flashlight from the front seat. He saw Skyler still lying with his fallen friends. He was in mourning. Tyler almost lost it right then and there. He knew exactly how Skyler was feeling and prayed desperately he would not have to mourn like his companion was. Tyler massaged the top of Skyler's head. "I know, boy. Come on. Help me find Mike."

Skyler jumped to his feet, and Tyler could swear that he saw determination on the dog's face. He led Skyler to where the blood trail started. Skyler's instinct immediately took over. He ran down the trail leading to the lakefront. He stopped to sniff a few times and then proceeded up a hill across the path.

Tyler was close behind Skyler, with Jim bringing up the rear. Sirens filled the air letting them know backup was on its way, but it would be too late. Skyler led them to a parking lot on the other side of a picnic area. The lot was empty except for the pool of blood that Skyler was circling.

"Find her boy," Tyler encouraged.

He ran around the lot, sticking his nose in the air, trying to get another clue to where Mike might have gone. But her trail ended there in the dirt.

Jim caught up with them. "What did you find?"

A dejected look on his face, Tyler could barely speak. "Nothing." Jenny and Paul passed Tyler on the path to the parking lot. They didn't bother questioning him. They could tell the news wasn't going to be good. Tyler walked back up the path to Mike's house and into the living room. Jason had her, and Tyler didn't even know if she was dead or alive. Anger consumed him and without warning, he slugged the wall and embedded his knuckles into the plaster. He pulled his hand back and looked at his bloodied knuckles.

"I know you're upset, Tyler, but that's not going to help Mike." Jim looked at his hand and then to him. "Let's get back to the office and see what we can find out about Jason."

CHAPTER FIFTEEN

Mike felt herself being tousled about. The pain in her shoulder almost caused her to black out again. She was weak and unable to focus her eyes. Jason was saying something, but she wasn't coherent enough to understand him. She was in a small room with dim light. Jason brushed the hair back from her eyes.

"Jason, I need a doctor," Mike murmured.

"I'll take care of you, Mike. I promised you I would."

"Where are we?"

"That doesn't matter."

Mike tried to look around the room. There was a small nightstand with a lamp. The shades were pulled on the window, and she could see the front door. She realized they were in a hotel, but where she had no idea.

"Jason, I need a doctor. Please."

"You don't . . . need . . . a doctor!" Jason was having difficulty controlling his temper. His words were measured and brimming with anger. "I said I would take care of you."

Jason reached for the makeshift bandage that he had wrapped around her shoulder. She winced as he pulled the bloodied cloth back and exposed her wound. She lifted her head and tried to look at it, but seeing her own blood was making her ill. *The irony,* she thought to herself. *She dealt with mangled flesh all the time, and yet this was the second time the sight of her own blood had the ability to make her sick.* She remembered back to when Tyler had cared for her on the tailgate of her truck. *I love you, Tyler. I hope you know that,* she thought before collapsing back on her pillow.

"I've got something I can give you for the pain, Mike. I've got to get the bullet out, and I know it's going to hurt."

"No. I don't want to take anything." Mike didn't want Jason giving her any drugs. She clenched her teeth the instant she felt Jason touch her shoulder. She balled her right hand into a fist and began taking deep breaths. She could feel him rooting around in her arm and even felt him scrape her clavicle with something. Tears rolled down her cheeks and she began to cry silently. Her shoulders quivered, causing Jason to yell at her.

"You've got to lie still, Mike."

"I'm trying!" she cried back.

Never in all her life had she been in such pain.

Jason moved deep inside her wound, causing her to cry out. He had retrieved the bullet and then dropped it on the bed.

"Got it!"

Blood started streaming onto the bedspread. Quickly, Jason tossed alcohol onto the wound, which made Mike scream. It was the last thing she would remember for awhile.

IT HAD BEEN THREE HOURS SINCE MIKE HAD disappeared. Nathan had arrived on the scene in record time and started gathering evidence. He lifted several fingerprints from Mike's house, but the one he hoped would be pay dirt was the bloody one on the knob of the front door. He took blood samples from the pool on the bathroom floor and made impressions of the tire tracks that seem to lead away from the blood in the parking area where Skyler had lost the scent.

It only took an hour for Nathan to confirm what they already knew. The bloody fingerprint belonged to Jason Billings. That put him at Mike's house after the altercation. That was enough for a search warrant.

Jim and Tyler were now driving to Jason's house. They rode in silence. There was nothing to say. They both knew the situation was bleak. Tyler continued to plead with God for Mike's safety.

They pulled up to Jason's home and looked around. Nothing seemed abnormal. Jason's car was just where Jim had seen it hours before, and there was no sign of him anywhere.

Skyler jumped from the back of the truck and walked beside Tyler. The two men cautiously approached the front door, making sure they both had plenty of cover in case Jason was inside and started shooting.

Jim yelled, "Jason, it's Jim. Open up! We have a warrant."

Nothing.

They banged on the door and waited a few more seconds. Convinced that no one was inside, Tyler tried the handle. It was locked. He stepped back and shoved his boot into the door and watched it fly back on its hinges. He and Jim braced themselves once again for gunfire, but the house remained silent.

"Come on, Skyler, find Mike." Tyler encouraged the dog into the unfamiliar surroundings. He was hoping he would pick up Mike's scent. Skyler sniffed around but came up with nothing. They continued to search the house for anything that would tie Jason to the other murders. The place was a mess. Stacks of newspapers cluttered the floor. Takeout food cartons were all over the kitchen counters, and the bathroom looked worse than most gas station latrines. Tyler made his way to the bedroom and again found nothing but piles of clothes and an unmade bed. He opened the door to the closet and was hit with an acrid smell. A hamper was on the floor of the closet, and when Tyler lifted the lid, the smell assaulted his nostrils at full strength. Inside the hamper were clothes covered in blood.

"Jim . . . in here. We got the son of a . . ." Tyler caught himself, but realized how quickly his old nature was creeping up on him. First, it was the fist through the wall, now the language, and Tyler was already devising in his head what he would do to Jason Billings when he caught up with him. He knew he needed to call on the Lord for strength and self-control, yet that was the last thing he wanted to do. He wanted the hate he had for Jason to simmer inside him. He wanted to make Jason pay for what he had done. Instant justice is what Jason Billings deserved. Tyler would continue to pray for Mike's safety; he knew only God could help her now. But as for himself, he wanted to hold onto his vengeance until Jason was caught.

Jim stood by Tyler as he carefully removed a shirt from the hamper with the corner of a hanger. "What are the chances that this blood matches that of one of our victims?" Tyler said as he let it dropped back into the hamper.

"We've got him, Tyler."

"A lot of good that's going to do Mike."

"Come on, man, you've got to remember that she was what he wanted all along. I don't think he's going to kill her like the others. That was just to get her attention."

"And if she doesn't give him the attention he wants, then what?"

"Mike's smart, Tyler. She'll figure out something. She's a fighter."

Tyler sighed. He didn't know what would be worse for Mike—dying at the hands of a madman or giving into his demented behavior in order to stay alive.

Just the thought of it made Tyler twitch. The wire hanger dropped from his hand and clanged on the hardwood floor. Tyler bent to pick it up and saw something sticking out from the back of the closet. He stood up and parted the clothes hanging on the rod.

"Oh, God, no." Tyler moaned.

There, on the back of the closet wall was a collage of newspaper clippings, Polaroids of the victims, and photos of Mike and Tyler together. Tyler's face was x-ed out in all the pictures, and small cut up photos of Jason were put in their place. In the center of the collage were two pictures with the words *this or this* in bright red letters. One of the two pictures that Jason was comparing was a shot of Mike and Tyler taken the day they were out on the lake. Of course, Tyler's face was covered up with a picture of Jason's. The other photo showed one of the victims, but this time it was Mike's face pasted over the picture. The message was obvious. Either Mike would allow Jason back into her life, or he was going to kill her just like the rest.

"Don't worry, Tyler. We'll find her before that happens." Jim tried to be reassuring and regretted that his words sounded empty and hollow.

They had all the evidence they needed to put Jason away for good, but it would be for nothing if Mike ended up being his last victim.

MIKE WAS IN AND OUT OF CONSCIOUSNESS for the rest of the night and all the next day. Jason was lying beside her, on the bed, admiring his prize. She felt him stroking her but was powerless to resist. A few times she asked for water. Her mouth was so dry she could barely swallow. Jason tried to help her sit up, but the pain wasn't worth it. She would allow herself to drift back into the fog that was surrounding her. By the next morning, her shoulder was on fire and her body was covered in perspiration.

Her eyes fluttered as light streamed in through a couple of broken slats in the window blinds.

"How are you feeling this morning?" Jason asked, as if he couldn't see for himself.

"Something's wrong. My shoulder's on fire, and I feel like I'm burning up. Please, Jason. You've got to get me help."

"But I took care of it. You should be feeling better." He stormed across the room frustrated with Mike. He raised his voice. "You're doing this on purpose. You're trying to trick me into taking you to the hospital."

"No. I promise it's not a trick, Jason. Look at me. I'm not making this up. Please, just get me some help and I'll say whatever you want me to say. I won't even talk to anyone." Her speech was labored but controlled. She knew she had to make him understand that this wasn't a trick.

"I'm not stupid, Mike. All gunshot wounds have to be reported. The minute I walk into a hospital or a doctor's office I'm a goner."

"But we are the police." Mike had spent what conscious moments she had the day before trying to devise a plan that would get her the help she needed. Explaining her strategy to Jason took all the energy she had. Her words were low and thready, but getting him to agree was imperative.

"Look, we explain we are the police and are on an undercover assignment. We're following some drug traffickers and got caught in some crossfire. We can't give up our position because we've been working on the case for months. We just need my arm taken care of, and then we can follow through with our investigation. They won't need to report it to the police because we are the police. We show them our badges, give them fake names if we have to, and get out of there as fast as we can."

"It will never work. It will seem too suspicious."

"It can work, Jason. Look ... where are we?"

"None of your business."

"Jason, all we have to do is go to some little back road's clinic. My arm's infected. I'm sure of it. We just need a doctor that can treat an infection and give me some medicine. We don't even need to go to a hospital."

"And what if the doctor starts asking you a bunch of questions? How do I know that you're not going to give me up?"

Mike tried to sound as sincere and as desperate as possible. "Because all I care about right now is feeling better."

"What about Tyler?"

Mike gave him a disgusted sigh and tried to sound angry. "What about him? He's had almost two days to find me, and he hasn't. Either he's not trying hard enough, or he doesn't really care." Now her words softened. "I know you care, Jason. I could feel it last night. The way you laid next to me and took care of me. That's all I ever really wanted, Jason. I just wanted someone who would love me." She almost vomited. Jason's touch was disgusting to her, but she had to keep playing with his emotions. She had to keep him off balance if she was going to get her way.

Jason was considering Mike's plan. He looked at Mike, who was lying helpless, obviously not getting any better. She definitely didn't have the strength to run from him. As long as she kept her mouth shut, they could make her scheme work.

Jason pulled out his gun, pounced on the bed, and rested the barrel underneath Mike's chin. His actions startled her, causing her to shake.

"Okay, Mike, we'll give your plan a try. I'll find some place where you can get patched up, but I'm warning you. If you try anything—anything at all—I will kill everyone in the place and finish you off as well. If I can't have you, no one will. Understood?"

"Understood."

Jason pushed himself off the bed and began undressing in front of her. Mike turned her head aside. "Don't look away, Mike. You might as well see what you've been missing all these years."

Mike rolled her head back to where Jason stood. He was trying to seduce her, but it only made her ill. She rolled her head from one side to the other and feigned another lapse of consciousness.

She heard Jason moving around the room, gathering up his things. He left the room for a moment but returned quickly with her duffel bag.

"You need to get changed. Walking into some doctor's office wearing only your pajamas is going to be a little too conspicuous." Jason pulled jeans from her bag and laid them on the side of the bed. He glared at Mike and began untying the drawstring to her sweatpants. It didn't take much to tug the oversized sweats from her hips. The look on his face was repulsive. Mike started shaking— not from the cold but out of fear. Her legs were covered in bruises from the beating that Jason had given her, but it didn't seem to lessen his interest.

"Um, um, um. If we only had a little more time," Jason taunted her before he grabbed for her jeans and yanked them over her legs. She helped as much as she could, wanting to minimize Jason's touching as much as possible. He fastened her jeans and then leaned over her and placed a kiss on her lips. "We'll have more time for that later, once you're feeling better." He backed away from her with a laugh. He pulled a blouse out of her bag. Mike couldn't handle any more of his touching, especially since she knew she had nothing on underneath her camisole.

"I can't even think of moving my arm, Jason. I'll just leave this shirt on. Besides, most girls wear these around as T-shirts anyway. It won't look out of place."

Luckily, Jason agreed.

He helped Mike sit up as she cradled her arm against her stomach. The wave of nausea only lasted a minute. She knew the only way she was able to push it down was with the thought of getting some help.

Jason crossed the room and pulled a few things out of his bag.

"What's that?"

"Something else to ensure that we're not recognized in case we get stopped somewhere. I'm sure by now our pictures have been sent to every P.D. in the state."

He pulled out an electric trimmer, scissors, hair gel, and some kind of aerosol hair dye. Mike looked first at the items and then to him.

"They'll be looking for a man with brown hair traveling with a blonde with shoulder length hair, not a bald guy and a girl with punked out hair." He smiled as he picked up the scissors. Then he started chopping at her long tresses, dropping the clumps of hair on the floor in front of her.

Tears rolled down her cheeks. She was beginning to think it would be easier to give in than to fight back. It wouldn't take much for Jason to finish her off. The thought lasted only for a moment. A vision of Michelle danced inside her eyelids. *No! I will not be a victim. I'll fight him until the bitter end!*

When Jason was done, they looked completely different. He had shaved his head bald and had streaked her now short hair with black and hot pink dye. She looked like a teenager on her way to a heavy-metal concert. He knelt in front of her and put her tennis shoes on her feet. When he was done tying them, he asked. "Are you ready?"

She nodded her head.

She stood slowly, Jason's arm firmly around her waist, causing her pain. Her ribs were tender and her legs were stiff. Her memory of Jason's assault rushed into her thoughts. She slowly hobbled to the door. When Jason pulled it open, the bright sunshine made her eyes squint in reflex. She had no idea what time it was or where she was. She had been unconscious when they got to the motel, so she had no idea how far they had driven. Jason led her to a car she didn't recognize. It wasn't his.

"Whose car?" she asked as he opened the passenger door and slowly lowered her to the seat.

"I took it from processing."

Jason crossed over to the driver's side.

If he took it from the impound yard, there would be a record of it. Tyler would know what kind of car they were driving. Hope sprang in her anew.

Jason entered the car and put the key in the ignition. "Oh yeah. I took it after hours; there's no record of it, if that's what you're thinking."

Mike wanted to cry. Jason's attention to detail had been meticulous. It was going to be challenging for Tyler to catch him. *God, you know where I am and what clues Tyler needs to find me. Help him, Lord. Help him put it together.*

They drove out of the sleepy town and down the main highway. The road sign up ahead told them of three destinations. The last one on the list was the clue that Mike needed. It read, Shasta Lake 210 miles. Jason was taking her to his houseboat. If that were true, it might be his only slip-up. He was using something personal and traceable. Hopefully, Tyler and Jim would figure it out before it was too late.

TYLER WAS GOING CRAZY. THEY HAD NO leads whatsoever. They knew Jason was indeed the killer because of the evidence found at his place the previous day. But had they missed something?

In his mind, Tyler replayed all the steps they had taken.

Before finishing their search at Jason's, they checked his phone for any messages. The only two programmed numbers on the phone were to his mother and someone named Carla.

"Who's Carla?" Tyler asked Jim.

"Carla's his sister. But she wouldn't be any help to us. She's been in a mental institution for years. Jason's dad was a drunk. He came home one night and beat her up so badly that he scrambled her brain. She's been in Sherwood for at least ten years."

"But he has her number saved on his machine. He must talk to her," Tyler suggested.

"Don't count on it. He still has his mother's number saved and she died two years ago. We'll check it out to be on the safe side. I just don't think it will amount to anything."

"Was he close to his mom?"

"As far as I remember, there wasn't a lot of love lost between them. He blamed his mom as much as he blamed his dad for Carla's condition. He felt his mom should have done something to protect Carla from the violence."

"Why didn't he?" Tyler asked in a clipped tone.

"I don't know, Tyler. That was a long time ago. I don't remember all the details."

"Come on, let's get back to the station and see what Jenny and Paul have found out."

Tyler continued to replay the day's events over and over in his mind.

He stopped by his house to drop off Skyler and check in on Hailey then headed back to the station. The rest of the night and the next day produced nothing. Time was running out. Tyler knew what that meant for Mike.

Tyler's phone rang, interrupting his thoughts. He saw Nathan's number appear on the screen.

"What do you have for me, Nathan? I hope it's something good."

There was a long silence before Nathan answered. "I'm afraid not, Tyler." Again, silence. Tyler clenched his jaw, waiting for what Nathan had to say. "The blood at the scene . . . I typed it. It matches Mike's." Tyler's shoulders sagged with the news.

"No way it could match both her and Jason?" Tyler was grasping at straws.

"No. Jason's records show he is B negative. The stain was A positive, just like Mike's." Nathan waited a minute before giving the added information he had found. "The blood swab taken from Elizabeth Jordan is B negative also. I just thought you should know."

Tyler hung up the phone without even acknowledging what Nathan had said. He thought back to the cut that Jason had explained away at the boat launch and the bandage he found floating in the water. Jason hadn't cut himself on the license frame of the car. He'd been bitten by Elizabeth Jordan, another clue that Tyler had missed.

Jim didn't ask. He was sure from Tyler's reaction that whatever Nathan had discovered wasn't good.

CHAPTER SIXTEEN

Mike tried to keep her eyes open and figure out where they were, but Jason was taking back roads, knowing exactly where he was going. The fire in her arm continued to burn, and sitting up in the car was putting a lot of pressure on her ribs. She wasn't sure how much longer she could take the pain.

She had drifted asleep when she awoke to the sound of tires popping gravel. Opening her eyes, she saw that they were parked in front of a small white building with blue trim. She leaned toward the passenger window, trying to read the sign. In large blue letters it read, Veterinary Emergency Hospital.

"You're taking me to a vet?" Mike moaned.

"You said yourself that you just need someone who can treat the infection and give you some medicine. Besides, he's less likely to know the protocol for gunshot wounds."

Mike tried to get him to reconsider.

"It's this or nothing, sweetheart. Take it or live with the pain."

His words were calloused and void of feeling.

"Fine. Hopefully he isn't some quack that tries to treat me for rabies instead of infection."

Jason pulled out the gun that he had stowed in his pocket, making sure that Mike saw it. "Remember our deal. You do anything stupid . . . and no one will walk out of that building alive. And as you can see from looking around, it would be awhile before anyone called it in—by then I would be long gone."

Mike looked at her surroundings. Jason was right. They were in the middle of nowhere. No one would hear the gunshots or see Jason coming or going. She wasn't sure what she would do, but right now, relief from the pain was her main objective. She would have to wait and see what the situation was like inside before she could figure out a plan.

Jason helped her from the car and again went over their story. They had decided Mike would do most of the talking. It would seem more believable if it were coming from the injured party. They walked into an empty waiting room that was separated from the rest of the building by a scratched-up blue door and a beveled glass partition. Mike walked up to the partition and her heart sank. There, sitting at the reception desk, was what looked to be a girl of about thirteen years of age. The girl looked up from her Algebra book and said, "Can I help you?"

Mike swallowed hard. She realized she would be unable to do anything that was deemed suspicious. She couldn't take the chance of this young girl getting hurt. Mike cleared her throat when Jason squeezed her upper arm. "We have a little emergency here. Is the doctor in?"

The girl surveyed Mike's bloodied bandage and punked out hair. She already looked fearful. Hopefully, Mike would be able to reassure her everything was all right.

"It's all right, dear. I'm a police officer. I just need to talk to the doctor." Mike forced a smile.

"Da—d!" the girl yelled. "Dad, someone's here to see you."

It took a moment before a middle-aged doctor appeared behind the girl. "They're police officers, Dad." She lowered her voice to a whisper. "And one of them is hurt."

"May we come in, Doctor . . ." Mike glanced down at the business cards that were being held by the paws of a bear statue. ". . . Dr. Raines. I'm feeling pretty weak, and I'm not sure how much longer I can stand here."

He hesitated for a moment, which was a moment too long. Mike collapsed against Jason. Jason quickly grabbed her up into his arms and looked at the doctor for his answer.

"Bring her in." The doctor quickly opened the scratched door and directed them to an examining room. Mike looked at Jason with a wink. She had staged the fainting to gain entrance. Even Jason had been convinced by her performance. Jason placed her on the cold, stainless steel table. It was not the size of an average human examination table, and Mike's legs dangled off the end. The stretch on her legs and rib cage made her moan. She played it off as if she were coming back to her senses.

"What's happened, and why are you here?" The doctor looked from Jason to Mike. Jason looked at Mike and gave her the go ahead to explain the story they had rehearsed.

"You see, Doc, my partner and I have been running surveillance on a drug trafficking group that is working in this area. Well, we got a little too close the other night and got caught up in some gunfire. We don't want to give up our location because we're close to bringing the whole operation down. But they know they injured one of us. I'm afraid they'll be looking for us at the local hospitals. If we show up there, our cover will be blown. My partner was able to weed out the bullet, but I'm afraid the wound has gotten infected. I just need you to finish patching me up and give me some meds for the pain and the infection."

Jason stood nearby making sure that the doctor got a glimpse at the badge attached to his waist and the holster underneath his jacket.

The doctored sighed. "I don't know. We're supposed to report all gunshot wounds to the police."

"But we are the police," Jason butted in.

Mike cut him off with words that were calmer. "I know policy says you have to report this, and that's fine."

Jason darted a look at Mike. *What was she saying? Was she going to take her chances and expose him?*

"We're just asking for a few hours head start. You see, we're afraid the reason this ring has gone so long without being exposed is because there is an inside leak. If you call our department now, we're sitting ducks." Mike paused to see if the doc was buying it. She hated herself for sounding so convincing, but she had no choice. Jason warned her of the consequences if the situation went sour.

She continued. "Look, only our direct superiors know our cover names, but even then we can't be too careful. We'll give you those names. All we ask is that you wait at least two hours before you call it in. That will give us time to get back to our location. "Mark," she turned her attention to Jason, using a fictitious name. "Give the doctor the name and number he can call."

"What county did you say you were from?" The doctor still looked at them suspiciously.

"We're not from a county. We're from a drug trafficking task force out of Washington, D.C." Mike winced from real pain. She was using what little energy she had to convince the doctor of their story. "Look, Dr. Raines, I don't think I can handle this pain much longer. Please help me. If we catch these guys, you'll become a local hero."

Mike heard a "WOW!" from the corner of the room. She turned to see that the teenager from the reception's desk had followed them in and heard everything they had said. "Imagine that, Dad—you a hero."

Her presence reminded Mike why she had to remain believable.

The doctor looked at her with steely eyes. "What's your name?"

Jason started to answer the question, "She's—"

The vet quickly interrupted him. "I asked her," he said, pointing at Mike. Jason looked at Mike, knowing a slip of the tongue would blow everything. He put his hands on his waist and pushed his jacket back just far enough for her to see his gun. It wasn't the gun that Mike focused on, but the lining of his jacket. She was sure it would match the fibers she and Nathan had recovered from two of the victims. She felt a moment of numbness when she thought again of the victims that Jason had used as part of his sickening game. She shook off the feeling and turned to answer the vet's question.

"Hailey Tom. My cover name is Hailey Tom."

It was one of the few clues that Mike could leave unbeknownst to Jason. He had no idea that the cover name she had chosen happened to be a combination of the names of Tyler's sister and father. She prayed that when the doctor found out he'd been had, the code name would make its way back to Tyler.

"Okay, your partner can take a seat outside. Lisa will stay so she can assist me."

Mike knew Jason would never go for that, so she rebuffed the doctor. "I'm sorry, Doc, he stays. Company policy. If you use any kind of anesthetic on me, he has to stay to make sure I don't mutter anything while I'm under the influence of medication."

Jason was impressed. Mike was actually defusing any chance of escape for herself. Maybe things were going to work out after all.

Finally, the doctor started to assess the wound. He gave Mike an injection of something that made her feel detached before he started working on her shoulder. He examined her arm closely, taking time to clean it out thoroughly. He removed a bone chip that had broken off from her clavicle and used several stitches to close it up. Mike was groggy and barely coherent when the doctor was finished bandaging her up. She was feeling queasy again. She couldn't remember the last time she had eaten anything and could feel the medication fighting with her insides. The doctor was talking to Jason, giving him different packets of medicine and explaining their uses.

"Now this stuff is pretty strong. One pill should do it, but if the pain gets really bad, she can take two. I keep this stuff on hand because I get my fair share of farming accidents. Usually nothing major, but it helps the locals not to have to drive all the way into Modesto for help."

Jason was distracted talking to the doctor. Mike tried to use this window of opportunity to slip another clue to Lisa. She whispered to the girl, "Do you have any Oreos or Vanilla Wafers? My stomach feels uneasy."

"What? What did you say?" Jason walked to Mike's side quickly. The anger in his voice was about to blow everything.

"She asked for something to eat because her stomach feels queasy," Lisa answered, fear evident in her voice.

Jason took a deep breath and looked at Mike. He held her hand in his and tried to look sincere. "It's just that you look so pale, sweetie. Are you sure it's just food that you need?"

"I'm going to be fine now ... Mark. The doctor has been so helpful."

Jason's outburst had caused Lisa and Dr. Raines to tense up. It took a moment for them to relax.

"I'll go see if I can find you some cookies or something," Lisa said as she left the room.

The doctor continued to give Jason instructions for the medication and a bag of extra bandages. Mike smiled to herself. She had been able to leave another clue behind. If only the girl would remember what she had said.

Lisa came back with a couple packages of Oreos and handed them to Mike. "They're my favorite. I keep a stash of them here so I can have a snack when I do my homework." Lisa also held up a bright pink shirt with snaps down the front and laid it on Mike's stomach. "I brought you a shirt that you could change into. I think it will fit. That one looks pretty bad." Lisa smiled at her. "It would be an honor to know that a policewoman was wearing one of my shirts."

Mike couldn't control the tear that ran down the side of her face. "Thank you, Lisa. You've been such a great help."

Jason looked at the scene and knew he had to get Mike out of there. The medication was making her weepy, and she might slip up if she was there much longer.

"Okay, partner, it's time we get back on the road." Jason walked over to Mike who was still lying awkwardly on the exam table. He helped her sit up. The doctor saw the way she grabbed her side and walked over to her.

"Do you have other injuries?" He looked at Mike intently.

"They're minor, Doc, really. The impact of the gunshot caused me to stumble back. I fell on something that did a number to my ribs. They're a little stiff, but they'll be fine."

"May I?" The doctor glanced at her torso.

Not sure what to do, Mike looked at Jason. Before she could answer, the doctor reached for her camisole and slid it up far enough to see the intense bruising that had discolored her side. He looked at her. "They're probably broken."

"I know, but it's not like you can do anything for them, right? That's why I didn't bother you with them."

"I could wrap them for you. It won't take away all the pain, but it will make it a little easier for you to move around."

"That would be great." Mike smiled at the doctor and glanced at Jason. His jaw was clenched and he was beginning to get antsy.

"Do you want some privacy? I can ask Lisa and your partner to step outside. It appears as if the effect of the medication is wearing off." The look he leveled on Jason was questioning. The doctor was getting a little less friendly and a little more inquisitive.

"You know what, Doc, if you could just give us some extra bandages, Mark can do it for me when we get back to our location. We're really pressing our luck being out in the open this long in broad daylight."

"If that's what you want." The doctor waited for her to change her mind. When it was obvious she wasn't, he reached for more bandages on the shelf and put them in the bag he'd already handed to Jason.

"Thanks, Doc. We really appreciate this."

"Don't let her kid you." He looked sternly at Jason and continued, "She's in an incredible amount of pain. If you care for your partner, you'll make sure she gets further medical attention. Broken ribs are nothing to fool with."

"I'll make sure she gets all the attention she needs, Dr. Raines." Jason's words sickened her.

"Did you need help putting the shirt on, Hailey?" Lisa asked shyly.

"That would be great, Lisa. I'll just go ahead and cut off this shirt since it's pretty trashed."

Lisa helped Mike slip the shirt sleeve over her hand and up her arm. She gently pulled it over her bandage and across her back. Mike was able to move her other arm back far enough for Lisa to be able to pull the sleeve up and over her other shoulder.

"If you cut my shirt straight up the middle before you snap this one, I should be able to just slip it off from underneath the other shirt."

Lisa looked nervous. She held the scissors at the edge of Mike's shirt. "Are you sure you trust me? What it I slip?"

"I trust you completely, Lisa."

Lisa clipped at the shirt until it was completely in half. She then quickly snapped the front of Mike's shirt, making sure never to let the camisole fall open. She reached inside Mike's new shirt and clipped the bloodied spaghetti straps. Lisa tugged on the bottom of the shirt and tried to pull it off of Mike, but it stuck on something. She tried again a little harder and Mike winced.

"I'm sorry, Hailey, did I hurt you?" Lisa's eyes were as big as saucers, and she looked like she was about to cry.

"No, I'm fine. I think my shirt is caught on the bandage, though."

Lisa walked around behind Mike and carefully lifted up the back of the shirt. Her eyes widened at the bruises and welts she saw, and she looked to where her dad was still talking to the other officer. She quickly loosened the T-shirt from the bandage tape and stepped back in front of Mike.

She mouthed to Mike without making a sound. "Are you in trouble?"

Mike caught Jason out of the corner of her eye. She reached around Lisa with her good arm and smiled as she gave her a little hug. "Yes ... I promise I'll write you when this is all over and tell you how it turned out."

Mike and Jason were back in the car and finally on the road once again. Lisa squinted through the window and tried to see the license plate number. The way the car was positioned and the way Jason backed out, she couldn't see it all, so she studied the car. As soon as they were gone, she turned to her dad.

"They were lying, Dad. I know they were." Lisa was almost in hysterics.

"Why Lisa? Why do you think they were lying?" He had his own suspicions, but he wanted to know what his daughter thought.

"Her back, Dad. Her back looked horrible. It was covered with bruises and welts." Lisa was sobbing, almost unable to speak. "I asked her if she was in trouble and she said yes. She was in trouble, Dad, and we didn't help her. Why did she lie to us? Why didn't she tell us she needed help?"

He held his daughter to his chest and tried to hush her crying. "I think

185

she was protecting us, Lisa. She knows something that we don't. She did what she had to do; now let's see if we can do something to help her."

TYLER AND JIM WERE ON THEIR WAY TO VISIT CARLA. They knew it was a shot in the dark, but they had to try. When they called the institution, they found out that Jason had been out to visit her earlier that week. Maybe he told her what he had planned.

When they got to Sherwood Institute, they were greeted by a large woman in a business suit with a serious look on her face. "I'm Dr. O'Neil. You must be detectives Henderson and Thompson. I'm glad you're here. Your interest in Carla was brought to my attention because of the trouble we've had with her the last few days."

"What kind of trouble?" Jim asked.

"Behavioral. She's never been a problem in the past, but she's been extremely agitated and difficult to control the last few days."

"Can you narrow that down? When would you say that you noticed this difference in her behavior?"

"That's the strange thing. It happened right after her brother's last visit, which is so unlike her. She always looks forward to him visiting, and usually she is at her best after Jason's visit. We've tried asking her why she's so upset, but she doesn't seem to be making any sense. We called Jason to let him know but got no answer."

"Did you leave a message?" Jim asked, knowing no messages were on Jason's machine."

"No. We try not to leave messages unless it's an extreme emergency. We don't like to worry family members unnecessarily. We had hopes that her behavior would improve."

Dr. O'Neil led them to a room at the end of a long hall. She entered a code at the door before pushing the door open. "Carla, you have some visitors. They're friends of Jason's."

At the mention of Jason's name, she responded, "Jason's bad. Jason's bad."

Jim and Tyler approached slowly. Carla looked at Tyler and smiled.

"Oh, I think she likes you, Detective Henderson."

Carla continued to smile.

"Carla, my name is Tyler, and I'm a friend of your brother." Carla frowned immediately.

"Jason's bad."

"Why is Jason bad, Carla?"

"Jason's bad." Carla began to rock in her bed. She crossed her arms against her chest. Tyler noticed the leather restraints on her wrists.

"Carla, why is Jason bad?"

"Jason's bad ... but you're not. Will you visit me?'

"Sure I will, Carla. Did Jason say he wasn't going to visit you?"

"Yeah, Jason's bad. He's going away and won't take me. Jason's bad." The rocking continued.

"Gentlemen, I don't want her to get too agitated. It takes too much to calm her down," Dr. O'Neil warned.

"I understand, Doctor, but I'm afraid Jason Billings is in a lot of trouble. I can't go into details with you right now, but it is imperative that we find him. Carla may know where he's gone."

"Mooning. Jason's gone mooning."

"See, that's what I mean," Dr. O'Neil said in frustration. "She keeps saying silly things like that."

"That's what she's been saying?"

"Yes, that and she keeps alluding to the idea that her brother is gay. Her thoughts are so confused right now. I'm not sure what to make of it."

"She said he's gay?" That one really threw both Jim and Tyler.

"Well ... she keeps saying Jason loves Mike; Jason loves Mike." The looks on the detectives' faces told Dr. O'Neil there was some truth to what Carla had been saying. "You mean he really is gay?"

Tyler turned to the doctor. "Mike is a woman, Dr. O'Neil, and we believe that Jason has abducted her."

She covered her mouth to silence a gasp. "I had no idea. We just thought that Carla was experiencing some kind of setback." The doctor was trying to digest this new information.

"Can you remember anything else she's said? Anything that didn't seem to make sense?" Jim questioned the doctor while Tyler turned his attention back to Carla.

"Carla, where is Jason?"

She looked at him and smiled. "Jason's mooning? Jason loves Mike. Jason is mooning."

It clicked for Tyler. "Carla, are Jason and Mike honeymooning?"

"Yes." Her eyes grew bright and then they dimmed. "Jason's bad. He's not going to visit me. He loves Mike. He doesn't love me anymore. Jason's bad."

Carla was quickly becoming agitated again. Dr. O'Neil gave Tyler another warning. He placed his hand on Carla's. "It's okay, Carla. I'll visit you. I'll be your friend."

Carla was inconsolable. Her rocking got more pronounced, and she was beginning to cry. She kept repeating that Jason didn't love her anymore. Dr. O'Neil put an end to Tyler and Jim's visit. They all gathered in the hallway, Tyler disappointed that he still didn't know where to look for Jason and Mike.

"I'm sorry, gentlemen, this is obviously upsetting her, and her health is my first priority." As much as Tyler wanted to push the situation, he knew he couldn't. "I promise, if she says anything else, we'll write it down and call you. This all sounded ridiculous to us, but you seem to know the missing pieces." The doctor excused herself and left Tyler and Jim standing in the hallway. Tyler's pager went off, and he looked at the number on the readout. It was the case number they had assigned to Mike. Tyler ran to get his telephone that he had left in the car.

"This is Tyler. What's up?"

"Man, we've been trying your cell. Where are you?"

"We were in a hospital and phones aren't allowed. I left it in the car and put on my pager. Do you have something?"

"I think we do." Andy's voice was on edge. "It's too much to tell you over the phone. How long before you can get here?"

"We're on our way. Just tell me—you haven't discovered a body?"

"No, but we might have a location where Mike and Jason were."

Tyler and Jim roared back to the station, lights flashing and sirens blaring. Andy heard them arriving before they burst through the door.

"What do you have?"

"Okay, listen to this. We just got a call from outside of Modesto. Seems a vet in the area reported a suspicious occurrence that involved a woman, a man, and a bullet wound." Tyler looked stunned. "We've got a number here of the vet, a Dr. Raines."

Tyler snatched the piece of paper out of Andy's hand and went to his office. He dialed the number and then punched the button for speaker phone so Jim could hear as well.

"Dr. Raines' office."

The voice sounded like a little girl.

"This is Detective Henderson from the Emerald Lake Police Department. I'm calling in response to a report Dr. Raines filed with the Modesto Police Department."

"Hold on. I'll get my dad." The little girl's voice seemed to crack, as if she were about to cry.

"This is Dr. Raines. With whom am I speaking?"

"Detective Henderson from the Emerald Lake Police Department. You may have some information regarding a case we're working on."

Dr. Raines got worried. *What if he was endangering the lives of two police officers because he was exposing them? What if what they said was true and there was someone on the inside that was working against them?* He had to be sure before he divulged too much information. "Detective Henderson, I have reason to believe that the people I encountered earlier today may be in trouble from their own superiors. I want to be very careful

188

and not say anything to the wrong parties that could endanger them further. Can you tell me what you know about the two people that might lead me to believe I am doing the right thing?"

Tyler took a breath. It was all he could do not to yell at the man to give him the information he needed. Jim saw this and intercepted the call.

"Dr. Raines, this is Detective Thompson. I am working with Detective Henderson on this extremely sensitive case. While I cannot divulge department information, I can give you a description of the people we're seeking. "Jason is six feet, two inches tall, has a muscular build, with brown hair and brown eyes. Mike has shoulder length blond hair, about five feet two inches with blue eyes. We believe that Mike has a bullet wound."

"These aren't your people then. Your descriptions are completely off. The people I saw were male and female."

"Mike is a woman, Dr. Raines. Her real name is Michal," Tyler interrupted, trying to control his tone. "Do you think they could have been in disguise? They could change their hair color and their appearance. But what about their sizes? Do they fit the descriptions according to size?"

There was a muffled noise on the other end of the line. It sounded like Dr. Raines was talking to someone else. He came back on the line and answered. "My daughter says the woman's hair was dyed."

"Did your daughter talk with the woman?"

"Yes, that's why we thought they might be in trouble." Dr. Raines was ready to divulge what he knew but hesitated. "Look, Detective Henderson, I don't mean to sound disrespectful. I'm just not sure who to trust."

"I understand, Dr. Raines, but time is not on our side. The man we believe you might have seen is armed and dangerous. He has already killed four people, and we're afraid Mike Madigan might be his next victim. Are you sure there isn't anything you could share with us? That you feel comfortable telling us? If not, I'll have no choice but to send an officer to your place of business and have you and your daughter arrested for obstruction of justice."

There was a heavy sigh over the phone. "I don't want that. Lisa's upset enough as it is. She's sure the lady is in danger. She's terrified."

"How old is your daughter?"

"Fourteen."

"May I speak to her?" Tyler was ready to jump out of his skin. He knew this was the lead they needed. He just had to stay calm enough and not frighten the girl.

"I've put you on speaker phone, Detective Henderson, and Lisa's right here."

"Hi, Lisa. Your dad says you're really upset by what happened today."

"I think he beat her. I think that's why she didn't try to get away. I think she was afraid of what he might do."

"Why do you think he beat her?" Tyler asked, choking back his own emotions.

"She had bruises and welts all over her back. She even has some broken ribs. She made up some lame excuse about falling down, but I don't believe her. When the man wasn't looking, I asked her if she was in trouble and she said yes."

Tyler swallowed hard. The thought of Mike being battered brought tears to his eyes. "Did the man hear you?"

"No, I only mouthed the words to her. She said yes, but made it sound like she was answering a different question. When I saw the bruises on her back, I panicked. She seemed so nice, even if she looked kind of creepy. "

"What do you mean by creepy?"

"Her hair was dyed black and had pink streaks through it. It was really short and choppy looking."

"How do you know it was dyed, Lisa?"

"Because there are black marks on the table where she was lying down."

"She was lying down? Was she okay?"

Dr. Raines answered this time.

"The gunshot wound to her shoulder was infected. I had to clean the wound and stitch her up. She was also limping, and like Lisa said, she looked pretty banged up."

It took a minute for Tyler to digest this. If this were Mike, she was alive, but in what condition he wasn't sure. "Is there anything else you can tell me? Anything she might have done or said that sounded odd, like she was trying to give you information?"

"She gave me her name, but it wasn't Mike."

"What was it, Lisa?"

"Hailey. Hailey Tom."

Tyler dropped into his chair and put his head in his hands. It was Mike.

Jim took over the questioning, seeing that Tyler was in no condition to talk. "It's Detective Thompson again. Did she give you any idea where they were going or maybe where they were staying?"

"She did tell us to give them at least two hours to get out of town before we called anyone. They made up a story about being with a task force and gave us a phony number to call. When I dialed it and found out it was fake, I called the police. Maybe she was giving us a clue about where they were going."

Dr. Raines could hear Jim's frustration over the phone. "You've got to understand, Detective, she was very believable. If it weren't for Lisa, I think I would have believed their story hook, line, and sinker."

"What did the man look like, Dr. Raines?"

"He fit the description you gave me except that he was bald."

"Is there anything else, Dr. Raines, anything at all?"

"There is one thing," Lisa said quietly. "She was kind of queasy after the medication my dad gave her. I know most people eat crackers when they have an upset stomach—at least that's what the nurse offers you at school if you don't feel good. But she asked for something else."

"What was that, Lisa?" Tyler composed himself enough to speak.

"She asked if I had any Oreo cookies or Vanilla Wafers. Isn't that strange?"

"No, Lisa, that's not strange," Tyler said with a sigh. "She was giving you a clue. Those are the names of her dogs."

Tyler thought about how they had found Mike's two precious Labradors. It was going to crush her . . . that is if she survived.

"There's one more thing, Detective Henderson," Lisa spoke up. "I saw the car they were driving. I couldn't get the whole license number, but I saw the car pretty good."

Lisa gave a description of the car: dark blue, two-door, trunk—not hatch back, and the letters WAT were on the license plate.

"Do you know what kind of car it was?"

"I think it was a Camaro, but I'm not sure. It was pretty old and really dirty."

"Dr. Raines, Lisa, I can't tell you how helpful you've been. Would you mind if I called back if we have any more questions?"

"That would be fine, Detective."

"Detective?" Lisa spoke up. "Would you let me know how she is when you find her? She said she would write me when it was all over, but she might forget."

"We'll be in touch." Tyler disconnected the call. He didn't want to promise the girl anything. How would he explain to her if Mike didn't . . .

"Tyler . . . Tyler." Tyler sat with his head sunk between his shoulders, his eyes focused on the ground. Jim got Tyler's attention. "She's alive. That's more than we knew twenty minutes ago."

Tyler knew they were making progress, but not quick enough for him. Jenny ran the description of the car and the partial plate. Moments later, they had a possible match. The car fitting the description was listed as being in the county impound yard. They called the yard clerk to check it out. He confirmed the car was missing.

CHAPTER SEVENTEEN

Mike was beginning to feel a little improvement in her condition. She pretended to be asleep, while watching the road signs as they passed by. Shasta was still two hours away, and she was beginning to get hungry. She rolled her head over to face Jason. When she tried to move her arm, she realized that he had handcuffed her to the seat belt.

Jason saw her discover her predicament and smiled. "You're awake."

"I'm hungry. Are we going to stop before we get there?"

"Get there? How do you know where there is?" Jason said, keeping his eyes on the road.

"I just figured we were headed to Shasta, to your houseboat."

Jason roared. His laughter made Mike nervous. She just assumed they were going to Shasta. She knew it was only a matter of time before Tyler and Jim would find out that Jason owned a houseboat on the lake and because of the path they were traveling, they would realize that was where they were heading. "Well, if we're not going to Shasta, then where are we going?"

"Like I'm going to tell you? You think I'm stupid, don't you?" Jason's voice was getting louder. He didn't like it when Mike acted superior, like she was smarter than him. He began to yell and then swung at her, hitting her right across the face. She curled up close to the door and tried to avoid his lashes, but again she was a sitting duck, unable to avoid his tirade.

"You think I would be dumb enough to take you to a place that Jim and Tyler can trace to me? You underestimated me, Mike. I mean, come on, you guys are the idiots. I was right under your noses the whole time, and you never even suspected me. Well, I'll show you . . . I'll show them. They hired Tyler because he was some hotshot detective from the big city. Tyler doesn't know anything, and I'm going to be the one to prove it to him. He's never going to find us, Mike. Never! Only one other person knows about this place, and there's no way they'll question Carla."

Jason was dripping with sweat. He had worked himself into a frenzy. Mike silently cried in the corner of the passenger seat, wiping the blood from her nose on the knee of her jeans.

"Here." Jason tossed one of the packages of Oreo cookies that Lisa had given her. "Eat these."

She didn't reach for the cookies, her appetite a thing of the past.

"I said, eat!"

With shaking hands, Mike opened the package of cookies. She brought one up to her mouth and tasted it along with her tears and the blood that continued to trickle to her lips. Staring at the wrapper, she thought of Oreo, 'Nilla, and Arnie. She had to fight back tears at the realization that they were all dead.

She tugged at the handcuff that kept her secured to the car. She closed her eyes and again talked with God, her only companion. It was strange. She should be angry with God, but she wasn't. How could she be? Her conversations with him were the only reasons that she didn't give up. That and the thought of seeing Tyler again.

They drove for at least another hour before Jason pulled off into the dirt lot of a roadside gas station.

"Okay, this is the deal. You go in with me, and you don't say a word. If you try to say anything or do anything, I will kill whoever is in there, you understand?"

Jason had found his way to control her. She already knew of four people who had died because of her. He knew she would not endanger the lives of others. He was in complete control.

Mike was thinking about what she could do as Jason circled the car. Quickly, she crumpled up the Oreo wrapper and stuck it in her pocket. He opened her car door and knelt down next to her seat. He unlocked the handcuffs and looked at her with eyes of warning. She stood up slowly, her legs stiff and her side still throbbing. At least her arm was no longer burning.

"I need to go to the bathroom, Jason. I'm not feeling so well." Her words were timid, not sure how he would react. He didn't answer. He just held her hand tightly while they walked into the mini mart. He looked the place over and then walked up to the counter.

"Hi. How are you doing this evening?" Jason's demeanor was polite and pleasant. He saw the questioning looks they got when they walked in and realized their get-ups were a little intimidating to people. He tried to put the store clerk at ease. "May I have the key to the ladies room, please?"

The elderly lady behind the counter handed him a key with a large pink pom pom on it. "Thank you so much."

She returned Jason's smile.

As they walked to the bathroom, Jason clenched Mike's hand harder. "I'm warning you, Mike, don't try anything." Jason turned the key in the lock and pushed the door open. He glanced in himself to make sure there were no windows. "I'll be standing right here."

Mike walked in and glanced around. The bathroom was set up perfectly for what she was going to try to do. She said a quick prayer, hoping she was doing the right thing . . . then she started make heaving sounds. She tried to make it sound guttural and loud enough that Jason would hear. In the meantime, she wetted several paper towels and began ripping them into pieces.

She made sure they were good and wet before carefully placing them on the back of the door. They stuck perfectly. She worked as quickly as she could, continuing with the sounds of a person who was violently ill. When she was done, she looked around for the one thing she was sure she would find in any unkempt bathroom. She pulled a piece of chewing gum from next to the sink and began chewing it. She actually gagged with the thought of what diseased person might have chewed it before her, but she knew she had to take her chances. She stuck the sticky substance onto the back of the Oreo wrapper that she had shoved into her pocket and stuck it to the back of the door. She stood back to see what she had done. *Please, Lord, let someone see it.* Without wasting any more time, she relieved herself and then splashed water on her face and poked herself in the eye. She had to make the tears look real. When she appeared at the door, Jason looked at her and almost seemed sympathetic. He stepped into the bathroom and glanced around, and then he shut the door. As they walked back to the counter, Mike gasped.

"Jason, I left the key in the bathroom." His jaw set and his eyes intensified, but he controlled himself. He grabbed some junk food from a few different shelves and then headed for the front counter.

Jason smiled at the clerk and again in his politest tone said, "Ma'am, I'm sorry to say that my wife here left the bathroom key inside the bathroom."

Mike jumped in. "I'm sorry, ma'am. It's just that I was feeling so ill that I forgot to grab it before I shut the door. I'm sorry."

Jason eyed Mike. She had broken the rules. She had spoken when he had told her to be quiet.

"That's all right, deary. We have a master key. Don't worry yourself about it. You know, we have some Pepto-Bismol in the second aisle."

"That's all right, Ma'am. It's nothing another seven months won't cure." Jason explained with a wide smile on his face. He put his arm around Mike and hugged her, knowing that he was causing her pain, but she knew she had to grin and bear it.

"Well, congratulations, you two." She smiled politely as she glanced at Mike's ring finger.

"Thank you. We're pretty excited ourselves."

"Are you sure you're okay, honey?" She looked intently at Mike. "You don't look too good."

"Actually, maybe you could give me some advice." Jason's hold on Mike tightened. He reached his hand across his body; she knew he was reaching for his gun. "You see, I've had a terrible time with swelling and blotchy skin. I'm not sure if there's something I can take for it or not. I can't even wear my wedding ring anymore; the swelling has gotten so bad."

"Well, I don't know about the blotchy skin, but to keep the swelling down, you need to get plenty of rest. Put your feet up when you're sitting down. Take care of yourself," the elderly lady said with a smile.

"I guess I'll have to wait until I get home for that. We have quite a bit more traveling to do."

"Thank you, Ma'am, for your help. You have a nice day." Jason wasted no time ushering Mike out of the mini mart and back to the car. He opened her door and shoved her into the seat. Her body protested as pain shot through her. Everything hurt equally. Jason cuffed her to the belt and slammed the door. He got in, turned the ignition key, and screeched out of the parking lot.

"What was that all about? I told you not to say a word!" Jason was clenching the steering wheel, causing his knuckles to turn white.

"I had to say something. Did you see the way she was looking at me? She noticed right off that I didn't have on a wedding ring, and my face isn't exactly star quality at the moment. I covered for you!" Mike yelled back. "Maybe I should have just cowered behind you and really given her cause to wonder. Then she could have called the cops and—"

Jason grabbed the back of Mike's short cropped hair and dragged her across the console. "If you think I need your help, you're wrong! Now shut up and do as I say from now on." Jason shoved her back into the passenger seat. Mike didn't dare cry. If she started now, she would never be able to stop. Instead, she prayed herself to sleep.

THE ELDERLY LADY HELPED A FEW MORE CUSTOMERS before she remembered to get the bathroom key from the ladies room. The market was empty, so she quickly crossed the distance to the back of the store. She unlocked the door with her master key and saw the pink pom pom lying on top of the towel dispenser. She stepped inside the bathroom to retrieve it as the door closed quickly behind her. Mike's message made of paper towels still hung on the back of the door. At first, the woman couldn't understand why anyone would make such a mess, until she made out the words. *Help me* was written in paper towel strips with an Oreo wrapper stuck in the middle.

"Oh my ... oh my. Oh dear ... I knew it. I just knew it." She shuffled to the front counter and reached for the phone. "I need the police. I think I just saw a woman who was being kidnapped or something."

The dispatcher for the area tried to understand what the elderly lady was saying, but she was talking too fast, and she mumbled her words.

"Ma'am. I'm sending an officer right over. He'll be there in just a few minutes." The dispatcher assured her that help was on the way.

TYLER AND JIM HADN'T MADE MUCH PROGRESS since their conversation with the Raines. They had a police sketch artist draw Jason and Mike as Lisa and Dr. Raines had described them and had their pictures sent out to agencies all over California. Jim had to talk Tyler out of driving aimlessly towards Modesto. Tyler felt helpless staying in one place while Mike and Jason were getting further and further away.

Another day had passed, and they still didn't know where Mike was or where Jason was heading. Tyler checked in with Hailey to let her know he would be spending another night at the station.

"We still don't know, Hailey. We really haven't gotten any leads since they stopped at the vet's . . . I will, the moment I hear anything. How are you doing? I'm sorry I brought you here just to leave you stranded at my house . . . I know, but I still feel bad . . . okay, as soon as we know anything."

Tyler stretched his sore muscles. He stepped outside and looked at the darkened sky. *Where are they, Lord? Where are they?*

Jim came rushing to the door. "They've been spotted about forty miles outside of Redding."

JASON KNEW EXACTLY WHERE HE WAS GOING. There was no other way for someone to find the out-of-the-way dive Jason pulled into unless that individual had gotten lost on the main highway. There was a light on in the office and a guy standing behind the counter. Mike could see him through the tear in the curtains that covered a window held together with duct tape.

"I'll be right back," Jason said as he climbed out of the car and stretched. He was back in a minute and pulled the car to the end of the building and around to the back. He pulled the bags from the back of the car before opening Mike's door. He unlocked the handcuffs from the seat belt but left the other end attached to Mike's wrist. Jason flipped on the light and walked into the dilapidated room. Mike's eyes traveled from the wallpaper pealing off the walls to the torn-up green recliner in the corner. The bed had a faded red bedspread on it and was sunken in the middle. There was a mouse hanging out of a trap next to the dresser and cobwebs in every corner of the room.

"What did you expect? The Ritz Carlton?" Jason asked when he saw her expression. He lay down on the bed and stretched his arms up behind his head. "You might as well get comfortable. We're here for the night." Jason patted the bedspread next to him.

Mike's heart began to race at the gleam in Jason's eye. Every muscle in her body ached, and the acid in her stomach was rising in her throat. She desperately needed to take a shower, but to put herself in such a vulnerable position would not be smart. She limped over to the cracked mirror hanging over the dresser and stared at the face of someone she didn't even recognize. She touched her swollen cheek and felt the cut on her lip then pulled at the short black hair that looked nothing like her own. Some of the dye came off in her hand. She was glad to know that it wasn't permanent. Not that it really mattered.

She hobbled to the recliner and carefully sat down. Cradling her left arm in her lap, she tried to sit up straight so she didn't put further strain on her ribs. "I need to take something to deaden this pain. I can't stand it any longer." Other than the medicine the vet had given her when he stitched her up, she had restrained from taking anything. She had wanted to keep her wits about her and knew the medicine would weaken her senses. Now, she no longer cared. She was in pain, in a scummy motel room with Jason; and if medicine could shield her from what might happen next, she would prefer that to being coherent during the rest of the night.

Jason held open his palm. There were two pills in it, and he held a half empty Coke can. She looked at her choices. She could probably do with one pill, but two pills would make the night go quicker. She thought for a moment and then took both pills, threw them to the back of her throat, and chugged the warm soda. She sat with her eyes closed, waiting for the medicine to start taking effect. The sound of running water broke the silence. Jason emerged from the bathroom and hovered in front of her.

"You need to get cleaned up. You look horrible." Jason actually sounded disgusted with her, as if she had done this to herself. The defiant side of her would not let her ignore the comment.

"No thanks to you," she muttered, her head down and eyes closed.

Jason grabbed both her forearms, pulled her out of the recliner, and shook her. The sudden jolt to her arm made her head spin. "You just don't know when to shut up, do you? You think you're smart, don't you, Mike? Well, let me remind you who holds all the cards here. Me! So, shut your mouth and do as I say!"

Jason pulled Mike into the bathroom. Mike got her first look at the dingy room. The paint was peeling off the walls and mildew was everywhere. Tiles were missing from around the shower, and the sink was being held up by a two-by-four. Steaming water was running in the bathtub, the color of the water slightly yellowed from rust.

"Get in."

Mike didn't move.

"I said, get in!"

Mike loosened the jeans she was wearing. When she leaned over to step out of them, a dizzying sensation sent her into the wall. She had to swallow back the urge to throw up. She continued to undress, the effects of the medication getting stronger. She sat in the dirty water, clenching her knees to her chest while Jason sat on the toilet ogling her. There was no way she would give Jason the show that he wanted.

"Jason, could you please leave? I feel like I'm going to be sick again."

"I don't think so." Jason didn't budge. "You'd be fine if you would just let yourself relax." His leering was repulsive.

Mike might have faked her illness at the mini mart, but what she was feeling now was very real. She retched slightly. "Please, Jason, just move so that I can use the toilet if I need it." Even her privacy was beginning to take a backseat to how she was feeling.

"I'm not going to fall for that. As soon as I leave, you'll—"

She could hold it no longer. Mike leaned her head over the side of the tub and spewed what little she had in her stomach. Jason jumped back, but not before his shoes were splattered.

He started swearing and ranting while Mike held her side and retched once again.

"Ah, man. That's it for me." Jason yanked off his boots and threw them in the corner of the bathroom. "You made this mess. You can clean it up."

Jason walked out and slammed the door. Mike stayed in the hot bath water but moved closer to the toilet. She could tell she wasn't finished yet. She sat curled up in the water, crying as her head hung over the edge. The smell of the bathroom alone was enough to make her sick. The bathroom, her condition, her situation, her life—all of these conditions made her feel hopeless. *I can't take much more, God. I'm ready to throw in the towel. Please do something.*

JIM WAS FILLING TYLER IN ABOUT THE PHONE CALL they had just received. "An older lady, at a mini mart, in the town of Cecilville. She described them and the car. When the police showed them the composites, she confirmed it was them."

"Is she believable?" Tyler questioned. "Did they show her the picture first, and she just agreed, or did she describe them?"

"She called it in. She said at first she was suspicious of the couple and that the girl looked like she had been roughed up. But get this—she said the girl used the bathroom and then accidentally locked the key inside. When the lady went to get it, there was a message on the back of the door." Tyler's doubting look was vanishing. "It said, 'Help me' . . . and had an Oreo wrapper stuck to the door."

Tyler dashed to the map they had been working on. They were in Modesto last, and now they're in Redding. Tyler thought about it. "He sure is taking his sweet time. He must be staying off the highway, driving back roads or something. Because unless something happened along the way, they certainly aren't taking a direct route."

"My guess is he's staying off the main highway. He knows by now that we've alerted the highway patrol. He's keeping a low profile, but he's definitely heading north."

Tyler grabbed at his jacket hanging off the back of his chair. "I can't stay here any longer, Jim. They're getting further away. We need to pursue them."

"But we don't even know what road they're on or the direction they're going." Jim tried to calm Tyler.

"Well, I can't do anything from here, this far away. I'm going to head north. You can keep me posted on anything that comes up, but at least I'll be closer to the situation if we're able to get a good lead on them."

"Tyler, you haven't gotten any sleep since Mike's been gone. Why don't you wait until morning? Try to get some rest, at least lie down for a couple of hours. I've got a pilot buddy that owes me a favor. I'll call him and see if he can fly you to Redding. I'll make car arrangements and everything for you. Just get some rest before you take off. You're not going to do Mike any good if you end up driving off the road or into someone else because you've fallen asleep at the wheel."

Tyler leaned against the wall and rubbed his eyes. He knew he was mentally exhausted but also knew he wouldn't be able to get any sleep even if he did stick around.

"Tyler, it's going to take you a good eight or nine hours of driving to get to Redding. I'll call Carl and arrange for you to fly out at 5:00 a.m. You'll be there before 7:00, hook up with the locals, find out what they know, and maybe even talk to the store clerk if you want. You're not going to accomplish much more than that if you take off now. Please, just wait until tomorrow."

Tyler wrestled with another night of sitting around and doing nothing. "Okay, call him now. If he can't do it, I'm leaving tonight."

Jim walked around his desk and flipped through his Rolodex while Tyler headed to the washroom. He used the facilities and splashed cold water on his face. He went back to his office to see what Jim had been able to arrange.

Jim looked up. "It's all set. Carl will fly you out at 5:00 in the morning. Now, go lie down in the break room, and I'll arrange transportation for you when you get there."

THE WATER WAS GETTING COLD AND MIKE was shaking. She stepped from the tub onto the cold, clammy floor. She looked around for a towel, but only saw a torn beach towel hanging from a nail on the back of the door. She dried herself off with it the best she could and painfully put her clothes back on. She reached for the roll of toilet paper and wadded it up to mop up the vomit from the floor. Throwing the mess in the toilet, she cupped water to her lips and rinsed her mouth of the taste of bile. She glanced up at the small window in the bathroom. Yesterday, she would have considered attempting to fit her small frame through the little opening; but tonight, all she wanted was fresh air. She pulled on the lever and the window dropped open with a thud. The chain attached to it only allowed about a six-inch opening.

Jason pushed the door open. "What are you doing?"

"Getting fresh air," Mike responded with no feeling in her voice, her eyes expressionless. "Don't worry, Jason. I'm not going anywhere. You win."

Mike limped to the bed and curled up into a ball. She clutched the pillow to her chest and cried. She wasn't feeling much pain; she wasn't feeling much at all thanks to the medication. She liked it this way. She didn't look like herself or feel like herself. She just wanted the whole thing to end.

CHAPTER EIGHTEEN

Tyler hadn't slept, but he was raring to go. Jim got him to the airstrip by 4:30 a.m. Carl was doing his final check when they arrived.

"Thanks, Jim. I couldn't have handled all this without your support."

"You know how you can repay me? Bring Mike back."

Tears welled in Tyler's eyes. "That's what I intend to do." They exchanged a handshake that extended into a hug. "You promise to check in on Hailey? I called her and she knows what's up, but I would feel better knowing someone was checking in on her."

"I understand."

Tyler was walking towards the plane when Carl gave him a wave.

"Hey. A Lieutenant Mitchell will pick you up at the airport and take you to their station. He'll let you look over the report the store manager filed, and then he'll hook you up with some wheels."

Tyler waved his acknowledgment and stepped up into the small Cessna.

MIKE WOKE UP CUFFED TO THE FRAME OF THE bed. She could hear Jason in the bathroom.

She scanned the room for her bag, but it was just out of reach. She sat on the edge of the bed, not sure where she would find the strength to face another day.

"You're up," Jason said as he stretched a T-shirt over his head and fastened his belt. She didn't answer. He uncuffed her and tossed her bag at her. "Get changed." She started to walk to the bathroom. "Not there, here." Jason sat back in the recliner and leered at her.

"Jason, stop." She tried to walk by him but he grabbed her arm.

"Don't walk away from me. I told you to get changed." Mike turned her wrist but couldn't break Jason's hold.

"Why? Do you want to see your handiwork? Is that it?" Mike turned her back to Jason and lifted up her shirt part way up her lower back. "Is this what you want to see, the bruises and the welts?"

He stood up and moved closer to her. "You know I didn't mean to hurt you." He pressed the words to her ear. "It's just that you keep pushing me away, making me feel like I'm not good enough for you. I don't want to hurt you, Mike, but I'm not going to let you go either. You'll remember. You'll remember how it was. And I'm going to be here when you do."

TYLER LANDED AT BENTON AIRPARK IN REDDING, and as promised, was greeted by Lt. Mitchell. He was also able to meet with the store clerk and listened as she told of her encounter with Jason and Mike. Lt. Mitchell drove Tyler to his substation where he had a rental car waiting for him.

"I hear this isn't the typical abduction."

"No . . . it's not." Tyler knew he would've been just as determined if the victim weren't Mike, but he was sure he wouldn't be so empty emotionally.

"So, tell me about her."

Tyler broke a smile. "She's the most obstinate woman you would ever meet. She's pigheaded, stubborn, and incredibly smart. She's beautiful and passionate and . . ." Tyler couldn't continue; his heart was in his throat.

"It sounds like if anyone can make it, she can. She's already figured out ways to let you know what direction she's traveling in."

"I know. That's what I keep banking on."

MIKE AND JASON WERE ON THE MOVE AGAIN. Jason had realized the clock was ticking and they needed to get a move on. Mike knew it was God's intervention that was keeping Jason from assaulting her sexually. Jason assured her that when they arrived at their destination, they would have plenty of time to reaffirm their love for each other. Mike tried to play along as best as she could to his talks of love and romance.

Before leaving town, Jason had swapped license plates with a car that was parked behind the motel. He had also used a garden hose out in front to wash off the car.

Mike sat in the passenger seat and tried to analyze Jason. The jumps in his behavior were hard to understand. One minute, he was beating her and threatening to kill her. The next, he was talking about his love for her and how sure he is that she will one day return that love. It was as if he was living in parallel worlds. One was reality, where he knew only force and threats would keep Mike in line, and the other was fantasy, in which they were lovers who had been separated by time and people. She knew she had to play along.

She could feel her strength returning. It wasn't much, but if she could make it another day, she was sure she would be able to find a way to either escape or turn the tables on him. She had one thing that he wanted more than anything—her love. She would use it as a weapon against him. She would just have to wait for the right moment.

TYLER HADN'T BEEN ON THE ROAD MORE THAN twenty minutes when he got a call from Jim.

"Tyler, Dr. O'Neil called. He said that Carla was talking again. She couldn't make out what she was saying, so I'm driving over there now. Just thought you should know. I'll call you when I'm done and let you know if she says anything new."

"Did you reach Frank yet?"

"No. We've tried and tried, but his cell phone must not be working."

"Did you check in with Hailey this morning?"

"Yeah. She sounds fine. She's really worried about you, though. She's afraid you're going to get yourself killed."

"She's been afraid of that since the day I joined the force. She knows better. I'm not going to do anything stupid."

"Can I take your word on that?" Jim asked concerned.

"I'm fine, Jim. I just needed to put myself closer to the situation. Let me know what you find out from Carla."

"Will do."

Tyler went back to driving and studying the map he had unfolded on the passenger seat. He was on a frontage road that drifted back and forth alongside the main highway. He was sure that Jason was steering clear of the interstate, otherwise he would have been spotted by now.

He stopped off in Weaverville and Cecilville to show Jason and Mike's picture at a gas station and a few truck stops. No one had seen the two or a car matching its description. He was headed out of town when he saw a rundown motel alongside the road. His gut told him to stop, so he pulled in and went to find someone in charge. No one was in the little office when he stepped in, so Tyler rang the old bell sitting on the counter. His eyes followed the cracked molding around the ceiling and came to rest on the smut magazine sitting on the counter.

"Yeah, what do you want?" A sullen looking man came out from the back room. He looked to have two days growth on his face and a cheap cigar dangling from his lips.

"I'm with the Emerald Lake Police Department."

"Never heard of it."

The man's belligerence let Tyler know he wasn't going to be much help. "I'm looking for two people who might have stopped through here in the last day or so." Tyler pulled the police sketch from his pocket. "Do they look familiar to you?"

Recognition registered on the clerk's face. "So what if they do? What's in it for me?"

Tyler was ready to reach across the small counter and level the guy, but he knew that would only cause him to clam up. "I can tell you there might be a big reward in it for you." He lied. "The man is wanted for four counts of murder. You help us find him, and you could be compensated."

The cigar in the man's mouth switched from one corner to the next. He rubbed at his bristly chin and said, "He told me he was running from her husband."

"So they were here?" Hope soared in Tyler.

"Yeah. Last night. He said he would pay me a couple extra bucks if I lied if anyone came looking for them. Said she was running away from an abusive husband who was out looking for them. They left this morning. Paid for the room last night but never did pay me that extra he talked about. Just took off."

"Were they still driving a dark blue Camero?"

"Yep. Washed it off with the garden hose this morning."

"What room did they stay in?"

"Number ten."

"Can I see the room?"

"It's twenty-five dollars a night."

"I'm not going to stay in it; I just want to see it."

"Stay in it, see it—it all costs the same. Twenty-five dollars."

Tyler didn't want to waste time arguing with the man. He handed him the money and took the key. The clerk started following him out the door.

"Where are you going?" Tyler asked.

"I want to make sure the room is in good condition and make sure they didn't mess it up at all."

"Well, I just paid twenty-five dollars for the room. It's mine for the day. You can check it out when I'm gone."

The clerk gave Tyler a disgusted snarl and chomped down on his cigar before turning and walking back towards the office.

Tyler put the key in the lock and said a prayer.

JASON PULLED INTO THE PARKING LOT of a fast food joint in Yreka. "Let's grab something to eat." They had only been traveling about two hours, most of it in silence. "I'm starved."

When Jason pulled into the drive-thru lane, Mike's heart sunk. She thought they would be going in. She was thinking of some way to leave another clue even though she had no way of knowing if Tyler had gotten the other ones, but she had to keep trying.

All of a sudden, Jason shouted at her. "Get down!"

"What?"

"I said get down!" Jason shoved her down toward the floorboard of the car. "Stay down there until I say you can get up."

Mike watched Jason's eyes dart between the rear view mirror and the side mirror. He was watching something, but Mike didn't know what.

The patrol car pulled into the parking lot, driving alongside the drive-thru lane. It stopped parallel to those waiting in line. Jason was next and had to drive up beside the patrol car. He reached for a ball cap from behind his seat and pulled it down snugly on his forehead. "Don't move, Mike, or someone's going to die."

She still didn't know what was happening—that is, until she glanced out the window from her place on the floor. She could see the light bar of a patrol car. The police were right next to them. The cocking of a gun turned Mike's attention back to Jason. "Don't try me, Mike."

A restaurant attendant walked in front of Jason's car and around to where the patrol car was idling. She handed them a tray holding two coffees and a bag. "Have a good day, officers." She quickly returned to the restaurant.

"Okay, that will be $9.87." The attendant was talking to Jason.

He handed her a ten dollar bill and told her to keep the change. He took the bag she was offering and slowly pulled away from the window. He glanced in his rearview mirror to see what the cops were doing. One of the officers appeared to be staring directly at him. Jason casually looked from right to left, before pulling into traffic.

The officer glanced at the license number. "Hey, Jerry, what was the plate numbers on that Camero we heard about the other day?"

Jerry swallowed the piece of Danish he had just bit into and grabbed the flyer. "It's only a partial. WAT. Why?"

That Camero that just pulled out, the guy seemed kind of strange, but his license was 159GNP."

"But the flyer says to be looking for a male and female."

"Yeah, I know. There was just something about that guy."

The officer stirred his coffee and pulled back out on the highway. "The problem with being a cop is that after awhile, everyone looks suspicious," he said.

"THEY'VE BEEN HERE, JIM, NO DOUBT ABOUT IT. There are bandages in the trash and another Oreo wrapper on a side table." Tyler looked around at the dump that he was standing in before closing the door. "Jason gave the clerk some story about running from an abusive husband. I'm going to contact Lt. Mitchell and have his guys come over here, and then I'll be on my way. It's obvious they are still traveling north. I just wish I knew where they were headed so I could get a jump on them."

Tyler was talking to Jim as he roamed the perimeter of the building. He saw an Impala parked behind the motel and glanced at the license.

"Jim, we might have a new lead. I'll call you back in a minute."

Tyler went to find the clerk. It took a couple rings of the bell before she showed up. "Do you own the Impala out back?"

"Yeah, why?"

"What is its license number?"

"You couldn't write it down for yourself?" The clerk continued with his non-compliant attitude.

"I think the man I'm looking for took your license plates—that is, unless your plates have the letters WAT in them?"

The clerk rushed out the door and around the back. He let out a stream of expletives before turning to Tyler. "I just put the registration tags on last week. Had to pay a fine because I was late."

"Tell me the number and I'll make sure we get them back to you."

"159GNP."

Jim's voice mail picked up immediately. Tyler remembered he was going to see Carla, so he probably left his phone in the car. "Jim, Jason's changed the plates on the car. The new number is 159GNP. Can you be sure to get that broadcasted? They left here only a few hours ago, which means they can't be far. Let me know when you get this message."

Tyler was back on the road when he received Jim's call.

"I've already notified everyone about the license change. How'd you figure it out?"

"He took the plates from the motel clerk." Tyler passed a sign: Yreka 40 miles. "What did Carla have to say?"

"A lot of the same. She talked about Mike and mooning, and wanting to go, but she did say something that she didn't say before."

"What's that?"

"She seemed to be talking about caves."

"Caves?"

"Yeah. She talked about them being scary and dark, but then she talked about another one that wasn't. One that she wasn't afraid of. Do you think Jason could be heading for a cave? There are all kinds of them in northern California."

"Why would he head to a cave? Surely he doesn't plan on hiding out in one." Tyler was thinking out loud.

"It didn't make much sense to me either." Jim seemed distracted momentarily. "Hold on a minute. I have another call."

Tyler kept turning the idea of a cave over in his mind while he waited for Jim to return to the phone.

"Tyler, they've been spotted at a drive-thru in Yreka."

"What? That's only forty miles from me." Tyler's foot immediately pressed harder on the accelerator. "Who saw them?"

"Two cops at the end of their shift. They said they were waiting for their order, saw the car, but since the license plate didn't match, they let it go. They were in their station when the update came through. They're positive it was the car but said there was no female in the car, at least not that they could see."

"Thanks Jim. I'm going to call Lt. Mitchell and see if he knows anything about any caves in the area. I'll be in touch." Tyler didn't want to think about the possibility that Mike was no longer with Jason. *What if he dumped her off somewhere? What if she's . . .*

Tyler called the station, but Mitchell was out in the field. They put Tyler on hold while they patched the call through.

"Tyler, I'm glad you called. Where are you?"

"I just passed a sign for Yreka. I'm about forty miles away."

"I should be able to catch up with you in about twenty minutes."

"What for?"

"I think we're getting close, and I want to make sure we have the manpower to apprehend this guy."

Tyler's heart was pounding through his chest in anticipation. "Look, Lieutenant, do you know anything about caves in the area? We kind of have a unique situation." Tyler went on to explain the few clues that Carla was able to give and the fact that she was now talking about caves.

"I don't know anything about any caves, at least none that haven't already been turned into tourist attractions. But I'll throw that info back to the station and see if anyone else comes up with anything."

"Okay. I'm heading for Yreka, I'll hook up with you there."

MIKE SAW THE SIGN FOR THE OREGON BORDER. "Where are you taking me?"

"A nice little place that I found. I think you'll like it."

"You realize you'll add another charge to your rap sheet if we cross state lines?"

Jason laughed. "If they ever catch me, which they won't, I think they'll be more concerned with the murder charges than crossing state lines."

Mike hated Jason's cavalier attitude. He actually thought he was going to get away with this.

"So, you're going to hold me as a prisoner somewhere?"

"Maybe at first, but you'll see. You'll come to love it as much as I love you."

TYLER ANSWERED HIS PHONE ON THE FIRST RING.

"Tyler, it's Mitchell. We think we know where they're headed."

Tyler immediately called Jim to fill him in on Mitchell's suspicions.

"Mitchell has a hunch. If Jason is heading for the Oregon border, Oregon Caves National Monument and a small town called Cave Junction is less than twenty miles from the border. That's where Mitchell thinks they're going. Is there any way you can go back to Sherwood and see if Carla recognizes either of those names?"

"Sure. I'll see what I can do." Jim hung up the phone with Tyler, immediately called Dr. O'Neil, and explained what they needed.

"I'll call you right back," was her quick reply.

Jim paced the office waiting for the call. He phoned Hailey and let her know they were getting closer and that Tyler sounded good. Just then, Frank burst into the station looking like he was going to collapse.

"What happened, Jim? What happened?"

Jim sat Frank down. "I'm sorry, Frank, that we couldn't tell you sooner. No one knew where you were."

"I was in Bakersfield at a breeding ranch. Arnie knew that and so did Mike."

"But you didn't answer your cell phone."

"What?" Frank reached into his pocket and realized his phone was off. He was not used to the conveniences of modern technology and hadn't realized that the battery had gone dead.

"What's happened? Where's Michal?"

After being filled in on what was happening, Frank began weeping uncontrollably into his hands. When he had arrived home from his trip, he was greeted by a police officer and crime scene tape. The officer didn't explain what happened, only that Jim had been trying to reach him.

The relief he felt from Jim's assurance that he felt Michal was still alive dimmed when he found out that Arnie and the dogs had been killed. He was afraid that Jason would have no reason to spare Mike's life.

His sobs were silent, but his heaving shoulders spoke of his devastation. Jim told Frank all that they knew, including the fact that they were picking up momentum.

"Jim, Dr. O'Neil is on line three." Jenny pointed to the flashing light on the phone.

"How'd it go, Doctor?"

"Cave Junction—she recognized Cave Junction." Jim could hear the smile on Dr. O'Neil's face.

"You're sure?" Jim knew they couldn't afford any mistakes. They were too close.

"Yes. I talked a few minutes about national parks and national monuments, and she didn't respond at all. I talked about touring caves and asked if she thought that would be fun. She told me they were too scary. Then I mentioned Cave Junction, and she lit up like a Christmas tree. She started talking about how Jason was going to take her there. How he was going to let her visit again someday, once he and Mike got there. She went on for some time about a cabin in the woods and roasting marshmallows. It has to be it, Detective. She recognized the name instantly."

"Thank you, Dr. O'Neil. This is just the break we needed."

Frank looked up with bloodshot eyes; Jim silenced the question on his lips with an upraised hand. He had to relay the information to Tyler.

"Tyler, Jim. It's Cave Junction. Carla talked about a little cabin and roasting marshmallows, stuff like that." Jim heard the shout of excitement from Tyler. "Tyler, do you have backup?" Jim was afraid Tyler was going to go in commando-style and get himself killed.

"Yes, Lt. Mitchell is following me with three of his detectives. He's already notified the Oregon State Police and the FBI. They are going to join up with us as soon as we cross state lines. "Jim ..." Tyler's words got serious. "I know you and Hailey are not the praying sort, but I could use all the support I can get."

"I've got someone here that needs to talk to you, Tyler." Jim's words were equally sober. Frank took the phone from Jim's hand and with a quivering voice spoke to Tyler.

"Tyler, you bring my little girl home. You hear me?"

The sound of Frank's voice crumbled Tyler's composure. "I promise, Frank. Because when this is all done, I'm going to be asking you for a favor of my own."

Tyler had to make the conversation short. He couldn't allow himself to fall apart now, not when they were so close. He called Mitchell to give him the update. They were headed to Cave Junction.

MIKE SAW SIGNS GO BY FOR MEDFORD and Grant's Pass. They seemed to be going west now, but she couldn't be sure.

"So will you tell me where we're going now?"

"I guess it won't hurt anything since we're almost there," he said as he stretched out his legs and rolled his head. "Cave Junction. It's this little town I stumbled across a couple of years ago. I liked it because of its privacy and seclusion. I thought it would be a great place to escape from it all. But I couldn't imagine being there without you."

"So what are we going to do there?"

"Live there. What did you think?"

"You have a house there?"

"Yep. But don't think Tyler's going to be able to find it. I bought the house using my mom's maiden name. I had a friend do some title work on the house and made it look like it changed hands a couple of times, but it never really changed ownership. They would have to know exactly what they're looking for to find it; and let's face it, they're not that smart." The grin on Jason's face spoke of victory. He already felt as if he had won.

Another hour or so had passed when they finally pulled down a long, narrow driveway hidden in the dense forest of its surroundings. They stopped in front of a typical A-frame log cabin. Jason shouted with excitement at finally arriving at the finish line. He quickly crossed to the passenger side of the car and unhooked the cuff attached to Mike's seat belt. He bent down and lifted Mike into his arms. She winced as he clutched her side and tried to wriggle loose from his hold.

"What are you doing? I can walk just fine!"

"I'm carrying you over the threshold. Isn't that what newlyweds are supposed to do?" He tightened his grip on her to get her to stop squirming.

"We're not married, Jason."

"Not yet, but we will be." He carried her up the front steps, oblivious to her discomfort. He fiddled with the lock and finally stepped through the doorway. "So, what do you think?" He set Mike down and let her take in her surroundings.

Mike was stunned. She had imagined a dilapidated old cabin with broken windows and weathered boards; but instead, it looked like something out of a designer magazine. Sleek modern furniture filled the living space. Tailored fabrics and crisp white woodwork covered the walls and windows. Jason led her through the kitchen and showed her the outdoor spa. A massive fireplace, made completely of slate, was flanked by floor-to-ceiling windows. He watched as she gazed from one room to the other.

"I knew you would like it. It cost me a small fortune, but you're worth it. You're worth everything I had to go through to get you here." Jason pulled her close to himself and began to kiss her passionately. He wrapped her in his arms and held her close. She struggled to get away, but Jason was so much stronger than she was in her weakened condition. Finally, she moved her mouth and ground her teeth into his lip.

Jason cried out from the pain and pulled away from her. He looked at her with enraged eyes. "Why did you have to do that? Why do you insist on spoiling everything I do for you?" He was shaking her with every word that he spoke, causing her head to snap back and forth.

"Because I hate you!" Her words brought his shaking to a stop. "Do you hear me? I hate you. I will never love you. I don't want this." She swept her arm around the room. "And I don't want you. "

"Then I guess I'll just have to teach you not to be so ungrateful." He dragged her across the room to a small closet off the back of the kitchen. "Maybe after spending some time in here, you'll begin to appreciate what I've provided for you." He shoved her into the small enclosure and slammed the door shut. Her shoulder smashed into a crossbeam and sent her to her knees. She thought she was going to pass out from the pain as she reached for her bandage. It was beginning to feel moist. Her wound was bleeding again. She heard a locking mechanism slide into place and could feel the darkness that surrounded her. A door slammed, and she could hear the screeching of tires. She rubbed at her lips with the back of her hand, trying to remove the taste of Jason from her mouth. She sat far back in the closet and kicked at the door, hoping to get it open. As hard as she tried, it wouldn't budge, and she didn't have the strength to continue.

Her mind wandered while she was in her cramped prison. She thought of Tyler. She thought of her dad and how unfair life had treated him. *Help him, Lord. He needs to know you love him.* She tried kicking at the door again. *If I could just get outside. Run. Hide. Scream for help, something.* She wasn't sure how long she'd been in the closet when she heard a door slam. Jason was back.

Jason unpacked the groceries he'd picked up at the local market. He wasn't afraid of being seen. The town's people knew him as Wayne, a quiet man that kept to himself. He had visited his place every so often, but never stayed long enough for people to get to know him. After putting the groceries away, he went back outside and drove the car further down the driveway, out of plain view. When he was done, he unlatched the lock that had held Mike captive.

"Now, we are going to try this again," he said as he pulled Mike up from the floor of the closet and drew her into his arms. She didn't fight back physically but had to concentrate to keep her nausea at bay. "Now . . . let me show you the bedroom."

With a firm hold on her waist, Jason led Mike up the stairs. Glass doors opened up into a bedroom decorated in stark grays and blacks. The contemporary appeal was lost on Mike; to her it felt cold and repulsive. Jason led her into the master bathroom area that was cavernous. He showed her a closet that he had filled with a new wardrobe just for her. Then he led her back to the bed.

He began to pull at the snaps of her shirt.

"Jason." Mike tried to sound enticing. "Why don't we christen the Jacuzzi? I feel all grimy from the long trip, and I'm still kind of stiff. The jets from the Jacuzzi would feel so good right now. They would help me relax."

"All right. I'll help you get undressed." He pulled at the button on her jeans.

"Is there a swimsuit in there?" Mike asked as she pointed to the closet.

"Yeah, but what do you need a swimsuit for?" He pulled at her zipper.

"Jason, you want me to love you, right?" He pulled back for a moment so he could see her face.

"Yeah."

"I can't just flaunt my body like some other women do. That's just not me." She was trying her best to sound sincere. "I've never been with anyone other than you. I just want to take this slow. One step at a time. You understand, don't you?"

Jason was sexually charged just from their conversation. His chest was heaving with his excitement. "I understand." He walked over to the closet and pulled out a black bikini. "I've wanted to see you in this for over a year." She took the skimpy garment from him and stepped into the bathroom. *Forgive me, Lord, for what I'm about to do. I just don't see any other way.* She tied the bikini and slipped it over her neck. It was a little loose, but there was no way she could reach behind her neck to tighten it. She looked in the mirror at her red-blotched bandage, her unkempt hair, and her bruised body. She looked like a mess and only wished that Jason could see her this way instead of through his own lustful eyes.

She stepped from the bathroom, holding two plush towels against her stomach, trying to conceal what the bathing suit did not. She was glad to see Jason had donned a pair of trunks. He moved close to her and caressed her bare shoulder. She shuddered, causing Jason to look at her with disappointment.

"I just wish I wasn't so battered and bruised. I wish I could look nicer for you. I'm sorry. I just feel self-conscious right now."

"That's okay, Mike. You always look beautiful to me." He wrapped his arm around her as they descended the stairs together.

THE OREGON POLICE AND FBI MET UP WITH Mitchell and Tyler at the state line. They understood the sensitivity of the case, and because of that, allowed Tyler to proceed with them. Mitchell, on the other hand, was considered extra baggage. Tyler extended his hand to Mitchell and thanked him for all the help he had provided.

"She's going to make it, Tyler. You've just got to keep the faith." Mitchell gave him a firm handshake. "My wife and I will be praying for you."

"I appreciate that." Tyler was disappointed that Mitchell was getting cut loose. He was a Christian, and the few conversations he'd been able to have with him had encouraged him more than Mitchell would ever know.

Tyler rode shotgun with FBI Agent Samuels. The Oregon Police were already canvassing the town of Cave Junction, coming up with possible locations where Jason might be hiding out. They had it narrowed down to two places and were on their way to check them both out. They hoped to have it nailed down by the time the FBI arrived.

CHAPTER NINETEEN

Jason opened the French doors that led to the deck and Jacuzzi. The deck was multi-tiered with the Jacuzzi on the top and stairs descending to two other levels. It was surrounded by dense forest, not another neighbor in sight. Jason took the towels that Mike was holding and tossed them on a nearby chaise. He admired the way she looked in the bikini and let out a low moan. Walking over to the spa, he tossed something into the water, and then pulled his gun from the small of his back and laid it nearby. "Don't take any chances, Mike. I'll use it if I have to."

"What was that?" Mike asked as she pointed to the pebbles descending to the bottom of the tub.

"A little something to help you relax," he said as he moved closer. "The aroma is supposed to work as an aphrodisiac." His eyes danced with anticipation.

Jason stepped into the Jacuzzi and stood in the middle of the rolling water. He helped Mike down to the first step. She paused to acclimate herself to the temperature. She gazed around, appearing to admire the beauty of the view, but she was actually looking for the best way of escape. She could run back to the highway and try to flag someone down, but there was always the chance that Jason would be able to follow her with his car. No, her best chance was the forest. If she could distract Jason somehow, she could run for the forest and try to get lost in the density of the foliage and underbrush.

Jason pulled her further down into the water. He held her close, but she quickly pulled away. Sitting with her back against one of the jets, she sighed. "This is what I need. My muscles hurt so bad I could cry."

Jason looked away. She could see that he struggled with a sense of guilt. He knew it was his fault that she was in such pain, but he tried to ignore the facts. He draped his arms around the padded rim and allowed his head to fall back. Mike massaged the muscles in her legs. She hoped they would have the strength to get her far away from here. It took only a few moments before Jason made his way over to where Mike was sitting. "Here, let me do that." Jason knelt in the water and began to massage her leg.

Mike felt like she wanted to crawl out of her own skin. Jason's touch was anything but soothing. She couldn't handle it anymore. She jumped to her feet, causing Jason to grab at her.

"I just need to stand for a moment. The water was getting too hot."

Jason pulled her back into the water. "Maybe it wasn't the water that was getting too hot." *I can do this,* she chanted to herself. *It's a matter of survival.* Mike wanted to survive. *I will not end up as Michelle did. I will fight until the bitter end.* Jason began to press up against her, trapping her against the wall, his hands searching for the ties of her bikini. She reached for his roaming hand and brought it up to her lips. She began to kiss his fingers, trying to be as seductive as she could manage without being sick to her stomach.

"What are those?" Mike pointed to what looked like small planters with no plants that were placed around the Jacuzzi.

"They're outdoor speakers."

"You mean we could be listening to music?" Mike knew they were speakers. She was hoping she could get Jason to go into the house to turn them on.

"Sure. Do you want to hear some?" Jason started moving from the tub. This would be her chance.

"That would be wonderful. How romantic." A smile creased her face. Jason thought it was because of him, but it was the adrenaline that was beginning to build in her at the thought of running. Jason stepped out of the tub and moved to the French doors, but he didn't step inside. He merely reached through the door and picked up a small remote that was on a nearby shelf. Mike wanted to scream. Her heart was racing, ready for her to leap from the tub and the chance to make her way down the steps, but Jason never allowed her out of his sight. She realized she would have to be more convincing.

RADIO TRAFFIC FILLED THE CAR. Tyler listened intently as the FBI agents decided to move in on one of the locations just as they rolled up on the scene. There was yelling and banging. The commotion was difficult to decipher without a visual. When the disturbance calmed down, an agent returned to the airwaves.

"No go."

"They're not there?"

"No, sir. We might have stumbled upon a harvester, but nothing on your suspects.

Tyler sighed with disappointment. The two FBI agents continued to pass information back and forth. They would be turning it over to the locals, but it was still a find to them.

"Okay, Henderson, let's hope they're at the other location," Agent Samuels said as he pulled back on the main road.

MIKE DETACHED HERSELF FROM THE PERSON THAT WAS now acting out the things that Jason wanted from her. She scrambled to think of something more she could do. Going for the gun was out of the question. There was no way she would be able to get to it before Jason.

Again Jason pulled at the bottoms of her bikini. She grabbed for his searching hands and pulled him under the water. She began to kiss him fervently under the surface. They came up for air, but Jason clearly was turned on by it. He pulled her back down with him, and this time she swallowed a mouthful of water. *Maybe this could be the distraction.*

Mike catapulted to the surface and started coughing uncontrollably. She grabbed for her throat and gasped for air.

"What is it? What's wrong?" Jason yelled at Mike. She continued to cough and gag, unable to talk. Convulsing, she leaned over the side of the Jacuzzi. Jason spun her around so faced at him. She was turning purple.

"Oil," she gasped. "I . . . swallowed . . . one of those pebbles." Her words were broken and barely audible.

"What can I do?"

"Milk . . . need . . . milk." Mike was hardly able to choke out the words. In an instant, Jason jumped from the tub and ran to the house.

Mike reacted the second he disappeared through the door. She leapt from the tub, grabbed for the gun, and ran full speed down the first flight of stairs. She was descending the second flight when Jason reappeared on the deck.

"Noooo!" he shrilled like a wounded animal.

Mike didn't stop, she just kept running. She felt the branches tearing at her skin and jagged rocks cutting into her feet. She didn't know how far Jason was behind her. *Would she have enough time to stop and take aim, or would he be on her too quickly?* she asked herself as she kept running.

CARS WERE PARKED ON THE EDGE OF THE HIGHWAY, along with an ambulance and a medical team. If Jason was in there, he would not go without a fight. The agents and officers exchanged positions as they advanced on the house. The first officer on the scene gave the thumbs-up. The identified car was parked to the side of the house. Everything else was strangely quiet.

Tyler was with the officers that were flanking the east side of the house. They were beside the elevated deck and could hear what sounded like a hot tub rumbling and soft music playing, but no voices and no signs of movement.

They rounded the deck and climbed the stairs. The Jacuzzi was on, towels were nearby, and a shattered glass was on the deck. The door to the house hung open, and after careful positioning, the officers swarmed the house from all sides. Tyler raced up the stairs to the second level of the house and found a pile of clothes on the floor, but no Mike.

"Clear. Clear. Clear." Each officer cleared the rooms one by one, but Mike was nowhere to be found.

MIKE TOOK COVER ON A LEDGE, BEHIND A LARGE boulder. She was bleeding from head to toe, and a gash on the bottom of her foot made running any further impossible. She waited. Jason would come into view soon. She would only have one shot at him.

He ran into the clearing, deciding which way Mike might have gone. She lowered the gun and took aim. Just as she was ready to pull the trigger, she lost her footing. Her finger pulled the trigger, but she missed Jason completely. She tumbled from her perch and saw him coming towards her. She scrambled to get to her feet and retrieve the gun from the twigs and leaves. She swung around to aim, but it was too late. Jason lunged at her, knocking her back to the ground, causing the gun to cartwheel deeper into the ground cover. He slammed her face into the hard ground.

"You idiot. It could have been good. You would have adjusted. Now you've ruined everything." He spun her around so he could see her face. "Now, you've given me no choice."

Jason straddled Mike and wrapped his hands around her throat. She clawed at his hands, trying to peel his fingers back from her neck. Kicking and squirming, she tried to get free but it was no use. She dug her fingers into his face, causing him to groan. Blood trickled from his cheeks, but he didn't relinquish his hold on her neck. She could feel her oxygen being cut off. She didn't want to die, but she was no match for Jason's enraged strength. *Please, Lord, take care of Dad and Tyler. Send Tyler someone to love.* She regretted that she never had the chance to tell her dad or Tyler about her recommitment to the Lord. They would never know the comfort that God had given her in these last few days.

She no longer struggled. She felt her body collapse against the cold, wet ground. She had no strength left. She heard a shot ring out before she closed her eyes.

A CLOUD OF OFFICERS AND AGENTS DESCENDED onto the clearing. Tyler reached Jason and Mike first. He pulled Jason off Mike, looked at her battered body and cried out. He put his ear to her mouth and felt the flutter of air. "Don't leave me, Mike! Don't you dare leave me!"

The medical team was on the scene in seconds. The four attendants surrounded Mike and began working on her immediately. Tyler sat above her head and stroked her hair. "Don't give up, baby. You've fought too hard to give up now." He listened as the attendants passed information back and forth with a local hospital. Agent Samuels stood nearby as the investigative team took pictures of Jason and documented his wound. Jason was killed with a single shot to the head. The sharpshooter did his job with precision.

An oxygen mask was strapped to Mike's face. Her complexion was gray and looked void of any life. Her many cuts, abrasions, and bruises were visible due to the scanty swimsuit she was wearing. One attendant threw a thermal blanket over her, covering her exposed body. Tyler caught his eye. A silent "thank you" passed between them. After Jason had been photographed, Agent Samuels reached into Jason's pocket and found the key to the handcuffs dangling from Mike's wrist. He tossed the key to Tyler, who quickly removed the cuff.

Everyone on the scene knew Tyler's relationship to the victim. They felt as if they had failed their mission. Losing a victim was unacceptable in their book. Not knowing if Mike was going to survive was weighing heavily on all of them.

She needed medical attention immediately, but in the wooded area where they were located, Medivac was out of the question. They would transport her as soon as she was stable.

Mike was carefully rolled onto a back board and then lifted onto the gurney. It took six men to carry the gurney over the rough terrain. They slid her into the back of the ambulance, four attendants taking their positions around her.

"You're welcome to ride in the front," the medic that was in charge said to Tyler.

"What are her chances?" Tyler asked, desperate for some hopeful news.

"The doctor will be better equipped to answer your questions." The attendant turned. Tyler grabbed his arm to regain his attention.

"But what do you think?"

"Depends on how much fight she has left in her."

The doors to the ambulance closed, and Tyler quickly jumped into the front seat before it sped away. His hands were shaking as he dialed Jim.

"We got him. Jason's dead."

Jim could tell that Tyler was emotional. "And Mike?"

He turned to see the medics working on her through the Plexiglas partition. "It's too early to tell." He swallowed hard. "They're taking her to Harbor University."

Jim didn't know how to respond. Frank stood by, anxious for some information. "Stay in touch."

"Yeah." Tyler clicked off the phone.

Jim looked at Frank. "I don't have any answers, Frank. I can tell you she's been injured, but I'm not sure to what extent."

"But what did Tyler say? Is she going to make it?"

"It's too early to tell."

While Frank tried to absorb the information, Jim got on the phone to Carl. He arranged a flight for Frank, Hailey, and himself to leave in thirty minutes.

TYLER SAT IN THE CORNER OF THE EMERGENCY room waiting and praying, his head between his hands, his elbows on his knees, and tears streaming down his face. He would look up every time the electric door was activated but would resume his praying when it closed.

Agent Samuels stood by the admittance desk with another agent; Tyler never got his name. They had procedures and reports to file, so they spoke together while waiting for some answers.

The electric door swung open and a white-clad doctor approached Samuels. Tyler sat up straighter. The two men turned and walked towards Tyler.

"Detective Henderson, this is Dr. Byrnes."

The customary handshake ensued.

"I understand that though you are not a family member, you have a special relationship with Ms. Madigan."

"Yes, Doctor . . . how is she?"

"Let's step inside." Tyler didn't feel like he breathed the whole time they walked the corridor. Finally, Dr. Byrnes turned to him as they came to stand beside a large white door. "Ms. Madigan lost consciousness due to lack of oxygen. At this time, we cannot determine the length of deprivation. Though her brain activity looks good, we will not know for sure if any damage has been done until she regains consciousness."

"But she's going to make it?"

"Yes. She has numerous other injuries that will need our attention, but she is going to survive. There is the possibility of surgery. Our concern is internal bleeding. We are still waiting to get those test results."

"Can I see her?"

"We're still attending to her contusions and abrasions. If you'll wait here, a nurse will come and get you when they're done."

"Thank you, Doctor, thank you." Tyler couldn't say enough to the man who had brought such good news.

The doctor walked into another room, and Tyler turned to Samuels. "I have to let her father know. I'm going to run outside and call Jim really quick. Promise you'll come and get me as soon as I can see her."

"Of course, I will." Samuel leaned against the wall while Tyler jogged down the corridor.

"Jim, I can barely hear you."

"We're at the airstrip. Carl is flying Frank, Hailey, and me up there. We'll be there soon. How is she doing?"

"Let me talk to Frank."

Jim passed the phone to Frank. He looked as if he had aged ten years over the last few hours. "How is she, son?"

"She's going to make it. They still don't know the extent of her injuries, but she's going to make it, Frank, so keep praying."

"I will, Tyler, you bet I will." Frank could not control the tears that moistened his eyes.

WHEN TYLER REENTERED THE WAITING ROOM, Samuels was standing there. "What are you doing out here?" Tyler nearly shouted. "You're supposed to be keeping watch for me."

"They needed to take her into surgery. She was still struggling to breathe, and the x-rays showed she has a punctured lung. The doctor will come and get us when it's over."

Tyler raked his hands through his hair and paced up and down. He felt as if he were going to jump out of his skin. He needed to see her. He needed to see for himself that she was still alive.

An hour and a half passed before Dr. Byrnes made another appearance. "She's doing fine," he said as soon as he met Tyler's eyes. "Her breathing has improved immensely. We still have her on oxygen so that she doesn't have to struggle too much. Her larynx is severely bruised and swollen, making it difficult for her."

"But I can see her now?"

"In about twenty minutes." Tyler's shoulder's sagged. "I know this is difficult for you, Detective Henderson, but we need to think of what's best for the patient at this time."

"I know, Doctor. It's just that I haven't seen her for days."

"I understand. I'll send someone to get you as soon as possible."

Twenty minutes had barely passed when a young nurse tapped Tyler on the shoulder. "Are you Detective Henderson?"

"Yes." He stood up quickly.

"I can take you to see Ms. Madigan now."

Tyler followed her down the corridor, not even noticing the throng of reporters that were now gathered outside. She stopped at the door and turned to address Tyler before he entered. "She still needs to be moved to a permanent room, but Dr. Byrnes wanted you to be able to see her as soon as possible."

"Is she conscious yet?"

"Not yet, but feel free to talk to her. It helps if patients can hear a familiar voice."

Tyler slowly pushed open the sterile door. He crossed to where Mike lay under a crisp white sheet, with an oxygen mask around her face. He reached for her hand. "Mike . . . it's me . . . Tyler. Honey, you're going to make it, so you need to wake up." He brushed his hand across her cheek and leaned down close to her face. He placed a kiss to her forehead and said a prayer of thanksgiving.

Mike trembled, causing Tyler to straighten up. She pulled her hand up to her face and tried knocking the oxygen mask off.

"No, Mike, don't do that. You need that, sweetheart." Tyler pulled her hand down to her side.

Mike started lashing about. She felt something on her face, someone grabbing at her hands. It must be Jason; she still must be struggling with him. She finally opened her eyes and saw Tyler standing before her. The realization that it was the man she loved brought her thrashing about to a stop.

"It's me, Mike. You're okay. You're safe now."

Tears started falling from her eyes. The last few days swirled around her. She wanted to find out about Arnie, Oreo and 'Nilla. Where was her dad? What about the vet and the little girl—were they okay? Where was Jim? She tried to speak, but her throat felt like it was filled with shards of glass. Her words were strained and obviously painful to utter.

"Don't try to talk, Mike. Your throat is pretty messed up."

She thought about Jason's other victims and instinctively reached for her throat. She didn't feel any bandages.

Tyler realized what she was doing and put her at ease. "No, honey, you weren't cut. You just have some bruising and swelling. "

She remembered. Jason had been hovering over her and then she had heard a shot. "Jason?" She struggled to say the one word, fear in her eyes.

"He's dead, Mike. He can't hurt you or anyone else any more."

A nurse with an attendant came into the room. "Ms. Madigan, how are you feeling?" She talked slow and loud, as if Mike were deaf. Mike tried to smile. "Well, we're going to move you to your own room now, okay? And then Dr. Byrnes will be in to see you." Again, Mike answered with a weak smile.

Tyler followed them as they rolled Mike to a room on the third floor. He pulled up a chair beside her and reached for her hand. He stared at her, afraid to blink, afraid to rest. He didn't want to let her out of his sight.

It wasn't long before Dr. Byrnes stepped into the room. He reacquainted himself with Tyler and then turned to Mike. "Ms. Madigan, I'm going to ask you a few yes or no questions, so all you'll need to do is shake your head, okay?"

She nodded in reply.

The doctor's questions were very basic at first, and then he delved a little further. "Now, I'm going to ask you to do a few things and to answer some questions. Keep your answers brief. I don't want you to put a lot of strain on your throat, but I want to see what you remember."

Because of Mike's loss of oxygen, Dr. Byrnes was looking for any signs of complications. He asked her to complete basic tasks, like raise her right arm and wiggle her left foot—actions that involved motor functions as well as comprehension. Then he asked her questions and had Tyler ask her some as well.

She answered everything without hesitation. The doctor finished his evaluation and then looked at Mike with a relieved expression. "Young lady, you should consider yourself one lucky person. When you came in here earlier, your condition was quite grave. Your recovery is nothing short of a miracle."

Mike knew that. She felt that. But she was not surprised. God had brought her through so much. She knew he would not bring her this far to allow her life to slip away now.

It was less than an hour before Jim, Frank, and Hailey arrived. Frank stepped into the room first, looking pale and tired. Tyler stood up and slowly let go of Mike's hand. He crossed the room and embraced Frank. Frank fell apart in his arms.

"I was afraid I was going to lose her just like Michelle. I was so afraid."

"I know, Frank, me too. But she's going to make it. She's pretty banged up, but she's going to be okay."

Frank stepped closer to look at his sleeping child. He looked past the black hair and the bruised skin. It was his Michal and she was beautiful to him.

Tyler stepped out of the room to give Frank some time with Mike. Hailey embraced Tyler the minute she saw him. Her puffy, red eyes were signs that she had been crying, but now she played the part of the tough guy. Tyler gave Jim a firm handshake and a knowing smile.

"You should see all the reporters outside, Tyler. It looks like a three-ring circus. It's all over the news too."

Mike was not going to be happy about that. He would tell her eventually, but now was not the time. "Don't say anything to Mike. It will only upset her."

"No problem, Tyler," Jim said with a hand to his shoulder.

"You look horrible." Hailey spoke the obvious.

"Thanks, I love you too."

"So how is she?" Jim asked soberly.

"She's a sight, but the most beautiful sight I've ever seen."

"What are her injuries?" The detective in Jim was coming out. He wanted the details.

"The ones I know about? A couple of broken ribs, a punctured lung, a bruised larynx, a bullet wound to the shoulder, and multiple bruises, abrasions, and contusions."

"What happened?" Hailey whispered.

"I'm not sure, yet. In fact, I'm not sure I want to know. There's no one to prosecute, so she doesn't have to relive the ordeal in order to make a statement. It will be up to Mike if she wants to talk about it."

The three of them talked in the hall for a few minutes before Tyler got antsy. He excused himself and slipped back into Mike's room. Frank was sitting beside her bed. Mike was asleep. Tyler pulled up another chair and sat across from Frank.

"She looks like a whipped puppy." Frank's words were barely above a whisper.

"I know, Frank, but she did it. She didn't give up."

"Does she have any permanent injuries?"

"It doesn't look like it. At first the doctor was worried about oxygen deprivation, but he examined her earlier and acknowledged that her recovery is nothing short of a miracle." Tyler rubbed at his eyes as he spoke.

"Tyler, you need some rest."

"I'm fine, Frank, really I am. I'll grab some sleep while she sleeps, but I want to be here when she wakes up. I don't want her to be alone."

There wasn't much that Frank and Tyler could discuss. Neither one of them wanted to speculate on the ordeal that Mike had endured. They talked for a few more minutes, and then Frank stood to leave.

"Jim arranged for hotel rooms for the four of us. I think I'll go catch up with them for now, but I'll be back." Tyler walked Frank to the door. They embraced like father and son.

Tyler moved his chair closer to Mike's bed. The shift nurse came in and checked Mike's vitals.

"She's strong."

"The strongest," Tyler commented.

"My name's Angela, and I'll be Ms. Madigan's night nurse. I'll be in a few times throughout the night. If you need something or become anxious about anything, you can press that button on the side of her bed or come and get me at the nurse's station. You're welcome to use the other bed if you want to lie down. I'll be back later."

She left the room and dimmed the lights. Tyler laid his head against the back of the chair.

MIKE TRIED TO FOCUS, tried to remember where she was. Her eyes wandered around the room, and she realized she was in a hospital. Her eyes brightened slightly when she saw Tyler slumped in a chair.

"Tyler, get rest." Mike's voice cracked as she felt for the oxygen mask on her face.

Tyler was awake immediately. He stood up and leaned over Mike's bed. She looked at him for affirmation.

"You did it, Mike. You made it. You're going to be all right."

Mike again pushed the oxygen mask from her face. It was making her feel claustrophobic.

"Hey, honey. You need to leave that on. It's making it easier for you to breathe right now."

Mike stared at Tyler, feeling as if she were in a dream. She was afraid if she closed her eyes, he would be gone and Jason would be there once again tormenting her.

Tyler could see the fear in her eyes.

"It's okay. You're safe now."

She smiled as she let the feeling of safety envelop her.

Tyler played with the pink streaks in her hair and smiled. "This is kind of fun."

Mike turned away from him. "It's ugly. I want it gone." She fiddled with her mask again. Tyler covered her hand in his and pulled it away from her face.

"Mike, you need to leave that on."

She turned to Tyler with a penetrating stare and asked the question that had haunted her during her capture. She was certain she already knew the answer but had to know for sure. "Arnie ... Oreo and 'Nilla?"

Tyler dipped his head. "I'm sorry, Mike."

Her lip quivered as she tried to hold back the tears.

"Come on, Mike." Tyler pressed his finger to her lips. "Don't think about that. You need to conserve your strength. You need to worry about you right now."

Mike pulled the mask off again, so Tyler pushed the button for Angela. It only took a minute for her to appear.

"Hey, girl, how you doing?" Angela crossed the room and smiled broadly at Mike.

"She doesn't like the mask too much. Does she still need it?" Tyler asked.

"Here." Angela moved the mask to the top of Mike's head. "Let's see how you can do without it for a little while." Angela stepped outside for a moment. Tyler stroked Mike's face, helping her to relax. She looked like she had fallen back asleep when Angela returned.

"How's she doing?" she whispered to Tyler.

"She's fine," Mike answered for herself, though her eyes remained closed.

"You are one spunky girl, aren't you? I like that." Angela checked Mike's vitals again. "Okay, I called Dr. Brynes, and you can dump the mask," she said with a smile. "But let me know it you start having difficulty breathing. I'll be back a little later. Call me if you need anything."

"Actually," Mike said, stopping her. "I need to go—" Her throat tightened and cut off her words but Angela got the point.

She helped Mike with her I.V. line and walked her to the bathroom. It was slow going. Mike had a gash on the bottom of her right foot that took five stitches, and it was making it difficult for her to walk. Once she was settled back in bed, Angela slipped out of the room.

Mike inched herself to one side of the bed and asked Tyler, "Will you lie next to me for a little while? I want to talk to you about something." Mike was still feeling panicky. She needed to feel Tyler nearby.

"I'm pretty sure that's against hospital rules," he answered with a raised eyebrow.

"And since when does Tyler Henderson follow the rules?"

Tyler only chuckled as he lowered the rail and scooted in next to her. He reached out to hold her and felt the stiffness of the bandages across her ribs. He fumbled with his hand, not knowing where to rest it. "I want to hold you, but I'm afraid I'm going to hurt you."

Mike reached for his arm and rested it across her hips. "You could never hurt me, Tyler."

They lay next to each other for a moment before Mike spoke in a whisper. "I wanted to talk to you about something."

"You don't have to, Mike." Tyler wanted to assure her that they didn't need to talk about anything until she was ready.

"No, I need to tell you something. Remember . . . the last time we talked I said I wanted to tell you something?"

"Yeah."

"Well, while you were with Hailey, I had a long conversation with God, and we got a few things squared away." Mike started crying. "And then . . . when I was lying there . . . and I didn't think I was going to make it . . . my biggest regret was that you and Dad would never know that I was going to be okay. No matter what happened, I knew God was taking care of me."

Tyler was stunned. "And even after all you've been through, you're not mad at God?"

"No. God was the only person I could turn to. He was there with me, Tyler; I could feel him. Every time I felt like giving up, it was as if he gave me the courage and the strength to continue. I won't say that I didn't get angry with him at times, but I knew I couldn't turn my back on him. I couldn't have made it if I were alone. He protected me, Tyler."

"Protected you from what?" Tyler heard the anger in his voice. He was struggling himself with what God had allowed Mike to endure.

"From Jason." Mike's voice got even quieter.

Tyler didn't understand how it was that Mike had felt protected when Jason had brutalized her.

"Tyler, the whole time I was with Jason, he never . . . I mean he didn't . . . Tyler, he might have roughed me up, but God never allowed him to hurt me sexually. I wanted you to know that."

Mike's throat was sore and her strength was gone. Stunned, Tyler's own throat was in a knot, preventing him from saying anything. His mind had already conjured up horrible scenarios where Mike would've been forced to perform for Jason. It was truly incredible that he had never been able to force himself on her. It was clearly the hand of God that had protected her.

In a matter of minutes, Tyler could hear slow, measured breaths. Mike had fallen back to sleep. *Thank you, Lord. Thank you for your protection, and thank you for making yourself so real to Mike.*

As Tyler drifted off to sleep himself, complete peace enveloped him, and he was finally able to get some rest.

CHAPTER TWENTY

Mike had finally convinced Tyler to go back to the hotel to shower and get some real rest. She spent some time talking with her dad and shared his sadness at the loss of Arnie and the dogs. Arnie had no family, so her dad would have to make arrangements for his burial once he returned home. Mike tried not to think about Oreo and 'Nilla. Her only hope was that they hadn't suffered.

Mike visited briefly with Jim. He would go home today. He needed to tie up loose ends with the case. She thanked him for keeping an eye on Tyler during the ordeal.

"You know that Tyler's a handful. I knew if you weren't around keeping an eye on him, then I would have to." Jim gave her a sincere smile. "I'm glad you're going to be okay, Mike."

"Thanks, Jim."

Tyler was back at the hospital in little more than an hour. He showered and shaved but had no need to sleep. Hailey was with him, looking a little nervous about meeting Mike for the first time under such adverse conditions. Tyler couldn't believe the sea of reporters they had to navigate through in order to get to the hospital door. He would have to prepare Mike before it was time for her to leave.

He knocked on her door softly before entering and then stepped into the room with Hailey at his side.

"Mike, I have someone I would like you to meet."

Hailey felt out of place. She looked at the battered woman in the hospital bed and had difficulty relating her to the person that Tyler had described.

"Hi, Hailey. I wish we could have met under better circumstances."

Mike's self-consciousness matched Hailey's nervousness. They shared a few awkward moments but soon relaxed in each other's company. Hailey began to tell Mike stories from Tyler's youth: embarrassing and funny moments, all at Tyler's expense. Finally, it was time for Hailey to leave. She would be flying back with Jim today. Tyler walked her out to the hall where Jim and Frank were waiting. Tyler asked about Skyler, and she assured him that he was fine and would be waiting for him when he got home. Hailey gave Tyler a hug, holding him especially tight.

"Hey, what's wrong?" Tyler could sense her fear. He looked into her eyes that were ready to overflow.

"It's just that I was so afraid that you were going to end up getting yourself killed. I was so thankful when I knew you were okay and she was okay. I guess I didn't think about the trouble she had been through until I saw her, and now that I've seen her, I can't even imagine what she's had to overcome." Hailey's tough exterior faded.

"It's okay, Hailey." Tyler drew her close. "Mike's been through a lot, but she's going to be fine. We're going to be fine—all of us." Tyler looked at her with a smile.

She embraced him again before walking away with Jim.

Tyler and Frank spent the afternoon going in and out of Mike's room. Between examinations, the checking of vitals, and visits from doctors, Tyler had spent little time with Mike and none of it alone. When Tyler saw Angela walking down the corridor carrying a large shopping bag, he was surprised. Angela was the night nurse from the previous evening. *Why was she here now?*

"Detective Henderson, how is our patient doing?"

"Good, other than the poking and probing."

"I know. Isn't that crazy? We tell people to get their rest and then we bother them day and night."

"So, what are you doing here? I thought you were the night shift."

"I am, but Mike asked a favor of me last night."

"A favor?" Tyler wasn't sure he understood.

"Yeah, so why don't you and her father go make yourself scarce for about an hour and then come back. I think Mike wants it to be a surprise."

Tyler wasn't sure what Mike could be up to. "She's not asking you to break any rules, is she? I mean I'm not going to come back and find out she's checked herself out."

"No, nothing like that."

"Okay, Angela. I'm taking your word on this. Frank and I will go down to the cafeteria and grab a bite to eat, but we'll be back in an hour."

TYLER ENDED UP SPENDING HIS TIME on the phone, while Frank sipped coffee in a booth, trying to relax. Tyler talked with Lt. Mitchell, Agent Samuels, Jerry Bridges, Mike's immediate supervisor, and of course, Nathan. Nathan had only gotten bits and pieces from the station and what had made the news, but now he pumped Tyler for details.

"I still don't know a whole lot, Nathan. Mike and I haven't really talked about what happened." Tyler listed her injuries and the fact that she was covered from head to toe in cuts and scratches. "Tell you what, when I get back to her room, I'll have her call you so you can talk to her yourself. Her voice is pretty trashed, but I know she'd like to hear yours."

Tyler made a few more phone calls. Jenny and the guys at the station were still in shock that Jason had been the one responsible for the string of murders and amazed that he employed such radical lengths to win Mike back. They all felt guilty that they hadn't noticed something in Jason's behavior that would have stopped him before he had taken the matter to such extremes.

By the time Tyler was finished with all his phone calls, he and Frank had been gone over an hour. When they reached Mike's room, Tyler tapped on the door. Angela opened the door for him and waved them in.

Tyler was nearly speechless when he saw Mike. "Wow!" was all he could say.

Mike was sitting up in bed. Her eyes sparkled with excitement as Tyler stared appreciatively at her. Gone was the black and pink hair. Though her shoulder length hair had been hacked off, Angela did some trimming of her own, giving Mike a stylish cut.

"I thought the color was permanent," he said as he stepped closer.

"Naw," Angela cut in. "He just used some cheap spray-on stuff. Most of it came out pretty easily. I did color Mike's hair, so it might be a shade different from her original, but it will grow out slowly. "

"What do you think?" Mike asked, looking a little disappointed.

"I think it looks great." Tyler stepped closer and touched her golden locks.

"Thanks, Angela. This helps me feel somewhat normal again."

"You are so very welcome. I'm glad I could help." Angela glanced at her watch and said her good-byes. "I'll see you tonight, Mike." She gathered up her things and left, brushing past Frank, who was still standing in the doorway.

"What do you think, Dad?"

He smiled widely. "You look just like you did when you were a junior lifeguard."

She smiled and turned back to Tyler. "So you're sure you like it?" she asked him again.

"It looks great, Mike, why?"

"Like Dad said, I haven't had my hair this short since I was in junior high. It feels so strange."

"Well, it looks great. You look great." Tyler pressed his face close to hers. His kiss was slow and gentle. He wanted Mike to know how much she meant to him, how much he loved her, but he didn't want to push her. He knew she had a lot to deal with emotionally and wanted to help her through that and take things slowly.

The three of them talked for awhile before Frank excused himself. He was satisfied that his daughter was going to be okay and decided to head back home. He had some arrangements that needed to be made and knew Tyler would appreciate having some time alone with Mike.

An hour later, Mike woke up from her nap to see Tyler stretched out in the chair next to her bed. She scooted up against her pillows so she could sip on some water. Her stirring caused Tyler to awaken. He stood and stretched.

"When do I get to go home?"

"Home ... I don't know," Tyler said as he plopped into the chair.

"I want to go home, Tyler. I want to get out of here. I mean, I don't even know where I am.

"You're in Oregon."

Mike remembered back to when they crossed the state line. It seemed like an eternity ago. "I just think I would feel so much better if I could get to familiar surroundings."

"I'll talk to Dr. Byrnes and see what he thinks."

"Today, okay? I want you to talk to him today."

"She's back, ladies and gentleman; the stubborn and bossy Mike Madigan that we've all come to know and love is back, barking orders once again."

Mike lowered her head. "I don't mean to be bossy. I just want to go home."

Tyler heard the change in Mike's tone and wanted to kick himself. "I was only teasing you, honey. Of course, you want to go home." He moved over to the bed and hiked his legs up on the side. He lay his head back on her pillow, and she rested her head on his chest. He played with her golden hair.

"Did you ever think I wouldn't make it?" she whispered.

"A hundred different times. I would think of the brutality that we realized Jason was capable of and begin to lose hope. But then I would remember how strong you are. I knew you wouldn't give up. I knew you would keep fighting."

"How did you find me?"

"Your clues and God."

"Really! You were able to use my clues?"

"Yeah. But I've got to tell you this: You were so convincing at the vet's office, he believed you. It was his daughter that insisted you were in trouble."

Mike thought back to the chances she took while there. She knew she was toying with the lives of two other people if Jason discovered the clues she was leaving. She was thankful that everything turned out okay.

"Lisa was wonderful. It was because of her that I was able to tell her I was in trouble. She's the one that figured it out."

"But giving Hailey Tom as a fake name and asking for Oreos and Vanilla Wafers was ingenious. When she told us that, we were convinced."

Mike's heart ached at the loss of her best friends.

"I'm sorry, Mike." Tyler knew she was thinking of her beloved dogs and the other innocent lives that were taken.

"I know. It just hurts."

Tyler changed the subject. "Remember when Skyler had a fit the night we were having dinner on the deck?"

"Yeah."

"Well, when I went to look around, all I could find was what looked like my own footprints, even though I didn't remember walking around that side of the house. I let it go, but now I think I figured it out. Jason and I both wear the same boot. It's a basic boot that thousands of cops wear."

"You really think he was watching us?"

Tyler hesitated before telling Mike about the collage of pictures he and Jim had found in the back of Jason's closet.

"I don't understand, Tyler. I mean I know he was upset when we broke up and always said he would win me back, but that was ages ago. I never thought he was so deranged. I knew he had rage issues, but I had no idea he was capable of murder. I should have seen it. I should have done something. He was right. This is all my fault."

"No . . . no! You're wrong!" Mike could hear the anger in Tyler's voice. "I'm not going to sit by and let you blame yourself. This is all Jason's doing, not yours."

Both Tyler and Mike were quiet. Tyler had to get control of his anger. He hadn't meant to be so hard on Mike, but there was no way he was going to let her take responsibility for Jason's actions. Mike was still dealing with the idea that three other people died because of her rejection of Jason.

After a moment, Tyler continued explaining to Mike how they were able to follow her path: her message at the mini mart and the motel as well as the patrol officer at the drive-thru.

"When we realized you were going to be traveling across state lines, we called the Oregon Police and the FBI. In a matter of hours, they had your location narrowed down to two possible houses. Unfortunately, they raided the other one first; otherwise, we would have reached you sooner."

"I'm just glad you found me when you did."

"Me too." Tyler kissed the top of her head and rested his beside her.

They relaxed for a little while before Dr. Byrnes came by on his rounds. "Well, don't we look different today?"

Tyler got up and shook the doctor's hand. "Doesn't she look wonderful?"

"Indeed she does." He picked up the chart at the foot of Mike's bed and glanced over the notations.

"Then when can I go home?" Mike blurted out before she went into a coughing spell.

"Well, let me take a look at a few things first, and then I'll make my evaluation. You did just have surgery, you know?"

"I know, but all I have to do is concentrate on my recovery, and I think I can do that better in my own home." Her voice was raspy but convincing.

"I'll take that into consideration." He smiled at her and began his exam. Tyler once again stood in the hall, waiting for the doctor's diagnosis. Dr. Byrnes called Tyler back into Mike's room and told him he would sign her release tomorrow. Because of the extenuating circumstances, he agreed with Mike that her recovery would be better served in familiar surroundings. The doctor recommended that Mike get some counseling once she was home and feeling better.

"You're a tough young lady, Ms. Madigan. Without that determination, I'm not sure you would have made it."

Mike thanked the doctor for her release. Tyler shook his hand and added his thanks as well before the doctor left.

Mike was elated. She felt as if she'd been gone forever. "Would you mind doing some shopping for me, Tyler? I need something that I can wear home."

"Sure, but do me a favor. Call Nathan. I told him I would have you call him this afternoon. Then you can get some rest."

Tyler left while Mike dialed the phone.

"Hey, Nathan."

"Mike! It's so good to hear your voice. How are you doing?"

"Surviving."

"Tyler said you were pretty banged up."

"Yeah. I've been better."

"So, when are you coming home? I don't mind covering for you, but the brass is beginning to miss you around here."

"And you're not?" she tried to banter back.

"Well, sure I am. No one understands my warped sense of humor like you do."

Leave it to Nathan to make her laugh. "I'm getting released tomorrow, but I'm not sure how long before I'm back at work."

"Take your time, Mike. I was teasing. I'm just glad you're okay."

"Thanks, Nathan." She sighed. "Do you know if the families of the other victims have been contacted?"

"Yes." His tone was somber. "They were told. There were some mixed reactions. Some were glad Jason was dead; others wished he had been made to suffer."

"Do they know I'm involved?"

Nathan's reply was slow in coming. "Mike, it's all over the news. We weren't able to silence this story."

She hadn't even thought about the media. She just wanted to go home to her quiet house by the lake and rest. Now she wondered if that would even be a possibility.

"Mike, are you there?"

231

"Yeah. I'm here." Her words were softer and harder to hear.

"It's going to be okay, Mike."

She was sure she heard a catch in Nathan's voice.

"Are you okay, Nathan?"

"Yeah . . . but I've got to tell you, I've never been more terrified in my life. I saw up close and personal what Jason was capable of and the thought of him—"

"It's okay, Nathan, I'm going to be fine."

Mike quickly finished her phone conversation with Nathan before her emotions got the better of her. There was a definite bond between them. Their friendship ran deeper than others would even suspect.

WHEN TYLER GOT BACK FROM COMPLETING the shopping list that Mike had given him, he found her standing by the window, staring at the crowd of reporters. "Why didn't you tell me about the media circus outside?"

"I was going to, but I didn't want to give you too much time to dwell on it before you had to deal with it." Tyler put down the shopping bag and walked over to where she was leaning on the window frame. He carefully wrapped her in his arms. "Don't worry about it, Mike. They'll go away the minute the next big story hits."

"We're still going home tomorrow though, right?"

"Yeah. I got everything on your list, though I have to ask . . . are you planning on wearing anything under the stuff I bought because I didn't see any of *those* things on the list."

Mike laughed. "Of course, I am, dummy; I just didn't ask you to buy them. Angela's bringing me some things later tonight."

Mike turned around in Tyler's embrace and looked him in the eye. "When are you going to ask me what happened?" She looked at him as if it were a challenge.

"I'm not. It doesn't matter to me."

"How can you say that? How can you say it doesn't matter?" She tried to walk away but he stopped her, not letting go of her hand.

"I didn't say it didn't matter, Mike. I said it doesn't matter to me. There's a difference."

She walked silently to her bed and crawled beneath the covers. She stared at the wall feeling a little insecure, wondering where she and Tyler would go from here. She knew he loved her. He had told her that more than once. And she knew her feelings for him were genuine, but she would only be fooling herself to think their relationship wasn't more complicated now.

She felt Tyler lie on top of the covers and curl up beside her.

"Did Jim tell you I suspected Arnie?"

"Yeah, he told me."

"How could I, Tyler? I knew Arnie wasn't capable of murder, yet I let my paranoia convince me that he was guilty. He was only trying to protect me. In his simple way, he thought he was helping."

"Mike, you couldn't have known. Nathan explained to me your reasoning. It was a natural response."

"Jason used him. Jason told him he was sent to protect me. Then when he didn't need Arnie's help anymore, he killed him."

"So what happened?"

Tyler now realized that it was Mike that needed to talk about her ordeal. He had revealed that it didn't matter to him, but to her it was a barrier that stood between them. She sighed heavily as her mind rolled back to the moment the nightmare started.

"I thought it was you at the door. I was actually picking up the phone to call you when I heard the knock. I was so stupid; I wasn't even thinking. I opened the door, and Jason was standing there. I was irritated that he would come over after an incident that had happened earlier that day."

"Jim told me," Tyler whispered.

"When I realized it was Jason responsible for the killings, it was too late. He had the upper hand in the situation. I tried to run; that's when I saw Arnie. That moment of shock paralyzed me. I was unable to get away. Jason dragged me back to the house and to my bedroom. I resisted. That's when I got the broken ribs. When he was done roughing me up, he told me we were going away, that I was to pack a bag."

"What happened in the bathroom?" Tyler asked quietly.

"Arnie's behavior earlier that night had worried me. I realized he had a code to the alarm on the door, so I took my gun into the bathroom with me when I took my bath."

"Arnie had your security code?"

Mike realized she had never explained that part of her reasoning to Nathan. "When we put in the security doors on the houses and the kennel, we made all the codes the same to keep it simple. Arnie had the code."

Tyler understood even better how Mike could have thought that Arnie was the killer. He listened as Mike continued to explain.

"I knew my gun was in the bathroom. All I had to do was get to it. When I went in to change my clothes, I had my chance. But Jason saw the gun. We struggled. I knew I was going to die, because while we wrestled for the gun, Jason had turned it on me. I was able to move at the last minute; that's how it got me in the shoulder." Recounting the moment made Mike shudder. "I don't remember much after that. I was in and out of consciousness. When I finally came to, I was able to convince Jason that I needed a doctor. That's when he took me to the vet's office. He warned me that he would kill everyone if I tried anything. When I saw Lisa sitting at the counter, I knew I had to go along with him."

"Next time you're taken hostage, don't sound so credible. If you and Lisa hadn't communicated, I don't know where we would be right now." Tyler was trying to be lighthearted, but it made Mike mad.

"Don't you understand, Tyler, if I had tried anything, Lisa and her dad would be dead right now."

"I know, I know. Of course, you did what you had to do and it worked." Tyler held her tighter and quickly changed the subject. "Your graffiti at the mini mart was a stroke of genius."

"I could only hope that Jason wouldn't follow me into the bathroom." Mike thought for a moment. "But how did you find me? That was the last piece of evidence I was able to leave, and we ended up clear across the Oregon border. How did you figure out where we were going?"

"Jason's sister."

Mike knew about Carla and her mental state. Tyler filled her in on the clues that Carla had given them. "She has no idea how she helped us. When she started muttering something about caves, caves that weren't scary, the officers from Redding put it together. When Carla recognized the name Cave Junction, everything else just seemed to fall into place."

Again, Mike was silent. Tyler waited a few moments before asking, "Do you want to tell me what happened at the house?"

Mike shivered. "He planned it, Tyler. He planned it all. He bought the house and had it decorated for the time we would be together. That's what he kept saying. That's when I started losing hope. He started touching me and kissing me. I couldn't take it anymore, so I bit his lip and told him how much I hated him. He locked me in a closet after that. He left me there for awhile. I think he went into town. When he came back, he wanted to start where he left off." Mike's words grew quiet. "So, I consented to his plan. I tried to sound seductive. I told him I was sorry for hurting him and that I wanted to start over. He took me to the bedroom and wanted to have sex, but I convinced him to let us go outside and use the Jacuzzi. I figured if I could convince him I was having a good time, I could somehow try to make a run for it."

"How did you get away?"

Mike explained how she pretended to swallow the oil pebble and how Jason had panicked and ran inside for the milk. "I grabbed the gun and ran. I don't think I've ever run so hard in all my life. The trees and bushes were shredding me to bits, but I didn't care. I ran until I got the gash on my foot; then I hid behind the boulders, waiting for Jason to step into the clearing. I aimed at him and then lost my footing. He was on me immediately, except this time I knew he wasn't going to stop. I knew I was going to die."

Tyler held her tighter. "I'm sorry I didn't find you sooner. I'm sorry that I wasn't there for you."

Tyler was exhausted from Mike's account. He had seen the multiple bruises and cuts that covered her body. He could only begin to comprehend the emotional torture she had endured as well.

"It's okay, Tyler," Mike said trying to sound stoic. "Like I said, God protected me from the one thing he knew I would not be able to endure. The bruises and the scratches will go away, but I don't think I would have been able to live with the memory of . . . " Mike's voice broke.

"Oh, Tyler, I was so scared. It was so awful. I hurt so badly that I wanted to give up, but I knew I had to keep trying. I had to keep fighting and figure out how to get away. I couldn't let Dad live through something like this again."

Divulging the painful details of the last few days caused her to break down in sobs. Gone was the strong exterior, the I-can-handle-anything persona. Tyler knew it was inevitable, but Mike being the independent person that she was, had tried to keep it all inside. She tried to pretend that she was doing fine and glad to be alive. Her breakdown had been expected by everyone but Mike.

CHAPTER TWENTY-ONE

M ike had cried herself to sleep. When she woke up, she was surprised that her room was dark except for the fluorescent light above the headboard. She could see Tyler sitting in the shadows, trying to read by the minimal light in the room.

"What time is it?"

"9:00 p.m."

"I guess I kind of lost it, huh."

Tyler moved from the chair. "You didn't lose it. It was a natural response. It just took you a little longer to realize you were human." Tyler ran his finger down the bridge of her nose and gave it a little bop before giving it a kiss.

"Has Angela come yet?"

"Yeah, she said she would check back around 10:00, and she left that bag for you, if that's what you were wondering."

"Could you bring it to me?" Mike slowly scooted up to a sitting position.

Tyler picked up the little pink bag from the counter across the room and gave it to Mike. She rummaged around in the bag and then put it aside.

"What . . . you're not going to show me what she got you?" Tyler arched his eyebrows and gave her a devilish look.

"Not on your life." Mike threw the tissue box from her bedside tray. Tyler caught it and laughed. He couldn't take his eyes off of her.

"What are you staring at?"

"You're laughing. It's good to see you smile."

Tyler yawned and stretched. He rubbed the back of his neck while he moved his chair closer to her bed.

"Go to bed, Tyler. You look beat, and you have a long drive ahead of you tomorrow."

"Actually, we're flying home."

"Flying?" Mike look disappointed. "But I wanted to stop by and see Lisa. I wanted to thank her for all her help."

"I'm sorry, Mike, but I already arranged for Carl to fly us home. I figured the drive would be too long and too hard on you. Besides, I just want to get home without incident. With all the press running around, we would need a police escort just to get to the highway."

Mike knew Tyler was right, but she was disappointed just the same. "Then I need to call Lisa tonight. I don't want her to think I forgot about her. I wouldn't have survived if it weren't for her help. What time is it again?"

"Almost 9:30."

"Do you think it's too late to call?"

"I don't know many teenagers that go to bed before 10:00. I think it would be all right." Tyler reached for his phone and recited the stored number to Mike.

"Hello. Is this Lisa?"

"Yes," was the shy reply.

"Hi, Lisa. This is Mike Madigan. I'm the woman you helped the other day."

"You remembered. You remembered to call me."

"Of course, I did. If it weren't for you I could have ended up a lot worse."

"Are you okay?" Lisa dropped her voice to a whisper. "I was so afraid for you. When you left here, I was so angry that we hadn't done more to help you. I knew you were in trouble, and I didn't do anything to stop that man."

"Lisa, you did the best possible thing. You called the police and told them what you knew. If you hadn't done that, they never would have found me. I called to thank you for everything. You saved my life."

Lisa was speechless. She had felt so helpless when Mike had left. It took Lisa a moment to get up the courage to ask Mike how she was doing. "The news said you were found in Oregon and that you were in grave condition. Are you okay now?"

"I'm pretty banged up, but I'm beginning to feel a little better. I'm going home tomorrow. I had wanted to stop by and see you on the way, but we're flying home instead of driving."

"Maybe you could come and visit another time." Lisa's voice was hopeful.

"Or maybe you and your mom and dad could come and visit me. I'm sure my dad would love to thank you himself."

"It's only me and my dad. My mom left us a few years ago."

Mike could hear the sadness in Lisa's voice. "I know how you feel. My mom left my dad when I was nineteen."

Tyler could see that Mike was connecting with Lisa just by hearing her end of the conversation. Mike and Lisa talked for a few more minutes before Mike hung up the phone.

"Sounds like you two hit it off."

"Yeah, she seems like she's a pretty together young girl." Mike was reflecting on how she felt when her mom left her. She knew it had to be different circumstances than Lisa's, but she remembered the pain and the confusion she felt. "I think it would be nice to have her over to the house, you know, once things get back to normal."

"Normal!" Tyler chuckled. "I tried finding normal. Small town, slower pace . . . and look where it got me."

"And where is that, Detective Henderson?" Mike stuck her chin up in the air and crossed her arms against her chest. Defense mode was evident in her body language.

Tyler moved in really close, his face just inches from hers. "In love with the most beautiful woman in the world." His words completely disarmed her. She framed his face with her hands and kissed him as only a woman in love could.

"ARE YOU READY?" Tyler asked as Mike looked up at him from where she was sitting in the wheelchair. She knew the chair was procedure, but it made her feel like she was center stage, one place she was not comfortable being.

"As I'll ever be, I guess."

Mike could see the crowd of reporters on the other side of the automatic doors. The chair triggered the sensor that opened the door and exposed them to the throng of people. They were immediately assaulted with flashbulbs and microphones. Questions were being yelled at her from all directions, and she was beginning to wonder if she would be able to make a statement. Tyler had encouraged her to, saying it would be the only way for the reporters to get their story and for her to get some privacy.

"If everyone can be quiet for a moment, Ms. Madigan has a statement that she is ready to make." Tyler held up his hands and got the crowd's attention. "Ms. Madigan has agreed to make a statement in exchange for some solitude. She is still recovering from her ordeal and asks that you respect her privacy. There will be no follow-up questions. She just wants to go home and continue recuperating."

With that said, Mike cleared her throat, as best as she could, and recited what she had already practiced that morning.

"Dad, it's her. She's on T.V." Lisa had been watching the television while preparing lunch for her and her dad. It was the first Saturday in a long time that they had not worked. Dr. Raines hurried to the living room and watched the news conference with Lisa.

"First of all, I would like to thank the many people responsible for helping me: the police departments of Emerald Lake, Modesto, and Redding, and the FBI. I would especially like to thank Detective Tyler Henderson, Detective Jim Thompson, Lt. Mitchell, and Agent Samuels. These men were able to put together the smallest pieces of evidence that eventually led to my abductor. I would also like to thank Mrs. Ethel Banks who gave the police valuable information on my whereabouts. I am convinced I would not be here today if it weren't for the courage of a young lady named Lisa Raines. She and her father helped me when they themselves were in danger. Lisa was able to stay calm and collected in a very difficult situation and because of that, she was able to give the police the information they needed to obtain my location. Lisa, if you're watching, I could never thank you enough for your care and courage. You are a special young lady. Thank you."

The reporters could tell Mike was ready to finish the interview and started volleying questions at her. "How did you cope at the hands of a madman, Ms. Madigan?"

"I relied on God and the prayers of others."

"Are you saying you had a religious experience during your captivity?" another reporter interjected.

"No, I'm saying that it was God that gave me the strength and the endurance to make it. Without God, I would have given up long before it was over."

"What is the extent of your injuries, Ms. Madigan?"

"Did you hear her, Dad? She said our names . . . on T.V. Can you believe it?" Lisa excitedly asked her dad.

"She's right, you know. You are a very courageous young woman." Lisa's dad pulled her into a hug. "I'm lucky to have you taking care of me. I couldn't do it without you."

Lisa's eyes began to well up. Her father deserved so much better than her mother had ever given him. She would do whatever she could to make her dad feel loved, because he deserved it. He always made her feel special. He was the best father and should have the very best.

TYLER WAS TRYING TO PUSH MIKE'S CHAIR THROUGH the mob. He had said there would be no follow-up questions, but the hungry reporters hollered them out anyway.

"It is true that you fell in love with the police officer that rescued you?"

"Okay, that's enough. Ms. Madigan is trying to be polite, but I don't have to be. That is none of your—"

"Yes, it's true," Mike answered back.

Tyler turned to Mike, surprised that she would answer such a personal question.

"When was that, Ms. Madigan?" The reporter pushed a microphone right in her face.

"From the first moment I saw him."

Tyler looked at Mike in astonishment. She only smiled back at him while he helped her from the chair. She had never told him that. She had never admitted that she had felt sparks from the moment they first met. She had been so cocky with him and had shown him nothing but contempt. Now, it was as if the crowd no longer mattered. Tyler had to know.

"Why didn't you ever tell me that?"

"What . . . and miss out on the dinners, the flowers, and an afternoon out

239

on the lake? No, if I were going to be won, you were going to have to work hard for it. Besides, you were too sure of yourself. I didn't want you to think I was a pushover."

"But, Mike . . ." Tyler leaned on the frame of the car, needing answers to his questions.

"Do we have to talk about this now?" Mike looked past Tyler to the reporters that were trying to move in even closer.

Tyler quickly shut her door and rushed around to the driver's side of the car. When he was inside, he glanced at Mike, who had a grin on her face from cheek to cheek.

"Why didn't you ever tell me?"

"Because you were already in a relationship, and I had to make sure that I didn't jeopardize that." Mike was referring to Tyler's commitment to God. Even though she had been struggling with anger and resentment towards God, she never wanted to put Tyler in the position to have to choose.

She looked at him with renewed strength and reached for his hand. "Now that God and I are back on track, you no longer have to choose. I think the three of us are going to make it just fine."

About the Author

Tamara Tilley resides with her husband, Walter, at Hume Lake Christian Camps in the Sequoia National Forest. Along with their children Christopher, Jennifer, John, and Alex, they have served on full-time staff and ministered at Hume for more than 14 years.

Tamara manages one of the retail stores at Hume Lake, which serves thousands of kids visiting the conference center on a daily basis.

Tamara is an avid reader and enjoys hobbies such as scrapbooking, card design, and enjoying God's creation from her front porch.

Other books by Tamara Tilley

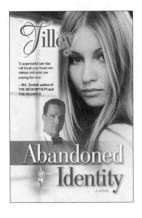

Abandoned Identity

"A suspenseful tale that will
break your heart one minute and
send you soaring the next."

M.L.Tyndall,
author of *The Redemption,
The Reliance,* and *The Restitution*

A corporate clash.
A complicated romance.
A shocking secret.
A dangerous journey.

Jennifer Patterson and Harrison Lynch don't see eye-to-eye. Since the day
corporate brought him in to fill the job that should have been hers, they've
been at odds. That is until one night when they are stuck in their corporate
offices by an unexpected blizzard and Harrison sees her in an entirely
different light.

But the next day, Jennifer does the unexpected—she disappears. Though
Harrison tries to find her, shocking news brings his investigation to an abrupt
end—but not his pre-occupation with the vulnerable woman revealed to him
one stormy night. Three years later, while vacationing on the California
coast, he sees her . . . he's sure of it . . . or is it just a figment of his imagination?

ISBN 978-1-58169-242-6

Other books by Tamara Tilley

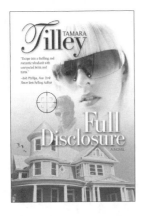

Full Disclosure

"Escape into a thrilling and romantic whodunit with unexpected twists and turns."

Bob Phillips
New York Times
Best-selling author

A quiet beachfront town.
An attempted hit.
A shaky romance.
An unexpected twist.

From the moment you open *Full Disclosure*, you'll be drawn into the page-turning action that unfolds as Ciara and Jack are thrown together by a hit man's bullet. Was the target meant to be the successful artist that Ciara grew up with, or the mysterious recluse who lives in a sprawling mansion down the beach?

You'll be swept into the action, intrigue, and romance that unfold in this quiet, beachfront community. The threat of permanent blindness for the artist and Ciara's lack of trust, which threatens to keep her locked within a wall of protection, cause them to seek God's direction in a more meaningful way than they ever had before. They knew God could meet their needs, but how?

ISBN 1-58169-205-6